CHAP'

'This *is the most desol*

I

'*Mon Dieu*, she's going!' screamed a guttural voice in broken French. 'P-u-s-h! Push hard! *mes amis*. HARDER. Keep within the poles.'

Wind-blown snow hampered the men, gritty eyes and curses accompanying the warnings ferried between them before the torturing gusts bore them away.

Far from comfortable, and annoyed at Shelley, Mary Godwin breathed on the glass, one delicate hand scrubbing away frozen condensation from the carriage window. 'I care not if I perish from the cold. I need air if only to dispel the stench from these ghastly rugs.'

She tugged fiercely at the window, fingers numbed through effort.

'How much longer must we suffer this wretched, snow-bound cart track?' Anxiety and anger fell on deaf ears, Shelley and Claire Clairmont equally dispirited.

The unsettled demeanour emphasised their predicament, time incarcerated in this vehicle stretching to infinity yet only an hour had passed.

Following an inane suggestion by Shelley, they had left Les Rousses around six that evening, hindsight proving to Mary that it wouldn't be good for her child, William – her little "Willmouse" barely six months old. She thought of the miles stretched before them, Geneva a long way off, the sluggish, interminable progress of the coach hardly easing the situation.

Someone had said, 'No small wonder the driver and his retinue are completely insane to embark on such a precarious route!'

Aware of the risks, eleven men agreed, reconciled by the age-old: Money speaks loudest when there is little to be had.

The road, in parts, climbed steeply and after only a mile or so snow had rendered the bleak landscape featureless, massive drifts presenting further obstacles: the pace slowed, sometimes reaching a standstill, the brute efforts of men and driver urging the horses forward, the poor beasts striving against the merciless wind as it buffeted them from all sides. Huge, sombre pines did at least break the sight-line as far as visibility would allow and so created a different aspect to the oppressive, unsettling white.

Will we ever see blue sky again instead of turgid, depressing grey mountains? An unvoiced thought, Mary aware that to say it aloud might promote one of Shelley's moods.

Tired, restless, her channelled thoughts grew more disagreeable by her deepening concern over the child, and further exacerbated by Shelley who appeared to revel in the situation. Then Shelley's penchant for the dark hours usually did promote a very different persona: a night person, he would often spend the time between midnight and dawn reading or musing over his writings. Acceptable if a bed happened to be at hand to which she could escape. Here in this creaking, floundering contraption, real comfort was denied. The carriage tilted alarmingly giving credence to the thought.

Mary and Claire uttered short, sharp cries of alarm. Only Shelley smiled and settled deeper into his corner.

The gale surged over the rim of the steep, rutted track, a bevy of urgent shouts punctuated with more expletives rising above the strident nickering of distressed horses. Unsettling sounds penetrated the blanket-coloured evening, whose pitiful sunset had been bled of what little light it offered.

'We will all perish!' Harsh, guttural tones embellished with fear curled in the frosty air from another of the half score men Shelley had hired to aid their passage. Instructed to support the battered coach, to excavate a path when the horses could no longer force a way through thickening snow, these fellows would earn what little pittance Shelley could offer them.

An air of uneasy calm prevailed, Shelley wishing he'd heeded Mary's caution to set off in daylight. Would a few more hours have made any difference? Unfortunately those who knew Percy Bysshe Shelley considered him a man who would rarely admit his error.

Lost in reverie, the gaunt, young and sometimes incompetent Shelley hunched forward as his almost permanent stoop demanded, appearing oblivious to the commotion.

Sinister Quartet

Books already published include :

Recluse
Demon
Treading on the Past
Through Dark Eyes
and the forthcoming : Jackdaw

And from Blackie:

Heart of Shadows – Lord Byron and the Supernatural
(co author – Mike Vardy)

SINISTER QUARTET

*Lord Byron, the Shelleys
and the Villa Diodati*

A Novel

by

Derek Fox

*Blackie & Co
Publishers Ltd*

A BLACKIE & CO PUBLISHERS PAPERBACK

© Copyright 2002
Derek Fox

First published in 2002

A CIP catalogue record for this title is
available from the British Library

ISBN 1 903138 17 5

**Blackie & Co Publishers Ltd
107-111 Fleet Street
LONDON   EC4A 2AB**

**Artwork for cover and frontispiece
designed and painted by
Rose and Frank Mafrici
e-mail: mafrici@learigg.freeserve.co.uk**

'My heart is in the vault, but it really matters not where my body parts are; my spirit is here and my body is no longer a concern to me. My true heart is my spirit and the physical heart matters not.'

Lord Byron

For JEB and LB
(They know who they are)
Thanks for everything

UNBORN

I am shadow, lacking substance. I wait to be given life.

I lurk within the deep reaches of the sub-conscious. In time, this essence will surface, gradually gain substance, become a breed of reality.

I will be interpreted in many ways – some will see me as human, others, sub-human, dependent on the conscience and ability of my creator.

It is a rare phenomenon to linger in this manner, but they say patience is a virtue. I depend on snatches of human concept, ideas nurtured by life's experience, its highs, its lows. For are we not all bred from an idea? In human terms, IMAGINATION?

A simple act of copulation can create an embryo...

Perhaps I am such, yet I loiter in the uncharted tunnels of the mind. It will hardly be a simple act of procreation that will give me life – it will be the very apotheosis of the mind, its ingenuity, its brilliance. When discovered, or remembered, *this will allow me, and others like me, to emerge.*

Shadows: Darkness – the dark beyond any concept of night is where I dwell, yet one spark will ignite my need to live, be a part of your world.

Ah, to be human, to be normal – whatever that means.

For now, I am mere fantasy.

'Shelley,' Mary said loudly trying to make herself heard above the wind, 'I warned you. Not one of your better ideas to start out so late in the day.' Intense hazel eyes demanded his response.

Claire answered for him: 'We had to come, sister.' She clung to the strap on the adjacent door pillar, her pained look obvious, each lurch prompting a breathy complaint.

Barely eighteen and slightly younger than Mary, her dark, sallow Latin features were partially hidden in shadow, eyes indicating a tolerable level of sufferance. 'Byron may already have arrived... and left.'

The mention of his name comforted her; it prevented her mind wandering down dreadful byways she agreed were too unpleasant to contemplate.

Beyond the flimsy coach walls nature represented a mounting threat, throwing up a frightful picture of coach, horses, men and occupants taking a tragic tumble over the rim to smash into a seething void overlaid with grey-white ghosts.

'Yes, he may well have arrived... and left.' Her eyes drifted to the opposite corner. 'Do you agree, Shelley?'

Tugging up the obnoxious smelling travel rug which didn't appear to deter her, Claire's continued irritability prompted: 'Given the choice I'd rather this than the heave and swell of the waves. We are at least on *terra firma*. We have arrived!'

'My decision to travel is right, Claire,' Shelley confirmed in his strange, high, slightly effeminate tone, a timbre which did not exactly instil the women with sufficient confidence in accepting him as their protector should anything God forbid go wrong.

They glanced through their respective windows, instinctively startled and irritated by snowflakes the size of pennies bombarding the glass.

'Our labourers are to be congratulated,' Mary remarked. 'One is forced to admire the brute force employed to maintain their own and our preservation.'

Shelley shrugged. 'I doubt anyone would lament our passing if we were all to perish on such a wild night.' He glanced at Mary, daring to add: 'Not least your father, Mary.' Before she could answer, he went on, 'Elysium, as we view our destination, is simply a word when destruction could be a mere fraction away.' A sigh followed, tinged with resolution. 'We have chosen and must agree it is more acceptable than the residue of shallow living we, uh, enjoyed in England.'

II

Family squabbles had taken their toll. Following the birth of their second child in January, Shelley had written to William Godwin, Mary's father, advising him of her continued health and that the child – his namesake – remained well. Underlying this tension, Shelley guessed, had been the strained situation aggravated by Godwin's unsupportive nature along with his dim view that Shelley had ruined his daughter's good reputation. Despite Shelley's missives – courteous to say the least – explaining their financial straits, Godwin still remained impassive. Thankfully, time did collapse his dour outlook yet did not allow him to condone the 'mistake' the young couple had made. He did, however, eventually forgive.

Shelley expected more from Godwin: in private he grumbled, 'The man's her father! It isn't good enough.' Obliged to write, his explosive reply from his heated pen pointedly reminded Godwin of how he, Shelley, deplored such unacceptable behaviour. Nor had Shelley wasted words: he blamed Godwin for injuring his own family in such an abhorrent way, and ensured the man felt his disgust when Godwin placed him, and his own daughter, on a par with 'prostitutes and seducers'.

Thus, by putting pen to paper it allowed such grievous thoughts to be held in perpetuity. *"Do not talk of forgiveness again to me,"* he wrote, *"for my blood boils in my veins, and my gall rises against all that bears human form, when I think of what I, their benefactor and ardent lover, have endured of enmity and contempt from you and all mankind."*

Had Mary been aware of the tensions between her father and Shelley? Godwin may have mentioned it. Despite her not remarking upon it, fundamentally, he argued, she must know. And she did, because it would later echo in her writings.

'Aye, we're all shunned creatures,' Shelley murmured, experiencing an inner turmoil he couldn't begin to account for. Godwin had proved a formidable antagonist, Shelley more than a little concerned over the man's determination in seeking to put an end to any relationship his daughter may covet. A fleeting thought – a premonition – creased his brow. It added to problems probably best explained through his own deep-seated guilt over Harriet, his wife, distraught following his callous desertion.

Guilt? Another cross to bear? Whatever his conscience dictated, Shelley prepared to deem it a warranted act and one easily justified to those around him. Easy to preach to the already converted!

Irrespective of cards life dealt, man is a free spirit and so free love and a bohemian lifestyle were acceptable. But then nature and the human mind, crammed with foibles and contentions, can sometimes be difficult taskmasters to appease.

In a sense, both Godwin's actions towards his daughter, and Shelley's own conduct towards his wife encouraged their flight, Shelley deciding they must depart in order to escape the painful humiliation of fickle mentality which regarded them as immoral – in itself ironic when taken in context.

Impulsive actions made Shelley realise he may have driven a deeper wedge between Mary and Godwin. Through various asides Mary made, largely blamed on her own depression, Shelley didn't doubt her wondering if she would see her father again.

Point: counterpoint. Would there be any winners in this chronicle of family squabbles?

III

A whimper rose from the bundle Mary clutched to her breast, this child, this *life*, another reminder to Percy Shelley of a family he'd abandoned. Seeking to dispel his guilt he turned away from what he saw as Mary's accusing stare, his pained reflection ethereal in the snowlit dark. The appealing arms of a leafless bush reached out and prompted him to think of Harriet. Why, dammit? The relationship had collapsed anyway!

'I wonder,' he said pensively, 'how long any of us are destined for this earth? As mere mortals we fight to live, eke out a pittance.' He grunted, drawing a questioning look from both women.

'Life is what we make of it, dearest,' Mary replied.

Unprepared to voice further thought, Shelley still felt the three of them remained condemned by Godwin. Consequently this presented a somewhat humorous slant, for Godwin nursed his own desires to practise Shelley's "free thinking". More irony to the predicament.

The cold impregnated, causing Shelley to abandon nature's insufferable force and solicit the more intimate confines of the coach, desirous of seeing himself in better light within Mary's eyes. Useless thinking about ghosts.

Mary offered a reassuring smile. 'Whatever distresses you, Shelley, you have left it behind.'

It helped. He returned her smile. It didn't prevent him being churlish. 'Is conscience to be shut off so easily? That which we do in our lives can return, be it pleasant or unsettling. It's always there, even out here it races in the wind, forms faces in the snow. See! There! On the window. Eyes, a mouth, sneering, defining our insecurity, our lack of continuity. We choose to come here, yet cannot escape the past.'

Mary disliked his brooding intensity, this dark batch of thoughts he was obviously not prepared to voice.

'Then why do we journey if not to escape?' she queried, the answer obvious. She avoided any reference to the arguments at home, and did her best to try and understand Shelley's mood, hope to curb his disturbed thinking.

How does one person ever really begin to know another? A thought with teeth. Mary accepted that only the reasonably privileged would be allowed to know what an individual decided they should know and nothing more.

Claire fidgeted, captive to their exchanges. 'Sometimes you can be so selfish, Mary. You casually ignore the fact that we are to meet Lord Byron.'

Mary's eyes flashed. 'You speak to me of selfishness. Dear sister, you mirror your own parsimonious attitude in what you state. We would not be in this unpleasant situation were it not for your scheming and infatuations. We should be enjoying the more pleasant climes of Italy.'

By not mincing words, Mary had very effectively slapped the offending countenance with the proverbial gauntlet. Self-gratification aside, she gained comfort in seeing how Claire seethed from what could only be the truth.

Claire's scathing look hinted that she would be willing to engage in what would undoubtedly be an argument. 'Oh,' she sneered, preparing for battle. 'And don't you for one minute think that your illustrious background prompted Lord Byron's interest in you, *sister*?' The last word was clotted with disdain, Claire intending it as a slur, rather than anything remotely smacking of fondness.

A user was Claire Clairmont: Mary knew it, so did Shelley *if* he cared to admit the truth. Mary doubted it.

Remarkably the ensuing quiet did allow Mary to agree that Claire could be correct. After all, Mary did not see this as an assumption, more a truth, effectively based on what the poet Coleridge had deigned to write to her. Admittedly his lines, his effort to promote Byron, had made her heart palpitate a little longer than any young lady ought to allow.

"If you had seen Lord Byron," Coleridge had written, "you could scarcely disbelieve him – so beautiful a countenance you scarcely ever saw – his teeth so many stationary smiles – eyes open portals of the sun – forehead so ample, yet so flexible, passing from marble smoothness into a hundred wreathes and lines and dimples correspondent to the feelings and sentiments he is uttering."

Lines from one poet concerning another, they held a wry amusing slant. Mary leaned into the shades in order to hide her own amusement from the other two. Truth, as is often intimated, will out, and privately she confessed to sharing Coleridge's vision. However, being the type of person she was, small, composed and more than a little sedate, in short a lady, Mary warned herself not to rise to the gushing accolades Coleridge had bequeathed. Or admit to agreeing with them.

Byron as a poet, a man of letters, drew Mary Godwin's admiration, and at her own insistence she'd prompted Claire to introduce her. Small talk suitably laced with a few compliments – she recalled there were such – hardly induced either herself or Byron to embark on any affair, and most certainly not of the type about which Lord Byron's predatory tactics upon the fey female preceded him.

Conceding he must have prior knowledge of her, whether or not gleaned from Claire, Claire being quick to convey any gossip, Mary guessed it may have been whispered by other well-meaning persons, close friends in fact. Armed with such tattle-tales, such personages may quite easily have referred to her as a "scarlet woman". Truth be told, her appearance and posture in no way prompted such acerbic comment. In fact Mary liked to think that Lord Byron not only admired her assurance but also her alert, accomplished mind.

As Coleridge had taken pains to point out – reading between the lines that is – it takes one to know one. And if true, why shouldn't she preen a little?

She hid her humour behind a gloved hand. Unbeknown to Claire, she'd read, in part, a letter her sister had sent to Byron, some phrases quietly fanciful in content.

"Mary is delighted with you..." Claire had written, "and is forever begging your address abroad. How mild... gentle he is," she went on. "So different from what I expected."

Untruths, or half-truths, penned to enforce Claire's own standing with Byron? Mary couldn't resist saying: 'You used me to promote yourself, Claire, even to the extent of fabricating certain phrases, taking them out of true context. I am right?'

Evidently displeased, Claire wouldn't rise to it, any anticipated argument by Mary rapidly diffused and, thankfully, interrupted by Shelley.

'Have patience, Mary.' Shelley had listened, animated by the brief exchange between them. 'Detours seem to be our lot in life. Dammit, I suppose we all admire Lord Byron for his dexterity with words. That aside, you both ignore how we were obliged to cut short our earlier tour two years ago.'

'Oh yes,' Claire said acidly, 'you mean when you sat astride that ragged-haired donkey to ease the discomfort of your sprained ankle. You should have looked where you placed your clumsy feet.'

He glowered at her, then at Mary, caring not that they understood his statement. 'Like fish caught on a hook we were decked, our chances of realising the community we longed for smashed on a rising tide of condemnation... *again!* Admit it, we did manage to engineer our own follies, realise our errors *without* Byron.' Shelley's lips twisted in a cynical smirk. 'Perhaps this time we can do it *with* him.'

Mary, hating what she judged as Shelley's irrationality, drew energy from the storm and if necessary would use it to qualify certain points. For a moment's peace she would have matched the cries of their helpers *and* the tempest had she thought it would prove worth-while. By keeping her tone moderately level she hoped it would take the sting out of Shelley's disjointed stab at humour.

'Lack of money, stupidity and illness made nonsense of the earlier tour, as well you know, Shelley. You, too, Claire. And besides, we were younger then, more foolhardy.'

Ignoring Mary's chagrin, Claire's interjection of, 'I agree,' unwittingly offered a little substance to Mary's statement. 'I believe,' she said, 'that this time we will succeed, *with Lord Byron's help.* One can learn much in two years.'

Not only did this add to her own confidence, it served to underline her feelings and confirm her ambition.

'You set such store by this man... this Lord.' Mary relaxed and re-inspected Claire, though perhaps through condescending eyes. She argued: 'Though I have met him, my understanding or, with your permission, *appraisal,* is that Lord Byron is a libertine, and an unreliable one at that. I suggest that much like us...' She faltered, hardly because of any embarrassment at speaking her mind; more because she realised she'd revealed something she had warned herself to avoid. And further because it made reference to her own and Shelley's unfortunate problems. She did, however, continue if only to justify a point. 'I suggest that like us, Lord Byron has been forced to flee England hard on the heels of a reputation that already precedes him. But then ostensibly he will have his reasons for being as he is and thus act in accordance with them. Like us, he may be searching for something he hasn't yet found.'

'Like *us*?' Claire teased, missing the innuendo entirely. She smiled testily at Mary as she fished for more, her comment directed at Shelley thus ensuring he was gathered into the conversation. 'How very precise you are, Mary,' she said. 'I agree we run from the truth of relationships in England, not least those of your own father.'

Full circle. Mary heard the echo of Shelley's comments aimed at herself, Claire now seeing fit to turn the screw a little tighter.

'What about my father? He has every right to voice his opinions. Free speech. Godwin wrote about it, and practised it; so by whose right do you, Claire, or you, Shelley, seek to malign him?'

9

It ranted through her mind, Mary little realising Shelley had been thinking along similar lines. Blood is thicker than water, so they tell us. But maybe water can act as a catalyst. Mary's mind had been torn and so had her heart. On the one hand, William Godwin, father; on the other, Percy Shelley, lover and perhaps future husband. So might it be that sentiment and love for Shelley, over-rode it – made blood as thin as water and so made it something easily stricken from her mind?

Did she really know him, or herself? Imagination can be an enigmatic beast.

Mary's turn to glower. Surprised, she noted that Shelley cast Claire a disparaging look, the two routed by Mary's outburst, and perhaps her cynicism. About to retaliate again, Mary found herself admonished by Claire.

'We should never forget that we are, in a sense, like Lord Byron.' Claire's shrill, mocking laugh, sounding more strident, confined as they were, gave weight to the rest. 'And undoubtedly apprehensive over what the neighbours will think!'

Mary's eyes matched Claire's for fire. She was prevented from answering by a whimper from William, his tiny hands struggling from beneath the shawl, flexing over her breast.

She welcomed the diversion, convinced this pest of a sister, had Mary exercised her prerogative, would have been left behind. A limpet, Claire had attached herself to them refusing grimly, despite hints, to be prised off and left to float in her own fantasy world. She'd cast her sheep's eyes at Shelley, and now if rumour turned to truth, she'd made a nuisance of herself with Byron, a man troubled with his own past and irksome memories.

Mary cooed to William, the child experiencing discomfort. 'My dearest puppy, are you hungry? Then we shall attend to your needs.' A tolerable silence – released from what could have been a protracted argument – gradually seeped in as Mary fiddled with the buttons of her dress and drew the infant to her nipple. As he suckled, she recalled the origin of the expression she'd used, thoughts returning to remarks made by her father...

IV

William Godwin, apprehensive about the circumstances surrounding his wife's illness, did eventually tell Mary about it.

'Sadly, your mother is unable to suckle,' he said. 'Fordyce,' he stifled a brief anger before adding a touch sarcastically, 'her *trusted* physician, warned her that she must cease feeding her child should her milk be contaminated.'

This duplicated similar words used by Percy following the birth of their little Clara.

Godwin had initially joined in with their humour when Fordyce had recommended using puppies to drain the abundance of milk from her mother's breasts, Mary Godwin herself a party to such. 'Sadly, though we weren't to know, it presaged the end,' Godwin said. 'Your mother was already mortally ill with puerperal fever. Fordyce told me of this,' Godwin added. 'Brought on by the retention of the afterbirth, he said. Apparently he attempted to remove it but –' Godwin's unfinished statement made sense of his grief and underwrote what he meant.

Mary understood his grief. She guessed her father had played a double act: alone, he would weep, yet when visiting with his wife his strength of will assured her all was well. Perplexing for any husband who considered a relationship as deep as the one they enjoyed, one which he obviously thought would never end so prematurely.

'Had the afterbirth been left to expel itself naturally, she might have survived.'

Mary remembered his wild, lost look. But then, she told herself, death is a great leveller; it can bring humanity to its knees, and oftentimes individuals can be fetched lower than that.

If I could only resurrect that which has been lost to me! she thought.

Such damning thoughts hurt: this flying in the face of the Almighty could never lead to any appeasement, or peace of mind. She should forget them, banish them. Let the infernal storm bury them!

The sins of doctors. Mary brooded over her mother's death, such thoughts precipitated by the very hands that had sought to rid Mary Godwin of the afterbirth. She wondered if those same hands could have healed, brought her back, and grew alarmed at the thought.

To escape from this darker tributary, Mary glanced at William and gently stroked his face. 'You will be safe, my William. I cannot, will not lose my treasure; not as I did Clara. *Or Mother.* Fourteen days is hardly sufficient to know a child, but it is more than enough to love one.'

Using William's shawl she angrily dabbed her damp eyes. 'A nightmare difficult to contemplate for any mother.' She cooed to him, his grimace testing her judgement in guessing whether or not he was smiling or complaining about soiled undergarments.

I will protect you, but it is the world at large you must fear. She made this promise silently, aware Claire looked on, her smug smile perhaps emphasising her own thoughts and memories, most of them presumably happier than those of her half sister.

Detached from the others, Claire considered blissful, more fruitful times. How many letters did I write to LB? she mused. The storm became secondary as she dwelt intensely on furious passions still smouldering within.

V

Ah yes, March, 1816, is when I began a campaign to ensnare my Lord Byron.

She'd seen George Gordon as prey, a man she felt could not refuse her initial taciturn advances.

Yet I was the only one who could heal his injuries, she'd told herself, failing to be convinced that what one believes can often be a far cry from the truth.

Claire Clairmont had given herself over to such passion, mentally and physically, and would challenge anyone who tried to tell her otherwise. Past events were over and she truly believed herself to be the great paramour of the poet lord's life.

Ah, the feelings we shared! I wonder, what would those smart, effete society ladies bedecked in finery and jewels have deigned to become, husbands or no, in their efforts to spend private time with you, my lord? And me, only seventeen then, succeeding where they failed. One ridiculous letter, sent to you at Drury Lane Theatre and signed "E. Trefusis" after a Cornish connection of father's was sufficient to whet your curiosity. My unstained reputation... placing my happiness in your hands... with a beating heart, I confessed my love, but above all, I tested that curiosity when I wrote, "It is for the piercing eye of genius to discover my disguise."

My passion for music dictated I played the piano and sang for you. They were your lyrics, Lord B, and you were beguiled. And yet I agree your comment concerning marriage in one of your many notes which precipitated our arranged meeting. You wrote something like, "I can never resist throwing a pebble at it as I pass by." One supposes it justifies your aim in life to break the fragile glass of every marriage you could. Or the hymen of every virgin.

'I believe you and I have much in common,' Byron said to me that first night.

It is where it properly started.

CHAPTER 2

'When, pois'd upon the gale,
my form shall ride...'

I

By candlelight in a quiet room housed in a country inn, hushed apart from barely heard sounds of revelry from the floor below, a few excited screams, laughter permeating from sundry other rented rooms. The subtle air dances with mischief, wine flows, and sherry, despite what he called 'its mothiness', being Byron's favourite tipple. She laughs at the quaint phrase, quizzes him about it.

'At the Abbey,' he says, 'Joe Murray, or one of the others would bring in the tray with the sherry decanter. More often than not the stopper would be left out and the moths would get in and drown. Either that or they were drunk.'

Claire laughs. 'And you drank it?'

'Why yes, it gave an added bouquet.' He taunts her with another smile, Claire unsure whether or not he is jesting. He catches the look. 'I assure you it's true. But then taste becomes academic after a while. I mean I will drink anything and everything if and when it suits. Including tea.'

And whether through the room's potency, its design, or their presence, Claire welcomes the poet who already treats her as "that odd-headed girl".

'So many letters I wrote you, my lord.' She smiles up at him from the stool upon which she crouches, fire flames creating subtle shades graced with intent. One hand plays across his left thigh. 'To imagine they brought us here to this haven.'

'That they did.' Byron, his pale, ascetic face emphasised by the subdued light, reflects on one letter he'd written to a friend, his smile directed at Claire, yet for quite a different reason. For he had written: "A man is a man, and if a girl of eighteen comes prancing to you at all hours, there is but one way."

He combs her dark brown hair with his fingers. 'Claire, your blend of humility and tenacity displays the essential arrogance of your nature. Girl, you invite rejection and yet you resent it. I admit I am weak when it comes to womankind.' He glances towards the bed, firelight prancing across the low ceiling. Their shadows merge, become one, parting only briefly before merging again. 'I warn you, dearest Claire. I fear this will lead nowhere.'

'My lord, be silent. There is but one place we wish to be, and that is here, now, tonight, the door closed from prying eyes.' Her smile smacks of conquest; being alone with her icon, her god, is all she seeks. 'Sometimes I would give anything to see their jealous faces, their down-curved, disapproving mouths.' She thinks: For me to tell the world my lover is none other than Lord Byron will more than equal the ambitions of Mary.

'You see, m'lord,' she trills, a promise in her eyes, warm shadows cavorting across unclothed arms, 'I have acquired the most literary lion of today as my lover. Time will show you that I love gently and with affection, that I am incapable of revenge.'

Further words prove useless. Claire rises to lay herself across his lap, nimble fingers undoing his buttons, massaging his ardour. Her head comes towards his chest. He bends forward to meet her, lips brush as her hand travels further. Byron moans, fingers snake about her bodice, popping buttons, tugging it down, Claire's soft 'Aahh' dies as warm air envelops her naked shoulders, her breasts. Her nipples harden, an integral part of the prelude to his rising, forcing her towards the bed to which she goes willingly...

Nor could she ever know that Byron's search for the deep love he craved would go far beyond her need for him.

II

Claire nursed her secret smile, still experiencing him deep inside her, aware also and very sure that she and Byron would be reacquainted soon.

To this selfish end she preyed on Mary and Shelley, her suggestions and scheming prompting them to arrange for their small entourage to meet Byron's on the shore of Lake Léman close by Geneva. She didn't doubt the decision to come here had been largely initiated by herself, and admitted privately that Mary could be right, and that she may have been a pest.

When they arrived and she faced him for the first time, perhaps she would tell him her good news and they would marry.

Her letters kept him informed of progress, but she had never received a reply. A new life awaited her in Switzerland, she decided.

True, Byron had said things, often hurtful things brimming with bitter recrimination, but Claire ignored them, blaming his restless spirit. Far easier to come up with some tolerable excuse than debate the ramifications of half-truths heard from others. And, of course, his non-compliance could easily be blamed on the fact that he'd found himself in debt, and become the butt of people's raw and often despicable comments. Yes, another reason for his sometimes curt dismissals. As soon as they met again in different climes and circumstances, Claire assured herself all would be well.

She dozed and dreamed, barely conscious of Mary and Shelley talking *sotto voce*, the tempest outside rising, falling, as her body and senses had that night, her animalistic passion meeting the poet's urgent demands, unabated fury melded for several, magical hours. Had she ever known passion could be so... so exact and exacting? Or even guessed that her chosen lover would meet her expectations?

Naturally she did, because she wanted to believe it. Because Byron had told her he loved her. But what she didn't realise was that Byron loved her for all the wrong reasons: his belief that love mattered in life's endless search for its perfection.

He would say later: 'I did not know that love was always there for me, that I should never have spent all my life searching for it. Claire was one among many: another love, yet nothing special. She knew this, yet demanded more. She was upset when I departed because she wished things to be more permanent.'

III

Through fluttering lashes Claire glanced at Shelley, lost in his own musings.

Enthusiasm drained, the decision to leave Les Rousses, to reject cheerless towns, infected landscapes, proved easy. Harassed by antisocial inhabitants, and the seediness of a France scarred by years of unrest, prompted their mutual agreement to depart this repressed area of Europe: it bore the weight of too many dead to allow it to breathe, its abundance of mass executions a damning indictment on the futility of war.

To Shelley, and Mary, sheer doggedness conjured visions of beauty beyond mountains that might prove unattainable. Surreal impressions romped in their sub-conscious, such pictures cultivated from their earlier tour: lush meadows, towering horizons and air that would enrich mind and body.

'Fresh, abundant, like breathing ice,' Mary once said to Shelley when they were alone on one of their many walks. Holding this dream, they tolerated the discomforts of those miserable French towns. This time determination and intent became the key to their hope of burying disappointment and disillusionment.

In turn, the three of them would discover that plans, like minds, are fickle, and present difficulties unlooked and uncalled for. But then all are masters of their own destiny in some way, shape or form.

In all walks of life, people are erratic in their thinking, often unable to reach decisions or stand by them. Humanity is contrary and sometimes its own worst enemy. Human nature belies the concepts of true living, especially living together, certain individuals torn in various directions for whatever inane reason.

There was Claire's implacable will driving herself and them forward: in her case, and not hard to guess, an egotistic fulfilment of her chosen destiny, a destiny which would not be denied in her own eyes, but certainly would be in those of another! Claire *believed* she had snared her Adonis, her man. Whatever she believed would be no less fraught than the moment when she would eventually realise the truth.

For something to say, Claire, without realising she demeaned Shelley, said, 'The practicalities of arranging our departure were fraught. Your efforts to locate a coachman willing to risk this... this mountain track were bad enough, but finding ten others who would walk with the coach, took too long.'

'At least I did find them,' argued Shelley, unprepared to be chastised. 'All you did was languish on a bed dreaming of... of other things.'

He sought Mary's help. 'We needed willing men to see us safely to our destination. I admit they are brave, and greedy, but don't shirk their tasks. I haggled and won. And I told you it would be less extortionate than the cost of staying at an inn.'

'Dearest,' Mary said, 'my one real objection is these stinking, threadbare rugs. It's a long night and our opinions, for what they are, have grown tiresome. To attempt the journey to Switzerland was folly even in daylight.'

Oh dear, she thought, afraid for her relationship should she say too much. Such is the non-compatibility of those who feel they are in love – it's easier to please, rather than argue. Are we that unsure of each other? Arguments, Mary accepted, were never the answer. But does my Shelley subscribe to that? She confessed she didn't know, and couldn't resist adding, 'Only the mad English would consider starting out at six in the evening!'

'You have a point, Mary,' Shelley hit back somewhat alarmingly. 'Do you not agree that some comfort can be had from this? The cold has purged us of the parasites and turbulent memories we strive to leave behind.'

Mary completed her ministrations with the child, slowly nodding at Shelley's words. Rather than create further problems between them she said, 'I marvel at the robustness of those trees.' She peered through another rough circle of cleared glass. 'I hope we are as robust.'

'They remind me of the Coliseum in Rome,' Shelley said, 'guarding the atrocities committed within.' He ached to hold Mary, yet was afraid Claire would take umbrage. Yes, hold Mary, tell her he loved her, have him purge his sudden presentiment of foreboding.

Mary made light of it. 'Quite apt, Shelley. For all its wild beauty, this is a terrible place, a wilderness of ice and rock devoid of any living creature.'

'Aye, a kind of purgatory.' Shelley's shadowed smile waned. 'Perhaps the souls of the damned are not consigned to some fiery hell but are ordered here to endlessly wander this frozen desert. Hear? They call from the mountain crevices and crags, insisting we join them. The horses will be attuned to 'em, their senses demanding they pull harder, and quickly bring us down from this cold tomb. Will such shadows lure us from our chosen way? The lateness of the hour does tempt such abominations.'

'Stop it, Shelley!' Mary's pulses quickened, a sick feeling settling in her lower belly. Outside, grey, unsettling spectres swirled – *Her mother screaming in pain as the fever took hold... Father berating all doctors...*

Imagination gripped, a seed planted, an idea to create someone who would be the giver of life, never one to destroy it. She willed Shelley to stem his mournful diatribe, her sternness tinged now with more than a little fear. Life. Death. But what of the in-between?

The stark image of a castle reared. Gripping the northern edge of a vast chunk of rock known as Magnet Mountain, this particular edifice awesome to behold in the twilight.

Recalled from 1814, all of them certainly younger, more impressionable, especially Mary. How could she forget, for the image appeared as clear now, as it had then?

Disintegrating walls, eroded by moss and lichen, which the locals termed 'mountain overgrowth'. Two command towers, smaller, rounded donjons – a kind of misplaced architecture that formed part of this medieval castle named Frankenstein.

Here were pulleys and palisades, porticos, observation posts, the structure's formidable walls anchored to the rock ; moat and a drawbridge, whose end stones emerged from the castle wall... and the deep, dark entrance tunnel that led into the very heart of the building...

Mary attempted to shake off the vision, the ice-rimed window presenting distorted faces, each representing her image of the castle, the people who dwelled there. On the wind she heard the local witch's warning, whispered to her one evening of their stay: 'Depart ere the chimes of midnight ring when ghosts, hobgoblins and other demonic sprites will play havoc with you, the unwary.'

Here again the dark tunnel, a hideous, malformed uterus that climbed into the womb of this... this invidious *Mother,* this castle perched upon its rock, housing within it the tombs of a few prominent members of the family Frankenstein. Housing within the means to... to give *birth?*

Frankenstein. A name to conjure with. Mary played it in her mind, wondering how she would ever forget it. Such a melodic ring. Frank-en-stein!

She masked her unfounded unease with an excuse, finding it easier to blame another. She said, 'Shelley, please don't harbour such thoughts, Claire is very susceptible to your imaginings.'

Claire's eyes bulged as she stared towards her own distant vision, her breath emitted in short gasps.

A confinement. Her own. And pain. For the sake of love?

An argument. With Byron. He said: '*Claire, you are never satisfied with anything in life, not just my lovemaking –*'

'Yes. YES I am.'

Shelley and Mary heard, looked concerned.

'*Oh, you're happy enough when it suits,*' Byron said, '*but it is always in your nature to complain.*'

'No. I never complain. And never to you.'

Mary touched her hand, finding it cold, and sweaty. Suddenly, more anxious over Claire's demeanour, Mary thrust the child at the bewildered poet. 'Here Shelley, take William!' She pressed her hand gently to Claire's cold cheek. 'Claire, you must ignore Shelley. His ghosts are inside his head, not here in this waste.'

Something might be. Ask this of yourself, Mary: *Where are your own ghosts?*

This whittled at Mary. She held Claire, seeking a *soupçon* of comfort, the awfulness of the thought refusing to relinquish its grip. Gradually Claire's breathing grew less worrisome, stressed gasps comparable to those of a puppy whimpering. She slumped against the tacky upholstery. About to remove her arm from around Claire, Mary sensed her involuntary shudder. 'Such visions stalk not only Shelley's thoughts,' Claire muttered, instantly turning away from the window unable to look upon the swirling drop into nothingness on her side of the coach. Addressing neither Mary nor Shelley, Claire said, 'I feel there is a creature which occupies the dark recesses of all our minds. It may be conscience, or the embodiment of all thoughts and fears we dare not give voice or form to. A portent of the future whose shape we cannot control.'

Mary, straining to catch what she said, was forced to agree. She thought again of her mother. *Something from the tomb... Or the womb. Some entity we nurture within ourselves but keep hidden. Something from the hidden shadows of the castle?*

Shelley took Claire's words to heart, certain malevolent images from his own past re-manufactured: of ghosts seen in the half-light of a room, on the edge of an eye.

Claire's phrases were a blight, and caused them all to see something that perhaps proved difficult to assess with any truth: a formless, detestable thing, a mind-ghost buried deep inside each soul.

The light in Claire's eyes continued dull: shadows obscured the light gained from one pitiful, flickering flame of a coach lamp.

'*A portent of the future whose shape we cannot control.*' The statement gained stature. Mary, taking William from Shelley, sought solace from innocence even though some featureless imp prodded her imagination.

'Shelley,' Claire whispered, a plea transparent, 'you are our protector now; we look to you to banish these foolish fancies.'

Shelley recognised this, aware how much they did depend on him. He smiled directly at Claire, the gesture noticed by Mary who read it as one of friendly affection rather than anything remotely suspicious, even when Shelley invited, 'Claire, come share my rug,' and beckoned her to join him.

As Claire slid across the seat, Shelley enfolded her in the rug. He drew her close and as though in defiance of what Mary might construe from his action lifted Claire's chin with his free hand and kissed her gently on the lips before settling her head against his shoulder.

Mary continued to rock William, pleased he'd settled after his feed. Easy to seek refuge in her love for the child yet loathe to think that he would grow into the corruption life may throw at him. She promised: It's up to me to safeguard and protect.

IV

'Of course there is one person more celebrated than I who will occupy a role of protector, Claire,' Shelley teased, his tone flippant, bringing Mary out of her maudlin thoughts.

Claire's satisfied sigh emphasised how she contemplated her own future. 'Whatever destiny holds for me with Lord Byron – ' she glanced up at Shelley, then across to Mary, 'nothing will ever replace this little family of ours, or the love that I hold for you and Mary.'

Mary nodded, to smile easier than voicing some crass remark. In all honesty, Mary did not wish to invite her sister's company, or seem over-enthusiastic. It did, however, make her ponder on how she might prevent it.

Shelley, failing to observe her tension, eased himself into a more comfortable position, as far as cramped conditions allowed. He tugged up the rug. 'If he be your protector, Claire – ' he gazed on her with obvious fondness, 'then, my dear, you are doubly fortunate to have the affections of so many worthy individuals. Let us declare that our futures will be as *we* make them... together. This duress departs only slightly from our intentions. We should look upon it as a door which will lead us from an impoverished past, into a world of new prospects.'

Shelley persuaded himself that such thoughts and opinions regarding their future had to be right. He agreed no man could be certain, but if we are all set on a certain course then surely tenacity and ambition will lead us to our intended goals.

'This time,' he declared, 'we will never return to the crumbled ideals and decaying regimes of a country through which we have travelled.' He hugged Claire, her dreams as flyaway as the swirling snow. 'Now, try to sleep for dawn will soon be upon us.'

After only a short time all but Shelley had lapsed into a restless slumber. Mutterings from the women as they chased respective dreams proved disruptive, sleep for him hard to find. He knew full well his charges must be protected. He could not do that if he were asleep. A lightening sky excited his attention. Unobtrusively, the attitude of the coach altered as the front dropped, men moving forward to assist with the braking.

Melting ice ran down the window, Shelley able to see and raise an arm to one of the men, to have it returned with a grin. A positive gesture, all guessing journey's end was nearly reached, the descent gradual, less bone-jerking, the banter from without light, humorous. Clearings appeared between the trees, became more profuse the further they travelled; slowly improving light revealed a squat wooden hut partially robed with new growth. 'A shepherd's,' Shelley decided, 'for only cows graze on the lower pastures.'

Tension eased: despite argument he preened himself, glad to be proved right in persuading them to make the journey. Contentment took the place of edginess as the unacceptable mountain winter now allowed glimpses of the herds returning. Patches of shrub and grass peeked from the suffocating blanket of white, the bad season finally giving out as the coach lumbered towards the lushness of an embracing valley.

Time brings its own rewards, Shelley pleased to have led them from the wilderness into a new sunshine.

Sadly it would be a blighted summer, but Shelley couldn't know it yet.

The sound of bells carried, caused them all to stir as they passed a herd of lethargic fat cows chewing spring grass. Here, houses were precisely placed in the landscape, brightly-coloured hues of roofs and open shutters greeting them; flowers trimmed a multitude of balconies, the land's undulations giving the impression all had been professionally landscaped, each configuration contradicting the indistinct, chaotic nature of the wilder climes so recently deserted.

'What a marvellous transformation.' Shelley's dark thoughts were displaced; still there, yet forgotten for the moment.

The environment breathed opportunity, became less a yoke about their fragile shoulders. Scents of meadow grass and flowers floated, mountain peaks stepped back into purple-hazed distance, their indefinable mystery shrouded by luminous shawls of cloud that added to the overall intransigence. Sunlight touched them, Shelley reminded of distant beacons. *"Look,"* they whispered, *"this is your dream, your destiny. Welcome."*

He leant forward to better appraise a seething mass of liquid-coloured light that united sky and land, an indigo surface like a carpet of spun silk. In the foreground a cluster of buildings, haphazardly placed with little regard to symmetry, a rightness about them which made his heart sing.

'See,' exclaimed Shelley, 'the lake!' He shook Mary properly awake. 'Our journey is done. Tonight we can enjoy a palatable meal *and* clean sheets.'

'A notion more comfortable than these wretched rugs,' a relieved Mary stated, stifling a yawn and throwing hers aside before checking on William.

Shelley leaned out of the window, the sweet air prompting a collective sigh of satisfaction.

Although lulled into that which is described as a state of false security, each would realise that, lost for now within the murk of their minds, footsteps paced. To whom they belonged prompted another question.

The date was May 15th 1816.

Ten days later, Lord Byron and Doctor John Polidori would arrive.

CHAPTER 3

'Beyond imagination's power.'

SUNSET. The rich colour of claret – the hue of blood – reflected in stagnant pools, imbuing the dust of Waterloo. Sunset and shadows – an image of a grey horse, a dark rider; a blot of shadow – perhaps the image of... a dog? – in a wasteland of mud; a calm sea breaking on a flat, wind-swept shoreline; dirty, grey-white buildings, the stench and humidity. A church.

A trick of light? Projected thoughts? Or real?

To the man sitting astride his horse it appeared *real*. He shaded his eyes as the mirage flickered, changed into something more definable.

On the 25th April 1816, George Gordon Noel, the 6th Lord Byron, walks with his friend Hobhouse towards a rough sea, where he boards the Dover packet bound for Ostend. Farewells over, Hobhouse watches the ship cantering over the swell, stating to others, 'The dear fellow pulled off his cap and waved it to me... God bless him for a gallant spirit and a kind one...'

And bless me – Byron shifted in the saddle – if the inn at Ostend did bid me celebrate it with a predatory spring. That their chamber maid rogered like a good 'un.

He smiled, the memory waning as his companion reigned in beside him.

'You look pre-occupied, m'lord.' The doctor's elegant fingers fiddled nervously with the reins of his bay. 'Haven't we seen enough?' He brought the horse round, both apparently impatient to leave.

Byron noted John Polidori's dithering, the way he sat his horse hardly that of an experienced rider. The movements irritated him. Half a mind to say something, he took a different tack, hoping to steer Polidori's attention to something less fearful than this battlefield.

'Y'know, Polly, I had no liking for Flanders, its voluptuous art, or its flat landscape.' He would later write to Augusta Leigh, his step-sister, that *"Reubens' women have all red gowns and red shoulders – to say nothing of necks."*

Byron would be reminded of this when he again set eyes on Claire Clairmont.

Dusting his coat sleeve, he stared across the barren expanse, gaze clouded to question. 'Level roads don't suit me; it must be up hill or down. Hell, Polly, those great *pavés* along which Wellington and Blücher drove Napoleon are an eternity of pavement...' Yet here, on the edge of Waterloo, he appeared dumbstruck, time spent in contemplation. 'Y'know,' he said, 'I've seen the plains of Marathon, and these are as fine.' Still taken with the awesome grandeur of plain, and distant fields, a fire burning in his eyes, his jaw set, he went on, 'I have this strange notion to gallop across this field, across this hell, this... this place of skulls.'

The words pricked at his composing conscience: *And Harold stands upon this place of skulls, The grave of France, the deadly Waterloo!* 'Yes, the third canto I think.'

Before his companion could respond Byron spurred his horse, its startled grunt cleaving the silence, horse and rider concealed by swirls of dust thrown up by beating hooves.

'Not another of his stupid whims.' Distraught, Polidori heeled the flanks of his own mount with such brutality the alarmed animal responded with a scream of pain and reared, the doctor almost sent toppling, a tight grip on the reins preventing a nasty fall as the horse plunged forward.

Eyes glaring, dark hair flying, mount at full stretch, Polidori was bound to let the horse have its head, his efforts to control it comical in the extreme.

Foolishness girded with silly superstition had promoted his unease, his mind disturbed by visions which smacked of recent, and awesome, reality. Attention diverted by flashing, barely seen images beneath the flying hooves, he saw – a glint of steel, stained with sunset's blood, an abandoned sword thrust like a grave-marker into a patch of mud; the flash of gilded buttons hanging by a thread from torn tunics; a boot, its spur rowel whirling; several sheets of paper – a lost letter never sent perhaps – trapped in the slipstream; an epaulette from another sodden, muddy tunic. And then he heard a sharp, shocking crack, his own startled cry emitted as hooves crushed bone. Shards of skull scattered, Polidori now more terrified as the gloom ingested the sound. Beneath his raiment his heart banged like a drum, that same rat-a-tat-tat a drummer boy would beat as the army marched into battle. Fear dried his mouth, the feeling of alone-ness in this wasteland of the dead forcing an adrenaline rush. He yanked at the reins, shoulders and arms screaming through effort. The horse skidded, nearly went down, its haunches buried in mud as it struggled to right itself. Polidori sweated, breath hard won.

He fought to dislodge grotesque impressions amassed inside his head, wondering if he was seeing the shades of vainglorious defeated, hammered into the field by ferocious hordes, rising, dead eyes lent a semblance of awful life by the visceral sun, their gazes falling on him like some collective accusation.

Accusing him of what? Being in this place with Lord Byron?

Viewing the terrible scene, Polidori cried out, seeking absolution, the cry overpowered by an unfamiliar song telling of battle, death and redemption. Yet he swore he recognised the Albanian war song, its raucous implication peaking, certain phrases lacking definition as the distorted lyrics carried on the breeze.

Puzzled, he raised himself in the stirrups to scan the sundered landscape, attempting to locate the source through choking dust. Try as he might, he could not shake off the visions of the dead rising to do battle, their voices united, the cant louder, the sound so much more disquieting. He coughed, desperate to clear his throat, the noise suspended in the dank air, the day's heat reduced, another cheerless reminder of his predicament.

'Damn you, Byron!' He waved the dust away, made it worse, only antagonising his situation. He couldn't see. And because of it, the mind conjured things which he hoped weren't really there.

The relentless tune besieged. Apprehensive, he urged the horse slowly forward, the mount snorting confidence. Eyes gritty through staring as he tried to locate anything that made sense in this impoverished place, Polidori shivered. 'Should leave,' he kept repeating. 'Go back, rejoin Fletcher and the others.' Foolhardiness and a sense of dedication intruded, made him see sense. 'Have to find the fool. Yes, find him, if only to reassure myself all is well.' He cursed his imagination. In this lonely place there must be something tangible to lay the images he'd beheld. 'So, who is the real fool?'

A dancing, grey, pastel-hued vapour obscured immediate surroundings; the fusion of late evening mist and dust soured his concept. Shadows lengthened, darker tints punctuated by a more solid object. 'Ah!' Not a joyous sound, it lacked conviction, even though Polidori hoped he'd glimpsed Byron. He called out: 'BYRON!' only the tinniest of echoes rolling back from the dull, diffused desolation.

'Where in Hell are you?' Unhealthy the way the word *Hell* took on a more sinister implication. He dithered, a feeling of intense cold unremitting. A breathy expulsion of air melded with the horse's sudden snort, as both sensed and saw a clawing, angular shape establishing itself through the murk. 'Mother of God!' The horse stopped of its own accord, sensing Polidori's fear. It backed off. The man gawped, unwilling to decipher the distorted shape's grim, darkly twisted hands. 'Pray I might lay the ghosts of childhood nightmare,' he whimpered.

Head averted, he found courage to peer between splayed fingers as that same child inside him might have done from beneath its bed covers. He saw – a tree! Admittedly rendered less a tree by cannon shot, but nevertheless a natural thing. Bark crumbled when he touched it.

On the edge of his relieved sigh, the galling tune increased in decibels.

Am I seeing things? Thoughts plummeted, the horse's startled whinny alerting him. Its breath curled in lazy phantoms linked to the encroaching mist. It lives. 'Holy – the shape lives!' It has to be Byron. Who else can it be?

Ghosts? He would reflect upon this on a night in the future, when the storms raged... For now, Polidori was forced to accept that nightmares had a habit of prompting truths, especially in such isolation. Further movement, the tune's cant debauched. It shredded his belief in what, until now, he wished to believe were healthy pastimes.

The noise crescendoed, its harbinger, the errant minstrel, gradually gaining more substance. The mist parted and closed behind the rider. Saddle leather creaked, a bridle chinked: the rider adjusted his posture, darker hues as solid as the tree. And less spectral.

Yet here amidst restless dead Polidori could not for the life of him reconcile it.

The horse broke into a canter, a laugh from Byron taken as a personal affront by Polidori. Passing the still agitated doctor, Byron dismissed him as though Polidori were part of the landscape rather than anything remotely substantial. Polidori was nothing of the kind, accepting and gratefully willing to acknowledge a companion, to laugh off silly thoughts in an effort to allay anxiety.

Byron slowed as the final, hummed bars of the song trickled away. He reined in. Turning, his smile was deprecating, and he tendered an audacious wave. 'Did you enjoy the gallop, John?' Excitement was evident, exhilaration more so. 'Truthfully, what did you think to my outrageous song? 'Tis but an Albanian war song, and I think fitting in such a place.'

Yes, thought Polidori. Oh yes, LB. Small wonder Mary and Claire nickname you *Albè*. It is a name that speaks of holier-than-thou preaching. You are one who courts the dead, and bathes in battlefield glory – the dark cowl of indifference worn about an enigmatic face.

Polidori reined in, scant feet from Byron, his condescending stare countered by the cynical air which Byron adopted. 'It would have been better had I understood the content,' Polidori said. 'I think it blasphemous to scatter tavern songs amidst the graves of fallen brave.'

'Pah! I'll wager a goodly number of fallen brave spent their final evening in a tavern singing much worse, their weapons primed, their target any maiden foolish enough to stray within range. 'Tis what I would have done.'

Polidori scorned the risqué humour. 'A form of combat with which you are well acquainted then.' His remark scorched a hole in the air between them.

Byron, unfazed by it, replied curtly, 'True, Polly. I have to say that I pride myself on my marksmanship.' A sardonic smile appeared, grudgingly given. 'Doctor John, despite the fact of your English roots, your humour and sarcasm surprise me. I admit y'sometimes dreary company has certainly been enlivened by my own reckless larks. It's apparent my actions have served useful purpose.'

Byron leaned towards the Doctor, and sounded deadly serious when he said slowly, pointedly, 'Yet even you are not privy to all my sensibilities.' A second disparaging look could hardly be avoided. 'I mourn the loss of any life in this vile place but –' Byron gazed into the mist seeing his own misspent youth, Polidori flummoxed by it. 'Most of all I mourn the loss of a dream. In this soulless land freedom has been trampled, buried with the bones of the vanquished.'

If Polidori did sense any reference to his own wilful trampling of the dead, he didn't show it. 'Freedom for who, m'lord? When have the lowly ever been free? Revolutions satisfy the vanity of the few, the most wealthy and educated.' Polidori deemed his opinion worthy of stating and wouldn't give ground. 'You consider yourself champion of the dispossessed, yet rank and privilege create an unbridgeable chasm whose opposite bank you'll never behold.'

Byron avoided Polidori's searching gaze. 'It's true I have known poverty and rejection.'

'But neither famine nor servitude... and you never will.'

Aware Polidori's words hinted at a greater truth, Byron patted the horse's neck. 'Walk on.' He called over his shoulder: 'Dispel your fears, John; we are done here, our carriage awaits.'

Doctor Polidori, a servant in the wake of a master he would not acknowledge as such, had little choice but to follow. 'And what, pray, do we do with the horses?'

'Why we leave 'em, my friend.' Such a serious remark bucked no retaliation. 'Dammit, man, it's where we found 'em. They belong here with their dead masters.' Dismounting, Byron uttered: *As the ground was before, thus let it be; How that red rain hath made the harvest grow!'*

'Beg pardon, m'lord?' Polidori heard yet remained confused by Byron's moods, his turns of phrase. Might he, too, have seen the harvest *grow*?

'Nothing. Mere musings is all. Too many shadows gather about me.'

CHAPTER 4

'Such partings break the heart...'

I

Dressed in a dark suit, Polidori, hair immaculately coiffed, refused to look upon the man reclining some little distance away on his ornate bed.

Still irked by Byron's attitude, he saw Byron as a petulant child who couldn't get his own way. You and your ideal standards, with an imagination that courts genius, not a stain or furrow on your alabaster skin. And I... *I* am your physician. He had sought the post, made himself a nuisance yet, if asked, wouldn't wish to admit it. Or the fact he could well be the petulant child. Seething from his exchange with the man others considered to be his mentor – a point Polidori would dispute – he said, without looking directly at him, 'You think me ill-informed, m'lord, and much less a connoisseur than your good self.'

He cast a cursory eye over the oversized interior of the diligence, its finery chosen as befitted a person of Byron's standing. Soon, Polidori assured himself, I will afford a silk covered couch *and* bookshelves to house my own choice of reading. Resentment permeated him, heightened his ambition. He wanted his own plate chest and crockery and an ornate bed. He turned away to avoid Byron remarking – as he assuredly would – on his abrasive smile, his remark intended more as a jibe than an observation.

Days ago, in this May of 1816, and out of this same window, he and Byron looked upon the lonely battlefield of Waterloo, the area, fitting enough to accommodate the carriage, fashioned by Byron after Napoleon's famous mode of transport. With its encumbrance of upholstery, it was still large enough to dine in, though Byron insisted upon dining outside whenever he could.

The jingle of harness intruded, as did the muted demands from three servants – including the one-time labourer, Fletcher, now elevated to the position of his lordship's valet – who trailed behind, there to attend to his lordship's welfare, look after luggage, and a menagerie of animals of varying sizes and description that included two parakeets and a decisively belligerent monkey.

Byron's penetrating, light grey eyes, either side of a handsome though rather thick nose, observed Polidori, who looked away feeling as if he were on trial.

Byron propped himself against a headboard decorated with gold scrolls and tails, silken cushions in disarray, his cool grin revealing white, regular teeth, appearing less white beneath his pale complexion. Still those veiled eyes would parry anything other than an initial first impression, the man fearful of allowing anyone other than the chosen to penetrate his façade.

Not yet in his prime – at twenty-eight what man would be, specifically when the elevated title *Baron of Rochdale* had been granted by reason of lineage? – his broad shoulders, his body and limbs were well-proportioned, yet slightly contradicted his small, patrician head and curly hair. His forehead appeared a little too narrow but high, and accentuated by Byron's shaving the hair away from his temples leaving the other glossy, dark brown curls to cluster over his head. This offered a fuller, defined look and hid the fact that his hair was thinning. Combined, every feature sustained an airy, graceful appearance and one that accentuated the massiveness and length of his throat and genius highlighted in his eyes and lips.

He was tired, but enjoyably tired. Certain aspects of the journey had been disagreeable, not least the tiresome breaking down of the coach, which hadn't helped his temper. Thank God he could write it out of his system; leastways it alleviated immediate discomfort and ultimately placed some of the burden on Hobhouse, his one trusted and reliable friend in a sea of uncertainty. Byron had written:

TO JOHN CAM HOBHOUSE, Bruxelles--May 1st 1816
My dear H,

You will be surprised that we are not more *en avant* and so am I -- but Mr. Baxter's wheels and springs have not done their duty -- for which I beg that you will abuse him like a pickpocket (that is – He -- the said Baxter being the pickpocket) and say that I expect a deduction -- having been obliged to come out of the way to this place -- which was not in my route --

for repairs -- which however I hope to have accomplished so as to put us in motion in a day or two.

We passed through Ghent – Antwerp -- and Mechlin -- & thence diverged here -- having seen all the sights – pictures – docks — basins -- & having climbed up steeples &c. & so forth ---- the first thing -- after the flatness & fertility of the country which struck me was the beauty of the towns -- Bruges first -- where you may tell Douglas Kinnaird -- on entering at Sunset -- I overtook a crew of beggarly-looking gentlemen not unlike Oxberry -- headed by a Monarch with a Staff the very facsimile of King Clause in the said Douglas Kinnaird's revived drama.

We lost our way in the dark -- or rather twilight -- not far from Ghent -- by the stupidity of the postilion (one only, by the way, to horses) which produced an alarm of intended robbery among the uninitiated -- whom I could not convince -- that four or five well-armed people were not immediately to be plundered and anatomized by a single person fortified with a horsewhip to be sure but nevertheless a little encumbered with large jack boots -- and a tight jacket that did not fit him -- the way was found again without loss of life or limb: I thought the learned Fletcher at least would have known better after our Turkish expeditions -- and defiles -- and banditti -- & guards &c. &c. than to have been so valourously alert without at least a better pretext for his superfluous courage. I don't mean to say that they were frightened but they were vastly suspicious without any cause.

At Ghent we stared at pictures -- & climbed up a steeple 450 steps in altitude from which I had a good view & notion of these *paese bassi*.

Next day we broke down -- by a damned wheel (on which Baxter should be broken) pertinaciously refusing its stipulated rotation -- this becalmed us at Lo Kristi -- (2 leagues from Ghent) -- & obliged us to return for repairs -- At Lo Kristi I came to anchor in the house of a Flemish Blacksmith (who was ill of a fever for which Dr. Dori physicked him -- I dare say he is dead by now) and saw somewhat of Lo Kristi – Low – country – low life -- which regaled us much -- besides it being a Sunday -- all the world were on their way to Mass -- & I had the pleasure of seeing a number of very ordinary women in extraordinary garments: -- we found the *Contadini* however very good natured & obliging though not at all useful.

At Antwerp we pictured – churched -- and steepled again -- but the principal Street and bason pleased me most -- poor dear Bonaparte!!! -- and the foundries &c. -- as for Rubens -- I was glad to see his tomb on account of that ridiculous description (in Smollet's *Peregrine Pickle*) of Pallet's absurdity at his monument -- but as for his works -- and his superb *tableaux* -- he seems to me (who by the way know nothing of the matter) the most glaring – flaring – staring -- harlotry imposter that ever passed a trick upon the senses of mankind -- it is not nature -- it is not art -- with the exception of some linen (which hangs over the cross in one of his pictures) which to do it justice looked like a very handsome table cloth -- I never saw such an assemblage of florid night-mares as his canvas contains -- his portraits seem clothed in pulpit cushions.

On the way to Mechlin -- a wheel -- & a spring too gave way -- that is -- the one went -- & the other would not go -- so we came off here to get into dock -- I hope we shall sail shortly -- On to Geneva.

Will you have the goodness -- to get at my account at Hoares -- (my bankers). I believe there must be a balance in my favour -- as I did not draw a great deal previous to going: -- whatever there may be over the two thousand five hundred -- they can send by you to me in a further credit when you come out: -- I wish you to enquire (for fear any tricks might be played with my drafts) my bankers books left with you -- will show you exactly what I have drawn -- and you can let them have the book to make out the remainder of the

account. All I have to urge to Hanson -- or to our friend
Douglas Kinnaird -- is to sell Newstead if possible.

All kind things to Scrope -- and the rest — ever
yrs. most truly & obligedly B

Byron's diamond-chipped stare detected Polidori's discomfort. Yes,
he deliberated, small wonder the farmer didn't expire from the
obnoxious concoction you poured down his throat, *doctor*!

'It may be fitting,' he suggested in that low tone he adopted,
'to administer the same physic you offered the farmer t'other day,
Polly. Your frail constitution contradicts your eagerness to venture
this far.' He eased himself , and shoved a silk cushion beneath him.
'That's better. Riding straddle legged across a saddle makes the
rump a little raw.'

'Do I detect a slight trace of your Scottish ancestry,
m'lord?' Polidori inquired. 'You have a slight impediment when
pronouncing your 'r's.'

Byron's eyes reached for the ceiling of the carriage. 'God,
man, not you. That silly woman Claire had the gall to tell me, and I
quote: "You have an engaging brogue, could it be a Scottish accent, I
wonder?" Unquote.'

'And you denied it?'

'Too right I did. Told her, though only in mock rage, that I
hoped not. I'd rather the whole damned country was sunk in the sea
– I with a Scottish accent! Enough of that. I'd prefer to forget the
bitch.' He didn't, forced to say, 'And d'you know what she wrote
me? Ended one letter with the words, "Farewell, dear kind Lord
Byron. I have been reading all your poems and almost fear to think
of you reading this stupid letter, but I love you."'

'Another follower,' quipped Polidori. 'You certainly have a
magnetism second to none.'

He caught Polidori's amused look. 'Tell you what,' he said,
'for a physician who is constantly sick – even at Karlsruhe we had to
linger because of your headaches and feverishness – '

'It gave you time to pounce on another chambermaid,'
Polidori shot back. 'So enhancing your reputation.'

'– and I sympathise due to my own illnesses,' Byron went
on. 'My confidence in you is sometimes lacking. Daresay your still

obvious paleness has been advanced by your unwillingness to ride t'other day.'

'*He'll be the cause of grief to you both, George.*' John Cam Hobhouse's words in reference to John Polidori, said to Byron before they left England. And Hobby always had his interests at heart. Hobby was there to be hearkened to, simply because he was rarely wrong, his beak nose, cupid-bow lips and acerbic wit masking a more lucid intelligence which made him a shrewd judge of character.

Blessed if you aren't correct, Hobby. Byron noted Polidori had ignored the reference to their gallop and turned away. Why, he thought, does the man want to enjoy the landscape when he so utterly maligned it only forty-eight hours before?

Byron used the welcome silence to reflect on his situation.

II

He had escaped from England and debt, and perhaps his own misinterpretation of love, in all its varied forms. Handsome to a fault, he enjoyed dressing like a dandy. Unlike Polidori, his hair, although dark, was more unruly, the curls wayward, adding to the sardonic amusement he experienced while watching the other man squirm because he, Byron, didn't answer directly.

Byron convinced himself that Nature could do little more for him. 'I should be grateful that she bestowed upon me a more inward spirit; at least it helps animate this body.' And yet, despite such gifts, it only served to make his lameness more conspicuous. Such a flaw also served to make him brood over this one blemish as most sensitive minds do, the nature of the defect intensified, made more damnably apparent to him. 'Explains my scepticism, cynicism and my bloody-minded savagery.' He managed a brief smile. 'But only when things don't go my way.'

Today, he felt might be a cynical day, with a few tidbits of humour thrown in for good measure.

A well-manicured hand fondled the sword cane leaning against what he termed "an uncommonly useless side table", useless because it didn't match the height of the bed. With his left hand he smoothed the long, loose trousers he preferred to knee-breeches. He barely moved save to sip from a small bottle, eyes dilating as the

Black Drop took hold, his mind and body invaded by its qualities, senses and manner grown more attuned to his surroundings. Opiates, taken in moderation, helped ease thoughts he would rather consign to the darkness and leave there. They also heightened the senses, threw everything into clearer perspective, offered a grander, yet often more sublime feeling of elation. The past weeks had offered the pleasure at being away from problems and so added to his anticipation on this, his second sojourn on the continent.

A Grand Tour for a *grand* man. And one which allowed him to indulge, please himself without the hindrance of that other life littered with fawning women and pretty boys.

And Darkness.

He didn't succumb to it but instead continued to study his companion: if asked he may well admit to being slightly envious of Polidori's dark olive skin, a natural contribution to his distinct Latin appearance.

Eventually, he said, 'Polly, for a man who is the son of Gaetano Polidori, secretary to the poet and dramatist Vittorio – Damn what's his name? Ah, yes, Alfieri – you lack the finer points. I mean the ones commonly used to infiltrate an hierarchy of literary excellence.'

Polidori dismissed it, replying equally casually, 'It may be I have sought you as my mentor to remedy that. We must all learn, my lord, if ever we are to make our mark in life. You forget that it was your good self who chose me to accompany you.'

Byron jabbed his stick in Polidori's direction. 'Let's say fate and your wretched pugnacity had a hand in it.' About to stretch out, he leaned down to massage his right ankle. 'Perhaps it is my notoriety you seek – I should be honoured.' He prodded his own chest to further promote his point. 'It isn't every day that such a person as I –' He reflected on the title the French authorities had bestowed upon him. 'Even the government of his Majesty Louis XVIII afforded me the salacious *nom de plume*,' said with an added sneer at authority. 'And d'you know it befits me to accept it. *"His Satanic Majesty".*' The phrase justified his authority, and was lent dignity. It was, as they say, intended. Byron, smiling broadly, sat up, squared his shoulders deeming the accolade fitting. 'That such a person as I is so recognised.'

Polidori nodded. His dark eyes met Byron's. 'I have already intimated, as have others, that your reputation precedes you.'

Byron changed the subject. 'What do you say to the countryside, Polly? That we were compelled to journey through Flanders, Ghent and all those other towns, constantly breaking down. Ha, no great diversion despite setbacks. The route along the Rhine is particularly interesting. This way, we see more of its beauty, and are able to take our rest when and where we choose.'

'Why is it I get the feeling you're not telling me something, George?'

'Your own lack of confidence, I presume. How the hell do I know? I do not seek purposely to avoid stating things; you should know me better. And apart from Hobby, hardly anyone calls me George. Sometimes Noel, never George. You were saying?'

Polidori reacted to this inviting prompt. 'That you always evade issues when it doesn't suit you to answer civilly.'

'How so? When have I not? I am the epitome of gentlemanly good manners.' He baited Polidori, guessing he'd failed to recognise this. 'The last time I visited these shores with Hobby, Fletcher and good old 'Bobby' Rushton we had a rollickin' time. You've seen Robbie, John, a handsome lad. O'course he's older now, even more handsome. Son of a tenant farmer at Newstead. My favourite page. Had him sleep in a small room that you could only reach through my bedroom.'

Polidori reacted to this with a sly turn of head, the inference obvious yet no suitable comment came to mind.

Byron wagged a finger. 'Dash those thoughts, Polly.' A ghost of a smile lingered. 'So, as I told Hodgson, I was happy here. I loves oranges, I talks bad latin to the monks at Mafra – you should see their library, Polly, it's one of the great ones of Europe. *And* I goes into society with my pocket pistols. What is more, I told him I swims in the Tagus all across at once. Tidal y'know, and not an easy swim even on a calm day. Strong currents splash around the walls at Fort Belem. And by God, Polly, I took t'swearing Portuguese. That made some of 'em sit up and take note. Visited Cadiz, too. Prettiest town in Europe, and the cleanest. Its women were the most seductively yet decently dressed in the world.'

'A feature that wouldn't escape your discerning eye.'

'Ah, you've guessed m'needs, John.' Byron stretched and yawned. 'Perhaps I could confess to it all being an act. Y'see it's expected of me, so I merely bow to the whims of others.'

'Is that right? Could it, I wonder, be the truth?'

'Make up your own mind.' It is Byron's only answer. 'I digress. What did you say before I reflected on my earlier tour?'

'Simply this, that you leave your native shores at the height of your literary and personal career. You have an English populace idealises you, they think you a demigod.'

'Ah! This then is the fundamental reason for your idealising – or might that be *idolising* me?' A smirk hardly begs an answer, rather confirms it. 'Think on, John: you with your Ampleforth Roman Catholic education may have gained an edge. Edinburgh University supplied your doctoral degree in medicine not s'long ago – how long?'

'Last year. I was nineteen.'

'One so young and courtin' s'many high ideals. Mm, we have a deal in common. I admit that I do admire your literary aspirations, wrought I'm sure by your father's connections. And you're right o'course. I did engage you as my personal physician and travelling companion.'

'At least that's settled.' Slight hesitation prompted Polidori to add, 'No sarcasm intended.'

'Whether or not you idealise, or idolise me, I care not, John. Despite my poetic genius, I am also condemned as the worst of men, especially in the eyes of contemporaries.' A disdainful snort indicated Byron's derision. 'They hate genius purely because they cannot assail to such heights. They resent me, yet all I want is to write good poetry, fulfil as many of my plans as is humanly possible. I grab life, Polly, my lines mostly written from the heart, from the innermost depths of my soul. Not always good, not always appreciated, but when I know it is good I want the praise it deserves.

'As a writer you do understand why we seek approval of our work. I seek the fame and fortune I believe is my due. I agree certain writings were good: hopefully current ideas will be better. Alas not everyone will think so, and some of 'em, my friend, are jealous –'

The pause defined the intention, Polidori instantly embarrassed.

'Yes, Polly, jealous. Some of 'em even wish me harm.' The jealousy of which he spoke would show a marked difference to the one he would discuss with Shelley in a few weeks' time.

A silence blundered in, Polidori trying to tell himself that Byron couldn't mean him, that he was jealous of Byron!

Byron stated: 'Would that I am allowed greater opportunity to prove meself, be honest with meself, and the world. Ah! Overnight, I became famous...'

The carriage lurched to a halt, each concerned as to the reason. Polidori watched an impatient Byron heave himself off the bed and limp to the window. 'Hate bein' disturbed when I'm in full flow.' Yanking the curtain aside he looked out. 'What the devil's Fletcher up to? I hope it isn't another infernal wheel showing signs of losing its mountings. That pathetic carriage maker, Baxter, should rot in Hell the amount he charged me for this... this... *hearse!*'

Tugging down his tight fitting olive vest, ensuring the soft collar on his shirt looked presentable, he said, 'How do I look, Polly? Collar straight. I dislike the starched cravats recommended by George Brummell.'

Polidori said, 'You'll do. Who's going to see you out here?'

Smoothing his dark trousers to maintain a tidiness, he said, 'You never know.' He beckoned. 'Come, John, I need air. Anyway, I reckon it's grown thick in here.' Impatiently rapping his sword cane on his left boot, he stepped back to allow Polidori to open the door. *Dogs and masters,* he thought. He said nothing, aware his earlier comments had at least proffered food for thought.

Stepping down, he winced, the damaged foot, legacy of birth, awkward, and a curse. Hence his massaging the ankle as it pained him today. Sitting too long cooped up? Maybe the ride, his leg locked in the stirrup. Who knows? 'Who cares?' A whisper, for this suddenly moody Byron assumed no-one did.

Looking towards the trailing wagon he queried the ever faithful Fletcher with a raising of a finely arched brow. Dusty from driving, Fletcher, who showed a strength not easily revealed in his stature, was more often a man who minded his own business. Known for maintaining his own counsel, he generally refused to get embroiled in serious conversation and to earn his keep tended to adopt the role of a good elder brother to Byron.

40

Patting dust from his clothes, he offered, 'A tree branch across the road, m'lord,' trusting his master would be satisfied. 'Not the wheel, or a spring, else you would've felt that I'm sure. Not t'worry; soon be on our way.'

Behind them, the second carriage, ripe with the stink of animals, lurched to a halt.

'Good.' Byron glimpsed at the wheels, tapped a couple with his stick. 'Not a wheel, or even some other infernal, mechanical thing.' Following his cursory inspection of the carriage, he headed towards a shaded grove. Above, an azure sky reminded him of his previous tour, today's air, as then, cooler beneath the trees.

I should never have returned to England. The thought denounced the truth in that he perhaps wrongly assumed the masses there may never have acknowledged his writing. *In which case he would have become just another rake abroad.* He contradicted himself, agreeing he did right in going back, 'If only to plague the bloody aristocracy by robbing them of their women!'

'Take your time, Fletcher,' he called. 'No hurry. We do not have to be in a certain place by a given date. We shall tarry here, enjoy the day. Have Rushton bring us some wine. I should take tea.' He patted his stomach, noting that a number of vest buttons appeared strained. 'Ah, tush, 'tis only temporary this weight thing.' Believing that made it easier to deal with and also forced him to defer the obvious: wine, women and debauchery; he agreed it may well be a combination best not intermixed. He grinned. 'Can't help meself.'

A quest for love. My God, why think it? Why feel bereft? I go through 'em like a shark cuts through water. Damn it, one hole's as good as another, so why not make a choice?

What of the future?

Claire Clairmont sat like a rock in his mind, Byron musing over certain missives received from the woman, especially those telling him of her willingness to tarry by Lake Léman to await his arrival. 'Damn her, she proved too willing. I'm right, no need to hurry at all.'

Glancing behind, he scathed at incompetence. 'John,' he ordered, 'close the door, don't want dust damaging the books.'

Polidori did so, hiding a belittling sneer from Byron. *One day,* he thought, *I will be great. I will show you all.*

For now, using his coat sleeve, he removed dust from the carriage door, the letters *L B* embellished in red upon the green and collecting a brighter hue. The gesture underlined the reason *he* wished to be great.

CHAPTER 5

'The heart – the heart is lonely still –'

I

He should have taken weak tea, eaten a few plain biscuits, but today, stomach aside, and the memory of his gallop at Waterloo plus his scoring points over Polidori, Byron decided to further indulge himself.

The shade of overhanging trees, the way the light played on the lush grass, reminded him of Newstead's park and added to this sense of well-being. 'Some things I do hold dear,' he mused. Aware of Polidori hovering close by, Byron leaned into the hole of a handy tree, annoyed that his blighted leg wouldn't easily allow him to take advantage of the lush grass and stretch out on the bank. He poured red wine from a bottle supplied by Rushton. Holding up the goblet, the liquid's hues pierced by the light, he said, 'Rich and dark, John. Like life's blood.'

'It seems you have a penchant for it, LB.' Polidori gestured across the copper-hued landscape, no longer melancholy, or decorated with battlefield colours. Polidori shivered despite the heat, memories of the reckless ride the other evening clinging like unwanted detritus. Removing his neck scarf, he wafted his perspiring face with it. 'Heat of the land, heat of man... Blast it, it's so hot. A place for the Devil I'm thinking.'

'I acknowledge the sentiment, John. Let us attempt to placate the spirits of the dead.' Tilting the goblet Byron allowed a few drops of wine to anoint grass and soil. Reciting other words said at Waterloo, Byron spoke up, making sure Polidori heard. 'Further red rain to make the harvest grow, a small libation to seek their blessing for our own endeavour.' He raised the goblet in a toast. 'To journeying, inspiration and adventures I know must come.' His eyes shone. 'Not forgetting women...may I never tire of them. *Not forgetting women.*' His voice trailed, the name 'Augusta' barely heard.

II

A letter. He recalls a letter, or a part of, which he wrote to Lady Melbourne. Perhaps he unwittingly hinted then that desire overcame sensibility. 'Dear God, is my mind so befuddled? Did I mean my sweet sister, or was it another? In any case it is apt. How did it read?'

> TO LADY MELBOURNE, April 30th 1814
> My dear Lady M.
> – You -- or rather I have done my Augusta much injustice -- the expression which you recollect as objectionable meant only "loving" in the senseless sense of that wide word – and -- it must be some selfish stupidity of mine in telling my own story -- but really & truly – as I hope mercy & happiness for her -- by that God who made me for my own misery -- & not much for the good of others -- she was not to blame -- one thousandth part in comparison -- she was not aware of her own peril -- till it was too late -- and I can only account for her subsequent "abandon" by an observation which I think is not unjust -- that women are much more attached than men -- if they are treated with any thing like fairness or tenderness.

How they'd assumed and presumed back then, in that winter when snow enclosed Newstead in its cold embrace. Yet cold was hardly a word to describe my admiration, my heart-felt love for a woman born of my mother and another father. Let 'em surmise, think as they like, because I will never lay voice to the truth.

I see them, hear 'em talking behind dithering little hands, all those society harpies voicing to their husbands how Lord Byron and Augusta Leigh tarried far too long behind the Abbey's closed doors with only Joe Murray and Nanny Smith and a scattering of other servants, mainly nonentities, for company. Wouldn't they love to learn that I did make love to Augusta, and she to me.

In the big four poster with the snow floating like swansdown on the lawns, melting to nothing, adding to the depth of the dark lake, its reflections sullied, like our profane love.

"Byron." She spoke my name, a whisper in the room. Apart, yet our two souls met, the distance between us only feet as we languished on the bed, hands touching, thighs... touching. Warmth, closeness, soft wet kisses heightening the passion...

Too cold for walking that day, yet even the weather, the ice, could never erase the carving on the elm. Nor could it ever eradicate our caresses, or the untold feeling of utter abandonment, and contentment. She welcomed me with a look, with her arms, her kisses, the warmth of her body.

Brother. Sister. Man. Woman. Is distance measured by an arm's length? Is it measured by blood? Transgression in the eyes of the law, in the eyes of... God.

True feeling, and need is all that matters. So tell me, why does real, profound love prove so elusive? Why is it only captured for a few scant hours behind the closed doors and thick walls of a building upon which only satyrs look? Do they curse us with their malignant glare, their knowing smiles? Are we a part of that world only for a few weeks?

And in every creaking door I still hear the sound of footsteps on the threshold... De Ruthyn wanting me... *Me* wanting... wanting...

His sickly smile, his fawning touch. A man twice my age, and daring to wink at my mother when he desired me!

'What do I want?' Deprivation is what I feel, is what I got. The love of a father eluded me, proved to me that such a different warmth wasn't to be. A wild jackanapes, a man always in his cups. The swine deprived Mother of a fortune, so what did he care about me? ME! Fortune hunter and poet, always trying to meet debts with words and false promises.

I saw him rarely and don't y'know I was totally unaware he was my father at the time. Too young I suppose, merely a child, and this man would visit, use the home as a stopping point between his jaunts, his spending sprees. Ah! Spending! He only came back for more money! Father? No... NO. Merely a strange visitor. No hand reached out in love, not even friendship. Others had fathers who played with them, taught 'em to shoot with pistol and long gun, who would walk, ride with their offspring. Not I. Never I. But then did I perhaps inherit his traits?

Maybe after all, there is something of Mad Jack within me.

Augusta understands. I have told her my feelings, what I truly desire. But only the Lord is aware of how much I told her. *Love*. One tiny word that means so much.

Wrong! I hear it spoken across infinity. Those professed learned fools quick to judge without first testing their own ubiquitous existence. All think it wrong, heinous because she is my half-sister. Went about with me she did. Damn it she was a Byron; daresay that drew me closest. I once asked: *'Do you think there is one person here who will dare to look upon himself?'*

I dared look upon Augusta... Perhaps saw myself. Call it forbidden love, for I did tell her that the great object of life is sensation.

I was her baby, and she treated me so. That husband of hers ill-treated her, so she sought solace with me. She'd do anything I wanted. Oh indeed, Gussie would do anything, answer to my whims. My "Goose" followed me everywhere.

> *'She was like me in lineaments – her eyes,*
> *Her hair, her features, all, to the very tone*
> *Even of her voice, they said were like to mine.'*

Tried to tell Lady Melbourne, unburden the problem. August it was. Attempted a letter beginning with "I want to tell –" Ended it abruptly with "No I won't." Was like being betwixt the Devil and the briny. I had Annabella on one side penning her declarations, Augusta on the other...

But it was never *wrong* with Augusta. We shared such a closeness that to some is difficult to understand. Best o'friends you might say, and never like brother and sister; not at all. Always, dammit! *Always* on the verge of being more than that, more like lovers. We felt it right to make love. Something destined to happen... So we let it. We gave ourselves freely, and the devil with the consequences. Call it need, lust, whatever you deem fit, yet it is the closest I came to fulfilment. Souls entwined. Forbidden? Yes, and being so the guilt attached itself, especially on Gussie's part, threw us in different directions.

Strange how desire forces one to undertake foolish things, crazy notions like carving our declaration on a twin-stemmed elm, only the two of us aware of its true implications. How her guilt increased because of the complicity, and tormented me by what we had done.

Power, the almost supernatural strength of will usurped by an even greater desire to love and be loved. I wrote of it, I revel in its memory.

"In the desert a fountain is springing, In the wide waste there still is a tree, And a bird in the solitude singing, Which speaks to my spirit of thee."

Yes, I penned such words. He smiles bitterly.

III

'My lord?' Polidori sounded concerned. 'Noel? I've been prattling away and I've a mind to believe you're not listening.'

Byron gazed at him, not quite seeing, unaware the doctor had spoken. He saw instead a winter landscape, heard Augusta calling, experienced only the warmth of two bodies coupled in desperation, gave himself to the longing that comes from souls eager to share everything their hearts desire. And to quell the loneliness albeit only for a fraction of time.

His name said again, in a deeper, more masculine tone.

'Eh? Ah, forgive me, John. I was lost for a minute or so. What was I saying?'

'Something about adventures yet to come. It's a fact your *need* for the fairer sex is hardly an issue.' Polidori paced, never privy to Byron's innermost thoughts and not expecting an answer. Totally unrelaxed, his attention settled on Fletcher and the others as they struggled to manoeuvre the offending branch from the rutted road. 'How much longer, Fletcher?' he called. 'I'm tired of this place already, even the shade is too hot. Though his lordship might not think that.'

Before Fletcher could answer, Byron interrupted, his opinion aimed at the restless doctor. 'Too edgy by far, sir.' He ignored his own unsettled state, the sense of euphoria lessened. Thoughts of Augusta he replaced in a corner of his mind especially prepared for them. 'I'm thinking that you see, *feel*, some unholy shadow that has somehow affixed itself to our party. A residue from –' he paused to lend more substance to his words, 'out there.' He gestured with a sweep of an arm. 'And to think this same sun that shines upon us illuminates a bitter, more morose Waterloo.'

And might those same shadows cling to your own soul, m'lord?

His conscience intruded, tempted an answer. Byron scanned the vast expanse of wilderness and trees. He blinked, shadows playing games with his sight. Thoughts of the past, of earlier sojourns... Things he would eventually write down:

'*"We had passed halfway towards the remains of Ephesus, leaving behind us the more fertile environs of Smyrna, and were entering upon that wild and tenantless tract through the marshes and defiles which lead to the few huts yet lingering over the broken columns of Diana – the roofless walls of expelled Christianity, and the still more recent but complete desolation of abandoned mosques – when the sudden and rapid illness of my companion obliged us to halt at a Turkish cemetery, the turbaned tombstones of which were the sole indication that human life had ever been a sojourner in this wilderness. The only caravanserai we had seen was left some hours behind us, not a vestige of a town or even cottage was within sight or hope, and this 'city of the dead' appeared to be the sole refuge of my unfortunate friend, who seemed on the verge of becoming the last of its inhabitants..."*'

Polidori whirled on Byron, whatever Fletcher had answered lost as he fired back: 'Do you gain satisfaction from losing yourself in thought and mumbling tracts of unsettling tosh? Not content to linger here, you insist upon promoting foolish fancy. Then again –' he frowned at Byron still sipping wine as though he had become totally free of care, his words, which Polidori quoted, '"– *perhaps the shadow has courted us since we left England's fair shores*"'. This fetched Byron's head up, steely light in the poet's eyes.

Using an overhang, and still attempting to shake off the dark traces infesting his mind, Byron tugged himself further up the bulk of the tree; he tilted the wine glass again, its contents once more committed to the ground. 'A creature of night dogs me, makes me compose lines... a *true* account of my last visit.' Not for the first time in his life, Byron felt the cold of years, heard the voices seeping from the stones of the Abbey, and saw the thing rising from the stone coffin...

He bit down on his knuckles, his back to Polidori, afraid he would hear more demeaning comments. 'Please God, let it be that I may relinquish my hold on it, or its hold on me.' He silently prayed for this to be so, yet doubted it.

'John,' he said, trying to sound calm, 'I merely reflect the mood that seems to have overtaken us all; aye, including me.' A slight tic in Byron's jaw became more pronounced. He gestured to the road where the others still toiled. 'Even Fletcher and the rest refrain from idle chatter; the animals strangely silent.'

Polidori, interested in the others, jumped at Byron's shoulder slap. 'Ah, you run from shadows, John. I wonder, what did *you* see on the field t'other evening?'

'We are ready for you, my lord. Doctor Polidori.' Fletcher broke the doubtful mood encroaching on the grove and the two men. Byron looked up, saw Robert Rushton and the Swiss, Berger, loitering behind Fletcher, both unsure as to what they should do, the younger and older man knowing their place sufficiently not to venture foolish questions.

Poor Fletcher, the fellow looks down. Trusted friend he'll always be. Even on the last tour I wrote to my mother from Constantinople and told her:

> Fletcher is a poor creature, and requires comforts that I can dispense with. He is very sick of his travels, but you must not believe his account of the country. He sighs for ale, and idleness, and a wife, and the devil knows what besides.

And even earlier, from Athens, he'd written to Catherine words that promoted a caring, considerate nature where Fletcher was concerned:

> Fletcher begs leave to send half-a-dozen sighs to Sally his spouse, and wonders (though I do not) that his ill-written and worse spelt letters have never come to hand; as for that matter, there is no great loss in either of our letters, saving and except that I wish you to know we are well, and warm enough at this present writing, God knows. You must not expect long letters

at present, for they are written with the sweat of my brow, I assure you.

One other image rose from that first sojourn abroad, the remembered heat of those days, suffered now, when he'd penned the words: "The heat has burnt me brown, and as for Fletcher he is a walking Cinder."

Other thoughts accompany this: those of that one "new Greek acquaintance" about whom he wrote: "He has called thrice, and we improve vastly. In good truth, so it ought to be, for I have quite exhausted my poor powers of pleasing, which God knows are little enough, Lord help me! We are to go on to Tripolitza and Athens together. I do not know what has put him into such good humour unless it is some Sal Volatile I administered for his headache, and a green shade instead of that effeminate parasol."

Ah me, he thought, was my Greek merely another dalliance in an effort to fulfil the ache inside? Thoughts, memories, dark holes in my conscious yearning.

Rushton out of them all, except for Fletcher, was another devoted attendant. 'That you are, Robbie, for you know my mood swings; you can guess this isn't the time or place to say anything. Best wait for orders, eh, Robbie? You feel better acting on definite instruction.'

Robert watched him, and knew Byron was aware of it. He would bet money that his lord would recall how he, Rushton, had pinched the maid off him back at Newstead.

'Time to leave,' Byron ordered. Together, they each went back to their duties, Rushton content to be doing something.

Byron, with one last gesture, flung his goblet, watched it arc up and then down to shatter on a clump of rocks. The sound caused a flock of black birds to rise, raucous cries mimicking the screams of the dying. So like the rooks at Newstead.

'There, that's done. Come, John. Onwards to the Rhine whose crags and cataracts I'm assured are filled with ghosts and goblins sufficient to give us all pause for thought, and –' a lascivious smirk appeared, '– whose inns I am reliably assured will satisfy *all* our needs.'

Like a twin shadow, Polidori trailed after Byron, the carriage's green blending often with the landscape, other times appearing stark against its dryness. Once ensconced inside, and away from the terrible heat, the doctor was able to compose himself. Slumping in a chair, he refused to even glance out of the window despite Byron's urging him to 'Take a last look.'

Beyond the dusty window, two horses – *surely not the same two as at Waterloo* – stared mournfully at the carriage as it departed.

Byron looked a second time. They were gone.

CHAPTER 6

'In solitude, where we are least *alone.'*

I

'I feel alive, John. The scenery stirs me: its rivers and mountains, a castle hidden in each dark, mysterious edifice lends a magnificence that is overwhelming.'

For nearly half an hour, Byron and Polidori had respected each other's need for privacy. Polidori sat on the sofa staring at nothing in particular, his journal balanced on his knee; Byron relaxed on the bed. The grind of carriage wheels on the dusty, weathered roads, the clopping of hooves, were distanced, merely sounds on the edge of consciousness. Occasionally, a scream from one of a pair of monkeys – Byron guessed the female – came from the other wagon.

Each man mulled respective thoughts. Polidori rose to Byron's comment – anything to detract from talk of battlefields or what they might contain.

'The mountains are majestic, but I wonder, are they the only peaks to which you allude, m'lord. I am aware of the fact that we're obliged to keep moving on because our welcome evaporates as quickly as morning mist over water.' He glanced over his shoulder as Byron swung his legs off the bed. 'Put more simply,' Polidori said, 'we are compromised by your need to fulfil a lifetime's ambition and bed every wench between here and the Arctic Circle.'

'Ah! One can try, John; one can at least try. Or die in the attempt.'

How far must I go to find that which I desire? Always the same thought, yet never a positive answer.

The dry, amusing comment birthed a rare smile from Polidori who, not to let the more capricious moment go, followed up with: 'I would have preferred to stay a while longer in Cologne but your dalliance with the innkeeper's wife curtailed that.'

'Don't forget the chambermaid. A pretty enough wench with and without her apparel.' He wandered about, picked up a book from the drinks cabinet, and put it down again. Retaining his good humour he quipped, 'The ruts in the road remind me of more preferable, more intimate ruts offered by womankind.' Still alive to the spirit of the conversation, he digressed. 'That apart, I did enjoy the architectural aspects of Cologne.'

'I agree.' Polidori laid his journal aside. 'And admit to enjoying a longer stay. I would have wished to have revisited St Ursula's Church and viewed the catacombs there.'

'Mm, a melancholy place. Indeed so when I think that the bones of eleven thousand young virgins are consigned to that dismal crypt. Such a waste.'

'Then it's a pity you didn't visit before, Noel, for I'm positive those maidens would have all gone to their maker with a more beatific smile. It pre-supposes the fact that to know Lord Byron is to know life.

'Tell me –' Polidori, contrary to his desire to lighten the conversation, sounded less jocular. 'Tell me, with your leaning towards death and its all-encompassing, and yet apparent finality, do you ever insist that life does overcome that which we know as death?'

'A riddle, eh? A conundrum to tax my beliefs? Are you asking: Do I believe in ghosts? If so, the answer is an irrefutable *yes*.' A gesture through the window, Byron encompassing the immediate, and the faraway world, he has, and still does inhabit. 'In England is a house, John, a fair piece of architecture with its follies and imperfections, its towers and dark rooms, and a vacant, yet all seeing West Front –'

Byron looked back into his past and felt an alien coldness surge through him; accompanying it, a memory. 'Do I believe in the hereafter?' Said as though he were talking to himself. 'A past populated with phantasms, wraiths, and one who walks in darkness, none but the doomed to look upon his face. Yes, John, assuredly so.'

Positive he has said enough he's adamant at not wishing to elaborate more despite Polidori's prompting. On the same tack, and anxious not to reveal too much about himself, Byron fired back: 'I wonder, John, is it the gloomy elevations of Castle Drachenfels on its looming outcrop that have turned your thoughts in this direction?'

Polidori headed for the wine cabinet. 'I believe I will partake of a little wine now. A Reisling, I think.' He purposely ignored the red. 'You?'

Byron refused with a headshake, still groggy from the two or three goblets imbibed back there, his greediness under such circumstances exacerbated by the heat.

Glass raised, Polidori savoured the almost amber colour as the light caught it. Sipping like a connoisseur he said, 'Yes, a fair bouquet. Light, crisp.'

'Authority on wine, too, eh?' Byron's comment, hardly intended as sarcastic, sounded a touch devilish. He couldn't desist and was not unduly surprised when Polidori didn't answer.

Engrossed in his tasting session, Polidori took his time. Half the contents drained, he said, 'LB, is it not the so-called vampire who is reputed to prey on the living, or more specific, lust after the innocent virgin?'

From the rear, the menagerie struck up an ear-splitting cacophony. Both men winced at the unbidden intrusion. Over the uproar, Byron shouted: 'You consider me animated by evil. That I use woman-kind selfishly. You think me as *undead.*'

All previous statements offset the argument, and gagged pre-supposed questions from one so naive in his outlook. Byron knew Polidori and would not offer him chance to condemn. For, in his way, Byron had answered such questions. Why make an issue when, in reality, the truth was known? The myth and folk-lore of the undead, for all he knew, had seeped throughout the length and breadth of the world.

Animal noises quickly ceased, the sudden quiet emphasising Byron's snorting laugh. 'Think me so, then dare I argue? I have lived more lives than a dozen men, whose shallow piety will outlive them. Yes, I have met such creatures in my travels and such association is hardly to be recommended.'

More invidious lines popped into his head. Doubtless he would write them down sometime...

"Where there is mystery, it is generally supposed that there must also be evil: I know not how this may be, but in him there certainly was the one, though I could not ascertain the extent of the other – and felt loth, as far as regarded himself, to believe in its existence. My advances were received with sufficient coldness: but I was young, and not easily discouraged, and at length succeeded in obtaining, to a certain degree, that common-place intercourse and moderate confidence of common and everyday concerns, created

and cemented by similarity of pursuit and frequency of meeting, which is called intimacy, or friendship, according to the ideas of him who uses those words to express them."

Rising abruptly, face clouded, he grabbed the red wine carafe and helped himself. 'Be damned, I am here to enjoy.' He quaffed a full goblet and refilled it.

'Vampires.' He turned on Polidori, startling him. 'Know that I have an aversion to such creatures and therefore insist they keep their own counsel, aye and their disturbing secrets.' Another drink, he dragged a hand across his lips. 'It may be that I know and have seen too much

'"This is the end of my journey, and of my life; I came here to die; but I have a request to make, a command – for such my last words must be. You will observe it?"'

'My lord?' Polidori sounded concerned. 'Those words? Did you intend to speak them aloud? Are you expecting to die?'

Byron frowned. 'We all die, Polly. But words? What are you babbling about?' He searched the other's face attempting to decipher something. 'Are you hearing things? What bloody words?'

Who, or what might be intruding? Had some vile form taken it upon itself to accompany them?

Byron remembered a paragraph here, another there. But from himself? All this talk of vampires and ghosts surreptitiously undermined his logic, his understanding. *Dark shape... a cowl... the folds in between...* The Friar. He is not necessarily a bad spirit, more a warning spirit. 'So am I then warned?'

Polidori could not fathom the phrases spoken out of true context. He felt the same as Byron, unsure where the discourse might lead. The very core of him dithered, promoted a distraction from the normal world, a world he wanted to hold on to. This coldness – perhaps the very same Byron had felt – denied him a reason why. He, too, paced, his face and body uncomfortable through perspiring.

'One presumes one's thoughts got in the way of our conversation.' Byron apologised. Eyes welded, both men silently admitting to themselves that something entirely hostile had entered the arena, their immediate awkwardness apparent, yet neither enlightened the other.

'Fear is a strange and terrible thing,' Byron said. He massaged his forehead, a sheen of perspiration dampening his hand.

''Tis infernally hot all of a sudden, maybe we pay homage to the Devil.' *No, not him, for he left you nought but debt.* 'No matter. Enough.' He scowled at Polidori. 'Tell me, John, which of us would you designate the more malignant presence? As a scientist you would know more about re-animating the dead than I.'

Another riddle, this time from Byron. They seemed to be avoiding the truth of their intentions, and, strangely or not, the intention was to uncover – truth.

Aware he couldn't hedge such a direct question, Polidori accepted he would be forced to go along with it despite feeling apprehensive. 'A loaded question, my lord, especially when addressing the length of time we've known each other. Can we presume to judge ourselves thus? The world turns; time adds to knowledge. It is only in due course of time we may accept that we are more learned. Indeed, modern thinking may enable us to read more into our own minds, and hence that of others. One day I may discourse on the latest scientific thinking in this field.'

Polidori's jaw clenched. He ignored Byron's reply of: 'Only when you have availed yourself more with the contents of your black bag. They do say certain substances empower the mind, allow us to gaze into the darkness of our own souls.'

A disdainful laugh followed, Byron wondering if that might be it. The distilled opium, the Velmont, coupled with the wine imbibed, may easily have rendered him incapable of rational thinking. He couldn't know Polidori had swallowed some. Could its residue be prompting imbecilic references to the past? Be adding to them in a manner he deplored?

An appraisal of a couple of books – Matthew Lewis's *The Monk* and Coleridge's *Poems* – left on the end of the sofa allowed Byron the excuse to avoid Polidori's professed innocent look. Had he noted it, he would have undoubtedly pursued a different argument.

Concluding he should bring the conversation to a close, Byron said, 'John, I beg, do not allow any *imagined* brooding presence to curtail our pleasure. There is a world out there, and we seek all it has to offer.' Pure afterthought prompted: 'Whatever it may be.' Tendering a sly wink he added: 'As much as we seek, *they* may even find *us*.'

Grabbing Polidori's wrist he pulled him to the window, Polidori at a loss. Any anxiety turned out to be short-lived.

'See,' said Byron, 'the mountains of Switzerland beckon.'

He failed to see disappointment on the doctor's face.

II

'Thank you, Rushton, that will be all for now. Go and eat.'

The dark-haired, fresh-complexioned young man tendered a curt bow to Byron and went to join Fletcher and Berger, already tucking into game pie, and supping beer, its coolness helped by Fletcher's dunking the small cask into a nearby stream.

Byron, seated at one side of a small table, Polidori sitting opposite, scanned the surrounding landscape close to Basel, a high, copper-coin of a sun hammered to the sky.

'D'ye know, Polly, that lad Rushton stole a servant girl from me.' He turned to view Polidori's reaction. 'Yes, I didn't doubt you'd be shocked, so was I. Susan Vaughan was the lass in question. Blamed my own vanity more than I blamed her, for ever thinking that I could ever be loved...'

It's what I seek. To be loved for what I am. It's why I prefer to shock because I dare not reveal my innermost thoughts.

His own mocking laugh followed such thoughts. 'And wouldn't y'know when heartless Susie departed my bed for Bobby's, I had a stone in me kidney. I told Hodgson, "If it had got into my heart instead, it would have been all the better."'

Remember Edleston? That stone still sits in your heart.

That I do. Cambridge. Sweet-voiced Edleston.

'You're reflecting again, m'lord.' Polidori stood, unable to read or even hazard a guess at the precise thoughts bedevilling Byron. Attempting to get him back on track, he said, 'By my own persuasion, I agreed to come to Morat. You might say my sense of history was piqued by your information relative to this place.'

'Yes, I remember telling you that Swiss forces defeated Charles the Bold here.' Byron's gaze dropped to the table, relieved his attention had been diverted from mawkish thought. 'Ha.' He tapped documents sitting before Polidori. 'A pleasure to see you've commenced your own journal, John.'

Seating himself again, and without looking up, Polidori dipped his pen into the ink bottle clipped inside a small leather writing case. 'I'm recording the history of this place.' He didn't tell Byron that he'd been commissioned by John Murray to write up a journal of the tour. 'Y'know, LB, I wonder whether it is your penchant for the dead that really has intrigued me, for here we relax on the edge of yet another field of carnage drinking in its –' Like Byron he scanned the dun-coloured fields. 'Words fail me. It's hardly beauty.'

Polidori jabbed his pen in the direction of a neat pile of bleached bones Lord Byron had painstakingly selected from a nearby small pyramid of them.

Despite his refuge in writing, Polidori felt irritable. Should he tell Byron that he was anxious to reach a more permanent place to rest, take stock? Pleased Byron's jibes had lessened, Polidori's nervousness still blurred what had passed for companionship, adopted when they had set out. Perhaps prudent the doctor had not overheard Byron's comment to Hobhouse regarding the fact that he, Byron, had made a mistake in employing Polidori as something as permanent as his physician.

'LB,' Polidori said, 'I'm afraid I admit to not understanding your fascination. You not only visit battlefields, but seem to have an inherent compulsion to collect their souvenirs!'

'I admit it. At Newstead, the dead were my companions for years. In my study my constant source of inspiration were the skulls of long deceased Canons whose permanent, bony smiles helped lift the gloomiest of days.'

Leaning back, Byron purposely looked serious merely to test Polidori's reaction. Po-faced, he said: 'I even supped claret from one of 'em, though I do confess to having a penchant for sherry.'

To Byron's delight, Polidori's rueful grin turned to a grimace. 'You... you drank from a... a skull?'

'Yes, me, Hobhouse, Scrope Davies, Kinnaird and the rest.' He proceeded to enlighten Polidori, whose shock had been overtaken by an eagerness to learn.

Polidori reasoned that if, by having insight into the behavioural patterns of this man, he could promote his own career, then why not listen.

'Perfectly true,' Byron said. 'Carousing, indulging in games with the opposite sex, kennelling my dogs in the chapel, aye even using the mortuary crypt as a swimming bath.' Another taunting smirk. 'Orders of the day, Polly, any day! And don't shake your head that way, just listen.

'It became a question of chance as to what would we partake of on a certain day. Good choice we had, too: riding through the park, boating on the lake, taking the wenches into the woods, boxing, fencing, tennis, pistol practice. Or –' He tendered a malign grin. 'Or playing with the bear and the wolf, assuming someone was foolhardy enough to loose their chains.' Byron paused, his smirk less than gratifying. 'Why Polly-Dolly, you've turned pale.'

Polidori looked disapprovingly at him and shifted uneasily. As Byron deplored being called George, Polidori was equally upset at hearing this bastardised version of his own name and voiced his displeasure: 'Please don't use that nickname; it's embarrassing.'

'Sorry, m'dear, promise not t'be so base in company.'

'Thank you for that small dispensation.' The doctor moved his chair nearer the table. 'A bear and a wolf you say?'

'Kept the bear in my rooms at Cambridge for a while; just a lark you understand. The stink was appalling.' Whilst he talked Byron studied Polidori, seeing the man's features flow from shock to downright incredulity. A real belly laugh rippled, his humour so entrenched he almost fell off his chair.

'You're lying.' The doctor's disbelief sat there, yet somewhere the half grain of truth Byron had fed him, grew.

'Polly, you should see your face.'

'Wh-what did they say? I mean the Masters? Surely they wouldn't tolerate that. I mean... a bear... in your rooms!'

'Kept me warm at night. Especially since there were no other *bodies* around.' He winked, an asinine grin still there. It faded when he thought of Edleston, the young choir boy, one secret he preferred to keep private.

'You mean you... you actually slept with... a bear?'

'Brought it home to Newstead. Bear and wolf made a fine pair. And cowards all; hardly any man would venture near 'em. Dash, they'd already run the gauntlet in order to enter the Abbey, but the cowards refused to renew their acquaintance.'

'Tell me about the wolf.'

'Not a real wolf but as good as.' Byron's sly grin stayed. 'Biggest dog you've ever seen though. Huge and black he was, with a set o' teeth like a mantrap. Called him Lyon. Devil took a piece out of my arse one time, or at least he had a damn good try. Thank God for thick britches and being a bit broad in the beam. No, John, you took your life in yer hands whenever you tried to court Lyon. Given the choice, I'd rather have the bear; big soft thing and tame enough to be a child.'

'You said you met at the Abbey? I gather you left the er, animals outside?'

'Aye, we had more favourable sport to occupy us. We gathered in yet another barren, low-ceilinged room with a Gothic vaulted roof. Only warmed up when we charged it with laughter, drunken carousing and screams. Nanny Smith turned a blind eye to our goings-on –'

'Nanny Smith?'

'Housekeeper, and a damn fine woman. Looked out for me she did. Just imagine, Polly, a gaggle of us carousing in the semi-dark with my skull cup sitting on the table.'

'Nanny Smith there?' Wry amusement accompanied Polidori's question.

'Not likely, she knew when to keep away.' Byron gestured to the centre of the table, Polidori so entranced by the story, eyes drawn and fixed on the spot where Byron's finger rested, a vision of the skull cup sitting there. Byron's knuckle rap nearly toppled him from his chair.

'You – you swine! I'm believing this.'

'And so you should, sir, because it is true, every word.' Byron sat quietly, distanced from immediate surroundings and Polidori. 'Yes, do believe, John.'

The intonation lent power to the words, Polidori transported to a cold, vaulted room...

III

...to a time where dark humour enabled baiting of contemporaries, darkness emboldening less wholesome pursuits.

The 'Order of the Skull' with its silver skull cup fashioned from the head of a deceased and disinterred prior.

'I was Abbot,' Byron revealed. 'Others included my friends Hobhouse, Wedderburn, Webster, good old Scrope Davies. And Matthews.' He added the name not as an afterthought but out of deep sincerity. His brow clouded, sadness evident, simply because those times were gone, the gang's indulgences remembered because it divorced him from the serious aspects of life.

Growing up had been both easy and difficult, so what better than to relive the drunken days, when cares were best left to others, and teenage indulgences, though seriously criticised by certain people, made them more worthy of trying? Indeed, if only to upset those *other people* that much more, for what teenager will enjoy himself if others cease to criticise?

'We went to Newstead and my famous wine cellar,' Byron said. 'Acquired *Monks'* dresses from a famous masquerade warehouse and, dressed thus, we recited verse. Not the bally classics either, more the wild, raucous poems to enrich our longing. We supped into the night, the lot of us stupefied by the contents from our wine-filled skull, plus several other bevies we saw fit to pour into it.'

'The raucous poems I can understand,' replied Polidori, 'given your recital at Waterloo.'

'Mm. I tell you, I found the skull while walking in the Abbey garden. I said to Tom Medwin how a strange fancy seized me of having it mounted as a drinking cup. I had it turned with a very high polish, leaving a mottled colour much like that of a tortoise shell.' His lips moved silently, afterthought prompting: 'I penned certain lines because I felt 'em apt. Listen.' He cleared his throat. '"Start not, nor deem my spirit fled: In me behold the only skull. From which, unlike the living head, Whatever flows is never dull." You hear that, Polly, I can never abide dullness!'

More laughter carried on the breeze, loud enough to disturb Fletcher and the others; the four carriage horses, eating their fill of oats and grass beneath a stand of trees further along the lane, stopped chewing.

'Lust and revelry, Dori, it's what you wanted to know, so here it is without any embellishments.' Standing, Byron tendered a mocking bow. 'I give you Byron, the man, and Byron, the lecher.'

The Lord struggling to survive. A man of few means, without money, certain things done for gain he would rather forget. Fame without *fortune.*

Stomping off, humour waned, he fixed upon one other of whom he'd barely spoken. 'Lucy.' He looked into the sun, aware that same sun on the other side of his world illuminated the decrepit pile of Newstead Abbey.

And Lucinda. Wild, Irish Lucy, hair as raven-coloured as the darkness he seeks to avoid. A word, a name, on the wind drifting across this other sea of dead. But Lucy is not dead, because she has returned to Newstead from Warwick.

He wrote to Francis Hodgson from Newstead in September, 1811:

> My dear Hodgson,
> I fear that before the latest of October or the first of November, I shall hardly be able to make Cambridge. My everlasting agent puts off his coming like the accomplishment of a prophecy. However, finding me growing serious he hath promised to be here on Thursday, and about Monday we shall remove to Rochdale. I have only to give discharges to the tenantry here (it seems the poor creatures must be raised, though I wish it was not necessary), and arrange the receipt of sums, and the liquidation of some debts, and I shall be ready to enter upon new subjects of vexation. I intend to visit you in Granta, and hope to prevail on you to accompany me here or there or anywhere.
> I am plucking up my spirits, and have begun to gather my little sensual comforts together. Lucy is extracted from Warwickshire; some very bad faces have been warned off the premises, and more promising substituted in their stead; the partridges are plentiful, hares fairish, pheasants not quite so good,

and the Girls on the Manor... Just as I had formed a tolerable establishment my travels commenced, and on my return I find all to do over again; my former flock were all scattered; some married, not before it was needful. As I am a great disciplinarian, I have just issued an edict for the abolition of caps; no hair to be cut on any pretext; stays permitted, but not too low before; full uniform always in the evening; Lucinda to be commander--vice the present, about to be wedded (mem. she is 35 with a flat face and a squeaking voice), of all the makers and unmakers of beds in the household.

My tortoises (all Athenians), my hedgehog, my mastiff and the other live Greek, are all purely. The tortoises lay eggs, and I have hired a hen to hatch them.

LUCY. *Another name carved on another tree. A beautiful day... alone together for once, the opportunities few.* Yes, I carved her name. Lucy, my only girl not related. I carved it with a small knife, my best knife, given me by a friend. The tree is near the house down a path on the right.

He sees it amidst others, dark trunks half in shadow, the rest in sunlight. He remembers the day he sat on the stone seat in the garden, how he picked a pink rose for Lucy, her cheeks so like it, how she had never looked more beautiful. They would take Patrick there on occasion and he would play as he and Lucinda talked.

'Pray, tell me, m'lord,' she says in her sweet, trilling voice, 'what of the future?' She looks longingly into his face, her own a mask of doubt, fear apparent in her eyes.

His features crumble, he touches her hair, strokes it, gazes on the little boy busy tilling a small heap of soil on the border by the white roses. Such a robust little chap, he looks up, aware he is being watched, his smile as open as his mother's, his brow and cleft chin as determined as his father's.

'Our future is there,' he says, still fondling Lucy's hair. 'It is all I can offer... for now.'

Will she accept this? Again the hurt is evident; she turns from him. 'I am only a... lowly... servant, sir,' she says, her voice subdued, earlier cheerfulness waned. Her stutter masks a sob. 'You bring me back to the Abbey, elevate my post yet I am nothing in your eyes, not like the grand ladies you mix with in London. That Shelley woman thinks me too lowly to be anythin' other than what I am.' She tries to hold his eyes. 'Yet there's one thing she can never take away. We met, we loved, and the result sits before you playin' in the dirt. 'Tis fine to carve a declaration on a tree, my lord... The tree will grow... but will what we 'ave do the same?'

And trees can be cut down, Byron thinks. He looks up, his view of the Abbey less pleasant. Eyes at windows, curtains repositioned: gossip making him only too aware of what they say. It is easy to have fun, but social standing will never allow it to become anything but mere dalliance. Isn't it the lot of his life?

'It is easy to say I love you, Lucinda, yet my position prevents me from making it anything more permanent. Respect is a by-word in these times, my own life subject to controversy, aye and pain. Would that I were a lowly farmer, a miner, then all about would say nothing about our relationship. Dearest, isn't it enough that I have you back again, and able to give you some permanence in the only way I can?'

She says nothing, merely nods. Taking Patrick's hand, she leads him through the gateway in the wall. Byron watches, a heat haze making them appear as ghosts, there only to test his determination...

In his heart he hears words written about another, but he ponders: Might I have written these to myself? They fit his mood and act as a blunt reminder that throughout his life thus far, he has achieved next to nothing in his relationships.

"It is my opinion that Mr B—— ought to marry Miss R—— . Our first duty is not to do evil; but, alas! that is impossible; our next is to repair it, if in our power. The girl is his equal: if she were his inferior, a sum of money and provision for the child would be some, though a poor, compensation: as it is, he should marry her. I will have no gay deceivers on my estate, and I shall not allow my tenants a privilege I do not permit myself – that of debauching each other's daughters. God knows, I have been guilty of many excesses; but, as I have laid down a resolution to reform, and lately kept it, I expect this Lothario to follow the example, and begin by restoring this girl to society, or, by the beard of my father! he shall hear of it."

Hardly himself, but it could well be. My standing denies me love.

Your father, m'lord? his conscience asks. Are you truly the B in your missive? Are you being detrimental to yourself? Is the woman Lucy?

Truth hurt. Resigned, he whispers: 'I did what I thought right, but now she is dead to me. So is the child.' Another name on the wind. 'Patrick.' The miles are unkind.

Polidori wandered over, standing so close their shoulders touch. 'And who is Matthews? Your words earlier betokened a fondness.'

Byron seized on the excuse to take his mind off Lucy and Patrick. 'My friend Matthews was a ringleader, a joker in his own way. Did some writing 'bout Matthews and a few others.

'So that, although I knew Matthews, and met him often then at Bankes's, he was my collegiate pastor, and master, and patron, and at Rhode's, Milnes's, Price's, Dick's, Macnamara's, Farrell's, Gally Knight's, and others of that set of contemporaries, yet I was neither intimate with him nor with any one else, except my old schoolfellow Edward Long – used to pass the day in riding and swimming with him – and William Bankes, who was good-naturedly tolerant of my ferocities.

'In our male orientated foolery 'twas Matthews foisted me with the title "Abbot". Bugger often played the *ghost!*' Byron flinched, memories painful. He clashed his fists together. 'Now, John, he is one, drowned and dead in the River Cam.'

His lordship mused, uncaring whether Polidori listened or not, the images of the past so plain as to be pictures laid before him.

'We were a company of some seven or eight, with an occasional neighbour or so for visitors. Hell, I've said this. No matter, we'd sit up late in our friars' dresses, drinking burgundy, claret, champagne, and what not, out of the skull cup, and all sorts of glasses, and buffooning all round the house... Matthews, the swine, always denominated me *the Abbot,* and never called me by any other name to the day of his death.

'He once threatened to throw Hobhouse out of a window, in consequence of I know not what commerce of jokes. Hobhouse came to me and said, that "His respect and regard for me as host would not permit him to call out any of my guests, and that he should go to town next mornin'." He did.'

Byron's spirits were lifted at such memories.

'It was in vain that I represented to him that the window was not high, and that the turf under it was particularly soft. Away he went.

'Matthews and myself had travelled down from London together, talking incessantly upon one single topic. We gets to Loughborough, and he insists: "Come, don't let us break through – let us go on to our journey's end." He was as entertaining as ever to the very end.

'During my year's absence from Cambridge, he occupied my rooms in Trinity, with the furniture. Jones, the tutor, in his odd way, told Matthews: "Mr. Matthews, I recommend to your attention not to damage any of the moveables, for Lord Byron, Sir, is a young man of tumultuous passions."

'Matthews was delighted with this; and whenever anybody came to visit him, begged them to handle the very door with caution; and used to repeat Jones's admonition in his tone and manner. There was a large mirror in the room, on which he remarked, "that he thought his friends were grown uncommonly assiduous in coming to see him, but he soon discovered that they only came to see themselves."

'Jones's phrase of "tumultuous passions," and the whole scene, had put him into such good humour, that I verily believe that I owed to it a portion of his good graces.

'I tell you Polly, once at Newstead, somebody by accident rubbed against one of his white silk stockings, one day before dinner; of course the gentleman apologised. "Sir," answered Matthews, "it may be all very well for you, who have a great many silk stockings, to dirty other people's; but to me, who have only this one pair, which I have put on in honour of the Abbot here, no apology can compensate for such carelessness; besides, the expense of washing."

'He had the same sort of droll sardonic way about every thing. When Hobhouse published his volume of poems, *The Miscellany*, Matthews would call it the "Miss-sell-any".'

Byron's mirth overwhelmed Polidori who, not having been present on these occasions, failed to see the humour of it. He did, however, nod and laugh a little in what he hoped were the right places.

'One of Matthews's passions was "the Fancy"; and he sparred uncommonly well. But he always got beaten in rows, or combats with the bare fist. In swimming, too, he swam well; but with effort and labour, and too high out of the water; so that Scrope Davies and myself always told him that he would be drowned if ever he came to a difficult pass in the water.

'Faith, but he was so. His head was uncommonly handsome, very like what Pope's was in his youth. His voice, and laugh, and features, are strongly resembled by his brother Henry's, if Henry be he of King's College. His passion for boxing was so great, that he actually wanted me to match him with Dogherty – whom I had backed and made the match for against Tom Belcher – and I saw them spar together at my own lodgings with the gloves on. As he was bent upon it, I would have backed Dogherty to please him, but the match went off. It was of course to have been a private fight, in a private room...'

Like Devil Byron's fight with Musters? The thought eased in. 'Aye,' he muttered, 'only that was enacted with a more fearsome weapon.'

'A comparison, m'lord?' Polidori enquired.

'Hardly that, more a murder of ideals, and burying petty jealousies with a sword thrust. A recollection is all, nothing to do with my reminiscences concerning Matthews. Let me finish, at least I'll get it off my chest, and mayhap gain a little more sleep havin' done so.

'Y'see on another occasion, being too late to go home and dress, he was equipped by a friend, a Mr Baillie, I believe, in a magnificently fashionable and somewhat exaggerated shirt and neck cloth. He proceeded to the Opera, and took his station in Fops' Alley. During the interval between the opera and the ballet, an acquaintance took his station by him and saluted him: "Come round," said Matthews, "come round." "Why should I come round?" said the other; "you have only to turn your head – I am close by you." "That is exactly what I cannot do," said Matthews; "don't you see the state I am in?" pointing to his buckram shirt collar and inflexible cravat, and there he stood with his head always in the same perpendicular position during the whole spectacle.'

Polidori saw the funny side, and pictured Matthews in the pose. 'Quite a card.'

'These were only his oddities, for no man was more liberal, or more honourable in all his doings and dealings, than Matthews. He gave Hobhouse and me, before we set out for Constantinople, a most splendid entertainment, to which we did ample justice. One of his fancies was dining at all sorts of out of the way places. Somebody popped upon him in I know not what coffee-house in the Strand – and what do you think was the attraction?'

'I have no idea,' Polidori said, Byron failing to see his boredom. But then, Polidori had ceased to become the centre of attention so there was little wonder.

'Why, that he paid a shilling, I think,' continued Byron. 'One shilling to dine with his hat on. This he called his 'hat house' and used to boast of the comfort of being covered at mealtimes.'

Polidori feigned a laugh and yawned. 'You obviously set great store by your friend, Matthews. I wonder, if you've finished your discourse, might we get back?'

'I agree,' Byron said, 'that certain yarns only appeal to those who were present, and that this "small talk" is hardly to your liking, but it is often good to indulge oneself now and then *despite* the damn'd company.'

It is true, ghosts all. And what of Newstead? Yes, I know too well of all the evil in that place. I felt their presence on so many occasions: I wanted to leave. Though I always will love the house I could not stay because of their presence.

Byron, irritated by Polidori's closeness, moved away, yet the doctor followed, attached like some irritant mollusc afraid he might miss something were he to detach himself.

Byron, highly amused by thoughts of Matthews and the rest, continued with an extra grain of humour. 'So, good doctor,' he said, 'you ask of bones. I see something amusing in that, you a man of medicine asking me of bones. Hah! You should realise there is comfort to be gained when coming to terms with the fate that inevitably awaits us all, even the hero out of whose bones I have but a quarter resting by yon table. I believe I shall send them to Murray.'

'Murray? Oh, your publisher.'

'He should gain a laugh from my dark humour. Good old Murray. I shall send them to him with the words...' Byron mulled it over. 'Ah yes, I shall say: "Enough to make a quarter of a hero, rather than a set of knife handles". How does that sound?'

Polidori deplored the comment. 'You speak ill enough of the dead, therefore 'tis no wonder you run scared of them. You offend them, LB; their spirits determined to plague you.'

'You must blame my degenerate ancestor for that. "Devil" Byron, for that is what they called him.' His sudden turn of head startled Polidori.

'*Devil* Byron? Damn me.'

'Ye may well say that, for he was damned. Aye maybe all the Byrons for their transgression. Bugger built a castle t'other side o' the lake at Newstead. Practised all manner of chicanery and worship, aye and debauchery. Screams and noises the manner of which you've never heard floated across that stretch of water over many nights, and many years so I'm told. Joe Murray said as much. Used t'be his retainer as well as my own. Good man, Joe. But he won't be buried with Bos'n that's for sure. Had a tomb dug out in the grounds but he mumbled something like "If I want to be buried with dogs that's my choice, not his."' Byron laughed. 'As I said, a man who knows his mind. Like me.'

'I'm amazed you know what you want. By the by, who's Bos'n, a mad seaman?'

'Not by a long shot. Y'know, I wrote one will and stated in it, "The body of Lord B. to be buried in the vault of the garden of Newstead, without any ceremony or burial service whatever, or any inscription, save his name and age. His dog not to be removed from the said vault." So, Polly, let me say I know what I should like.' Voice lowered in deference, he said, 'Bos'n was the best friend I ever had. A Newfoundland dog, a comic, a playmate and a saviour. Him and me would play games. I'd be out in a boat on the lake and he'd sit on the bank watching.' Another smile of recollection. 'All of a sudden I'd yell and roll out the boat into the water. I tell you, Bos'n was in like a shot to rescue me. That dog was so strong he'd have me out o' there in a trice.

'Aye, Bos'n.' Byron's eyes watered. 'Silly hound got into a fight, had his ear near tore off, got bit all over. Came loping back to the Abbey all wild-eyed and frothing at the mouth. Joe and Nanny Smith went crazy telling me I shouldn't go near him for fear I got bit and went mad.'

'Did he? The dog I mean?'

'I wiped the foam off him, and he let me. Me and Bos'n... I knew he wouldn't harm me. Died days later.'

'I'm sorry,' Polidori said, debating whether or not to pursue the original discussion. Realising he might be treading swampy ground he deviated by saying: 'This Folly Castle, did you ever visit there? I mean, given what you state went on in inside it.'

'I still have a penchant for discovery, it's part of my makeup to discover... things. I visited many times because to me it was a place of great mystery and sometimes felt threatening. I loved to visit despite the threats. Strangely, I felt at home there. Whether or not it was down to the darkness within me I cannot tell. I had to prove something to myself. Yes, I felt at home there despite everything. But I still carried my pistols. Sometimes a bible in my pocket. They were my comforters.' He fell into thought again, accepting that none, including himself, could do anything towards destroying the dead.

It posed other questions: What might the dead be if not echoes of our former selves? Our need to lay the ghosts of family, of kin ere we can ever move forward, be less antagonised by such awful contemplation?

'I confess that I should have hated the place so entrenched in my forbear's evil turn of mind, yet I never did. I used to enjoy my visits. I tried desperately to never admit my fears simply because I felt other places were far more threatening to me.'

'Other places?' Polidori tried to assimilate further hidden meanings behind what he'd heard, or more precisely that which the poet had revealed. 'Perhaps,' he said, 'I am now beginning to gain insight into the man.' Concluding enough was enough, he wandered back to the table and picked up his pen.

A curious Byron followed. 'Tell me, John, what do you write?' As a tutor might, he stood immediately behind Polidori. Disliking it, Polidori shifted position and so avoided sight of Byron.

'Well?' prompted Byron.

Polidori half-turned, looked up, and immediately shielded his eyes, the sun now directly over Byron's shoulder, the latter's shadow thrown across the table. Disturbed by such overpowering presence, he turned away. 'I already told you, but to reiterate I'm compiling a journal of our travels, describing places of interest, adding clarification as I think befits...'

He still didn't mention Murray's commission, content to wallow in blatant subterfuge for the reason of not wishing Byron to accuse him of spying on him, the poet lord, the one about whom everyone desired to know.

A man of some dignity, it did go against Polidori's business-like manner, yet arguably not if it meant he would benefit his own literary career. John Murray would help promote that.

'LB, I will suggest that you're not the only scribe who has an enviable command of the written word.'

Byron must have detected a hint of covetousness and excused it. Unlike him to miss the opportunity, he decided to bide his time before making Polidori squirm. Instead, and being as it were, well-versed, he teased the doctor, throwing him when he admitted: 'I wholly accept that.' He sat, smoothed his waistcoat, and spent a few seconds placing papers in order. He tapped them. 'Another canto of my epic *Childe Harold*. Relate a line of yours so I might appraise it.'

Polidori shuffled in the chair, aware he was bound to recite something if only to learn. 'If you wish,' he said quietly.

'I insist.'

Clearing his throat, Polidori referred to his writings, and extolled: '"Arrived at Mayence. Saw along the Rhine many fine old castles."' He glanced at Byron. 'I'm also thinking something like... er... Ah yes.. "The Rhine is a magnificent river winding through valleys with wooded hills cloaked with vineyards either side, and castle turrets peeping above the treetops."' A further quick glance at Byron. 'Your opinion?'

Byron flicked through his own pages, retrieved one sheet and recited: '"A blending of all beauties; streams and dells, fruit, foliage, crag, wood, cornfield, mountain vine, and chiefless castles breathing stern farewells from grey but leafy walls, where ruin greenly dwells."'

If the term "cleaving the air with a sword" was ever apt then this appeared to be the precise second when it would truly rip ideals into shreds. Polidori looked thunderous. He tried to cap his rising angst by managing a tight-lipped smile, his fists clenched beneath the table. He trembled with inner rage.

'Merely an example, Polly. It er, may need a few slight changes, not sure if I'm wholly satisfied. Do read me another of your gems.'

Attempting to keep the spoiled child in check, Polidori eased out another biting grin. 'Of course it is still in my head you understand. I mean, not yet written.'

'Understood.' Byron was aware Polidori guessed what was happening and enjoyed it all the more. 'Continue.'

In a tremulous tone and without glancing at Byron, Polidori recited: 'Of all the castles seen, Drachenfels appeared the most forbidding with its crumbling, dark walls encased in encroaching greenery... *et cetera, et cetera.*' The purposeful interruption of his own narrative proved very marked, his tremor stark, his unsettled demeanour borne out in Byron's condescending look.

Appearing like the cat that got the cream, Byron answered calmly: 'Not too badly written, m'dear fellow. Has its merits.' Pale hands resting on his own sheaf of papers, he slowly shook his head. 'Polly, I am sure you can do better. Don't feel too harshly about it. Here, allow me to tender another example. And don't misunderstand; writers work in different ways... you have yours, I... *I* have mine.

'Take note. "The castled crag of Drachenfels frowns o'er the wide and winding Rhine," and so on. You are welcome to read it if you wish.' A shrug. 'Your trouble is taking me too seriously. It is only intended as constructive critique.'

The comment poured more distress on Polidori's already injured ideals. He couldn't bear Byron to request he read another segment and gathered up his book, writing case and pen before scuttling to the coach.

'Too hot, I... I'm tired. Excuse me,' he called back. Yes, he was tired, sick and tired of being made to appear the lesser man. It was a plain fact to which John Polidori would never admit.

'FLETCHER!' Byron called.

Fletcher, resting on a tree stump, rose and hurried to his master. 'My lord?'

'It seems that once more our good Doctor has a desire to be on the move. Prepare the horses, there's a good fellow.'

Byron scanned the landscape; he watched Berger and Rushton tote table and chairs away before he collected the selected bones and placed them in a leather valise. With the view across the field in mind, further lines occurred to him, lines he may or may not incorporate in his epic. Spoken aloud: 'Time to leave this proud, patriot field,' the lines could well underscore his love-hate relationship with death.

At the coach, bag in hand, he halted beneath the open window. Deviously, he quoted in a purposely deeper, more disturbing tone: '"Here Burgundy bequeathed his tombless host... Unsepulchered they roamed, *and shrieked each wandering ghost.*"'

Thumping the coach work, his tone rendered normal by a chuckle, he suggested: 'Perhaps we should leave here before darkness falls, Polly-Dolly. Who knows we, and our new found friend –' Byron rattled the bag, the clunk of bones snapping sinister '– may yet gain sight of Geneva.'

CHAPTER 7

'Thou seest me not pass by...'

I

Lake Léman, a slender, trailing hand in water; languid, the boat floated gently only slight distance from the shoreline, the air keen, vibrant, making life worth living, reflections distorted by a lulling swell.

Beneath the surface a carpet of multi-coloured stones of varying shapes and sizes: these had been polished smooth over centuries, most smothered with weed, myriad green hues merging from light to dark.

Mary conjured the waving tresses of a mermaid's hair reminiscent of an artist's impression she'd seen in a book of myths.

Darting shoals of tiny, silver fish broke the tranquil lake's surface.

Above the trees across the lake she had earlier made out the red roof of a small, humble villa. Upon making inquiries she learned it to be the *Maison Chapuis,* its terraces, and what appeared to be vineyards bisected in haphazard fashion by an upward path. On the shoreline she'd detected a port for mooring a boat.

II

They had settled in Sécheron on the outskirts of Geneva, choosing the picturesque lakeside *Hôtel d'Angleterre*, the first coaching inn on the way out of the austere walled city. Run under the watchful, fussy and very efficient eye of Monsieur Dejean, the establishment – reputedly one of the best inns in the area – had three storeys and catered ably to the more delicate palates and tastes of the 'true English gentlemen' and their ladies. It was spacious and non-pretentious: set back from the lake on its north side, it offered an unencumbered view of the Alps, and the majestic Mont Blanc. Elaborate gardens extended to the water's edge and its own harbour. Boats and boatmen placed themselves and their transport at the disposal of guests.

'See,' Mary had pointed out, 'the park leads to the road from Geneva to Lausanne. Perhaps we might visit Lausanne, Shelley?'

Shelley had simply nodded. Concerned about their finances, he felt it better not to argue and so dash Mary's plans. They were here – a minor miracle. 'Very impressive,' he said of the hotel. And we have the benefit of staying outside the city gates. We can at least be certain the hotel offers its greatest advantage for night revellers.'

Shelley delighted in this and told Mary. 'I am sure Lord Byron will enjoy the fact because it remains exempt from the curfew imposed by the city elders. They order the gates closed at ten p.m. sharp. I am a night person, and such an hour would be too early to suit.'

In the days following their arrival, Mary and Shelley found occasion to stroll in the narrow, cobblestoned, and ill-lit streets of Geneva's old city. They browsed in bookstores, spent much time in awe and admiration of both watch and lens makers – Mary bought Shelley a telescope, the man excited enough to insist upon using it at every given opportunity. They shopped for balloons and kites, primarily for Shelley, the child inside, or perhaps the seeker of truth, never completely hidden.

In her diary over ensuing nights Mary made reference to the town, particularly alluding to the discomfort of walking over its rough stones. *"The houses are high,"* she wrote, *"the streets narrow, many of them on the ascent, and no public building of any beauty to attract your eyes, or any architecture to gratify your taste."*

She mentioned the three gates, and underlined the time they were closed. *"No amount of bribery can open them."*

They had walked on the promenade of the Genevese, a grassy plain planted frugally with trees. Shelley was intrigued by the small obelisk erected to the glory of Jean-Jaques Rousseau.

'Would you believe,' he told Mary, 'that the local magistrates, successors of those who exiled him from his native country, were shot by the populace during the revolution. Ironic isn't it that Rousseau's writings contributed to that revolution which, in turn, gave enduring benefits to mankind. A life impregnated with conflict, and he still had the power to change opinion.' He'd sighed as he gazed on the obelisk. 'What price life?'

'Yes,' Mary had answered, 'I agree Rousseau's writings produced benefits to mankind.' Perhaps she was thinking of Byron when she said it, for it seemed obvious that the poet and Rousseau were married to the same ideals. The term *free thinkers* seemed apt, for both had practised and preached, and written about, certain taboo subjects that only individuals of like mind would accept.

Such thoughts remained so, yet Mary imagined they would yet be resurrected. She had met Byron, looked upon him, and perhaps, if admitted, might be said to be in awe of him. Or – *frightened*?

III

Distinct from town life, Mary revelled in the countryside, and likened it to her love of England's 'green and pleasant land'. She basked in its warm sunshine, the humming of sun-loving insects. From the hotel windows they could view the lovely lake, blue as the heavens reflected within it, and sparkling with golden beams. Its opposite, vine covered shore, sloped, yet, this early in the season their lacklustre detracted from the beauty of their prospect. Beyond them rose the various ridges of the black mountains, Mont Blanc, a jewel in the midst of its snowy Alps.

The water excursions attracted, Mary so enamoured that they hired a boat every evening around six o'clock.

The one thing tending to mar such recreation, to blight their otherwise positive outlook, was Claire's inordinate impatience. Despite having cajoled Mary and Shelley into coming here and not forgetting Mary and Shelley's constant enquiries alongside Claire's own pestering of hotel and post office staff, Lord Byron had not yet arrived. Shelley and Mary were thus more put upon to try and keep the unhappy, petulant girl suitably entertained.

From the water, Mary, having reclined in a more or less self-induced silence, said little to her companions. Instead, her gaze strayed more and more to that secluded spot on the far side in which nestled such an alluring villa.

Privately she saw it as the epitome of all that they may have missed by means of pleasant habitation and so conjured small, intimate rooms in which they could relax, read, and discuss personal things. Claire would have her own room, and the doors would lock.

'I am grateful,' she eventually said, 'that the passage of time has served to distance us from the stench of horses and the ridiculously small confines of that carriage. And not least travel sickness.'

The others agreed, especially Claire, the trio basking in new, more enlivened and welcoming aromas: a glut of exhilarating scents of new mown grass, flowers and spring blossom curled across the evening lake to instil a greater sense of well-being.

'I am less bothered than you, sister,' Claire offered. 'At least those blankets kept out the cold.'

'And we are divest of thick, winter clothing,' Mary countered. She wrinkled her nose. 'Those malodorous blankets entrapped our own body odours. Good Lord in his heaven, so many endless hours passing without benefit of soap and water. Do admit, Claire, lighter clothing and access to water for washing does promote a happier mood.'

Shelley's white shirt rippled in the warm breeze, Mary's light blue dress a well-chosen match for their surroundings, while Claire's startling maroon ensured she remained prominent against the blue of the lake and green textured backdrop.

Mary leaned over, unmindful that one lace sleeve became soaked as it floated on the surface, her left hand and forearm immersed in cool water.

Eyes narrowed against a sudden glare, and almost as if she were speaking thoughts aloud, she said: 'I believe I shall collect pebbles from the lake's bottom as I would pick wild flowers from yonder meadow. Strangely the bed of the lake appears within my grasp.'

Drawing closer to the almost flat surface, she narrowed her eyes attempting to see beyond reflected cloud shadows. Uttering a surprised 'Oh!' she was startled by the apparent deformity of her arm swallowed by the water. 'The water is so soft yet I am of the impression that it is powerful enough to crush bone.' She turned to Shelley. 'See, Shelley, I am almost dismembered, one part of my arm appears quite separate.'

'Most certainly a welcome break in our routine.' Claire's humour carried, despite her preoccupation. The willows lining the bank added their own amused chuckles as the breeze tickled them.

Mary closed her ears, absorbed as she was by the suddenness of reality: a limb suspended, hanging free of encumbrance, devoid of body, brain, or nerves to give it life, yet buffeted gently by the current as though given new life.

Fascinated by Mary's detachment, Shelley and Claire, too, leaned over, Shelley warning Claire to remain at her side of the boat. 'Or we may capsize.'

United in this way, they all stared, individually aware of different images. 'Like pictures in a cold fire,' Shelley commented, 'the ash forming caverns and peaks with perhaps that one dying ember of red.'

Mary closed her eyes, the sun behind her lids forming aureoles of red, the heat burning – akin to a stare from other eyes welded in her imagination.

The whole appeared merely an abstract vision where warmth and coldness combined, a lukewarm allusion perhaps to how their lives had been, and would be lived.

Claire looked up. 'Tell me, Shelley, what is it *you* see beneath this flexible skin?'

'What does anyone see beneath?' Shelley's comment lacked his usual interest. He sat upright, a fresher, profound thought urging. 'Here we have a world in which creatures from the dawn of time reputedly live. Many, I have read, are dreadful, grotesque in appearance, unfit for human eye to behold.'

Claire hugged herself. 'Shelley, why pretend to see something unpleasant in our surroundings? In the coach you spoke of the souls of the damned, about them being sent here... calling us all to join them.' She eyed him suspiciously. 'It frightens me.'

Then, as though a cloud had dispersed, and without further recourse to her fears, she added brightly, 'But then you could always join those so-called monsters down there. It is only a small step out of the boat. Just think what might have happened had I not heeded your request to remain on my own side.' She chuckled mischievously.

Shelley offered a courteous bow with head and shoulders and joined their levity. A grin surfaced. 'So, madam, you reprimand me for trying to add a touch of the unknown to our voyage. It was hardly intended to annoy or upset.'

'Oh you –' Claire attempted a playful slap at him, almost losing her seat had not Shelley grabbed her, her shrill scream startling water birds who set off in a wing-flapping flight further upstream.

Satisfied Claire was comfortable, Shelley shifted position to ease his numb buttocks on a seat which, despite several cushions, had grown extremely hard. 'I am curious, Claire. What would you do if I were to undertake such a foolhardy step?'

The smile proved anything but flattering, yet it teased, Claire's careless attitude along with her besotted state prompting: 'Hardly a problem, Percy, for I am sure Mary and I shall not be left to flounder for long. We are quite capable of taking an oar each.' Her painted smile looked slightly contemptuous.

'You apparently see something in the lake that I cannot.' Shelley, at this juncture, and despite what he offered by way of an apology, seemed put out. With the knowledge that he, not Mary, encouraged Claire and acutely aware of Mary's sometimes niggardly toleration of her half-sister, he was shocked to realise that Claire's inferring she could do without him contradicted what she'd already implied in England before they sailed – other than her anticipated meeting with another certain poet that is.

'Yes I can,' Claire retorted dreamily. 'Since by your oblique reference to Byron, I admit to seeing his features.' She giggled behind her hand. 'Man, or monster, I view him wearing a silver crown studded with the lake's diamonds.' She fluttered her eyelashes at Shelley. 'Of course it may be *your* reflection I see, Shelley.'

'Should I be flattered, Miss Clairmont?'

Claire gazed towards shore. Impatient, she added for both Mary and Shelley's benefit: 'I feel sure Lord Byron must arrive soon.'

On an entirely different plain, Mary only partially heard the conversation, certain phrases disturbing. Prompted by a ripple, some movement, she stared again at the water, her arm jerked out instinctively, some pre-emptive notion that a threat lurked amongst those beautifully hued stones urging the action.

A face? Impossible. A corruption in the water, what it contained. Already she had witnessed her arm become disjointed.

Surely then a similar effect could be caused by something else? Hadn't her father mentioned light refraction?

Her heart fluttered, pain nagged above her eyes, the sun's glare blamed as it sat balanced like a huge ball on the tip of a mountain.

And even that might tumble off and fall into a bottomless pit, swallowed by a darkness she abhorred because it resurrected her father's demeaning of her own and Shelley's circumstances.

As it reflected the dying of life.

So much for Rousseau, Mary mused. His *Confessions* lessen in their implication when compared to the candour of my father's details. No hypocrisy written or intended in *The Rights of Women.*

Circumstances? A child born out of wedlock... A human creature born without the trappings, or the blessings of the church. Or the child she had lost, now merely food for grave worms. Oh would that it, too, might be resurrected.

Foolish thoughts, whimsy? Seeds planted through simple discussion, the sometimes inexplicable vagaries of imagination.

Shelley's voice sounded distant. She heard: '...not well, dearest?' He grasped her arm, his fingers warm on her flesh after the vagaries of the water. 'Mary, are you unwell?'

Claire made a few concerned noises, barely audible in that she still dreamed of Lord Byron riding in on a huge horse to snatch her up and bear her away.

'Mary?' Shelley again.

Turning slowly, fearful that some hideous entity would rise up and take her from him, from William, and from the world, she managed a tight smile. 'I... I am all right.' Uttered without real conviction. 'Perhaps if we return I can rest. It's the heat, I'm not used to it after the raging cold of the tiresome journey.' She glanced at the water aware it conflicted with her feelings. Her heart beat loud, so loud she guessed the others would hear it.

'I should get back for William, he's due his feed. I cannot expect the hotel staff to offer the same sustenance.'

A white lie: William's feed was not due for at least another hour, Mary having fed him barely thirty minutes before they had embarked on the trip. Thankfully, since arriving here, her son's health – worrying to say the least after that horrendous journey – had greatly improved, the colour returned to his cheeks.

Of course, she knew Claire must guess the excuse. But then I am not beholden to her, nor will I rely on her. Her whims and fancies will one day destroy her optimism.

So might my own, she thought. She arrested this, arguing, maybe a little cruelly: I don't need puppy dogs to take surrogate sustenance from me.

Nor did she share Claire's adulation for all things Swiss. To her the inhabitants here lacked grace and vivacity and did not enter society. Having taken few pains to acquaint herself with the inhabitants in Geneva she did at least extol the greater equality of class as compared to England, and the refinement of manners among the lower orders, as well as their Puritanism.

Totally divorced from them all out here, the rapidly cooling day gave vent to wisps of vapour playing across a surface animated by rising currents of air that, albeit momentarily, formed and reformed into strange, human-like forms about the boat.

'Look!' Shelley exclaimed. 'The lake's creatures escape their watery confines, no longer content to remain below us. They adopt other forms and surround us. D'you think them capable of overwhelming us?'

Claire's silence alerted Mary. 'Enough, Shelley,' Mary admonished, face paler than normal beneath a slight sunburn. 'It is time we made for the shore, kindly take up the oars.' A quick, sidelong glance at Claire emphasised her concern.

How quickly an idyll can change into something culpable and much less acceptable in the predominantly awkward atmosphere, not helped by the diminishing light. Shelley emphasised a certain reluctance to do as bidden. Petulantly fitting the oars into the rowlocks, unaware the left oar hadn't properly seated, he gripped both and pulled back violently. With a clatter, the offending oar jumped from its precarious seating, the suddenness of it unbalancing Shelley who tumbled backwards into the prow, feet in the air, arms akimbo, shock and surprise evident.

Seconds stretched, a stunned silence prevailed until Shelley, cursing wildly, attempted to untangle himself from his own legs, somehow lodged beneath the seat Claire occupied.

Claire tried not to laugh, the awkward moment's expletives from Shelley eventually buried in shrieks of laughter from both women. The sounds carried, turning the heads of others relaxing in their boats some distance to starboard.

Shelley, upright again, rummaged for the lost oar fallen in the bottom of the boat, thankfully not in the water.

Mary tried to stem her laughter, hoping to prevent Shelley going into a sulk. Unfortunately, her giggles prevailed much longer than Claire's. Satisfied no harm had been done, and that the incident did not add to an already strained situation, especially where Claire and Byron were concerned, Mary said, 'Take us back, Shelley.'

Pulling away with a will, both oars fixed properly, Shelley glanced at Mary, then at Claire. 'I don't mind being the object of so much mirth.' He attempted unsuccessfully to hide his own grin. 'At least, Claire, it proves a point: I am needed.'

Claire, underscoring her superiority in the friendly battle of wills, fired back: 'I daresay Mary and I would have managed to shout help had you gone overboard!'

Laughter still flowed, the creak of the boat, the swish of the oars creating its own ambience as they headed towards the dock.

Once there, and taking Shelley's hand, Mary stepped from the boat. Laughter subdued, she still saw that intense image glimpsed in the water, each tiny wavelet having distorted its startling features.

Claire, almost tumbling, caught Shelley's arm and managed to gain the bank making rather more of clinging to Shelley than Mary would have liked. She looked across the water, deliberately avoiding sight of Shelley giving Claire a hug.

Evening shades threw unsettling blotches across the lake, the darker silhouette of the hotel broken by golden light from its rooms and salon, the gold drowned in the water, further dashes added here and there as more oil lamps were lit.

Like a monster with myriad eyes, it lay within the lake, waiting. Mary, turned away quickly, hating the track her thoughts walked – *down the shaded, stone tunnel of a grim castle.*

As Claire turned she uttered a startled 'Oh', her gaze settling on a dark figure as it detached itself from the trees. Her heart fluttered. Picnic basket abandoned, and to the surprise of the others, she hiked up her skirts and set off running up the slightly sloping bank.

'My lord... MY LORD... It's me. It's Claire.'

The sound slapped across the lake and its surrounding buildings. Mary glanced at Shelley, both simultaneously whispering: 'Byron.'

At once they joined Claire, Mary detecting the disappointed slump in Claire's shoulders, the pout as she turned, one foot stamped. 'He is not here.' She looked close to tears. Then she turned back and gestured. 'It was Lord Byron I am sure.'

The gathered gloom made it more difficult to pinpoint any real definition. Tree shadows cavorted as the breeze waltzed amongst them, the descending night, its chill, and the fact they all wore thinner clothes, forced their huddle. Mary gripped Shelley's hand, felt him squeeze it, and wondered who Claire had seen.

A resident perhaps? Could have been Byron, she supposed, but then what if it had been someone else? Something from her imagination, given a restless kind of half-life. A someone not yet ready to be born?

ON THE EDGE OF CONSCIOUSNESS

Fools, they think me human, a thing of flesh and blood.
Do they not know that I crave blood?

Do they not realise that I am born already, a creature of night lent reality by a poet seeking his destiny? His words alone will truly create ME.

Even the poet may not know to what he has given life: not be aware that I share his darkness just as the creatures of the night at his English home shared it... And still do. For once created, given substance, we linger in man's innermost fears, compel him to bring us forth, in the night hours, in the shade, on the dankest, miserable days.

He spoke of not feeling fear in Folly Castle, that building erected by his damnable kin. The vain fool is wrong! Even then I courted him yet stayed behind out of reach, out of sight, but I breathe bad air and exude the stink of the charnel house. I know *he experienced something diabolic.*

Laughter. I hear it in the night wind. An echo of another phrase, from a pretty, unstable and foolish woman.

Mad. Bad. And dangerous to know.
Which one of us might it be?

I see the other woman peering into the trees. She wants him.

Not yet, my pretty. Not yet.

CHAPTER 8

'Tis to create, and in creating live...'

I

'AGE?' The question in the hotel register asked. 'Age?'

Tired, and impatient to retire to a proper bed instead of that uncomfortable thing in the carriage, and to be rid of that leech, Polidori, Byron scribbled an answer. He wrote: *'One hundred!'*

Badgered by images from his past, not least a postscript he'd added to a letter addressed to Hobhouse concerning his daughter –

> P.S. — If you hear of my child — let me know any good of her health — & well doing.

But the mind plays tricks and he is wont to think of himself again, and the fun they all may have when together and drinking, discoursing about the fairer sex. So he added –

> Will you bring out Pausanias's Description of Greece (Taylor's ditto) when you come — I shall wait for you at Geneva — don't forget to urge Scrope into our crew — we will buy females and found a colony — provided Scrope does not find those ossified barriers to "the forefended place" — which cost him such a siege at Brighthelmstone — write at your leisure — or "ipse veni".

It was midnight on May 23rd, the basest of all hours when one is tired and aggravated by a loathsome last lap, and not least by having to make banal conversation to Polly-Dolly who, in Byron's opinion was exactly the kind of person to whom, if he fell overboard, one would hold out a straw to know if the adage were true that drowning men catch at straws.

Bleached of energy, Byron would meet the wrath of the unamused hotelier M. Dejean when the latter woke him later to demand that he correct his age in the register. For some other guest has written beside it, which Dejean quoted in stilted English, "'I am sorry you are grown so old. Indeed I suspected you were 200 from the slowness of your journey. I suppose your venerable age could not bear quicker travelling."

'Sir,' Dejean said, 'it is hardly fitting to harbour such notations in *my* register!'

Despite his irritable state, Byron had smiled. 'At least, you have two humourists in the establishment, monsieur.' And promptly ushered the man away. 'Tomorrow, sir, I will amend my entry. For now. Let me rest.'

He didn't know then that nearly two weeks earlier, Claire Clairmont, with the Shelleys, had taken the cheapest rooms on the top floor, and that she had been anxiously awaiting his arrival, and had prayed that Byron had not misled her as to his destination.

So besotted was she that Claire had taken liberties by rummaging through *poste restante* at Geneva, eventually pleased and reassured to find a letter addressed to John Polidori.

She had written to Byron begging, "Pray write, I shall die if you don't write." This from London. Later from Paris, excited about the prospect of a reunion, she wrote again but rather than herald any thoughts of sexual entrapment, she couched it thus: "I had ten times rather be your male friend than your mistress."

Byron had grinned. Considering he had coaxed Caroline Lamb into dressing as a page boy, the thought of a less sylph-like Claire conjured a heavier image, and an amusing one. Claire dressed as a man he could not, for the life of him, truly envisage.

'I am indifferent to her,' he said to himself, at once wishing to admit certain growing antipathy. 'In fact, and in truth, I loathe her.'

Ironically, it echoed his feelings towards Caroline. 'Such damned hysterical admissions of love, her need to be servile. Damn me, every word, every comma and full stop could have been penned by Caro.'

Thankfully, Polidori did have his own room, Byron now able to at last give vent to his true feelings.

'The demon and his lovers.' He sought the small mirror on the equally small dresser, his tired image somehow less wholesome in the flickering lamplight. 'Yes, fiends the both of 'em.' He stared at yet another note left for him from Claire. A note of welcome.

'And she directs me to reply to this under cover of Shelley. "For I do not wish to appear in love or curious,"' he quoted with scorn. 'Let her wait, I am all played out and think of her as merely another dalliance. Sunday is mine. I shall keep to myself, pretend she does not exist.

'As for Polly-Dolly, he may share her if he wishes.' Byron fell onto the bed agreeing it was indeed of much finer vintage comfort-wise than the one in his carriage. 'More loose wheels than a horse loses shoes.'

II

Claire Clairmont paced her room: such a small, pathetic room practically under the eaves, so close to them in fact she could hear the wretched birds' claws scratching at the tiles.

'Why has he not replied to my notes? I know he's here but will have little or nothing to do with me.'

It helped to talk like this, alone with no-one to argue with but herself. And yes, she would do that, talk, argue and contradict, discovering and rediscovering every reason beneath God's sun for her lord not to have responded.

'It cannot be that he will not see me. He is tired after his journey.' But a whole week tired? If argued, it did not ring true, her excuses for him merely that.

Granted she had heard about Byron's wry, amusing comment about his age entered in the hotel register. In fact, it was she who had penned the joke in the register about him grown so old. She smiled, saying: 'Well, heaven send you sweet sleep – I am so happy.'

More days would pass before Claire would meet her lord.

III

Like Claire, John Polidori moped.

'I am as good, as clever, as proficient at writing as Byron. *I am!*'

Jubilant about his early association with Byron, he'd written to Fanny, his favourite sister, stating, "... I am with him on the footing of an equal..."

Sad that such quality waned, yet this vain, selfish, sickly man demanded that assurance: he hated walking in Byron's shadow, being the butt of jokes. And he disliked vehemently the nickname Byron would insist upon using. God, it made him sound like he was a parrot.

The view across the hotel grounds and lake from his tiny hotel window should have inspired him, instead it made him more insensitive and spiteful simply because, if he dare admit it, he would never hold a candle to the prolific poet genius. It did, however, reward him with a glimpse of a couple, heads close in conversation, walking beneath the willows near to the water's edge. 'Might that be the Shelleys I wonder?'

He had only glimpsed them so could not be sure, yet he had heard rumour to the effect that they had run away from England to escape the wrath of Mary's angry father.

'Married? Or not?' He balanced the question, again aware of hearing Shelley's penchant for the ideals of free love. 'Quite enlightening if true.'

It gave more credence to his determination to adopt a Byronic character, and thus, in his mind, such adoption may lead him to a more benevolent lifestyle.

Polidori, by nature dashing, reckless, often impetuous with a predilection for tilting at legendary windmills, also liked to think himself a man of honour. A compassionate individual, at least he believed so, he was also very sensitive, proved by the fact that he despised being made fun of.

'I will not bow before Byron. Or Shelley.' Convinced he was their equal, he was afraid to accept any constructive help either may offer.

A foolish man, he would not at this time admit the fact either to himself or others. 'I am a genius.' He smiled at his own reflection in the window glass. 'For who else could win such an accolade as being one of the youngest men ever, at nineteen to attain a Degree in Medicine?' He preened, he strutted, he admired himself in the free standing mirror against the opposite wall. 'Black suits me, don't y'know.'

All ego and very little, if any, self-esteem and totally lacking a sense of humour, he hadn't the sense to know the latter, in itself, would bring out Byron's mean streak.

Byron doted on practical jokes, marked by some of what Polidori had heard – and suffered – on the way here. Yet following such incidents, Polidori still did not have the sense to realise that had he joined in, made himself the butt of being singled out *by design*, he would have won more than Byron's friendship, he would have won his esteem. Did he now regret this? Hardly so, for in one of his frequent, petulant outbursts he'd demanded of his employer: 'Just what do you do, aside from penning poetry, that I, John Polidori, cannot do?'

To a man of Byron's temperament, this could only be termed a challenge. Initially, Byron had laughed, almost demanding without saying it – do you really wish to know? He'd sneered, the curve of his lip heralding: 'First, my friend, I can hit with a pistol ball the keyhole of that door. Secondly, I can swim across that river to yonder point – and thirdly...' He'd paused for emphasis. 'Thirdly, I can give you a damned good thrashing.'

In short, the barbed comments, threats if you will, so belittled Polidori that, like Shelley, he sank into a semi-permanent sulk. So why, to do himself good, did he not reflect upon this? Reflect and learn that at nineteen he could not insinuate himself upon Lord Byron without first passing certain tests? He failed miserably, incurring Byron's self-effacing wit alongside the man's wrath at his own expense.

It was perhaps deliberate that Byron did not reveal the fact that Polidori's inadequacies intensified the poet's longing for Augusta. Deprived as he was of her loving presence and wordless understanding and that the beauty of all he saw felt muted, it came out more subtly in a lyric, the very words of which, had Polidori deigned to think harder about, would have given him a clue.

"The Castled Crag of Drachenfels" had four verses, each ending with a rhymed couplet lamenting an earthly paradise less perfect without her. And yes, Polidori had at least collected some references to Byron's fondness for his sister, yet had simply coupled it only to blood ties, nothing more. Not a matter, he warned, to discuss with such an ennobled personage.

Emotional volatility alone in Polidori had been the cause of grief to them both, Polidori too blind and self-centred to see it. Now all he could do was attempt to match probably the self-same thing he believed inherent in Byron.

An icon, a man to copy, and so establish some kind of parallel regime, Polidori went to his wardrobe and removed a suit. Hung overnight to allow the creases to fall out, once dressed in it, the suit would make him appear presentable. A white scarf wound about his equally white, winged collar and finished in the neatest bow, would lend a little colour, the whole image he wished to attain perfectly promoted. He did that and posed before his mirror.

'Mm, very striking.' Not least he accentuated it with a comma of dark curl which he fetched down with finger and thumb to lend his tanned face more prominence. 'And –' he said to the reflection, 'And I even won the appointment as private physician to an English lord? Dammit, Lord Byron claimed I was *irresistible!*'

Everything, every statement, every barbed comment, so conveniently pushed aside, he paced to the door and back, to the window and back, attempting to tell himself that he would win through and be accepted by society as a whole, in a way he wanted, and not least by Byron and Shelley. 'They must!' He snapped his fingers. 'Ah, I have it! I shall talk with Mary Godwin, she will help me curry favour.'

Polidori hadn't met her yet, but then Doctor John was nothing less than a determined man.

IV

Mary Godwin wrote home on the 1st June:

> You will perceive that we have changed our residence since my last letter. We now inhabit a little cottage on the opposite shore of the lake, and have exchanged the view of Mont Blanc and her snowy *aiguilles* for the dark frowning Jura, behind whose range we every evening see the sun sink, and darkness approaches our valley from behind the Alps, which are then tinged by that glowing rose-like hue which is observed in England to attend on the clouds of an autumnal sky when day-light is almost gone. The lake is at our feet, and a little harbour contains our boat, in which we still enjoy our evening excursions on the water. Unfortunately we do not now enjoy those brilliant

skies that hailed us on our first arrival to this country. An almost perpetual rain confines us principally to the house; but when the sun bursts forth it is with a splendour and heat unknown in England. The thunder storms that visit us are grander and more terrific than I have ever seen before. We watch them as they approach from the opposite side of the lake, observing the lightning play among the clouds in various parts of the heavens, and dart in jagged figures upon the piny heights of Jura, dark with the shadow of the overhanging cloud, while perhaps the sun is shining cheerily upon us. One night we enjoyed a finer storm than I had ever before beheld. The lake was lit up — the pines on Jura made visible, and all the scene illuminated for an instant, when a pitchy blackness succeeded, and the thunder came in frightful bursts over our heads amid the darkness.

Another Sunday recreation for the citizens is an excursion to the top of Mont Salve. This hill is within a league of the town, and rises perpendicularly from the cultivated plain. It is ascended on the other side, and I should judge from its situation that your toil is rewarded by a delightful view of the course of the Rhone and Arve, and of the shores of the lake. We have not yet visited it.

There is more equality of classes here than in England. This occasions a greater freedom and refinement of manners among the lower orders than we meet within our own country. I fancy the haughty English ladies are greatly disgusted with this consequence of republican institutions, for the Genevese servants complain very much of their scolding, an exercise of the tongue, I believe, perfectly unknown here. The peasants of Switzerland may not however emulate the vivacity and grace of the French. They are more cleanly, but they are slow and inapt. I know a girl of twenty, who although she had lived all her life among vineyards, could not inform me during what month the vintage took place, and I discovered she was utterly ignorant of the order in which the months succeed one to another. She would not have been surprised if I had talked of the burning sun and delicious fruits of December, or of the frosts of July. Yet she is by no means deficient in understanding.

The Genevese are also much inclined to puritanism. It is true that from habit they dance on a Sunday, but as soon as the French government was abolished in the town, the magistrates ordered the theatre to be closed, and measures were taken to pull down the building.

We have latterly enjoyed fine weather, and nothing is more pleasant than to listen to the evening song of the vine-dressers. They are all women, and most of them have harmonious although masculine voices. The theme of their ballads consists of shepherds, love, flocks, and the sons of kings who fall in love with beautiful shepherdesses. Their tunes are monotonous, but it is sweet to hear them in the stillness of evening, while we are enjoying the sight of the setting sun, either from the hill behind our house or from the lake. Such are our pleasures here, which would be greatly increased if the season had been more favourable, for they chiefly consist in such enjoyments as sunshine and gentle breezes bestow. We have not yet made any excursion in the environs of the town, but we have planned several and when you shall again hear of us, we will endeavour, by the magic of words, to transport the ethereal part of you to the neighbourhood of the Alps, and mountain streams, and forests, which, while they clothe the former, darken the latter with their vast shadows.

Adieu! M.

CHAPTER 9

'Earth's troubled waters for a purer spring'

I

Alone, trying to relax in the rented Villa Chapuis – the one she'd noticed that day on the lake – Mary wondered, not without consternation, about the images she had conjured both in the coach during their abysmal trek across the mountains, and those she had seen in the lake.

Darken the latter with their vast shadows.

The phrase threw up further undesirable images, but she had sealed the letter ready to post. 'No matter, I shall be able to enlighten them at home once I have stayed here a little longer.'

Did she regret leaving the hotel? Certainly the villa cost less than the rented hotel rooms, with the added benefit that here they could be themselves without pretence extended to other, mainly English, visitors.

She recalled the doctor visiting on the Sunday barely a few days before she, Claire and Shelley decided to leave. Again, relaxation had proved to be futile when she heard the slight tap at her door.

II

Her caller introduced himself, his beguiling smile hardly off-putting, his dress immaculate. 'Doctor John William Polidori, physician to Lord Byron, at your service ma'am.'

A word, a name amidst all the rest: not her caller's name, but a poet's. It had a certain ring to it.

'Please, come in.' Mary waived his apology about intruding on her privacy. 'Shelley is out walking, so I have a little time. And be assured, a friend of Lord Byron's is a friend of mine.'

Might she have detected a slight *moue* of annoyance from the doctor? If so, was it any of her business? Deciding no, she invited him to sit in a chair by the window, the early afternoon sun lighting his countenance, Mary taken by the dark, moody complexion.

'So,' she said, opening the conversation, 'you are the good doctor my sister Claire spoke of recently? I am pleased to make your acquaintance.'

Polidori stood. Acting like the gentleman he craved to be, he took her hand and brushed it lightly with his lips, dark eyes never leaving hers. 'It is I who should be honoured, Mrs Shelley.' He took his seat once more and, quite relaxed, crossed his legs.

'I trust I am not inconveniencing you too much. Perhaps I should have sent a note first asking you to see me.' He wouldn't have done any such thing, instead endeavouring to adopt Byron's way of sometimes turning up unannounced. The mention of the poet's name had almost surely precipitated her inviting him in.

'I, er, should also question, if I am permitted of course... Your, er *sister*? Claire is it? I thought... Forgive me, but I did think she was you, and that –' He laughed, the sound a trifle false. 'And that you were she.' He motioned over his shoulder towards the window. 'That is, I thought I saw Mr Shelley and, er *you* walking in the gardens prior to my coming here.'

He felt embarrassed, every word a sudden hurdle in his urgency to become more acquainted with her. 'Surely not your sister?' He raised a quizzical eyebrow and smiled again to cover his *faux pas*.

From her strained look, Polidori deduced he could well have upset her and chided himself. 'Please,' he said, 'do excuse my obvious assumption. I fear it is a mistake I often make.' He rose. 'I shall leave. Another time to suit?'

He hoped to call his own bluff, amply rewarded when Mary said, 'It is of little consequence, think nothing of it, doctor.'

Mary allowed her eyes to drift, not quite yet ready to look at him directly. Her first impression led her to believe he was somehow clumsy in his own introduction, and not suited to conversation other than perhaps small talk. That he was young and inexperienced did not take any assuming, for he had already proved this.

'I should also correct you on another matter, sir.' She stared at him, unafraid of any reaction whatever it may be, and said, 'Mr Shelley and I are not yet married.'

The silence, for the short duration it lasted, didn't go unnoticed, Polidori hoping to make it less embarrassing by stating:

'Certain gossip is hard to dismiss, Mrs... er, ah... Presumptuous I know, but may I call you Mary?'

'And you are John?'

He felt better at her acceptance and thanked her. Yes, a very good foundation. 'It is difficult I know, Mary. I mean, here am I a complete stranger turning up on your threshold and expecting... expecting... so much. Perhaps I should tell you a little about myself; that way we will hardly be complete strangers.'

'I am aware... John,' she said hesitantly, 'that Claire knows of you inasmuch as she sought news of Lord Byron's coming. She, er, ascertained that you had written a letter to the manager of this hotel.'

Polidori nodded. 'Yes, I have also heard of Miss Clairmont's dare I say, infatuation with LB –'

'LB. How quaint. Does he mind being called so?'

Polidori could think of much more to tell her but being the gentleman he again declined in favour of a more acceptable retort. 'Among other things, but I do know he dislikes being called George. He doesn't mind Albé.'

'A quaint name, derived from LB I take it.'

'He has a need to burst forth now and again with Albanian war songs, so –' He offered an open palm gesture.

'I see.' She didn't tell him she already knew this from her meeting with Byron in London. He had told her of his earlier trip, and of the music and songs he'd learned. She made a point of being evasive on the subject when prompted with:

'How well do you know Byron?'

'I know *of* Byron.' She was aware now that she may have a fencing match on her hands. While this went on, Mary silently queried: How much do you know, doctor?

That he had presupposed her walking in the garden with Shelley gave vent to slight unease. Although outspoken like her father, Mary decided to act in a naïve way, thinking it would support her act of being, for now at least, a deserted maiden.

He looks at me with sheep's eyes, she thought. She fidgeted, smoothed down her blue, bouffant skirt, dusted her sleeve, silly things, anything to take her mind off what she judged to be Polidori's sadly obvious fawning.

He cleared his throat. 'Perhaps you and I could, er take a stroll, join with your... Meet up with Shelley and Claire. I would very much like to confer with another great poet.' He was waffling, and knew it, but couldn't stop himself.

'Oh,' Mary feigned surprise. 'I didn't realise you were a poet, Doctor Polidori.' She looked away, then back again. 'Or perhaps you meant Lord Byron?' She kept her face perfectly still without a hint of baiting him. In doing so, she couldn't help but notice the vaguest flicker of annoyance. Had she touched a raw nerve? Might Byron, despite his mysterious absence, still be at liberty to inveigle the doctor's susceptibilities?

Polidori cleared his throat a second time, a nervous habit, and a precursor to answering, time taken to compose what he felt a perfectly acceptable answer, one that wouldn't reveal too much.

Before him sat a not unattractive young woman he guessed to be around twenty years of age, his own age so close as not to matter. The highlights in her hair, tastefully taken off her face, and held neatly with pins at the back, collected the sun's gold through the lattice, made the texture burn with a truly richer hue, a slight hint of crimson where yesterday's sun had caught her enlivening her otherwise pale complexion. A gold, lace shawl draped about her shoulders enhanced the whole, Polidori enamoured practically at first sight when she had opened the door to admit him. And no, it would not be fitting should he rise to her comment and throw out some callous, uncalled for remark, even though he felt like doing so.

Can I never be free of the man? Such thoughts aside, he said, 'Dear lady, I have been known to er, put pen to paper and compose a few lines. Why on our way here, Byron and I compared notes –' He couldn't stop the slight tic beneath his right eye, a sure sign of his annoyance, and of his fabricating certain aspects of the trip. He hoped she would not detect it.

'And did his lordship offer any helpful comment? Oh forgive me, John –' She leaned over and touched his hand out of instinct, believing she may have uttered the wrong thing. 'I meant should you have needed it. Not having any knowledge of your writing as I do of Byron's, it is hard, as you must understand, to comment, or compare. Again, I apologise.'

Polidori laughed, the sound strained and lacking humour. 'Mary, please, I am far from offended. I acknowledge how difficult it can be when knowledge is lacking when referring to the contents of my verses. I... I do agree that I... I am not in the same league as LB, but then one has to start somewhere and grow in stature.'

'That is precisely what I meant, John. And thus if Lord Byron is willing to comment on your work, I am sure you will benefit from what he has to say.'

Oh, how cute you are, he thought. So quick, so infuriatingly persuasive in your sentiments, all spoken with an accompanying smile, a fey sidelong glance. Yes, a drug indeed, and far better a soporific than the collection I carry in my bag – the same one Polidori remained convinced Lord Byron '*borrowed*' from.

'In response to your request for a stroll,' Mary said, 'I think not.'

The moment he heard this Polidori's respect for her climbed.

'Of course not. I shouldn't have been – forgive my impertinence.' He changed the subject and again talked of his own and Lord Byron's journey here, ever alert to her reaction whenever he mentioned Byron, emphasised when Mary's colour deepened through what could only be an unexpected blush. One other thing, too, she had not told him that she had even made the good lord's acquaintance, Polidori guessing that she must have done. In a way, through her behaviour she'd as good as told him.

He hid a smirk behind a well-placed hand, unable to recall whether or not Byron had said anything about Mary other than a casual comment about meeting them here in Geneva.

Damn the man. Whatever he wanted, he got. Byron need only snap his fingers and they all come running, women and men.

So did I. Why am I here? He fought shy of answering, certain knowledge gained warning him not to answer, or ever admit that he might not only wish to walk beside Byron, be an equal, but wish... something more intimate. They were both young men, and by his own admission, Byron sought love, his need to express it in any way he could bringing Polidori to a belief that life is a search for that often elusive quantity of caring and sharing.

Polidori admitted he struggled through sludge like that on the battlefield. Would that I were older, more Byron's age, and know what he knows, have penned what he has penned. Done what he has already accomplished.

Isn't it the lot of man, sometimes, to walk in the shadow of others without recourse to one's own prowess? Polidori's thoughts drifted on this course. Should he mention his degree to Mary? No, no, too presumptive and too... too conceited. 'We –' he managed to say, 'visited the field of Waterloo. Lord Byron has a penchant for battles and battlefields, uniforms, weapons and, surprisingly, bones.'

In the water... an arm... reaching... part skeletal... partly fleshed... waiting for someone to rebuild it, give it life.

'Bones?' she repeated, the echo lingering in this sparsely furnished room with its one wardrobe, two chairs, and the small table with an obvious defect down its central plinth – a scar marring what would otherwise have been a presentable object.

She glanced towards the cases and trunks stacked in the corner, one of Percy's jackets draped over a case adorned with colourful travel labels.

Polidori diagnosed a certain anxiety within her but rather than question her well-being, he stupidly added to it, saying: 'Byron collected a pile of 'em and threatened to write his publisher with words to the effect of "another set of knife handles". He –'

Mary stood abruptly. 'Please, doctor, no more. Speak of less unsavoury things, I beg.'

She felt she sounded like some vainglorious prima donna, but determined to keep up the pretense despite the way her mind ran into depths of quivering, enigmatic shadow. And in there, somewhere, beneath the stones that lay within the lake of her mind, something moved... something omnipotent, demanding life.

The thoughts of her own father's indignant attitude, his sometimes overpowering presence, scared her. So, too, had her mother's death, Mary thinking her parent had gone too soon with no chance for Mary to get to know her.

Had she truly guessed, her own life ran parallel to Lord Byron's who, as a sorry boy of twelve come to England from Aberdeen, had never known his own father.

Experiments, she thought. Experiments with life, the way minds work, become fraught with the often inexplicit deeds and words of others, themselves knowing little but expected to teach their offspring.

From the moment we are born we start to think, to learn. Do those on the other side, those we cannot see, still live out their lives?

If they do, what will happen if we give them firmer substance by writing about them? Write them out of ourselves, share them with the world? For that which is written about can never truly die.

This one thought, this conjecture, caused her to sway. She felt her arm taken, vaguely aware of the darkly countenanced man assisting her. She pulled away.

'No! Who are you?' Everything vague... the room swam... figures loitered on the edge of consciousness. Father. Mother. Shelley. William. Claire. Lord Byron. And bones... in the water, reaching... as a child's arm will flex in the fluid contained within the womb.

A dead baby. Mary closed her eyes, and as quickly opened them, scared beyond description. Here a table, now. And a wardrobe. Coloured labels on a trunk, a creased jacket. 'Yes, it will need clothes.'

'I'm sorry?' A strange voice, but one she felt she recognised. A doctor. Yes, yes, Doctor... Frankenstein. *The castle. The old woman warning of demons.*

Had Lord Byron mentioned Yorkshire witch, Mother Shipton, cursing his family? Perhaps Claire could have conveyed the information. Mary couldn't recall.

Polidori sounded concerned, his voice compelling enough for her to distance herself from the disturbing thoughts of moments ago. Mary saw him, the room, reality. Yet why did he appear predatory? A threat? Not wholly recovered, Mary mumbled an apology and walked a little shakily to the door. 'Please, sir, I have matters I must attend, letters to write. You understand.'

Standing by the door, Polidori bowed, a short, sharp nod acknowledging her polite dismissal. He would not, dared not, question what she had said a moment ago about clothes, or who they were for. Her child perhaps? The one he had come across earlier in the hotel lobby with the young woman. 'Another time then.' He purposely made it a statement.

III

He stepped onto a landing whose ceiling pitched sharply to form the slope of the roof. Pictures of lake and mountains, placed at random, like the labels on the suitcases, added colour to the dingy confines.

About to say something, Polidori was interrupted by voices, feminine laughter, footsteps climbing the narrow, uncarpeted flight of stairs from the floor below.

Smiling, Mary looked towards the stairs and brushed past Polidori. 'Shelley. SHELLEY.' She hurried to wait at the top of the stairs, his familiar stoop preceding Claire.

Shelley matched her smile with his own, his arms outstretched to meet her. Holding her at arm's length, he looked concerned. 'You look pale, dearest.'

Another smile belied the truth. 'I'm all right. Some fresh air will do me good.'

'I've been walking with Claire,' Shelley said. He missed Mary's *moue* of annoyance, most unconcerned that such a statement should antagonise her.

Claire, piqued at being left out, stepped onto the top stair. 'Doctor Polidori, do you know where Lord Byron is today?'

Always *him*. Polidori disguised his indignation with a smile. 'I am sorry, Miss Clairmont, I'm afraid I don't. Have you tried his room?'

'I knocked and knocked until I was asked to refrain by one of the other guests. No-one answered the door.'

'Then,' said Polidori, tired of what could become irrelevant banter, 'his lordship is obviously out!'

Shelley came forward, Mary a step or two behind. He offered his hand. 'Percy Bysshe Shelley at your service, sir. Ex-Oxford and an atheist.'

Polidori felt it polite to laugh and shook the hand, introducing himself more formally.

'Byron's physician, eh,' Shelley said, in over-pitched shrill tones and sounding a little in awe.

If it wasn't for the stoop he'd be tall, mused Polidori, grateful that Shelley seemed more his own height because of the bowed shoulders. In fact, Polidori disliked others taller than himself. Not that Byron was taller, well not too much. Unfortunately, Byron made up for his shortcomings in many and varied ways.

Shelley, although tall and large boned, appeared fragile, the doctor taken by his luminous blue eyes and his boyish, round, pinkish face framed by flowing, rich brown hair – an animated face, filled with fire and enthusiasm. A man who exuded intelligence and, as Polidori would later discover, highly excitable.

Polidori, embarrassed to see how intently the haphazardly dressed Shelley scrutinised him, said, 'Sir, I have heard of your successes, and something of your er, reputation.' Polidori added compliments. 'At only twenty-two you're already a poet, an author, and by all counts, a brilliant conversationalist?'

'You flatter and mock at the same time, sir.'

He had presence right enough, and in those few minutes turned out to be honest and forthright, a man never afraid to mince words. 'Whatever you may have heard is probably true. As I said, I'm an atheist. Fools turfed me out of Oxford because of my leanings towards matters most people ignore through fear. To deny the existence of God is tantamount to treason in England, or anywhere as far as it goes.'

He turned abruptly, having forgotten himself. 'Ladies, please... We must be comfortable.'

Polidori, though invited, decided not to accompany them. He lent weight to a comment Mary made and said, 'Mary and I were discussing the possibility of a walk. I trust you enjoyed yours.'

Mary glared at him, then averted her eyes, thus avoiding the mirth in his. She wondered why he'd suggested it. Her heart told her one thing, her mind centred on another entirely. Logic against love. *Free love.*

The latter – implication or blatant suggestion – had upset the normal flow of their lives, emphasised in the shape of a hovering Claire, a woman afraid to miss anything.

She, too, had sheep's eyes. Mary thought for a moment, seeing Claire and the doctor together and decided she might attempt to match-make them.

Desperation borne from earlier, unsettling thoughts, provoked Mary's feeling of being closed in: she wanted to leave here for a while to gather herself. She longed to find somewhere other than this claustrophobic hotel with its compilation of too many eyes and ears, people who could never mind their own business, who would rather live another's life than their own – insipid individuals with tiny minds.

Perhaps I am changing. Shelley is good for me, alone we could do much. They'd walked together, deep in conversation, spontaneous laughter quarrelling with the breeze rustling the grasses on mountain slopes. And their lovemaking. Heights reached, two people together, the world locked out.

Maybe I do realise how Claire feels, for it echoes my own feelings.

She heard her name called. Then again. Shelley said, 'You're preoccupied, my love. But listen, it so happens Polidori and I have reached a compromise: we shall take out a boat and visit the other side of the lake, investigate the possibility of fresh accommodation.'

Mary's heart leapt for this was the catalyst she needed to snap her from tortuous thoughts, install a new, more invigorating meaning to the day, and their future.

Mary hoped that whatever shadows courted her would disperse.

Maybe. Maybe not.

CHAPTER 10

'I had a dream which was not all a dream'

I

With Polidori rowing, the oars didn't dip with quite so much gusto, yet despite it, the decision had been right, the situation less fraught, and certainly less so than their first sojourn on the lake.

Uplifted, Mary raised her head, the breeze off the water refreshing, her cheeks shining with health. "Willmouse" delighted in watching his father trail a hand in the water, Mary less perturbed, the time she'd done it so far away as to be non-eventful. There could be nothing beneath the surface to harm them and she trusted Shelley to hold their son. She was amused as Shelley searched the water for the silver, shining fish seen yesterday. Despite his exclamations of 'Look, Willy, there! A fish. Did you see it?' and 'Hundreds of them!', William stared in wonderment out of eyes the same shade of blue as his father, detecting darting movements as the boat cut through the tiny waves. Even water slapping the hull, lulled.

To leave Sécheron fulfilled a dream Mary upheld: that it would happen bucked little argument. Alongside, the fact that Claire had decided not to accompany them, made Mary undeniably more ecstatic. They were a family again, Polidori the odd one out, yet in a way partly accepted.

That Shelley's funds had dwindled pressed them to seek other accommodation. In tandem with the fact that their little group of three plus William, no matter where they walked, were followed by the curious stares of other guests. This alone emphasised their need to escape and seek privacy.

Taking Polidori's proffered hand, Mary stepped out of the boat, to saunter up the grassy path. Shelley she ignored, trusting him to look after William. She wanted this precious moment to herself, one thought describing her feelings: I am away from crowds and impertinent stares.

She revelled in freedom, absently watching as the doctor moored the boat.

Over here in the hamlet of Montalègre, it smelled different, the harsher aromas of the hotel left on the other side, and so were the disparaging odours from stagnant parts of the lake where, Mary had noticed, a few dead fish floated.

'We should have left "Willmouse" with Elise,' Shelley said as he tried to contain the struggles of a child who gripped his lapel in an effort to pull himself up. Shelley helped him, hanging the lad over his shoulder like a soft leather valise.

'Are you trying to wriggle out of your commitments as a father, Shelley?' Mary called. Looking back she was surprised to discover she had distanced herself by at least twenty yards. 'HURRY, I WILL WAIT,' she shouted, this type of call seriously considered unladylike within earshot of the hotel.

She gestured in the direction they'd come. 'You did notice the mooring? The dock?'

'We noticed,' Polidori said, speaking for the first time – other than making occasional small talk and a few observations – since they left the hotel. After all, he wanted the Shelleys to enjoy their interlude but for a reason – he hoped it would gain him favour.

He'd bristled at the way Claire's glancing at Shelley caused Mary acute anxiety. Thankfully, minutes before their departure, Claire decided not to accompany them. The look passing between Mary and himself conveyed much. Claire, turned on her heel and went to her own room, doubtless Polidori assumed, to think about Byron.

Not the fool he sometimes led others to believe, Polidori congratulated himself on assessing the situation. Thankfully Mary had recovered from whatever had possessed her in that despicably small room, her attitude pleasantly different. A relieved Polidori decided it wouldn't do for his first meeting with her to prove unacceptable: it did not prevent him thinking about relationships. He saw them as strange, utterly absorbing and hard to fathom.

Here was Mary on one side, not yet a wife, and Claire on the other without her lover. Not content with this situation, Claire insisted upon making a nuisance of herself with Byron who would not tolerate it. Of course, he could hardly leave out poor Shelley, the sometimes disillusioned poet who unwittingly sat right in the middle.

'One, two... three, four and five.' Polidori said well out of earshot as he counted the protagonists in the game. 'Hardly a *ménage à trois.*' Had he said it louder, he doubted they would have heard, William's baby laughter skittering across grass, ochre in

104

places where hot sun had burned it, the merriment loud enough to dispense with the need for over-caution.

'Five,' he said. 'Get rid of one,' and he didn't include himself here, 'it leaves four. A quartet. Two poets, one woman, and *me.*' His smile was both beatific, and sinister.

Mary called: 'See. Over there!' She leapt up and down, her excitement contagious. 'There! The roof over the trees. The tiny house I saw from the lake... it is *real.*' She turned to Shelley, embraced him, kissed William, a more vibrant light in her eyes.

'It is destiny,' she said. 'We can ask Elise Duvillard to accompany us, she can look after William.' Before Shelley could counter such exuberance, or complain about how much the Swiss nurse would want paying, he found himself unable to curtail Mary's happiness, not that he dare. Shelley knew how outspoken she could be, yet doubted Polidori did.

The scent of vines pervaded the air, a breeze waylaying the heightening temperature on this afternoon at the tail end of May. Mentally, Mary began composing her letter to England. At this time, she had no reason to think of shadows to mar her jubilation.

Shelley halted, shifted William to a more comfortable position in his arms. Waiting for Polidori to catch up, he decided it had taken them a quarter of an hour to walk the sloping path.

'Montalègre,' said Polidori, as he walked beside Shelley. 'It forms part of the hill of Cologny. Many voyagers have stated how overcome they are by its beauty. Apparently the name means "joyous hill".' He paused to give substance to his next comment. 'It has certainly brought joy to your lady, Shelley.'

'Indeed. Look at your mother, William –' He turned, holding the baby in such a way that the child could see Mary waving. '– see how happy she is.'

'Perhaps you have never seen so many vines,' Polidori ventured. 'We can drink ourselves silly.' In saying this, he didn't feel he overstepped any barriers. Revelling in the sheer magnificence of the area, Polidori wanted to unite with what he hoped were his new found friends in their capacity for living.

II

The two men and the child followed Mary as she threaded her way from one terrace to another, using flights of rustic stairs, their varying levels obscured by vines, as they meandered to the top of the hill.

Mary turned often, as did the others, to take in the fairly steep incline sloping quite sharply towards the luminous lake, every few yards offering a different outlook, sometimes more complex, yet more tantalising and more idyllic on the eye.

Could an artist capture this magnificence on canvas? Mary argued, probably. Even the sharp scents became more vital the higher she went. Below her, given the fact that the Chapuis property, not yet reached, stood at about the centre of the hill, the path to Montalègre twisted along the lakeshore and lay parallel to it. Across the lake, the Jura mountains drew their own purple, wavering line on the horizon.

A shriek burst upon the two men through a fairly thick tangle of foliage, the flora a bounty to behold.

'She has found it. Without doubt she has.' Shelley half ran, half walked, William jiggling, gurgling with every movement of his father's body.

Both men burst through this tangle of greenery to look upon the Maison Chapuis, its rustic pantiles lent differing hues by the glare, its grey-white exterior and shuttered windows smacking of a modest gentleman's abode. The garden, like the pathway, rambled, a clutter of plants and walkways, each path obscured by undergrowth. The two men dodged the denser overhangs, Shelley careful the branches did not scratch William. By the time they reached Mary both were sweating profusely.

How humble and unpretentious, Polidori thought as he laid eyes on the dwelling, convinced it would be an appropriate place in which to hide from the curious. Definitely a bonus for Mary.

I wonder what LB will think? Polidori mused. Given the fact that we're also condemned to take our sojourn at a hotel with an insufferable manager. Then, he had heard a whisper that a move might be in the offing for them, such was Byron's dissatisfaction.

'A very pretty villa in a vineyard,' Mary said. Laughter trilled, swift little handclaps promoting her elation.

Square shaped, with two storeys, the house from the outside was indeed, 'humble and unpretentious'. The three of them argued how many rooms it might have.

'Four,' said Mary, sounding a little disappointed. She brightened when Shelley guessed five, perhaps six. At least it will segregate us from Claire, Mary told herself. *If* she accompanies us. It would be a big if.

On closer inspection they found that four of its windows faced the lake on the western side, the area of the basement and foundations as they strolled around the place practically confirming it would have at least five rooms. More than enough.

As Mary walked, she wished for Claire to meet Lord Byron and stay with him. Mary desired privacy, and pictured herself and Shelley alone with their child, and the nurse. How utterly wonderful.

Surrounded by trees, the little house became hers in those few seconds, its location provincial enough for her needs.

The afternoon slid into early evening, the trio enjoying a ramble, feeling good because they'd decided it would meet their needs admirably.

A dying sun draped colours across the mountains; it played on summer leaves, on this fairy tale house, this nest, so intimate, so... so Mary. It became her Eden – a place for which she had longed.

Whatever she felt about Claire, Mary could hardly wait to tell her, the one consolation being that Claire would have her own room, be able to please herself.

Already she had composed more of her letter to the people back home. I hope Father will read it: it may make him more amenable towards Shelley.

From higher up the hill the sweet, harmonious voices of vine dressers sang monotonous ballads, the words floating on the breeze as it sighed towards the lake.

Through a gap in the trees, Mary pointed to an impressively appointed villa further up the hill. 'I wonder –' She turned to Polidori who had joined her and followed her pointing finger. 'I wonder who owns that fine looking place?'

'It's for rent,' Polidori informed her. 'M'lord Byron seeks another property. To be honest, I'm told he's negotiated for that very one –'

Mary arched her eyebrows. 'I see.' She gave nothing away.

'Yes, a few days ago, the twenty-sixth I believe. I gather the rent was too excessive. As much as twenty-five louis a month.'

'A pretty price.' Shelley stood to Mary's left, William reaching for his mother, Mary squeezing his tiny hands, tickling him. The baby screamed his delight, the sound carrying into the trees. 'Damn robbery if you ask me. Out of our pocket, Mary.'

A cool wind drifted up the hill. Polidori scanned the darker bulk of the villa. 'Byron's banker friend Charles Hentsch has interceded.'

'Should we know him?' Mary inquired.

'Hentsch? I shouldn't think so. You may have heard of him. He's the scion of a well-to-do banking family. Charming young chap. Older than Byron. Another with literary aspirations.'

'Like you,' Mary said. 'I see then that this gentleman is doing Byron favours in the hope that his lordship will give him the benefit of his literary prowess.'

'Happen he is.' Polidori deplored the obvious reference to himself. 'Suffice to say,' he followed up, 'Charles Hentsch has certainly introduced Noel to the er, *salons* of this city over the past days. The reasons are obvious why Byron wishes to leave the hotel–'

'I can well understand,' interjected Mary. 'Lord Byron's notoriety does make him, how shall I term it? A tourist attraction?'

'I bow to that, ma'am.' Polidori offered his curt nod. 'So, given that "attraction", Hentsch has completed a deal in order to allow his lordship a similar privacy to that of your own.' He looked back at the villa. 'It's apparently owned by one M. Diodati. It seems he is a member of a distinguished, highly respected Geneva family, most of 'em civil servants. A propitious deal it is, for the villa has been rented for –' He smiled. 'For a very acceptable one hundred and twenty-five louis... for six months!'

'Then Byron is to be our neighbour,' said Shelley.

Mary continued to tickle William, the child fractious. Does he sense something, I wonder? Mary hated the way her tummy knotted.

Shelley snaked an arm around her. 'It's turning chilly.' Mary didn't argue and allowed herself to be assisted down the steep path.

Claire will be delighted at Byron's close proximity. I won't. Why she allowed such thoughts to enter the equation she couldn't be sure, a sudden premonition given credence when she turned once again to look upon the Villa Diodati's mirror-like windows.

A daydreamer, Mary couldn't know that such thoughts would soon turn to irrevocable nightmare. And in the dying of the sun she half wondered whether or not she had glimpsed a face at the window of the room sitting just behind the balcony fronting the first floor.

On the tenth of June, Lord Byron would move his retinue into this larger, more impressive house, the Villa Diodati, situated higher up on the shores of Bellarive, its dark windows collecting the magnificent scenery like so many precisely placed paintings.

Mary shivered again and pressed against Shelley. Again those other words taunted:

Darken the latter with their vast shadows.

AN INVITATION TO A DIFFERENT WORLD

They arrive at last to their own destiny.

The waiting will soon be over. Yet it needs one other.

The one who courts ghosts... the same who will give my dark soul life once more.

How they will laugh, and provoke; they will promote jealousy, their natures so involved, so tied together both ethereally and ephemerally.

Life. Death. They will all touch both, their own fears provoking, invoking...

Meanwhile, I wait...

Not only for them I pray. Listen. Hear me. There is one other who will yet be born from the mind... an alter ego of more grave demeanour –

Days, hours, it matters not. I have waited this long, so where is the need to hurry? It is common fact that each and everyone must wait for the world to turn upon its axis, for something to happen.

As it does... Eventually.

CHAPTER 11

'Alternating attraction and repulsion'

I

Claire, determined to see Byron, stated, 'He should avoid me no longer.' Neither she, nor the Shelleys had seen much of him.

A more astute Mary, less weighed down with Claire's frustration, had another idea: Lord Byron spent his time enjoying the *salons* to which Hentsch had introduced him. She also knew he enjoyed sailing.

Wishing to bring about a meeting, she engineered it that Shelley's morning stroll brought them to a small, pebble-strewn beach not far from the hotel at the precise moment Byron, in a rented boat, approached the shore.

It was difficult not to mistake Polidori for the poet, for they were, at a distance, quite alike. Thankfully no-one mentioned this, Mary convinced Lord Byron would have been vexed by such an observation.

Byron preceded Polidori off the boat and stood facing them. He looked tense, his countenance ridged by a frown, an artificial smile on his lips.

Shelley, Mary guessed, was in awe of such a distinguished man and as Byron limped towards them she detected an awkwardness between them. Shelley, acting like the boy he sometimes could be, held out a trembling hand.

'Sir,' he said, then, 'My lord.' He sounded uncertain as to how to address him.

'Are you Shelley, the author of *Queen Mab*?' Byron inquired. He remembered the poet had sent him the work some years earlier.

Following the less than hearty handshake, she also detected reluctance on Byron's part, though not in an intentionally offensive way. Yes, m'lord, she thought, you are also in awe of my Shelley. Courteously, having had insight into Byron in London, she stepped forward.

'Two famous poets at last meet.'

Byron acknowledged Mary with a short bow.

111

Impertinent towards him? Mary thought not. Why shouldn't she say it? She was proud of Shelley. Although he hadn't yet earned such a reputation, nor was he as notorious as the man from Nottinghamshire, Mary knew he would be one day. 'It is truly a great encounter.' Her laughter trilled, broke the ice. 'I do believe,' she remarked pointedly, 'that the boys are both shy.'

Claire's over-eagerness didn't help. She gushed platitudes, threw out inconsequential phrases about the journey, the atrocious weather, and said, 'My lord, being a gentleman, I thought you might have contacted me sooner.'

Like a fey fawn she attempted to drape herself all over Byron, whose acute embarrassment caused him to silently appeal to Polidori for assistance.

The doctor gently took her arm and steered her some safe distance away, his conversation light. Mary overheard: '...lay my length in the boat, letting it go its way...'

Later, Mary would admonish Shelley for his high seriousness. 'You might have been less so, in such an illustrious presence. Despite your mumbling, he did at least invite you to dine with him this evening.'

Byron had indeed extended an invitation. 'We will dine on the terrace of Dejean's Inn.' Having looked forward to meeting Percy Shelley, he considered it proper to talk more intimately over a meal and wine, and away from others who he desired not to be present. Unfortunately, he invited Polidori to join them.

The doctor would write in his diary: "Dined, PS, the author of *Queen Mab* came; bashful, shy, consumptive; twenty-six; separated from his wife; keeps the two daughters of William Godwin who practise his theories: one LB's."

The facts were wrong. Had Byron read this he would have most assuredly decried the doctor for such obvious mistakes and surely would have told him, or at least have invited Shelley to correct the obvious *faux pas*. Shelley was not yet twenty-four; nor was he consumptive, yet Shelley's appetite for attention led him to allow others to believe this; in itself a great pity for he had already gained a band of followers second to none.

Ironically, too, Polidori overlooked the fact that Claire Clairmont was not William Godwin's daughter.

Strangely, and perhaps fortuitously, Polidori's last entry had, in a way, been correct. He had known of Claire being Byron's mistress, and detected allusions to this in the conversation. Rightly, or wrongly, the doctor, brain fogged by a surfeit of wine, had missed certain elements of conversation between the two poets, but remained adamant that both Byron and Shelley did talk, though not at any great length, of their relations with Claire, problematic or not.

Much to Polidori's disenchantment, the two poets developed an immediate rapport, both having warred against the laws of society, and so outcast as rebels. It made Polidori more hostile towards Shelley.

He also heard Byron invite the Shelleys and Claire to the villa. 'Come soon, we will have lunch,' he told Shelley. 'I shall send Fletcher as a reminder. In the meantime I will establish my presence there.'

'I vouch some could well be there already, m'lord,' Polidori said.

'You listen to too many tales, friend,' said Byron. 'We desert those shores to rid ourselves of unsettling demons.'

II

The following days were spent at leisure: Byron joined them on a few lake trips. Time eased by, yet not for Polidori, whose provocation of Byron, though accidental, resulted in numerous confrontations.

Polidori, no matter how he tried, was guilty of his own volatile temper. His diary reflected this when he noted, "Went on lake with the Shelleys... Lord B quarrelled with me..."

Subject to constant sarcasm by Byron, another incident witnessed an opportunity for caustic retaliation by the doctor. Again on the lake, a clumsy action by Polidori caused him to strike Byron painfully on the knee with an oar. With no desire to apologise, Polidori followed up with, 'I am glad to see you can suffer pain.'

'But none the worse for wear, Polly. Y'see, I don't harbour it as you. Pain heals –'

You think so, my lord? Physical, perhaps, but inside, in your mind? I doubt it.

'Dear God,' Polidori retaliated, 'I have never met with a person so unfeeling!'

A mood followed, Mary and Shelley made uncomfortable, anything they said – suggestions, jokes – made little or no impact, resulting in the trip being brought to a premature close.

III

Towards noon on a day in early June, they felt they had waited upon Lord Byron for too long already, Claire's mounting excitement verging on hysteria hardly blunted by a look from Mary.

Earlier, and following a further summons for the extended invitation of Lord Byron's to be fulfilled, a second message delivered by Rushton obviously underlined his master's intent. They set off on the relatively short, eight minute walk from Chapuis to Diodati.

Mary, Claire and Shelley walked in single file up the narrow pathway, certain frivolities occurring when they attempted to walk side by side up a steep flight of stone steps, Mary's shawl becoming entangled in a clutching branch. It startled her for a second or so, the branch taking on a semblance of clutching fingers.

'Mary, it's all right,' Shelley assured. 'There, see, all untangled.' To prove a point he broke the branch from the main trunk and threw it into the undergrowth.

'I'm being silly aren't I?' Mary laughed and hoping to avoid further looks, especially from Claire, walked on.

She was the first to duck under more overhangs and enter the villa's gardens. Awestruck by a less formal array of haphazardly planted shrubs and flowers, Mary enthused in the multitude of variegating colour. She enjoyed the scents, Claire and Shelley bowing to her ebullience.

Shelley approved, pleased she'd countered her mood on the steps. He did, however, wonder if Byron had anything to do with it, his charm so utterly testing. Such thoughts were buried when Mary grasped and squeezed his arm, her smile adding to his new-found well-being.

They dawdled in the villa's grounds.

Of course that had been a good half hour ago. Late or not, they neither knew nor cared, for they had not bandied their time idly.

Claire – still smarting from being ignored for days – allowed her inquisitive nature to best her irritation, saying, 'I am sure his lordship will not take offence that we inspect his gardens.'

Shelley was his usual self, the shyness experienced at meeting Byron obliterated without trace. Mary decided that his drunken return to their room in the early hours had been more than adequate to loosen his tongue and so make him more acceptable to Lord Byron's acidic wit and banter.

Her questioning him from waking until they had risen an hour or so later, though not too frequently to provoke an outburst, had brought little by way of information. This left Mary to wonder what may have been said. 'Boys will be boys', she quipped to herself, thinking that, in a sense, given one's reputation, she hoped anything more physical between them would not follow, infuriated by her own jealousy.

As for Polidori as *chaperon,* that could hardly be merited. Not him; for that man, if one overlooked the arguments between them, clung to Byron's coat tails like a limpet. Much as Claire did to Shelley's.

'Here we converge,' she mused out of earshot of the others, 'in wonderful seclusion, and about to visit our mentor, yet all for totally different reasons.'

More sights, sounds and fragrant aromas met them, causing them to linger and ponder, revel in this new location. Prior to entering the two-storey, grey stone villa with its substantial porticoed basement, they admired everything, comments bandied hither and thither.

Claire, unusual for her, took time to praise the gardens. 'Always a pleasure to see mature trees. And do look, such a variety of plants in the soil beds.' She confessed to not knowing their names.

A pace or so in front of the others, she ducked down entering pathways to discover stone seats partially hidden by overhanging hedges and shrubbery, making some risible comment at Mary over the latter's shawl getting tangled earlier.

Shelley, after commenting on the garden, and the narrow, rectangular pond that collected the house's reflection, marvelled at the elegant columns supporting the wrought-iron balcony running around three sides of this *rez-de-chaussée.* 'See how they lend a kind of equanimity to the dwelling. And look, I believe that must be the coat of arms centred on the railings.'

Indeed so, its twin beasts resembled lions, each head turned respectively left and right and overlooked by crowned griffons.

'I'm impressed, and of the opinion that nothing less would be entertained for such an eminent figure as Byron.'

He'd strained to read the Latin inscription on the coat of arms. '"Deus Dedit" it reads, as far as I can ascertain. "God and –"' He waived it and tendered a limp smile. 'My Latin isn't very good. Sorry. You have to admire the traditional architecture of the Swiss.'

Not that Mary, or Claire seemed bothered about any translation, Mary, at least, believing that if God had something to do with it, it couldn't be so bad. As to the architecture, both ladies agreed that the simple lines added to its miniature grandeur.

She smothered a giggle as Shelley, pacing backwards in order to study the upper storeys, nearly fell over his own feet. 'Look where you're going next time.' She followed his gaze, and positioned the fine lace shawl about her head to protect against growing heat. With her pale complexion she burned easily so was wary against taking chances.

As Shelley had done, she examined the villa's wide windows some of which were shuttered, the roof dormers closed against the day. At least, she argued, it dispels my unease when I beheld it from a distance.

From this angle there seemed to be three to the front, their curved tops almost like arched lids on a wide, tiled face. A tall chimney stood to the left, sited between two of the dormers.

Craning her neck in this way, Mary felt dizzy, the glare of the high, wide, sapphire sky overpowering, light and shade dancing, creating weird forms. She instantly looked down at the grass, the comparison more subtle, less distressing to the eye. Dwarfed by the house, she considered her own Chapuis much cosier by comparison. However, she wouldn't pre-judge, not before she'd had an opportunity to view the interior.

'Mary,' cried Shelley, 'just think what a marvellous garden from which to fly my balloons! And my kite!'

'So it is, Shelley. But won't the trees get in the way?' Mary didn't mind his childish preoccupation, in fact she accepted it willingly, telling herself that Shelley, *my* Shelley, is the man I fell for. It's wrong to want to change him, or anyone.

At this stage, Mary could not envisage that another creation would change the literary world, the populace who would read it, and herself.

Claire hurried to them. 'I congratulate Byron on his choice of abode.' Unable to curb her exuberance, she thought how easy life would be if she were to settle here with her lover, and in future, Byron, *my* husband. She smiled secretively, the others ignoring her slight eccentricities. They were, after all, used to them.

Loitering beneath the portico, they anticipated crossing the threshold, except that beneath it, out of the sun, the temperature had dropped a degree or so.

Slightly nervous, Mary was perhaps more attuned to the place than either Shelley or Claire. She sensed rather than felt the chill. Call it foolish whim, or fertile imagination playing tricks –

A doorway... a passage into the unknown.

'Good morning, Mr Shelley, ladies.' The stocky, ubiquitous Fletcher opened the Villa Diodati's heavy, ornate oak door and stepped back. 'Lord Byron is expecting you. He won't keep you long.'

The villa held a peculiar chill and their shivers persisted. Unlike days when you long to go inside, to escape the heat, welcome a cooler atmosphere, this had about it a more underlying cold, intemperate and a little alarming. Mary bore it for the sake of the others because they regarded it as a joke. Even Percy said, 'No fire, Fletcher?'

Claire didn't notice. Ignoring Fletcher, she crossed the marble-floored hallway, Mary and Shelley obliged to trail after her, as she marched through open double doors into the lounge, the swish of her white silk skirt a whisper in the silence of the room.

Unlike the entrance hall, the room radiated welcome, its comforting silence impregnated with the smell of wood smoke curling up the fairly narrow chimney, a warming glow welcoming rather than detracting.

'Here is your fire, Shelley,' Claire called over her shoulder.

'Look at that magnificent mirror.' Shelley, intoxicated with the opulence compared to the more humble situation of their own house, crossed to the fireplace to gaze into the highly polished glass of an ornate mirror above it. Twin, silver candlesticks positioned either side on the marble mantle complemented the wide, gilt frame surrounding the glass.

Mary shared Shelley's love of beautiful things and joined him. She gazed into the glass, her smile waning. She saw herself only briefly before a sudden shadow-shape presented itself behind and to her left. At first she thought it to be Lord Byron. But no, the visage presented appeared scarred, as though the person had undergone an operation of some magnitude, its eyes yellow, watery, speculative, yet hardly focussed, more of someone recovering from the after-effects of ether.

Her breath came in short gasps, Shelley assisting her to an armchair.

'I will be all right, Shelley. Don't fuss. I blame the heat.' It had been warm on the walk, and following the incident with the branch, and her brief dizzy spell, Mary had found herself perspiring, her body heat reduced by the chill of the villa.

Contradictions swirled in her mind, but she overcame them and managed to regain a reasonable sense of normalcy if only to avoid Claire's fussing. Shelley she didn't mind, but Claire's sense of nursing went beyond the pale. Her intentions were good, but a body could only tolerate so much.

'What ails you, Mary?' Shelley pressed. 'Do you need a physician? We could get Doctor Polid –'

'No!' A little sharp, but Mary insisted no doctor. 'Don't trouble yourself, I am quite well.' She wouldn't tell him how eerie it had felt gazing into the mirror and seeing... She couldn't be sure. A notion, an idea?

Claire paced, irascibility marked. She ran a hand over the fine marquetry on a chair, checked the velvet drapes at the windows, and marvelled at the polished wood floor running the perimeter of the room beneath what she decided had to be a very expensive carpet.

Excusing herself, and intent on escaping the mirror, Mary wandered into the main hallway. She stopped abruptly, a little 'Oh' of surprise, almost a startled breath, when she beheld the man dressed in dark apparel standing in the doorway of a room off to her left.

'Mary, I'm happy to greet you once more.' Lord Byron smiled. Hands held out, he came towards her, his shambling gait more pronounced as his booted lame foot clicked heavily on the marble floor.

Mary, feeling flustered, gave a slight curtsey and took Byron's offered hand.

'Madam, welcome to my summer home.' Byron smiled, a wide, welcoming gesture, his eyes, darker in the subdued light of the hall, reminded Mary of the shadows beneath the lake.

I wonder, she thought, what truly lies behind that gaze, Lord Byron?

Claire and Shelley must have heard him, proved by Claire hurrying to the door to stand for seconds in awe of the man she had bedded, and longed to do so again. And again.

She shuddered with anticipation, annoyed when she saw Mary in too close a proximity to Byron.

He spends too much time with her, so why not me? I am better dressed now, older, not the plump girl I was with my pale complexion and lank hair. She called, 'Albé,' and rushed forward. Had not Byron side-stepped she would have embraced him.

Not wishing to be embarrassed a second time, he gripped her hands, spoke her name and planted the briefest kiss on her cheek. He then looked beyond her at Shelley hovering behind.

'Come, Shelley, no need for shyness. Y'must agree we've overcome such pettiness. Remember that meal. The wine certainly loosened tongues and inhibitions. Grand, it was, sir. Famous!'

Byron turned and located Fletcher as the latter closed the front door. 'Fletcher, be s'kind as to fetch refreshments.' He turned to the others. 'What's it t'be, tea, or lemonade on such a glorious day? Or –' He leaned around Claire, so close they could have been Siamese twins, and said to Shelley, 'Or wine?' His smile held that quality of jokiness for which he was renowned.

Shelley reacted instantly. 'No, thank you. Lemonade sounds more er, refreshing.'

'Thought you'd say that.'

'Doctor Polidori not joining us, m'lord?' Mary couldn't resist asking.

'Polly-Dolly. No, 'fraid not. I say, were you expecting him? Had I thought on, I wouldn't't've sent him into town for the post. Expecting some funds. Can't entertain without 'em.'

'Polly-Dolly.' Claire tittered, muffling it behind a well-manicured hand. 'That's funny, Albé. Don't you think it is, Mary? Shelley?'

'I suppose he does resemble a doll,' Shelley said. 'He was very drunk when we dined, kept slurring his words.'

'Didn't we all?' Byron still retained his air of wry amusement.

A few days before, Polidori drugged and drunk, had provoked Byron by making a silly, effeminate pass at him. Byron had grown enraged, wishing he had heeded Hobhouse's warnings and kept the doctor away.

Should've eaten an apple or two, he thought.

He looked at Claire. Pity I agreed to meet her here, too.

The woman looked coy on purpose, totally unaware he was thinking of his embittered confrontation – of sorts – with the doctor.

IV

The night of their carousing, Byron tells Polidori, 'You're a damned leech.'

After eating, Byron watched the doctor slowly grow more drunk – not that he hadn't had his share. Now he staggers unannounced into the doctor's room, both inebriated to the point of falling down. It's said that when in such a state, the mind doles out truths no matter how unsettling they might be.

Polidori, attempts to disrobe: he staggers, hops, catches hold of items of furniture to prevent himself falling, and eventually slumps on the bed clutching his left boot.

'L...leech? W...what d'you mean? Is it vampires again?' A loud hiccup follows.

Byron lolls against the door, questions his own ability to stand without support, yet is equally determined to have his say.

'You always misinterpret things, Polly. Poor Shelley wondered what the deuce you were talking about half the time over our dinner with him.'

Another boot follows the first, both clatter on the floor. 'Talk tomorrow, need t'sleep. Too much of ev...every...thing I fear.'

'Not enough words to curtail your exuberance.' Byron tries to stand unaided and manages to reach a chair. 'Over-indulgence jades the senses, but airs the bloody truth.' He slumps onto the chair, locks his arms about it.

'A leech, my friend. Know what that is? Y'should being a qualified doctor an' all. They use 'em in medicine for bleeding. Hey, you can't sleep, I'm about t'tell you what *you* really are in terms of such a vile creature. I will re...redefine *leech.*'

He stands, the chair reliable support, his shadow looms over Polidori, the moonlit shades of the room creating their own uneasy aura.

Byron contemplates the drunken, splayed figure. This doctor is incapable of diagnosing his own problems let alone those of a patient. Too far gone to remove his trousers, Byron is surprised the man has accomplished the relatively easy task of taking off his shoes and one sock.

'*Hirudinea,*' says Byron, 'or the common leech. Better known as *Hirudo medi... medicinalis* – Didn't know I knew that, did you? Or that I could... could pronounce it. So-called because of its use in blood-letting. My 'pologies, I repeat myself.' On cue, he belched. 'Y'see, made to order. I repeated my – Oh for pity's sake laugh, Polly, lord knows y'did enough earlier 'til the malaise set in. What's wrong, jealous of Shelley is it? Me an'... and Shelley chat like old friends and you're left out. I don't doubt you're upset.

'And rightly, m'dear, one could easily term the leech a vampire. See, it first attaches itself before gorging on blood; the more it imbibes the more it swells, grows terribly obscene.'

Byron is loving this. He doesn't give a fig whether he's drunk or not. Or that Polidori can hear him; damn fellow's unresponsive anyway.

He thinks about all those weeks spent with this, this semi-comatose imbecilic doctor; how they have undermined his authority.

Byron lets go of the chair and lurches towards the bed. He sits, almost slides off it. 'I am pissed.' Laughing, he grabs Polidori's jacket sleeve to stabilise himself. Leaning over, face within inches of the doctor's, he studies its contours – the slack, open mouth, the half-closed eyes. 'I shall now proceed to enlighten you as to what I think.' He taps Polidori's cheek. 'Hey, come on, you like to talk, so listen.

'Party wasn't it? We met at that party. Whoever organised it and invited you should never be allowed to hold such a *soirée* again –' Slowly enunciating each word, Byron eventually regains command of speech patterns, and gradually senses himself growing more sober, his oratory far outweighing his own need to rest. A stickler for doing what he sets out to accomplish, his determination sometimes pushes him beyond what many would term "human limitations".

'Party for the elite it was. And you know what, Polly, ye took a fancy t'me. Don't try and argue.'

Polidori grips Byron's thigh. Byron slaps his hand away. 'Not me, Polly. Not me. All that fawning, the attention you paid me. We dabbled, had a bit of fun in the carriage, but no more. I grant I was impressed by y'knowledge, didn't know you were evil then, not then. I tell you true, I was flattered by your attentions, I mean all those compliments *you* paid me when I was largely only used t'women doing it. You certainly impressed me, Polly-Dolly, that y'did. Might say I fell for y'magnetic charm, eh? EH?'

'You... you impress *me*, Albé. I want –' Polidori sits up, supported on one elbow.

'Nothing from me.' Byron rises, mind less fogged, the threat from Polidori meaning more than just idle chatter, innuendo. 'Nothing, y'hear. Spending time with you in all those inns and taverns, aye even locked inside that carriage traversing some of the worst routes God ever carved on the land, enabled me to see into the dark side o' your evil nature. Talk of vampires... Very clever, John. Perhaps you were talking of y'self.

'I'm the fool here, for not listening to m'friends, not heeding them as I should. They warned me about taking you on, allowing you to catch m'coat tails and be towed along.

'Can't let go, can you? You're besotted with me... ME, one of the greatest poets who ever lived, a legend in me own time.' He leans over Polidori who, surprised at the sudden movement, falls back across the bed.

In this state, Polidori believes he is truly falling and grips Byron's frilled shirt front to prevent it. The material tears yet not hardly sufficient to part company. Byron, struggling against the grip, attempts to stop himself being pulled on top of the doctor.

'Please, I beg,' Polidori is tearful, 'stay with me, Albé. STAY.'

The air resounds with a crack, Byron's backhander causing Polidori to release his grip.

'You clinging parasite!' Byron wipes his lips as if to rid himself of the imagined taste of Polidori's lips, his obnoxious, wine-fumed breath. 'Think you to control me, Lord Byron? Think again, *sir*, and also know that I detest you, your company, the air you breathe.'

Backing to the door, afraid to take his eyes from the sobbing shape on the bed, Byron senses something more. The room feels charged with a different sort of atmosphere, moonlight touches the curtains which ripple in the breeze tumbling through the casement. Polidori's sobbing fades.

A corridor, a *salon*, tumbled *facia*, crumbled coving, tumbled, broken furniture. A legacy.

He is running, a chittering in his ears, all about him. He recognises the sound... a thousand... a million *crickets*! The familiars – for this is what they are to this lord – familiars of *Devil* Byron, his very late, unlamented ancestor.

A dark shade detaches itself from corners, from the wainscoting, the ceiling, each formless, mis-shaped slice merging into a whole. It follows yet it lacks eyes to see, or any that he, Byron, can make out. Raw, pungent evil exudes from it. He screams... loud... and long...

...and wakes up on the floor by Polidori's bed, the doctor's loud, snores enough to awaken... 'The dead.' Byron whispers.

His mouth and tongue are furred from a surfeit of wine, yet he has accomplished one thing this night – home truths have been aired, yet only by him, not Polidori, the man far drunker than Byron. Poor Polly-Dolly is unable to string more than a few words together.

Byron fears it isn't over, that his companion will forever fasten his metaphorical teeth into every ounce of flesh and thought that he, Byron, possesses.

'Dear God, I tell him how much I dislike him, try to destroy his affection, but it seems I increase it! Will I ever be free of him this side of death?'

CHAPTER 12

'Some living things to love'

I

'What ails you. Lord Byron?'

Claire, attentive as usual, leaned across the picnic rug to stroke Byron's leg. 'You seem preoccupied.'

It won a brief smile. At least they were alone, momentarily, Mary and Shelley, having eaten their fill of the picnic lunch, had taken it upon themselves to explore. As ever, the faithful Fletcher sat in attendance some one hundred feet away, and in conversation with Rushton who felt obliged to keep glancing over Fletcher's head towards Byron.

'Preoccupied? Perhaps I am. You read me well, Claire.'

'Do you want to tell me?'

Feeling less anxious over his thoughts about Polidori in those early hours, Byron leaned down from the bower upon whose seat he reposed, and stroked her cheek. 'Such tender, soft skin.'

'Almost as soft as a baby's?'

Byron offered a quizzical smile. 'A baby's? You couch it as a question for which you expect an answer?'

'Must you always counter a question with a question, Albé, without first answering the initial question?'

'Answering questions with too bold an answer can often get a man in trouble, especially so where a lady is concerned.'

Claire plucked a daisy, twirled it between her fingers. 'D'you see this tiny flower, my lord? See how rare and colourful it is?'

'More questions.' Byron poured himself tea and sipped it slowly. 'This drink is easier for my digestion, and doesn't allow frightful things to enter my mind. I should refrain from taking alcohol; it dulls the mind, reduces its capacity for logic.'

'Your mind was far from dull that night at the inn, good sir.'

'Ah, another hint of your promiscuous nature.'

'Ooh, I dare broach that when one such as yourself, and another like myself has a need, then 'tis up to both to fulfil it.' She

125

watched him beneath her dark lashes. 'I would tell you that one certain need has been fulfilled.'

'How? What can you mean?' Byron caught Rushton's look and lifted his hand in acknowledgement. Ah, Robbie, we've shared much, you and I, even women. And each other.

'You're less attentive again, m'lord.'

He sipped more tea. 'To what you have to tell me? Then say away, lady, tell me before you burst, for you have a look about you that seems not s'preoccupied, more... ah, fulfilled.'

'How clever you are. I am with child.' Claire sat up on her haunches, the gold of her dress almost the colour of the daisy's centre. '*Your* child, Lord Byron.'

He opened his mouth to say something and promptly closed it again. His colour drained; he looked beyond her towards the villa, its many eyes appearing to mock the situation. He could almost hear the stones saying: "She has you now. There is no Annabella in your way, and you know well Claire's intention to claim you. Have you no sense?"

'My lord,' Claire reached, took his hand, almost upsetting the cup. 'My lord, have you nothing to say? Surely you are pleased at such news?'

He found voice, initiated by a mounting rage; the day, his well-being, ruined by this one comment from this stupid, doting, insipid woman.

'Is the brat mine?'

He might well have physically slapped her, Claire's smile gone as swiftly as a wave breaks on shore. He followed this up with, 'There is no child of mine, save one, who can be ought but a bastard.' He glared at her. 'The Hell with you, woman, that you must entrap me.' He stood abruptly, the cup tumbling to land on the picnic rug, its contents staining the pattern. 'All the same! ALL the same! Everyone wants a piece of me, their own favoured bit to covet and cherish, tell the world that this is Lord Byron's heart, his soul –' He glowered at Claire, who shrank before it.

'Do you realise that even my own mother, Catherine, tried to belittle me, aye before others, too. And strap me, I loved her, as I know she loved me.' He paused briefly, picturing his wild, inveterate mother in her cups, her own selfish ways he now realised, passed on to him. 'Catherine had a dashed peculiar way of showing her affection, that she did. I have the scars to prove she hurled fire tongs at me, her own tongue as fire whenever she sought to make an example of her dear little boy with the lame foot!'

Claire tried to stand, her skirts preventing it. She thrust out a hand. 'Please, help me.'

Byron towered above Claire, as he had towered over Polidori that day when they had compared writings. He sought to make his presence known, and ensure all knew where he had passed, benefited from his touch.

Like some predatory panther, he stalked the lawn, came back, continuing to ignore Claire's reaching hand.

Fletcher and Rushton moved closer, Byron staying them with a hand. 'Leave it, it is not your concern. Go about your business. Where's Shelley?'

Fletcher seemed at a loss. Rushton answered: 'Walking, m'lord. I understand he and the lady are flying a few balloons.'

'Or he's peering at all and sundry through his spy-glass,' put in Fletcher.

'Ah yes, he's watching where they float no doubt. I remember seeing a couple fly over the villa.' He waved the two servants away, his preoccupation as nefarious as the woman who would not take her eyes from him.

Is there no-one here who wants me as I am? Does not one body wish to understand what damning family indictments I must carry?

Questions, m'lord? Aye, questions, for is there no more savage irony than my conversation with Claire, her revelation? A child! She is pregnant with *my* child? Aye, and if so, then Edleston, Matthews and the rest are still alive. *If so*, we will all continue to make sport at Newstead and Augusta will remain my unsullied half-sister!

Yes, I am preoccupied. Preoccupied with a welter of mincing idiots. I'm at their beck and call all hours.

Claire's simpering tone appealed: 'Lord Byron, I speak the truth, it is your child. We made love at the inn... At Piccadilly Terrace –'

'So right, dear Claire. But please spare me any notion that should I not be the father, it might perhaps turn out as another miracle. Madam, you wouldn't know the truth if it reared up and bit you on your rather prominent arse!'

He ignored her hurt. 'And do not, for one minute, believe I don't have any experience of that for one o' my dogs did the very same thing. I still sport the scar!'

Sobbing prevented further admonishment from Byron. Claire grabbed a table napkin, used it to blow her nose. Too late now, hindsight reminded that had she heeded his rather reluctant, indeed cold reception at their first meeting, and had not been forced to write: "One thing I am afraid of – you rather dislike me and may therefore be prejudiced on the wrong side," her future may have turned out markedly different.

To fall into any kind of liaison with Lord Byron would mark anyone's card in a way that defied optimism.

The idyll had been breeched, destroyed, whatever remained of today thrown out on the tides of indifference – that is to say Lord Byron's indifference. He had promised himself no ties, to seek solitude, a place to recuperate, to write. Here it seemed he had none of that, only some pale harpy accusing him of fathering another 'child of the famous'. Didn't they all try it on? How many will lay claim to my fame and titles in future all because the first cousin thrice removed might be able to prove they initially came from my loins?

'Stop it, madam. Cease snivelling and we may yet salvage something from this mess. And use a handkerchief.'

'I don't have one.'

'Oh, the lady hasn't got one. Well, m'dear, you certainly had the relative accoutrements to beget a child through trickery.'

'Trickery?' Claire snivelled.

Byron tossed her a handkerchief. 'For pity's sake use this. And yes, I do mean trickery. Meet one tart, you meet 'em all.' He knelt beside her. 'A man has needs, Miss Clairmont, but those needs do not mean that any woman he courts, or beds should produce a whelp every nine months. Tell me, what of the other brat you said was mine?'

'Other brat?'

'Damn it, woman, you know who I mean.'

She started crying again, Byron stalked off. 'No, don't leave me. Albé, please... He... he died. He only lived a few days.

You must know I never said anything. No-one ever knew he was yours because I... I wanted to protect you, your reputation. If any other knew of another child they would maybe not take to your writings, your poetry, for you write mostly about what is good, wholesome.'

'Good? Wholesome? My dear, if you did but realise what haunts my mind.' He knelt again, gripped her wrist, pulled her towards him. 'No. Madam, I do not wish to kiss you, merely tell you that were you to read my lines properly, and use your own intellect – if you have any – to read *between* those lines, then, and only then, would you comprehend the truer meaning of life, *my* life, as *I* see it, and as I would wish it!'

He let her go. On his feet once more, he placed his back to her, the look on his countenance a match for the severest storm. He searched the trees, the sky, the distant reaches of the lake far below. I'm cursed, he told himself. It's true, my whole wretched family, each generation, is doomed to fight for its life and soul. Can any form of love exist? Really exist? I am loath to even define the word. Yes, yes, it must. Gussie. Lucinda. And Patrick – a child of love and not some pre-ordained plan by a calculating bitch such as Claire. And there was Hugo. And Jacqueline. Both more tangible, and more caring in their own way.

'Go home, Claire,' he uttered through gritted teeth, the words dreadful in their tone and implication. He still did not turn, nor wish to look upon her despite her pleas. 'Return to England, find some... some sailor, some other wanderer –

Father, where are you now? Dead like all the rest.

'Yes, sweet Claire, find someone like that and live with him. As for that which you insist you carry inside you, then I am bound to accept *your* truth of it.'

Byron did turn, almost overbalancing when his ankle gave way. 'Damn my insufferable affliction! Claire, I shall at least pay for the child's upkeep, but *I will never marry you!*'

'MARRY YOU.' The phrase carried, caught by Mary and Shelley as they rounded the corner and ducked beneath a grove of trees.

They questioned each other, wondering if they hadn't misheard what sounded like a promise. Mary beamed; if it were true then she would be satisfied. Claire would have found her station in life, and she, Mary, would be free of an encumbrance.

Percy managed a brief smile, and allowed Mary to run ahead, obviously bursting to congratulate Claire and Lord Byron.

Some little distance away, Mary faltered, her exuberance lessened, her smile fading into a doubting frown.

Byron turned towards her, his features resembling the Devil himself. Without another word to either of the ladies, he limped off, bellowing for Rushton. 'More tea, Robbie! I'll be buggered if I let a woman best me.'

Claire gawped at the picnic rug, at the tea stains on it and wondered if that is what she had become, a stain on Byron's life, an intrusion into his privacy. Clumsily, and after a struggle coping with her skirts, she managed to climb to her feet. Grabbing a corner of the rug, she whipped back her arm and sent the whole picnic hamper, plates and other crockery smashing into the stone built arbour.

She said one word: 'MEN!' And refused to be comforted by Mary.

Shelley stood off to one side: he stared at Byron's retreating back, remembering their conversation about Claire, what she meant to them. His stomach felt jittery, especially when he looked at Mary.

II

He contemplates the grounds, the sloping contours of the land and wishes, how he wishes, that he could have inherited something as beautiful as this Villa Diodati instead of a derelict abbey in England.

'Aye, and even that's lost to me now; my good friend Wildman has it. May he make it live again for neither I, or my accursed forbears ever did.'

He looks down from the balcony, musing how everything could be so perfect, just friends enjoying a holiday in this sylvan setting. He'd wished he could stay forever, yet seeing the trio below – one man, two women, he regrets the decision. Is it the sum total of my life – men and women in one long, rousting, rutting search for that which eludes me?

Claire offers a finger wave which he ignores, continuing to look towards the distant mountains, and the dark clouds gathering over their majestic peaks.

The storm, when it breaks, is spectacular, the whole of the lake basin reflecting dancing light; it tangos from peak to peak, the rain and heavy, screening mist eventually blocking the view; thunder rolls like some giant's drumbeat, a forerunner to a battle in the clouds. 'And here on earth,' he says, the words absorbed by the storm.

He snatches up his pen. The Third Canto of Childe Harold's Pilgrimage lies before him. He scans that already written:

> *'The sky is changed! – and such a change! Oh night,*
> *And storm, and darkness, ye are wondrous strong,*
> *Yet lovely in your strength, as is the light*
> *Of a dark eye in woman!'*

'Always that,' he whispers again, and replaces the pen on its stand. 'That look, that condescending agreement in order to net me, to... *own* me. No my pretties, for this Byron will never be a chattel.'

Wherever he looks, whatever aromas drift on the breeze, he is reminded of two men, and other pretty boys who sought to own him. No, unfair, for it is not always so.

But this woman who still looks towards him, standing lost and alone in the rain, is something very different. The word *predator* perches like a vulture in his thoughts, and as such is a threat to his well-being, his need for privacy.

'How private can I be? I have placed myself in the public eye.'

For what? Fleeting fame? A name in poetry, verses of life, of love, of unfelt yearnings conjured because I haven't the time to fulfil all of them. 'Look upon this vain, selfish individual, world; tell him truthfully what you see.'

Byron rises, turns his back on the mountains, and the solitary figure in the garden. He briefly sees Fletcher hurry towards her with an umbrella, hears him urging her to come in. At last the landscape is empty of people, only the great might of the storm present – a warrior who vanquishes all ills, who will make the air fresh again, and he can breathe new life. He paces, unable to rid his mind of Claire's threat.

Conniving, and about as subtle as Polidori, both of them have used stealth to inveigle themselves into his life. 'And I have been too blind to see it. God, is it too late?'

He picks up the pen a second time from the writing desk by the window, taps his lips with it, before throwing it down. Manuscript pages waft in the warm breeze, yet it is hardly warm enough to ease the chill infusing both mind and body.

'I cannot function. One part of me urges I write, yet the other will not allow the words to flow.' He re-assesses the four lines,: the phrase *dark eye* suddenly a torture.

There, in the mirror on the chest by the door, a more profound image of a man, whose twenty-eight years of life are depicted in the frame, apparent behind those eyes, and in thinning hair, combed forward, its curls still wayward, its loss giving an impression of someone far older.

The maudlin mood grips. He runs fingers through his hair, too much forehead revealed as he combs it back. He blames a poor diet, and smiles coldly at the grim irony. For to gain a better figure and retain it, he must suffer other losses. What life offers with one hand, it takes away with the other. He hopes others are too considerate to comment, for embarrassment would be overwhelming.

'I am Lord Byron, Sixth Lord, therefore I must present a face to the world that is forever alluring.'

An imp of self-doubt surfaces, it contradicts other thoughts and is persuasive enough to make him accept truth and live with the same truth, let others see him how he really is. For is it not true, that when people like people, they like them for what they are and Devil take the consequences? Better to be what you are than live a life of pretence.

'If only I could do that.' The imp of the perverse, the brother of the pure, reverses the improbable decision. Byron believes that to behave in ways opposite to what is expected would be tantamount to a sacrifice on the altar of less positive ideals, certainly in this world.

The phrase erodes his resolve, Byron contemplates its worth and compares it to the truth of what he really seeks. Does it matter when you're dead? Better to leave a more lasting legacy in which I promote the opposite of what I really am. To a degree, at least.

He thinks of Hugo with fondness, wishing he were here to placate him, to... love him, offer respite from the spider's web of deceit and lies spun by Claire Clairmont.

Hugo. They met wherever, probably at some society ball, or some poetry reading when this one man stood out against all the swooning women.

Hugo. An aristocrat and a hairdresser, who allayed Byron's fear of baldness, who persuaded him to overcome it by giving him head massages, his dexterity covering the thinning. Hugo – very well known in the circles in which he moved, and one who only ever wanted male friends.

'Ah Hugo, you revered and gentle man. Do you recall our many happy nights together, how you would caress me, care for me, indulge me? A good friend, a best friend and always the faithful, excellent lover.'

He sits before the glass, the light and shade promoting a face that mirrors his soul, a need to break out and be himself rather than what others think he should be, the ones who engorge his heart and mind.

'Must I always walk in shadow, afraid to be myself?'

He is startled by a discreet knock.

'Who is it?'

'Rushton, m'lord. You ordered tea.' The voice is muffled by the door, the tone distant like other voices on the rim of memory. 'I 'ave some water biscuits. George noticed you 'ardly touched a thing at the picnic.'

Byron opens the door. 'Robbie, come, put it on the table.'

Rushton does as bidden and about to leave, pauses by the door. 'Anythin' further, m'lord?'

An age of recollected incidents, of chats in the privacy of Byron's dressing room at Newstead pass between them. Byron wants to say yes, but his state of mind prevents it and he simply dismisses Rushton. 'Leave me to my thoughts, good Robert, for I feel a need to compose.'

The door closes quietly.

Byron, wearied by thoughts of the past, pours himself some tea. He sits at the desk and again picks up the pen. Uncovering a fresh sheet of paper from beneath the jottings, scribbles and doodles, he lounges in the chair and muses for a minute or so before he starts to write.

The words penned are indiscriminate, an outpouring of hardly lucid thought. They speak of unease, of life, of wanting to find freedom from the imposition made on him by others.

"It is important," he writes, the pen scratching across paper like a whore's nails across his heart. *"It is important that all know I am not a bad person, merely confused because I am unable to be as I wish to be. I want to be a good person and to write good poetry, but my other problems have been, and still are insurmountable. In attempting to contend with them I can never be as I would wish myself to be..."*

He is aware of how he repeats phrases, but the outpouring is determined to have its say. *"I have been lover to many,"* he scrawls, *"yet wish I could be steadfast to one. Lucinda. Augusta. Jacqueline."*

He stops writing, the pen poised over the inkwell. 'Jacqueline de Prement.' The name is again, like Hugo's, spoken with fondness. 'You proved a good friend, and a good support in my writing.' He smiles in reflection. 'You were very patient, Jacqui, never wanted me as a lover.' The smile, now a trifle woebegone, lingers. 'It only happened because you were so supportive when I craved encouragement. In truth, I suppose I felt indebted to you.'

Ah me, and poor you, he thinks. 'You were not pretty, not even sexually attractive, but I owed you something.' His laugh undercuts the memory, Byron aware he had little else to offer Jacqueline other than himself, the penniless poet housed in a draughty abbey, or in some less than salubrious lodging in London.

'And you accepted that. I bless you for it, and am more aware now that you realised I had no feelings for you other than gratitude. My dear Jacqui, we enjoyed each other's bodies and revelled in our lust for those guarded, private moments.'

He stares at the paper, realising he has written it all down, the man becoming the writer once more, private thoughts there, on paper... and scored out! His pen scratches runnels in the paper until every word is obliterated. Sometimes it is better not to reveal too much, and the old saying: *Never put in writing that which you regard as secret.* A good yardstick, for there are always others who, once having sight of it, would use it to their own advantage.

Another sheet: more thoughts. *"Steadfast?"* A question. Answer: *"How could I be, it was impossible for I had not completed my search. Will I ever? Searching, always searching for what I could not have. Always I want more of everything... Nothing is ever enough.*

"I need to be more than I am but will I ever be given the chance?"

His next lines are prophetic, and his brow is as scored as the paper beneath the flying pen, deep lined with life, and thoughts of a life left to live.

"I demand so much more, and I am too frightened to think that I might have to leave this Earth behind without fulfilling all my plans. I have to do my best to achieve what I can, for I am not to know what time is left. My fame flies like chaff in the wind, there for a while, and will be gone... Sometimes I wonder, will my work remain when I am dust? Or will it, too, become as dust? Destroyed. And no-one will ever know of this Byron, the Lord Poet.

"To tell of my wildest dreams, my innermost secrets, my unfulfilled hopes, is my wish. The world should know the truth, and it is hoped that if I cannot achieve this, for whatever reason, then another with the power of the pen, shall do this for me."

'Mother. Dearest Catherine, what have you made me that I know not my own destiny, that I cannot ever find what I seek? Would that I could be that wonderful person, a someone who helps others, not belittles them in my quest to be a name.'

He thinks of Claire, her words. The child she carries. 'How can I be sure it is mine?'

I cannot, dare not take her word, for too often in the past I have listened to others and found trouble. Conversely, I do ignore them, and still invite trouble.

Polidori for one. 'Yes. I should have heeded Hobby.'

He scrawled on the bottom of the nearly full sheet of paper the words:

"I AM NEITHER VAIN NOR SELFISH. I AM ONLY WHAT LIFE MADE ME!!!!"

With a heartfelt cry, Byron slams down the pen. Snatching up the sullied sheets, he begins to tear them piecemeal until only scraps flutter to the floor.

He glares at them believing he has destroyed certain parts of his life. ''Tis true, for they will never come again.'

A knock at the door, and without any by your leave, John Polidori pushes it open with his foot.

'My lord, I heard you call out. Is everything all right?'

Byron looks up, an unwilling host to one he has maligned. And who, he knows, has maligned him.

SURFACING FROM SHADOWS

My good Lord Byron, think what you unearth by disclosing your thoughts in this way.

The days, like the nights, do lure me to the sad, the lost, the lonely for it is within these people I can be born, be given life, have... substance.

I travel the world in the hope of discovering the fickleness of souls: only then may I enter in, become as they are and thus make them strong again.

We are of the shadows, you and I, a darkness with which you are familiar, m'lord.

All I require is that you extend the invitation: I take another step nearer, am therefore ever-present, for I only require one word to be allowed to step over the threshold. The word is WELCOME.

CHAPTER 13

'The sufferings of mortality'

I

'You!' Byron looked up from his destruction of the papers. 'I thought you gone, *hoped* you were gone after your drunken ravings. And by what right do you walk into my chamber, sir? You are not welcome.'

Polidori, thick-skinned and as sober as ever, ignored the insults and stepped into the room. He looked at the floor. 'Dear, dear, a tantrum? Shall I send for Fletcher or maybe Rushton, he's younger. One of them can clear up the mess.' He sauntered to the table and felt the teapot. 'Cold. I'd hoped for some refreshment.'

From his coat pocket he fetched out a few letters. 'Here. All addressed to you. Collected them, at your bidding, from the post office. I'd guess there's a money draft in one of 'em.'

'I wouldn't be surprised at you having opened the wretched thing. Always you make a habit of wanting to know my business.' Byron perused the letters, and decided to put off opening any until he was alone.

He held Polidori with his famous steely glare. 'Know this, *Doctor*. I resent your meddling. If you heard anything t'other night, pissed as you were, then heed it, for 'tis what I believe you to be. I curse the day we met, and what's more, I do not want you barging in here on a whim simply when you feel like it. It's polite to knock and wait. Or didn't your esteemed father teach you any manners?'

'College habits,' said Polidori, pacing back and forth. 'You know that already, m'lord, such environs as Edinburgh and Cambridge can and do bring out the most questionable habits. One of yours was a bear from what you said.'

'Better company than at present.'

Refusing to be drawn into fresh argument, Polidori stated simply, 'I've apparently come at a bad moment. My error in thinking you wanted the mail delivering.'

Byron drummed his fingers on the desk. To anyone else, had they been present, extreme effort to avoid lashing out and slapping Polidori could be discerned in stiffening shoulders, his upright posture. And this fool, he's thinking, still persists in antagonising me. Can't the idiot ever take a hint?

'What ails you, *George*; not feeling lyrical today?'

Byron had half a mind to take the pen and score Polidori's face with it. Instead he gritted his teeth trying to maintain some sort of equilibrium.

Before either could do or say anything to add to an already charged atmosphere, Shelley's light, shrill voice intruded. 'BYRON. My lord, are you there?'

On a relieved sigh, Byron rose from his chair. He walked to the door, left ajar by Polidori, and opened it wide. 'Percy, my friend, yes. Come in.'

Shelley, about to do that, caught sight of Polidori and remained outside. 'My apologies for interrupting, I thought you might be alone.'

'We are, in a manner of speaking. This person is just a doctor, heaven help me, and so hardly merits a mention.'

The air congealed, Polidori's look emphasised in the way he fiddled with his hair, cheek bones lent more emphasis by a quivering jaw.

Shelley offered a passable smile, thinking to treat it as a joke. A glance at Byron told him different.

'Well, Percy, speak out,' prompted Byron. 'Y'didn't come to pass the time o'day I'm sure.'

'Er, no.' The man's shyness peered out through rapidly blinking eyelids. 'No, I er, came to ask... That is, I wondered if the weather's fair that is, if tomorrow you might c... care for a sail on the lake?' He edged further away rather than step into the room.

Someone who appears to accept me for what I am, thought Byron. Then I do have more in common with Shelley. The very fact Shelley had presented himself flushed Byron's mind of the detritus he'd been accumulating, and allowed a sense of well-being to surface.

'Grand idea, Shelley. We can collect our thoughts of last evening and continue our conversation about life and poetry.'

Polidori's literary aspirations fell to his boots. He dared to invite himself and thought better of it. 'Excuse me,' he said, striding past Byron and a bewildered Shelley, 'I have other matters pressing.'

'And one is, no doubt, a quick shot of whatever substance you choose from the bag.' Byron's sarcasm had been stated with good cause, his dislike rapidly generated to hate where the doctor was concerned, Byron dearly wanting to inform Polidori as to where the doctor stood in the scheme of things.

'I will see you at dinner.' Polidori excused himself again and edged past Shelley who hadn't the sense to move out of the way.

Shelley watched Polidori down the short corridor, and then at Byron's further invitation, stepped into the room. Byron closed the door.

II

'There,' Byron said, 'another problem partially solved. Out of sight, out of mind. Would you care for some tea? It's cold, but wet. Or sherry? I could have Rushton bring some up.'

'No, please, I am quite refreshed now, and wouldn't wish to promote another headache.'

Byron laughed and slapped Percy's shoulder. 'Nor I. By the by, I saw your balloons earlier floating over the house.'

Shelley blushed. 'Some may think it a childish whim, but I have this fascination for anything that defies gravity. I am also aware that balloons can help relate information about the weather. All to do with air currents, the way the wind blows, from what direction it comes. From my brief research today, I'm of the opinion storms are imminent.'

Byron collapsed in a chair, his foot paining him. 'Storms! I thought we'd already had some of 'em.' Shelley looked perplexed. 'Sit down, Percy. Don't worry about me; I jest. Tell me, did you know that two hundred years ago the poet Milton is reputed to have stayed here, or somewhere hereabouts?'

'No. No I didn't. I confess I haven't read him much. Coleridge, a few others, but not Milton.'

'Came close to missing this place.' Byron changed the subject, not feeling in a literary discussing mood. 'Looked at several properties including one owned by Madame de Staël. Hentsch told me she was exiled by Napoleon and hasn't yet returned to these parts. It's in Coppet, not that it matters, I didn't take it.'

'Apologies for the size of this room, it's narrow, but I like this south side with its view of the mountains. See how those vineyards tuck into the folds of the Jura? Marvellous views at sunset. Bit like a layered cake.'

'Sounds poetic?' Shelley had grown less tense, his smile prompting Byron's laugh.

'Seriously,' said Shelley, 'I dislike Polidori.'

'You don't surprise me. I, too, have reason to think that. What's yours?'

'Something I can't properly equate. It sounds vague, but I'm sure you understand that when you meet people instinct dictates whether or not you like or dislike them. It might be their manner, their pomposity even –' The more he defined it, the more Shelley's deliberation brought him to an obvious conclusion. 'He's too pushy,' he said. 'Overbearing. And –' He watched Byron for a reaction. 'And jealous.'

Byron slapped his own thigh. 'Strap me if you ain't hit the nail on the head, Shelley.' He told Shelley about his first meeting with John Polidori, and did mention the word *leech*, though wouldn't elaborate, deeming it sufficient to underline the more than literal meaning in context with Polidori.

'I get an impression he's trying to outdo you, m'lord.'

'It's an act, Percy. He thinks he's in love with me.'

'Love?' Shelley pretended shock. 'I don't understand.'

'Don't be naïve. You've expounded enough about your free love commune, and how the world should acknowledge same. Whatever form it takes, s'long as love and affection reside side be side, then what matter? Lust? Now there's a different thing.

'Understand that as far as Polidori's involved, he doesn't love me; it's simply the thought of rubbing shoulders with genius.'

Shelley shifted awkwardly, a precursor to: 'Excuse me, but isn't that a high opinion of yourself?'

''Course it is, but if I let Polidori believe it, and promote the feeling, then I have him eating out of my hand.'

'Do you treat all your acquaintances in such a way?' Shelley provoked.

'Only some, Percy. Only some.' Byron leaned forward to emphasise, 'But not you, my friend. You and I have much in common. We talk on certain levels, and I have no doubt we shall communicate much more before our trip is ended and we decide to move on.' Byron leaned back again, more relaxed than he'd been all day, certainly since the dispute with, and departure from, Claire.

'Jealousy, the bane of lives. Husband of one of my lovers really hated me for my involvement with her. He wanted to see me fall, no doubt laughed when I clouted a few obstacles. But I rose like a Phoenix, Shelley; I beat 'em all. That man was evil.'

'Name?'

'Of no consequence. Suffice t'say, he didn't fill my boots 'specially where his missus was concerned.' An impertinent chuckle followed. 'Yes, lots of people hate me for various reasons, most of 'em not worthy of mention. All comes down to the green-eyed god.'

'Are you never jealous?'

'Is there a point to your question?'

Shelley went to the window, on his way cursorily scanning Byron's writing table. 'I see you've been busy.'

'An idea I'm toying with. It's called *Don Juan.*'

'With your reputation, it isn't difficult to understand why. Autobiographical?'

'All work contains something of the writer; you should know that.'

'I do. Sometimes it's quite frightening to realise just how much of oneself we dare reveal, often unconsciously.'

Another target well hit, thought Byron, still remembering the lines he'd penned earlier and which now littered the floor.

'I daresay the original Don Juan had to tolerate a certain amount of jealousy, wouldn't you say?'

'What is the point, Shelley?' Byron hated evasiveness, so why didn't the man come out with it?

Shelley eased his collar. 'Hot in here.'

'Shelley!'

'Very well. Since our discussions, I merely wish to learn why a man such as yourself, can rarely have qualms should your ladies return to their former... er, partners. What I mean t'say is do you not see it as an affront to your prowess in the bedchamber? Or wherever the, uh, act takes place?'

Byron paced round the sofa, then to the window. He stopped within a yard of Shelley. 'Profound thinking, m'dear.

However, think on this...' The pause, too, was profound. 'Take yourself and Mary. It's obvious how deep her feelings are for you.'

'What are you inferring?'

'That you've found the one you seek. Look to Mary, see how much she abhors your time spent with Claire. It's love, Shelley, pure and simple. Me, I have never been jealous to the ignorance of all else.'

'Your reason?'

'It's a good 'un. I have never found the truth of love, Shelley. Never imagined a relationship lasting years. Annabella proved cold, calculating and so does Miss Clairmont, the latter a mere 'something to do' to pass the time.' Byron's next remark sounded barbed. He asked: 'Tell me, is that how you feel about Claire?'

It promoted a silence all its own, and to play for time, allow Shelley to piece together an answer, if he could... if he *dare,* Byron moved to stand by him. Together they scanned the grounds. 'Ah, the ladies of whom we speak are conspicuous by their absence.'

He gripped Shelley's shoulder. 'Well, have you any feelings for Claire? Don't be shy, your secret's safe with me. Faith, I wouldn't dare talk as I do if I didn't trust *you.*'

'Mary and Claire are relaxing in the lounge. Fletcher has taken them refreshments.' Shelley hesitated before adding, 'Claire is quite upset.'

'Over me? Or you? And perhaps knowing she can't have either!' He noticed how Shelley reacted, one brusque shrug indicating Byron remove his hand.

Byron did. 'Fickle ain't they?' He led and guessed Shelley disliked being so intimidated. All the while Byron remained evasive, wanting Shelley to tell him rather than be seen to be the enemy in whatever Claire had deigned to reveal to either Shelley, or Mary.

Soft scents streamed in through the open windows heralding a warm evening, the fresher breeze following the downpour making it easier to breathe. Outside the trees swayed gently, and from the hills above and behind, came the faraway chants of the villagers.

'There is a certain melody to all that,' Shelley said, 'despite its monotony. Mary and I became aware of it when we discovered Chapuis.'

'Ha, your little house amidst the vines. You declare your need, good Shelley, and prove to me that Claire is... is what? A different choice of confectionery? We all tire eventually, my friend, because we are never truly sure what it is we seek. Degrees of love, of affection. Most come to nought in the end. The house is comfortable I trust?'

'It's distanced from the town, quieter... and cheaper than the outlandish charges made at the hotel.' He looked at Byron. 'Despite our fencing with words and ideals, I cannot disagree with what you say. How far does one have to go to find true happiness?'

'And not be jealous?' Byron's eyes twinkled.

'Now you are baiting.'

'Got used to it with my tame bear.'

'Yes, you mentioned it the other day, amongst other things.'

Byron mulled this over. 'I'll be damned if I can recall one half of what I said.'

'I suggest, with your permission, that we leave this conversation to ferment. It will doubtless raise its head again.'

Byron smiled. 'Many times,' he said. 'If desire pays court.'

Didn't he have a similar conversation with Polidori? Of course. Damned prude, or so he'd have me believe. Unless he's drunk of course.

'Forgive my persistence, Shelley, but I'm dashed if I can leave this whole question of love and jealousy alone. You asked me a few minutes ago if I were ever jealous and I begged the reason.'

Shelley turned defensive. 'Merely conversation. One man trying to get to know another. From what you've revealed your *paramours* have been many and varied. Come, Byron, the law of averages states that you must at sometime have developed a more intense relationship with someone and been... jealous.'

'What a marvellous notion, m'dear. As I said, I see you and Mary in that light. You appear inseparable; every laugh, every sigh as one; even the air you breathe is shared with a closeness I envy. And I... I have yet to meet the true love of my life. Yet there is one *female* for whom I have undying affection.'

'Dare one ask?' Shelley, curious, sat in a wing backed chair. He liked to believe he could get to know Byron, the man behind the pen.

Byron looked upon Shelley with a seriousness that belied his earlier affability. 'One lady who is lost to me, I fear, and purely by reasons of station. In short, she's a housemaid and meself, well, I'm a lord.'

'And not prudent that you meet again, is that it?'

'It is what many of my pathetic contemporaries feel, but how can laws dictate human need? Christ, man, half the bloody county of Nottinghamshire, and a hundred others, the men that is, are rogering upstairs, downstairs, with scullery maids and any other female that winks at 'em, in truth the whole bally lot simply because dear wifey's offering her favours elsewhere.'

'To a butler, or a stable lad most probably,' Shelley offered. 'Some women revel in a bit o' rough. Strapped across a saddle, that sort o' thing.'

'You've been the route then?' Byron's turn to wink.

Shelley laughed. 'We all have our crosses to bear.'

His own humour curled, Byron really moved to want to call this man friend, their banter – whether serious or light – clearly the kind enjoyed by two equals. They each wrote poetry, and both loved sex.

'So tell me, who's the lucky maid?' Shelley sounded insistent.

Byron grew cautious, wondering if Shelley might tell Mary. Or Claire. Or both. On analysis, did it matter?

'Devil or no, y'may as well hear. She was my first true love. Beneath my status wouldn't y'know. All so ridiculous in that I could not acknowledge my love for her because of drawing that other goblin, ridicule, along with its pointing fingers. Naturally, there are some who know; staff at the Abbey for instance. Most are sworn to secrecy, but many a word is spilled from a tongue when ale loosens it. My manservant, Joe Murray's a bugger for that when in his cups. Fellow sings enough bawdy songs to scare the maids as it is.' Byron chuckled as he pictured Joe in the chair by the fire, conducting an imagined orchestra as he put his own, less salubrious words to well-known tunes.

'Obviously this Murray is well-respected. Tell me, Byron, would it, or does it, worry you having people discuss your er, private interests?'

'Not exceptionally so. Afterwards my reputation tended to overtake me. In all honesty, I hated the subterfuge, meeting in dark corners, sometimes in the grounds of Newstead where others rarely walked. I also deplored hurting her when she learned of my relationships with others.'

'That's love, m'lord, to coin your phrase. The fact you hate certain underhand tactics dictates so.'

'I suppose it is. Between you and me, I did love the girl with all my heart. One could easily term us soul-mates. I fear it was a love that would never be allowed on earth –'

'For what reason?' queried Shelley. 'Must we always kowtow to others' opinion?' Here Shelley's atheism emerged. 'What you're inferring is that if man cannot allow a certain thing to happen without provoking various degrees of unrest amongst the populace, God can. Byron, m'dear chap, I'm of the opinion that God is man-made, an invisible entity devised so that our shortcomings can be forgiven in order that we can carry on and create more. A vicious circle, my friend, and one not truly accepted in every race.'

'Then am I to blame in deciding the lady and I could never be together as I wished because I played on the fact that she deemed herself unworthy of me? Or is it perhaps that she would not reveal *her* acceptance of me knowing *she* was unworthy? And there's a kind of paradox! I conclude that some of her reticence is blamed on the fact that she had learned about my other philandering.'

He beheld the stern look Shelley presented, a look countermanded by a wayward twist of the lips. 'So, tell me, friend, is the power of the Almighty about which men speak so improbable that we can never learn the true meaning of love?'

Shelley thought about this, and said, 'Only individuals can decide their own worthiness. Ask yourself, what is prayer, m'lord. Is it us asking ourselves are we doing right? Appealing to that within us which is called the 'soul'? Come, sir, we make decisions – and rise or fall by 'em.'

'Food for thought, Shelley. I regret I'm able to do little about lost chances now.' Despondent again, he fought against it, refusing to let it take hold. 'Blast mawkish thought. Shelley, we've talked enough about me, what of yourself? I'd lay bets that you've had a few fair maids in y'time. Let's be honest with each other, eh?'

Byron sat opposite, willing Shelley to reveal a few dark secrets. 'You're a master at evading certain questions.' A knowing smile mocked. 'Come, man, I've observed Miss Clairmont following your every move. Fondled that have you? Had a hand up her petticoats, I'll vouch.'

Shelley blushed, disturbed by Byron's outspokenness.

Byron nodded a few times. 'Thank you, your reaction is noted; it's all I need to know.' He slapped his own knees. 'Let it go. We should join the others. Fletcher will have our meal ready.'

'What kind of man is Fletcher? Seems a bit dour t'me. Been with you long has he?'

'One o' the best, Percy. Good and loyal servants are hard to come by. His wife's a bit of a harpy though; took umbrage over my treatment of Annabella. Swore blind I was beating her –'

'Any truth in it?'

'Pah, fickle women again. Make no mistake, they're the power, think they can laud it over us, call the tune. Fletcher's a law unto himself when he owns to it. Stays on the outside. You'll notice he won't get involved with our revelries. Oh he'll hover and listen, and watch, but he won't speak out of turn and can be trusted. Protects me like... like a guardian angel! There, that kicks out on your observations about religion, and in truth, underlines 'em. We create our own angels, Percy – human or in here.' Byron tapped his own head.

'Tales abound concerning me, Percy. I like to think you wouldn't be here had you heeded them. Never as bad as I seem. They portray me as bad because of my professed vanity, my selfishness. I admit to doing many wrongs to many people, but I never meant to hurt, didn't set out to. Y'might say we learn from mistakes, and if we never make any, God what a dull life!

'On occasion, I sit and contemplate what I've done, what I might wish to do, sort of analyse the error of my ways and hope to correct 'em. You and I are intellectuals, Percy, always searching for the right thing, the right way. My insane quest to find love. My life up to now spent searching... Tell y'something, I had a dog who was more faithful than any man or woman. Hell, there is more to life than pleasure. I keep reminding myself that to do good is far more important and, despite your own views, we should believe in an after-life if only to purge the shocks and disbelief that's thrown at us in this one.'

Shelley interrupted. 'You mean, I take it, that we should all be prepared to meet whatever Maker is out there, in the hope it will understand why we do what we do?'

Byron glanced meaningfully at Shelley, more aware how serious he could be without the smile. 'For a moment there I had a notion you were being frivolous. Accept what I have said as truth, and hope to gain some salvation.' He grinned, leaned over and slapped Shelley's leg. 'But not tonight, eh?'

They both came from their seats almost simultaneously, Byron placing an arm about Shelley's shoulders. Shelley did not shrug it off.

'You say the little house is cheaper,' Byron said. 'That's good. Give you more peace o' mind not having to think where the next louis is coming from. I've travelled that road too many times and experienced the anxiety it causes.' Byron halted by the table and drained his tea, now cold. The biscuits went untouched.

Shelley preceded him from the room, Byron pausing only to look at the litter on the floor. 'Fragments of my life,' he whispered and closed the door.

CHAPTER 14

'A shadow tracks thy flight of fire –
Night is coming!'

I

The meal, despite Shelley's thinking to the contrary, turned out to be anything but strained; Lord Byron's enthusiasm and tall tales about their journey here – omitting any reference to certain dalliances – distilled any awkwardness wrought by the afternoon's events.

Polidori, the one Shelley expected to remain moody, surprisingly allowed the party atmosphere to stir his dark mood, his own contribution going some way to further lightening what could have been a silent, chastened gathering harassed by memories of his pitiful behaviour with Byron.

Claire tried countless times to catch Byron's attention. He refused to meet her eye, and instead insisted she take more and more wine. At least, he thought, if she won't be party to the party, I'll get the bitch drunk.

It worked, for Claire's primness soon melted, her rising, commodious laughter echoing throughout the darkening villa. Candles, fetched in by Fletcher and Rushton, chased away the more ominous shades. Except, that is, for the tall figure Mary was sure she glimpsed beyond the windows – the one with the pallid face, and staring eyes. *The one aching to be born onto the printed page!*

II

'I wonder,' said Byron, picking at the main course and eating barely enough to keep one of his pet monkeys alive. 'I wonder, amongst this gathering, who of us dare lay out their life story for all to wonder at?'

The statement, said without intending to sound discourteous, did provoke: it made the others sit up, earlier humorous asides and banter squashed to extinction. It could never have been a demand, Lord Byron assuming that each should be given an opportunity to mull it over before saying anything.

'It's a game if you will, for –' His dark eyes met each of theirs, his grin harsh, hardly amusing. '– we all tempt the fates which govern our existence.' He leaned forward, toyed with a knife, repeatedly tapping it on his plate before using it to cut an apple, the fruit left untouched, its peel exactly what it was – discarded skin.

'Take this –' He lifted the skin, allowing it to bounce and curl. 'How do we see it? What does it convey to you? And have some conviction, please. We are a gathering of writers, none of us, it is hoped, afraid to put pen to paper. We use our imaginations.

'Is it a sloughed snake skin? A rope?' He looked at Polidori. 'Something pretending to be that which it is not.' Again, not a question, Polidori purposely pouring more wine and so avoiding the marked stare.

'A lock of hair, perhaps?' Mary suggested. 'Floating amidst a sea of weed... in a lake... its owner drowned...'

'Mary?' Shelley thought about Mary's behaviour on their lake trip, the allusion very intense, and real.

'Hair of the dead.' Byron nodded. 'A pretty notion, I'll grant. Tell me, Mary, why is it the living tend to lean towards the dark of life? Is it that we all fear death? NO! Not death itself, but the way it comes? Might it creep upon an individual, that person completely unaware, and when it happens, they hardly have time to be surprised? Or then again, it might be, as in battle, a fear already instilled. Only by wit and luck do those unfortunate warriors, empowered to fight for their country, avoid the great leveller.'

'Or by God's will?' said Polidori.

'Why not, John? Belief in the deity can temper fear; those who die willingly go to their Maker accepting they will be greatly remembered for it; believing their souls will float in the ether until such time as they are recalled.'

Claire spluttered wine, mopped it from her dress with a napkin. 'Oh my, are you a believer in reincarnation, Albé? Do you –' She leaned forward, one hand nearly sliding off the table, her head jerking, drunken laughter dismissing it. 'D'you I wonder, run before your own fears and beliefs like a scared child?'

'What we learn in our formative years is attached for as long as we live.' Byron stared into the amber sherry, the glass held up, its crystal reflecting flickering candlelight, that part of his face distorted, a mobile, agonised mask.

'You, my lord,' said Claire without faltering, her voice loud in order that all would hear, '*you* are a monster.'

Byron didn't look up. 'Dark. Light. One part of me in shadow, the other bathed in golden glow.' Now he looked up, and met Claire's bloodshot eyes. 'Do you truly believe, madam, that I am the only *monster* in this room?'

Mary's intake of breath was heard by all.

Polidori ruminated on parts of his own conversation with Byron on the journey, and silently willed Claire to be quiet. It was the wrong thing to say to Byron, and the doctor sank lower in his seat.

Mary and Percy sought one another across an expanse of white linen scattered with plates coloured by leftovers. Had Mary been able to reach him, she would have gripped Shelley's hand, tightly

A breeze sprang up; it flattened the fire's flames before allowing them to gust up the chimney more rapidly; in the mirror above it, reflected shapes cavorted, but they could only be the drapes at the tall windows, more shadow reflections. Outside in the hallway, several wayward leaves blew in at the door, left open by Fletcher to ease the gathering humidity: they skittered across the floor, their sound like dead teeth chattering.

Portentous? Did they perhaps herald something far more pertinent than words might conjure? 'Listen,' Byron said, his tone lower, more sinister. 'Nature, they say, has a habit of playing its own tunes. Nature waits. It lures the unsuspecting into the common sense of false security. Then, and only then, will it strike.'

The words curbed Claire's sniggering. Heavy air lumbered in, thick with unspoken thoughts, acting as a precursor to something which, in its way, disturbed them all. People together, their own lives and what they had done during those years, now at the forefront of all their minds. Young people who had maybe lived more in their short years than many do in a lifetime, but nevertheless young people who had tapped the darker meanings of existence, or who would be forced to by whatever the future conjured.

If the 'other side' existed, the elements might force a reckoning. Question: Did any here feel enriched enough, or damned enough, even innocent enough, to gamble?

It was for each one as an individual to freely admit to Byron's question, but *dare* they?

Conscious of the deeper, more fundamental tributary the conversation was taking, Shelley interrupted. Sitting forward, elbows on the table, he started to offer certain observations in the hope they would all return to a less scathing mood, and dispense with insults.

'We are, as you say, m'lord, writers, so I suggest we return to our more literary style of conversation.' He pushed the wine towards Claire. 'Help yourself, my dear, but do, please, refrain from using that sour tongue you've developed recently.' Shelley followed up with his own peculiar laugh, high yet lacking humour. 'It's a party, and I'm thinking I should have brought balloons!'

Claire sulked – again. Shelley let her. Mary turned slightly away from her, sick of pandering to infantile rejection.

Shelley addressed Byron. 'Your penchant for less salubrious aspects of life precedes you, Lord Byron. You make reference to yon apple skin as being that of a snake. Goëthe's *Mephistopheles* calls the serpent that tempted Eve "*My aunt – the renowned snake*".'

'And I say you cite the Devil, good Shelley. How very perceptive, for he lurks in all our lives in one form or another. And you –' He looked up from the curled peel, now drying, more distorted, a cold grin sitting there as though someone had drawn a knife across an inanimate lump of clay. 'You,' he repeated, 'must be this aunt's nephew. A good enough nickname, I think. Yes, "Snake", for you have bright eyes, a slim enough figure and dare I say, noiseless movements?'

Shelley grunted. 'I believe that somewhere in your observation could lurk a compliment.' He raised his glass in toast. 'To a quick wit, and a brave fool.' He drank it down and slammed his glass on the table causing cutlery to dance, a few plates to rattle.

Byron returned the toast, Polidori did not, the two ladies – not that Claire seemed aware of anything by now – learned enough to not interrupt what might turn out to be an intense and enlightening conversation, or a more friendly argument between such closely allied scholars.

Polidori opened the match, dark eyes even darker in the dying daylight, the orb of the sun visible through the undraped western window, like the single, obnoxious eye of a cyclops staring into their well-ordered lives and hinting: Where to now, gentlemen?

'His Satanic Majesty sets the precedent,' Polidori said. He looked straight at Byron.

Byron offered a quick nod and raised his glass again, but didn't drink.

'I suggest, my lord, that you are the real snake, to wit a dangerous prankster whose tomfoolery, whether by word or by action, will generally force a dreary smile, or hollow laugh from those in your illustrious company.' Polidori glanced round, realising he had the floor, that every ear was attuned to him. 'A man who prides himself in extracting discomfort more than any playfulness in others; one who seeks to illuminate another's failure. I don't doubt it is always your lordship's intention.'

Claire, blinking in what she felt too harsh a light, heard and gasped at such wilfulness. She hiccuped and drained her glass. Mary admired Polidori for his bravery before their dignified host.

Byron, to Polidori's surprise, rather than rise angrily to such remarks, slapped the table and laughed. 'Keep the banter light, eh, doctor? Sometimes, Polly, you give as good as you take, well done. It can benefit an individual to gain the upper hand –'

Polidori relaxed a little, priding himself on the fact that he had scored a point in this ongoing battle of wills. The one-upmanship was short-lived.

'– but I fear failure is inherent in your make-up.' Byron's eyes shone in the light from the flickering candles. 'You see, those witless hangers-on who seek tutelage listen, and they learn, and then go away, relate to their families and friends my sometimes caustic witticisms. It gives me an edge, Polly, it is why I extend such invitations to people like you, in order that *I* can emerge the winner.

'Words, my friend, just words which, when strung together form compliments, information, and insults. Look at you, you're squirming, your ignominy as red as the claret you sup. Take heart, though, for the wine's a good 'un.'

A slow handclap interrupted what would have undoubtedly been another pregnant silence, Percy Shelley prompted by the wit of both men, to add his applause. 'I live, I learn, and let me say, shy away from revealing my life story, such as it's been until this moment, with either you, Lord Byron, or your contemporary here. I'm wont to admit that certainly yours, Lord B, forces my own into anaemic shadow.'

'Contemporary! You misunderstand, Shelley, Polidori is no such thing for he has a way to go before he matches either my own, or your prowess.' Byron glanced at the doctor. 'We stopped to take refreshment on our journey, John. We compared writings? And I only too willing to coach you –'

'Sir, you did nought but seek my shaming, as you do now. But –' Polidori raised a finger to make his point, 'you conveniently forget I was a brilliant student at Edinburgh, and published a play, *Ximines*, and a discourse on the death penalty before I'd reached twenty.'

Not to be outdone, Byron said, 'Then I suggest you attempt to follow your self-revealed brilliance by adding to your portfolio, Polly. A writer, any artist, is only as good as the work he is engaged upon, *not* what is past. In other words, Polly, you must better it!'

'And is your own work always so satisfactory, m'lord? Does it account for the scattering of torn paper in your room earlier? An idea that went wrong?'

'Private thoughts not intended for public consumption,' Byron explained. 'We all have them, scribbled down or not. Without wishing to belabour earlier comments, I say you shame yourself, doctor.' Byron glanced at Shelley, the younger poet wearing an amused smile, trying to guess what Byron might be up to.

Torment wore many guises, and it appeared that Byron and Shelley had singled out the easily upset Polidori, using him to replay all the aggravations they had suffered at Eton and Harrow.

'My poor Polly,' Byron said, 'you are too hot headed and passionate for your own good. And you have the unfortunate ability to get yourself into scrapes. For instance, what of your unrequited love for the young Genevan lady?' His eyes dared Polidori to rise to this, and so prove his point.

The doctor sat up. 'You... you heathen! I told you of that in strict confidence.'

'Aw, doesn't Polly-Dolly want his love life aired?' Byron mocked. 'Can it be that such desires are so secret he dare not reveal his lovelorn state?'

'It might be more fitting,' Shelley interrupted, 'if you were to invite the lady to one of our intended outings on the lake. Hire your own boat, make her captive to your infatuation.'

Mary, sensing the full-blown argument, interrupted. 'The apple peel, my lord, you overlooked my suggestion.' Her openness begged an answer. 'A lock of hair perhaps?'

Polidori offered the slightest nod of thanks for this interruption, having no wish to further promote words with Byron. To be singled out like this made him, at least in their eyes, some kind of enemy. Put out by his show of affection to Byron, he squirmed in his seat, praying Byron would not make reference to it.

His own 'secret' entries in his personal diary probably went some way to matching Byron's, for they hinted at an affection for Mary, so much so he'd appointed himself her Italian teacher.

"Read Italian with Mrs S," he'd noted on the 31st May: "Went into a boat with Mrs S and rowed all night till nine; tea'd together, chatted etc."

Mary acknowledged his silent thank you. In her way, she felt sorry that Polidori should be so put upon and decided she would talk to Shelley about it. When she came to write up her own account, the term 'in the highest and most boyish of spirits' came to mind for use. And she would chastise Byron for merrily threatening to tell her about the mysterious lady with whom the young doctor was madly in love. The man had been blatant enough to mention it in full company, rather than keep the secret. Yes, Polidori had every right to feel chastened and clung to the hope that Lord Byron might take the hint.

Thankfully, he did. Tired of baiting, Byron turned to Mary. 'So. Whose hair would you have it be, Mary?' He looked at the peel on his plate. 'It looks so lack-lustre, so bereft without a head. I hardly think one small plate, as white and pale as this 'un will ever warrant the colour of flesh, except...' He surveyed them again, toying with the peel as he did so. 'Except perhaps on the dead. And it brings us full circle. Life. Death. The hereafter.

'What does lurk out there?' Byron scanned the darkness of the window, and his own reflection thrown back by the night.

'Why you, my lord,' Claire said very seriously. 'You lurk there, as well as here in this cosy room. I am sure there are two of you, George Byron – Saint. And Devil!'

THE OPENING OF THE WAY

'Do you see now?' said the one dressed in night-black clothes. 'Hear how they quarrel?'

The other only nodded, for he was not as learned as the dark one, and was still devoid of the power of speech. The one who addressed him had at least been given some background by the English lord, and from such thoughts, things begin to grow.

Often they become real.

True, the lady had allowed thoughts to tumble around in her own budding, literary mind, yet had not imagined words to place on the tongue and lips of this one who desired to learn. And to live.

A name had been mentioned. A castle in the frozen mountains. In a place where demons walked and perhaps the dead were given a second chance.

Frankenstein.

'Ah, even now she thinks it,' said the dark one. 'If I work on the poet, it may mean he will continue this treatise on the dead, and how they come to be reborn, or created from the stuff nature placed before man.

'Male. Female. Procreation.

'It will soon be time for His Satanic Majesty to hold court. To bring down the storm on his gathering. And himself.

'Life is but a passing of time, yet from it, we can be given life.'

CHAPTER 15

'What is life, what is death?'

I

Byron had ordered the English-made skiff from Bordeaux.

'Unlike many of the hire boats available,' he told Shelley, 'this one, as you will see, has two sails and a deeper keel.'

'Is that good?' A preoccupied Shelley, head in the clouds as usual as they walked down to the dock, didn't appear interested.

'Listen, Snake.' Byron grabbed Shelley's arm. 'If you're ever in charge of a boat, safety is important. Weather is unpredictable and a boat such as this will afford greater safety in sudden squalls so heed it. I'm advised that Léman's waters can be whipped into a rough sea. Danger to life and limb, understand?'

'I'm sorry, Albé, forgive my lapse. Thank you for the advice.'

Byron's confidence in Shelley restored, he said, 'Come, we will test it out.'

Shelley, trusting Byron, was prompted to offer half the cost. 'If it is our intention, when not with the er, 'family' to venture out ourselves,' he told Byron. 'I think it fair to share.' His pause foreshadowed slight embarrassment. 'I will pay you as soon as I can; funds are low at present.'

'Noble of you,' replied Byron. 'I've already intimated my life's friends can be numbered on one hand.' He stuck out a thumb and laughed. 'That's you, Shelley.'

'At least I appear more solid than your other artistic fingers, m' lord. Thank you.'

The Genevan who had taken delivery of the skiff for them, smiled at their banter. A businessman who catered for the boating fraternity in which the area was proud to be involved, he told them in passable English: 'You have a fine boat. I dread to be the one who take money from two such notables, and they were to drown. My life it would be forfeit to every poet lover the whole world wide. No, good sirs, once on the lake, you will be safe *in* the boat; what you do *out* of it, is your own affair.'

His grin made them smile, Byron dropping several coins into the man's mahogany-coloured hand.

II

Having used the morning to relax and recover after the previous night's revels and arguments, they concurred that the heat of noon was hardly conducive to being tortured by a lake excursion. Unlike other tourists, they preferred the cooler, quieter time of day in the late afternoon and well into the evening.

Polidori had retired from their dinner party not long after Byron's betrayal of his trust. Around one in the morning, Shelley and Mary had opted to walk back to Chapuis.

This left Byron and Claire – much to Mary's surprise and relief – smouldering at one another across the vast expanse of table.

A breathy, boozy sigh preceded Claire's, 'Do I deserve an apology?'

Behind them, by the door, Fletcher stifled a yawn.

'Yes, Fletcher,' Byron beckoned him, 'you may clear away. Where's Rushton?'

'On the terrace, m'lord. Too shy for 'is own good, that lad. Gets a bit tongue-tied in company. I'll get 'im to help as soon as you've retired. Er, will Miss Clairmont be staying, sir? On'y I need to prepare another room.'

Byron spoke with his eyes, the thought conveyed to Fletcher as, *Don't be so silly, man. I have plans.*

Fletcher stepped away, waiting as Byron pushed back his chair and stood, one hand extended to grip Claire's as she tottered towards him using chairs for support.

'No apology for what I made clear this afternoon, madam, but I do respect your feelings and admit to being harsh. We'll discuss it upstairs.'

Supporting Claire, Byron passed Fletcher who avoided looking directly at him. Discreet to a fault, Fletcher was very conversant with Byron's liaisons and decided years ago that it didn't pay to criticise his lordship despite his own concepts of right and wrong.

He knew of Lucy, and the child, Patrick – hadn't he played with the lad, or at least walked him when Lucy and Byron had been deep in conversation in rooms that leaked when it rained and paid court to birds nesting in damp rafters?

'Play your games, m'lord,' Fletcher said as he watched his master and the woman disappear into the darkness of the hallway.

Rushton closed the front door behind him, and quietly joined Fletcher. 'They gone?' He looked sheepish. 'Didn't want to interrupt, seein' as I heard what was said today.'

''Elp me clear away.'

Rushton loaded a large tray he'd secreted behind a chiffonier. 'Hey, George, he isn't taking up with 'er again, is he?'

'Don't fret, Robbie; Lord Byron does what 'e likes, when 'e likes.'

'I know that.' Rushton leaned on a chair back. 'I reckon he's a touch crazy carryin' on with all these women. What does he want out o' life, George? I mean, you been with 'im more years, so y'must have thought about it.'

'My lord Byron takes some fathomin', Robert. Hard to tell what he's thinkin' half the time. Some things 'e does I don't approve of, but I'm only a servant trailin' an enigmatic master.'

'Bloody hell, George, that's some statement from you.'

'P'raps I've picked up a few of his nibs's traits. Christ, I bin on 'is coat tails some years. Joe Murray said t'me once, "Take it slow, an' don't antagonise 'cos that feller has one 'ell of a temper."'

'Don't I know it,' agreed Rushton. 'If I didn't get his clothes jus' right he'd bawl me out. Dress sense like a peacock 'e 'as.' Rushton mulled this over, his head inclined towards the dying fire. 'Pity he criticises 'isself like 'e does. That lameness bothers him, don't it? Don't know why; I mean the feller allus looks immaculate. Who cares about his limp?'

'Easy t'say, Robert. When folk aren't afflicted, they fail t'realise how it affects the one that is. Byron lives with it, and we have to live with 'is moods. Kind of full circle, ain't it? Now, let's get cleared up and get to bed.'

Rushton loaded some more crockery on the tray. 'Is 'e still rogerin' that Claire then?'

Fletcher dawdled, thinking, finally stating, 'If you was 'anded it on a plate, Robbie, what would you do? You and that lass Sarah Vaughan 'ad a 'igh old time at the Abbey.'

'Y'know about that?'

'I know t'pinched 'er off Byron.' Fletcher grinned. 'I reckon 'e admired you for that.'

III

Night curdles outside the window, a three quarter moon throws the garden into stark relief. Partially naked, Claire leans against the balcony rail waiting for her lord and master, her own hands cupping her breasts beneath a flimsy shift.

She turns, narrows her eyes, patterns of light and shade fooling her, the effects of too much wine failing to induce that same clarity of vision needed to appreciate the beauty of a shining lake. She peers, blinks, peers again. On the night breeze the suggestion of a voice whispering inside her head. Byron standing behind her? She turns, he isn't there, she hears him moving about inside the room.

She glimpses the pond to her left, a long slit in the earth, open and inviting in the warmth. How she longs to slide in, experience cool water on naked skin.

Hands caress her body, cup her breasts, tease her nipples, a hard maleness pins her to the rail, a moist tongue laves her shoulders, her neck... teeth nibble, cool air taunts her lower limbs as her shift is hiked up... She feels him, it, *against her skin, her body manipulated, angled forward over the rail... He's close, almost there... moans of pleasure... of pain as he enters her from behind...*

And the moon hides its face, the lake darker, the slit in the earth buried under the weight of darkness-

I had a dream, which was not all dream. Whispered in her ear even as her body is torn by the weight pounding into it. *The bright sun was extinguished...* The air cools, she cries out, sweat erupts in the generated, rising heat... *and the icy earth swung blind and blackening in the moonless air...*

Eyes closed, mind awash with this different passion, wine's bloody shades trickling across alabaster skin, her vision transfused with wild tumultuous thoughts, she grows aware of something huge close by, a sound of beating wings, of teeth lightly touching the pulse in her arched neck, a tongue licks greedily, and eyes the colour of... not blood... but fire – rich, flaring, condemning fire, grow to become the centre, the core of her being.

I am sure there are two of you, George Byron – Saint. And Devil! Her words a few hours ago.

God! Such pain... such pleasure. Exceeding anything ever experienced before. It is what I wanted: more than I expected. A new kind of love – her secret. He does want me, love me... does not wish to harm the child, so he does... does... Ahhh. The stories are true!

She begs for more... feels a hand on her brow, another gently pressuring her shoulder urging her to –

'Wake up. Claire, wake up.'

Her head pounds, a hum of voices... No, one voice. Lord Byron's voice. Through tormenting opaqueness she sees the form sitting on the bed, the whiteness of a shirt, a cravat hanging loose.

'You passed out.' His laugh is demeaning.

Trying to raise herself, she notes she is fully dressed, yet she feels used, her breasts, her lower regions on... *fire?*

A hand on her neck, lower. 'NO!' She pushes him away. 'You... YOU... what have you done to me?'

Byron rocks back, puzzled by her sudden attitude. 'Done to you? Why I had a hard enough time stopping your wild thrashings.'

'But... we... made love. You took me – I *felt* you *inside* me-e-e. You whispered words to me... And my soul cried out to you... YOU, MY LORD.'

'You dreamed.' He goes to kiss her, she retreats up the bed. 'I. Want. To. Leave.' She tries to rise on legs which won't obey. She falls back against the pillows. 'Oh God, I'm sick.'

Byron goes to the door, opens it and bellows: 'F-L-E-T-C-H-E-R-R-R.'

CHAPTER 16

'To those that walk in darkness; on the sea...'

I

Shelley's ribald laughter climbs, he lies practically prostrate in the bow listening to Byron's account of how drunk Claire had actually become.

'Swore blind I was rogering her,' Byron said. He eased on the tiller, the wind from the east billowing the skiff's twin sails. 'Fact is she was too far gone to believe I hadn't.'

'And did you?'

'No. As soon as we reached the room she fell across the bed. I made her comfortable. Only hook I touched was the one at the back of her neck. Loosened it so she wouldn't damn well choke. Nearly sick all over me as it was. Thank Christ Fletcher brought a bowl. Made it in the nick of time. Room stinks like a drain.'

'So what were you doing while she was sleeping?'

'Composing. I like the night, Shelley. Knew I wouldn't sleep, mind over-active what with badgering poor old Polly, and the rest.'

'We're alike, you and I, Byron. Night-time is a quiet time, allows the imagination to run riot. Most of *Queen Mab* was produced in the early hours.'

'No wonder you rejected kings, queens and statesmen in those verses, aye even God. "There is no God!" you wrote.' Byron looked beyond Shelley to the rising majesty of the Jura mountains, closer, more awe-inspiring. 'They dwarf even the might of man,' he said. 'Do you not feel crushed by their might, their presence? They cast their shadows on our sail cloth.'

'Clouds, mountains... they are all far bigger than man,' Shelley said.

'Yes but clouds disperse,' Byron said.

'And so does man, gone to dust.' Shelley studied the wildly flapping canvas, how it creased, how the folds straightened, forming – to him – disturbing shapes. First a face, then a blacker, less distinguishable form, almost, he thought, like some massive, flying creature. Now the face again, shaped proper, a suggestion of handsomeness suddenly grown ugly, deformed.

Clouds blotted the sun for minutes, each second stretched, both men forced to study their lowering, heaviness, praying the sun would win through.

The boat heeled as a sudden gust caught it, Byron yanking on the tiller, correcting it, but not before Shelley had nearly toppled from his seat.

Byron let go the tiller and helped him get seated again, the boat trailing to larboard, the west bank with more colourful buildings, rushing towards them. Byron set them back on course. 'The wind and sun is doing your tan good, Shelley. Enhances those freckles, too. What age are you? I mean, you look s'boyish.'

The skiff heeled again in the opposite direction.

'Have a care, Byron, this is partly my investment – when I've paid you that is.'

Late afternoon sun released from its cloud prison rendered the lake's surface a kaleidoscope of colour, the air as fresh and sweet as any they had tasted.

'A lull before the storm, perhaps,' Shelley shouted above the freshening wind.

'See that tight little cove yonder –' Byron nodded towards it. 'I aim to put in there, we can relax on the rocks, set the world to rights with our musings.'

Shelley, unhappy at a sudden choppiness, agreed. Perhaps he should have said he couldn't swim, but did not wish to appear less brave than Byron, a strong, confident swimmer Shelley had noted this several times having seen him streaming through the water like a dolphin.

Distanced now, Chapuis, the village of Montalègre and naturally Diodati, were hidden by the contours of the land. Other sails resembled hankies cast into the wind, left to bob in air currents off the lake's surface. Smoky blue heat haze curled between the trees, the area given a supernatural quality that struck the two poets in quite different ways.

Shelley's conjuring shapes and faces in the sails prompted his 'seeing' them again within the curl of branches; the static limbs of a dead tree resembled the antlers of a fighting stag; bushes swayed to the tune of the wind, the air grown colder as the inshore breeze caught them. Shaded, this particular spot – according to Shelley, who didn't comment on it – failed to meet his expectations.

The coolness made them shudder; it smacked of awkward silences obvious during their meal last night. He studied the vegetation, interspersed by yet more trees, their heaviness and looming intensity not helping his depression.

A clatter of falling rocks splashing in the water startled him, Shelley reminded of Mary's fascination with drowned pebbles.

Disembodied arm... hair floating... the apple skin like hair... Her unsettled look as he'd caught her looking towards the window last night.

Byron sensed none of this and moored the boat. 'That's done. Don't want the boat floating away; it's a long walk back.' He laughed. 'We could pretend we're pirates marooned.' He scanned the area, searching out a place to take their ease. He pointed. 'Yon flat rock looks as though it may be less harsh on the posterior than the narrow boat seats.'

At last, after a short, steep climb, they were able to settle, Shelley's view of the lake, and the distant opposite bank, and the deepening colour of the mountains urging his composing mind. The clouds remained a threat, the changing, effervescing light dowsed by them. It made him edgy.

'Shelley,' Byron queried, 'is something wrong?'

'No,' Shelley lied, 'should there be?'

'There is, my Snake – You don't mind me calling you that? Thought not. Your tone betrays you. It holds excitement and awe, and I'm bound to say, you look uneasy over our situation.'

It was true, for whenever Shelley, excitable as he was, found himself placed in a given situation, he would react accordingly. Soul-light streamed from his eyes, every mental emotion expressed in his pliant, ever-changing features.

Unlike Byron who could be very superficial sometimes, Shelley could be most profound. Unbeknownst to him at this time, Shelley's depth of thoughts, as well as their boldness, supplied Byron with exactly what he wanted, so a portion of Shelley's aspirations were infused into Byron's mind. Despite his purse having a limit, his mental wealth didn't, not only to Byron, but to anyone who decided to try their hand at literature.

'Snake,' Byron said, 'I really admire your genius. Every detail learned thus far is interesting. It appears your life harmonises with your spiritual theories, so why so uneasy? Surely I cannot cause your irritability?'

Two men together, marooned, their thoughts, for practicality's sake, as one. Poets, one recognised and famous, another who would struggle whilst he lived to attain such fame. He would never complain of the world's neglect, nor express any other feeling than surprise at the rancorous abuse wasted on an author who, to all intents, had few, if any, readers.

'Hardly you, m'lord.' Shelley stared at the waves surging towards the shore, the boat bobbing, the sound from its keel growling as it scraped the rocks beneath.

'You asked last night about putting our lives before the public gaze –'

'No, Percy, you misunderstood. I said: I wonder, amongst our gathering, who of us dare lay out their life story for all to wonder at.' Byron eased himself. 'Wrong choice of rock I feel. The rear's rather tender.' He looked for any reaction: Shelley wasn't amused.

'Snake,' he said, 'in the short time we have known each other, I consider us the best of friends. You're educated and offer much in the way of intelligence. To some extent we are of like mind, but I do detect –' Byron paused, gnawed his lip. 'I do detect a certain discomfort, even your own jealousy... Shades of yesterday, eh? Jealousy of my relationship with Mary. No, please, don't be angry, and do sit down rather than crouch like a frog unable to make up its mind which way to leap.'

Shelley did sit, legs splayed out before him. 'What are you inferring? First you admit we're friends and now you accuse me of being jealous of your actions towards my Mary.'

'As well as your actions towards Claire.' Seriousness of an even more complex nature took hold. 'I said yesterday that you must have at least tried with her. Like me, Snake, you have a penchant for putting it about. Reputations do precede people y'know.'

'I've a feeling you're talking about you again.'

'No, I'm trying to ascertain whether or not the child Claire states she carries, is mine or yours!'

Rising, cheeks flushed beyond what the weather could do, Shelley made his way down from the rock. Stumbling a little, he managed to reach the boat. 'Are we ready to sail?'

The air grew heavy as more clouds amassed to the east.

'Don't be a fool, Shelley.' Byron, from his vantage point gained an unlooked-for presence. 'You are a good man with a fine reputation. I trust you to keep secrets and hope our talk will go no further. A man with false pretensions – I mean Polidori – is no use as a friend, or an enemy. Believe me, I have many of the latter.'

Byron climbed down from the rock to walk to within feet of Shelley. The short distance might well have been a mile, Shelley's being accused making him more wary.

Byron said more, the wind slicing his words. He moved closer. 'Admit it, Snake, you are a ladies' man. There must be other children. I have a few scattered about... Come on, neither of us are celibate, we each have followers, women who will lay themselves before us if only to gain a taste of what it is like to bed the true artist.

'I envy your feelings for Mary. Though not an exception, you should have no need to seek comfort with others. And why should I condemn it? I'm so irrefutable. Better to speak the truth, Shelley, for only real friends can.'

Turning away, Shelley dallied with the consequences of what he had lately done. Yes, he could admit to having had relations with Claire, but how the devil could he know whose child she carried? Mary was no fool, and had probably guessed. But maintaining her own sweet innocence, and because they weren't married yet, Shelley assumed she would bear it.

'You speak of trust, Lord Byron,' he said, facing him. 'Libertine as *you* are, forgive me if *I* doubt your truths. I accept your reputation is a degree more questionable than my own.'

'I bow to your reluctance, Shelley. Let not what I say mar our friendship. I assure you, it will go no further than these encroaching trees. Listen, they speak their own tongues, and neither you nor I can understand such language.'

The swish and sigh of leaves in a cooling wind proved a point. 'Mother Nature,' said Byron, 'has ears, but not the language to repeat what she hears.'

Did the leaves in their chatter, pass on this vow of silence – this promise from one poet to another?

'Despite either of our infidelities, Snake, be a good husband to Mary, if it is your intention to marry her. Love her to the end, maintain whatever principles you have, for they are of the utmost importance. Pray, do not lose sight of your true aim in life: live it to the full, maintain your beliefs.'

'Faith, you sound like a preacher. Thinking of taking the cloth?' Shelley tried to remain serious, found it impossible, and started to laugh. 'Somehow, I can't picture you wearing any such raiment; completely out of character.'

Byron, flung out his arms and embraced Shelley. 'Damn right. I lived in an Abbey: it doesn't necessarily mean I took vows.'

'Only those you writ down for yourself and none other!' Their jocularity carried across the choppy water,

II

The bow wave's spray plumed, shot through with rainbow lights from a desultory sun attempting to dig a way through gun-metal clouds as Byron steered down the eastern shoreline towards home. The clouds chased them, the wind carrying an humidity that made them sweat.

White caps, a million white hankies flung up, splashed as waves broke: they reassembled, the gathering multitude heralding greater threat.

'Byron,' Shelley shouted over the wind, 'I'm told astronomers and astrologers have seen mysterious patches on the sun through their telescopes. Tried to spot 'em myself but my 'scope isn't powerful enough. Seems they've announced the end of the world for the middle of June. Time is short; it's almost that now.' Levity smothered concern.

'I heard something.' Byron turned, a jaunty peaked cap keeping his hair in place. Shelley, he knew, would say nothing. 'Swiss almanacs predict a wet summer of winds, rainstorms, squalls and electrical storms in this region. We'd best prepare for war, Snake. Batten down the hatches, put up the shutters and make merry. What's the betting that Polly-Dolly locks himself in his room?'

'I don't doubt it. For him it won't be the storm without, rather the one within.'

Byron frowned. 'I don't understand.' Then it tumbled. 'Ah, you mean our baiting him?'

It would not be their baiting of the hapless doctor that would perpetuate the dread, rather a gathering of many and varied elements that would make the whitecaps on the lake appear as insignificant as wedding confetti.

Such possibilities would make Lord Byron grow cold.

CHAPTER 17

'Of a dark eye in woman'

I

The year is 1816. The month *is* June. Mother Nature is a woman amongst many.

The weather is changing: an unseasonable warm spring has turned cold, driven people indoors to escape the persistent rains that only serve to obscure the normally expressive mountains in fog.

It is the year Lord Byron's world will match the uncleared ashes in the Villa Diodati's fire grate; a year that will witness a major global disaster.

One year earlier, the eruption of Mount Tomboro in that collection of islands bordering the South China Sea, unleashed a vast quantity of volcanic dust. Taken high into the stratosphere, the dust reflected sunlight back into space. Earth darkened, temperatures plummeted –

The Devil walked.

If not, then his children did.

II

Lord Byron, seeing this as some indication of his own dark soul and his accompanying losses – wife, child, possessions and his valued reputation – sought to capture it through the 'reality of imagination'.

Due to the inclement weather, the Swiss authorities had ordered all boats into port, so after the sailing trip with Shelley, Byron locked himself in his room. Refusing all but the most meagre of food and drink and, at his request no alcohol, he remained there, penning the literal metaphor of 'Darkness'. Lines that mirrored not only his own bleaker nature, but that of many. Some of these lines he'd already spoken aloud, Claire Clairmont being the receptor, hearing their echoes in her dream.

> *'I had a dream, which was not all a dream,*
> *The bright sun was extinguish'd, and the stars*
> *Did wander darkling in the eternal space,*
> *Rayless, and pathless, and the icy earth*

Swung blind and blackening in the moonless air.

'...The pall of a past world; and then again
With curses cast them down upon the dust,
And gnash'd their teeth and howled: the wild birds shriek'd,
And, terrified, did flutter on the ground,
And flap their useless wings...

'...And they were enemies; they met beside
The dying embers of an altar place
Where had been heap'd a mass of holy things
For an unholy usage; they raked up
And shivering scraped with their cold skeleton hands
The feeble ashes, and their feeble breath
Blew for a little life, and made a flame...

'Two... died – saw and shriek'd, and died –
Even of their mutual hideousness they died.

'The moon their mistress had expired before;
The winds were withered in the stagnant air,
And the clouds perish'd; Darkness had no need
Of aid from them – She was the universe.'

Each line, each wretched syllable, was forced onto the page, his life outpoured in one litany: unfulfilled hopes, dreams, fears for the future of his soul, all scratched out in ink as black as the darkness of which he wrote.

He thought of Caroline Lamb, a relationship good in its way, yet one that failed to portray all his feelings at the time. Confused feelings that refused to grant him what he deserved.

Yes, he pondered, should have felt better about it than I did, felt more love for her. Couldn't last. Were you as bad as I, Caro, other admissions curtailing our need for one another? Not love, then; only sexual appeasement. I shamed you, made you dress as a boy.

'By my reprobate father, I am condemned by one dalliance after another,' Byron scorned. 'Total happiness is elusive. Do I trust in Mammon? Does money, or lack of it, govern my days? Money and power? I scarce accept that.

'God help me, I tried to live up to the image I held in my mind of you, Father. A distortion of ideals, a someone to look up to. You took that away!' His eyes blazed. 'Yet I still want to believe that had I really known you better, you would have taught me how to be a real lord.'

Lord Byron: *His Satanic Majesty.*

'Like you, Father? I miss you though I never knew you. I was never your son, yet I'll wager your love would have helped me steer a better course.'

Like you, Father? An echo. Hardly so. We are but men. I'm the one who courts delusions, a mortal who wanted only to be cared for, loved as a man should be, without fear or favour, needing only trust and real friendship that emerges from heart and mind.

The clouds hid the moon that governed tides ordered to lash the lake into a frenzied sea of uncertainty.

Two died? Byron pored over his verses, eyes sore through staring at the paper. The pen tilted, ink spattered, formed a blot so like a winged beast – a predator.

Snippets of conversation drifted, told of his own and Polidori's invocation of evil – talk of vampires and ghosts, promoted by his time at the Abbey; his cursed family traits, his marriage, of sorts, to the icicle, Annabella Milbanke, his *Princess of Parallelograms...*

'Why did I marry you, Annabella?' More thoughts intrude. Because you were available to me? I only thought I loved you. You were the challenge to perk up this monstrous ego of mine. Bell, I thought you were worth fighting for. How wrong can one be?

I flaunted our relationship. Two identical gold brooches, each displaying a lock of hair. 'Not easy to forget.' Augusta and I wore them, the initials **A** and **B** displayed along with three incised crosses on them. Bell, you couldn't know it was our own peculiar sign denoting our sexual consummation.

'Bell, my Bell,' he breathed, 'did you know some idiot chose to christen me the "Divine Marquis" because of my rumoured obsession with the writings of de Sade? *And* because some dried-up maid had listened at the keyhole, heard my threat to execute such ideas.

'How I played you and Augusta against each other.'

He thinks of the day when he lounged on the sofa. 'I ordered you both to embrace me, and had the gall to humiliate you in the most foul language.'

More sexual games: more upsetting memories...

Such things alienated Hobhouse, and him my truest friend. In innocence, he learned of my tyrannies, menaces, furies and neglects, aye even real injuries I caused. Bad enough as it stands, but I lied to Hobby. Who can blame him for finding it difficult to believe such outrageous deceit?

And the child, my own and Annabella's – Augusta Ada. Dear God, when she was shown to you, you said, 'Oh! What an implement of torture I have acquired in you!' He mimics Annabella, earlier mirth dissipated.

He scanned the papers before him, convinced the blank verses would promote self-destruction. 'My obsessions lead me to court demons of my own making. Away, shades, allow me peace!' He ran a hand across his forehead, the late hour coupled with the unrelenting need to work making his head pound with the insufferable knowledge of all things.

Moonlight eased through banked cloud, the light casting his image onto the opposite wall – a flimsy, ethereal thing that clung only by the skin of its... *teeth*?

This had a profound effect, Byron reflecting on...

Turkey. A dry, arid hell; the wearisome horseback ride to the ruins... things not merely to think about but to write down. For posterity?

'I wonder, am I happy on this earth?' He weighed the question. Turning to his shadow on the wall, he said: 'Yes. *And* no. My writings assist, although certain beliefs, certain loves... *sex*... do nothing to bring me peace.' The laugh sounded crazed. 'All those elite of society thought me eccentric, so I let 'em. How did the fools know I was being myself? They would never allow me to belong to their world.'

Scornful, he pictures the 'dog' who trails in his wake. 'Should you choose writing as a career, Polly-Dolly, I pray do not scourge yourself with ideas as I do. I both love, and loathe you, doctor; that you know.'

In a small quiet, his thoughts refused any reprieve. 'Annabella? I am not so sadistic, enraged often, but never to the limits of raising a fist. *I am not like my mother!*'

Denial then. For Byron, when accused, would become the epitome of goodness. He would sustain a plea of innocence, and project and use it as argument. 'I have never done an act that would bring me under the law – at least on this side of the Water.

'Best you go back to your icy friends, Annabella. I wonder, are you the epitome of an innocence you shrewdly deny me? Why did I ever write:

> My Heart -- We are thus far separated -- but after all one mile is as bad as a thousand -- which is a great consolation to one who must travel six hundred before he meets you again. ---- If it will give you any satisfaction -- I am as comfortless as a pilgrim with peas in his shoes -- and as cold as Charity -- Chastity or any other Virtue.

'The things we do–' Byron sighs. 'The things we do we feel are right at the time. Here it is, a life in words. Who will read the life of this lowly lord of words I wonder?'

His mind is captured by yet another letter written to Annabella in February before embarking on this journey.

> All I can say seems useless -- and all I could say -- might be no less unavailing -- yet I still cling to the wreck of my hopes -- before they sink forever. ---- Were you then never happy with me? -- did you never at any time or times express yourself so? -- have no marks of affection -- of the warmest & most reciprocal attachment passed between us? -- or did in fact hardly a day go down without some such on one side and generally on both? -- do not mistake me -- I have not denied my state of mind--but you know its causes -- & were those deviations from calmness never followed by acknowledgement & repentance? -- was not the last which occurred more particularly so? -- & had I not -- had we not -- the days before & on the day when we

173

parted reason to believe that we loved each other --
that we were to meet again -- were not your letters
kind? -- had I not acknowledged to you all my faults &
follies -- & assured you that some had not -- & would
not be repeated? -- I do not require these questions to
be answered to me -- but to your own heart. -- The day
before I received your father's letter -- I had fixed a
day for rejoining you -- if I did not write lately --
Augusta did -- and as you had been my proxy in
correspondence with her -- so did I imagine -- she
might be the same for me to you. --

Upon your letter to me -- this day -- I surely may
remark -- that its expressions imply a treatment which
I am incapable of inflicting -- & you of imputing to me
-- if aware of their latitude -- & the extent of the
inferences to be drawn from them. -- This is not just --
but I have no reproaches -- nor the wish to find cause
for them. ---- Will you see me? -- when & where you
please -- in whose presence you please: -- the
interview shall pledge you to nothing -- & I will say &
do nothing to agitate either -- it is torture to
correspond thus -- & there are things to be settled &
said which cannot be written. -- You say 'it is my
disposition to deem what I have worthless' -- did I
deem you so – did I ever so express myself to you -- or
of you -- to others? -- You are much changed within
these twenty days or you would never have thus
poisoned your own better feelings -- and trampled
upon mine.

Ever yrs. most truly & affectionately, B.

'And what good did it do, this outpouring of my soul to one so
utterly contemptuous in her thoughts of me?'

It is night again, another day passed in the spinning of the sun. Byron
lit the lamp, flaring patterns adopting a sense of the grotesque.
Aspects of life gather, form layered shadows, clouds build inside and
outside his distressed mind. Humour is extinct. By explicit order to
Fletcher, he will see no-one, not even Shelley. Certainly not the

174

revered doctor. How it is that his wit drips with caustic ability whenever he thinks of Polidori.

With his pen he scrawls haphazardly: "Alternating attraction and repulsion, thine went astray and that was rent in twain."

It is, like his heart, broken. The ensuing days will prove how prophetic the words are when he comes to realise the truth of his existence.

CHAPTER 18

'A sufferer for my sins.'

I

June 15th – a ragged day, minds and bodies racked with partying again the previous night.

Risking the incessant drizzle, they walked, Byron and Shelley following Claire and Mary, Polidori regaling the ladies with his stories of his trips into town.

Nothing whatsoever had been said about Byron's self-imposed incarceration, for none dare, not even Shelley, the true friend. Yet after their carousing, Byron emerged with a more defined, positive look about him. He glowed with the need to write, his limp not so pronounced, his humour returned.

Mary and Claire were yards ahead of and below the others as they carefully eased themselves down the treacherous sloping paths to reach Maison Chapuis where Mary had invited them to take tea.

Polidori dawdled, Byron and Shelley of the opinion that he waited for them. It was possible Mary had told him to wait, thinking to talk to Claire privately on some matter – to Byron such a matter was obvious.

II

It had nothing to do with Claire's need to net Byron. Mary had decided, without consulting Shelley, that it was none of her business. Not least, she was concerned over William. So easy to leave him to the attentive nurse, but Elise could never replace her as a mother. Anxious to see him, and chastising herself for her neglect – Byron's charm having persuaded her and Shelley to remain at the villa due to the inclement weather – she yearned for the simplistic life she'd hoped for when they moved here. A routine had soon ingratiated itself, again simple and frugal. They would rise early, often read aloud, play games with William, eat almost nothing and look forward to either sailing or rowing on the lake, whatever the weather. Shelley's launching balloons always pleased William, Mary happy to see him smile in wonder as they floated up and away. So much in common.

The late evenings took their toll, time generally given over to Byron and Shelley setting the world to rights by dipping and diving into their respective works, discussing politics and science, even the weather. Whatever they discussed it left Mary to her own devices, or to be bored to distraction by Polidori's attempts at conversation.

A little is enough, she declared. His assistance with Italian lessons did help and prompted Mary to add *Tasso* to her impressive reading list, Polidori's romantic overtures more than inferring his designs to her. But Mary, at eighteen, told Polidori: 'I see you as a younger brother. I like you well enough, but, my dear doctor, I love Shelley.'

He hadn't liked her honesty, but must accept it. At least he didn't sulk, not that she noticed.

Now, determined to have her way, she marched ahead, unaware her decision would be countered.

Contrary as always, Byron again suggested they take refreshments at the Villa where Fletcher, or Rushton could wait upon them. He qualified it by stating: 'You, dear Mary, should not be obliged to wait upon us; you are one who should be waited upon.'

He shouted to Polidori, 'John, help Mary. Escort her back to the villa. Go on, m'dear, prove your gallantry.'

Perturbed at being singled out again for ridicule, Polidori did take up the offer. Being the gallant, and seeking to score a few points with Mary, he leapt the stone wall to the lower level, hardly realising the drop was some eight feet. His aim went wildly awry and his feet skidded on the rain-slicked stone path. Falling heavily, his face reflected intense pain as he clutched his left ankle.

Shelley, about to laugh, decided against it when he glimpsed a concerned Byron's face, any hilarity absent.

Shocked by the accident, the two women hurried to the doctor's aid, as did Byron. He looked stricken, his hasty and paradoxical behaviour lost on Shelley.

Gently easing Mary and Claire aside, Byron picked up the doctor. 'Percy, please run on, have Fletcher prepare cold water compresses. Go on, don't dither.'

Shelley trotted up the path, care taken where he placed his own feet amidst the clutter of branches, moss and leaves.

Byron marched into Diodati's lounge, Polidori in his arms. Lying him on the sofa, he fetched more pillows for the doctor's head. He fussed, and supervised, ensuring the ankle was wrapped as tight as Polidori could stand it.

'My profound thanks, m'lord,' Polidori said. Along with the others, he confessed surprise at the sudden change in Byron.

If this were to be the precursor to a more moderate change in Byron, Polidori was wrong to think it. That evening it would be different.

FROM MIND TO REALITY

The die is cast, my friend, our hour draws near.

Mental strain, and past lives conjure things from the abyss. We have need only to wait a short while before imagination becomes reality.

The storm gathers: I drink of its power.

And you? What of you? Will you bring down the lightning? Urge it to ignite your dark soul?

You are prepared. Good.

Together we will dance with demons. Let them enter, torment and –

GIVE. US. LIFE.

CHAPTER 19

'Till they drop blind in blood'

I

They gathered. It was a question of who that mattered.

Polidori, in his own room, availed himself of the contents of his black bag. The corked bottle mocked from the table. Fully dressed, he lay on his bed and waited for the opium extract to take effect.

The place held a strangeness: the hiss of rain bouncing on the walkways, splashing in the pond, every sound amplified... even the whispers.

Perturbed, he sat up. The room spun, vibrated as the first clap of thunder clattered mightily, yellow lightning burning away shadows across an eternity of seconds.

Lines, features on the window's glass, in the hang of the drapes, in the patterns on the wall, even in the patina of his skin as he stared in wonderment and awe at his own hands. Each line – fate, life, heart – forging new, more intense designs in dilating pupils.

Still groggy he managed to reach the door, his sprained ankle threatening a tumble.

Polly-Dolly.

A whisper-shout, the sound as a breath of wind clattering the casement.

'Byron?'

A lull, nothing else heard, only rain beating on glass. Life forms appeared to shamble about the confines of the small room, his own startled face illuminated in another multi-coloured cascade of lightning.

A bear, wicked claws collecting the light, lumbered towards him: on the other side a wolf, fangs bared, dripped the venom of his own fear from threatening jaws as it stalked... And the dead rose all about him, a horse pounded a skull into powder, Polidori's outflung arms trying to batter everything he saw into extinction. Not easy when life is already extinct.

A pile of bones took shape, formed the skeleton – a framework upon which to build. And build he did: as a doctor he found himself obliged to, placing each bone in order – tibia, fibula, femur, pelvis... On and on until he came to the skull, with its vestige of the living. Flesh formed, the dermis, the epidermis, all grey clay, pasty, sallow looking, and yet... yet the eyes gleamed from that rapacious face and... 'Oh my God, the teeth!'

'Vampires.' Some *thing* resembling Byron, yet Polidori retained enough sense to know it couldn't be. It turned towards him.

'Know that I have an aversion to such creatures and therefore insist they keep their own counsel, aye and their disturbing secrets.'

Byron's words scuttled back and forth.

'It may be that I know and have seen too much – This is the end of my journey, and of my life; I came here to die...'

Polidori cursed his habit, and himself for ever allowing it to become the craving it had. Imbibing the draught must be a warning.

'No more. NO MORE! It isn't you, Byron, you would never taunt me so.'

Pain flared up his leg, the ankle swollen, a threat. Polidori sat in a chair and registered the fact that maybe he was Byron, and that Byron had become him. Fantasy. And desire. A double-sided window, one clear, the other opaque, presenting images too frightening to contemplate.

Crowding thoughts went back, far, far back beyond childhood, beyond the womb, to the extensions of the universe where creatures of the night lurked, waiting their time to be born. And all... *all* balanced on the lip of a bottle that promised beautiful dreams.

Polidori grabbed the bottle and threw it at the wall. He watched it spin, lightning collecting it like... like a slowly floating balloon... taking it gradually, slowly to the wall, the explosion of its bursting dulled, thrown into mute insignificance as the thunder voiced its opinion. And there, flying, floating, a million tiny fragments of refracted light... like segments of torn paper scattered... The liquid showered out in a vast plume of multi-coloured nightmare, each droplet a demon, wings outstretched, fighting for control in the turgid, ozone-fresh air, each howling to be let in... to share their games, show him, all of them, the truth about themselves.

'Pavido fortique cadendum est!'

Polidori called out the Latin phrase, remembering it as something his father had quoted back in the doctor's formative years.

He scrabbled for the door handle, anxious to escape this claustrophobia, the words tied to the storm's tumult – "The coward and the courageous alike must die."

II

Claire Clairmont died a little, her dreams of a world of riches and refinement dashed.

'Is the brat mine?'

The echo made her heart ache; her eyes bled their own tears. 'How dare he say that to me? ME?'

Easy to forget entrapment. Am I really no worse, or better, than a Haymarket whore?

Had she known what he had written to Augusta, words to the effect that he was not in love... "but could not exactly play the stoic with a woman who had scrambled eight hundred miles to unphilosophise me", Claire would have considered her position more intently.

She was perhaps right with her acid comment at dinner the other night, for to know Lord Byron *is* to know a devil.

And what, pray, happened? Laughing, she had accompanied him to his room, yet afterwards...? She saw herself leaning naked over the balcony rail, rising to answer the pleasure-pain of being taken and yet... Yet Byron denied any part of it. 'Was it –' she uttered, shocked beyond reason – 'was it all in my mind?'

The disturbing realisation forced her legs to give way. She fell on the bed, determining whether or not to face him, question it. 'He... he toyed with my mind. Did he feed me... drugs?'

She couldn't recall drinking anything more following the meal, only wine, and she'd drowned herself in that.

'I can't. Won't go!' Claire was bereft. To venture downstairs, join the others, knowing he would be there lauding it, proved too much. Common sense dictated she remain in the room ... alone with her terrible thoughts, her rejection. The decision was not easy.

'He is bored with me.' It became fresh torture. 'And I am foolish enough to allow my besotted state to promote further mistakes.'

In the sullen quiet between the rolls of thunder, she determined to continue to help him in copying out his poems. She had promised, and even if he reneged on other promises made, Claire decided that she would not.

Obsession. Possession. Whatever term she used, she would at least be with him, near him, learn of his soul's plight through those writings. And she would still nurse the fact that her own hardly sophisticated worship tired him.

For a woman with her head full of Shelley's free-love lectures and Mary's views on the rights of women, Claire argued her position, and its impossible solution.

Instead of being a new woman... a fighter for women's rights, and independent, she had curtailed her own ambitions by being too... 'Too *possessive.*' More tears squeezed out, Claire striking at them in self-confessed anger, wiping them away with her hand. 'Why make myself dependent on a man who has never loved me?'

Like Polidori, Claire jumped, as blue, almost supernatural light illuminated the room, her heart palpitating at every driven drop of rain, every thunderous beat of Thor's hammer.

God's lightning ignited the room in intermittent jabs, and made a hideous mask of her sorrowful face.

What had Byron said to her, proposed to her before he'd shut himself away after his browbeating words out there in the garden? Only suggested that the child, when born, should be placed in Augusta's care. That *half*-sister who had made her own intentions towards Byron quite clear. Claire pictured them together, hidden away, doing... doing... 'Oh God!' She felt nauseous.

'No child of mine will ever be brought up in such an environment,' she told him, ensuring he caught each nuance as intended. Thankfully he'd agreed to her suggestion that the child – boy or girl – should stay with one or other of its parents until it reached the age of seven.

'I bow to that, madam,' Byron told her, 'but insist it would be best if the child stayed with me and you pass yourself off as its aunt.'

About to argue with him, she'd allowed him the benefit of the doubt and listened further to what he had to say.

'I only suggest it, in order that you may preserve your reputation.' Ever the gentleman.

'And what pray, is my reputation?' she asked herself, not having asked him. Loneliness of a type she had never felt before surged in. 'Am I so scorned because I thought only to love?'

The storm drowned fresh crying, the pillow wet with tears as she buried her face in it.

Claire fortunately didn't realise that on the twenty-ninth of August, she would depart this region, her bitter disappointment when Byron would not spare time to see her, or give her a parting kiss, merely another nail in the box within which she placed her own set of distorted ideals.

III

Mary and Shelley argued, naturally about Lord Byron, Mary angered at the amount of time Shelley spent with him in deep-rooted conversation.

'You leave me with... with that doctor,' she said loudly. 'I am sure he means well, but I grow sick of his fawning.' The appeal sat there like a half-opened book. He remained unprovoked by it. 'Shelley, you must understand *my* needs.'

The two had not yet braved the slippery path to the villa, an earlier walk having resulted in them both getting wet from a sudden, unannounced shower. Daylight had waned swiftly, the new storm disturbing Mary's sought-after tranquillity.

She looked about the small room at Chapuis, the house hardly grand enough when compared to the vastness of Diodati. To Mary, it didn't matter: by being here with Shelley and William, it ensured Shelley's being attentive.

In castigating herself for ever blaming Shelley, it made her realise what a foul, degenerative sin jealousy is. Conversely, without it, would true love of the type she felt for Shelley, be strong enough to rise above its somewhat tenuous foundations?

Perched on the edge of a hard chair, she suffered the discomfort, arguing it made her more determined to place her metaphorical cards on the pine table.

An aroma of polish over-rode the damp odours from curtains soaked by rain before Shelley, at her insistence, closed the window. She'd warmed to the sounds from above, of Louise Duvillard, 'Elise' – putting William to bed. Normally, Mary loved this part of the day, yet certain omens prevailed, Mary made more unsettled not knowing why. Nor could she determine exactly when it started. From being exuberant about finding this haven, her sense of well-being had been sorely tried, not least by Shelley's indifference to her needs,

They hadn't yet lit the lamps, the room and the small hallway off thrown into semi-translucent shades. She studied him as he sprawled in a similar chair turned out from the table. Preoccupied, his brow seemed darker in the subdued light.

'Shelley,' Mary said quietly, 'are you listening to me? I often wonder if you prefer Lord Byron's company to my own.'

His head came up. 'Prefer –? My heart, no! I regret you're having a need to infer such a thing.'

'Then why must I be treated as a third party, hardly ever invited to offer my own views? You and he are so... so enamoured with each other, I –'

The chair legs squeaked on the uncarpeted floor as Shelley stood. 'Enamoured? A strange choice of word, my love. Captured by, even enthralled by what he has to say, is more apt. He has helped me, Mary, is interested in my views. No, definitely not enamoured, for that implies love.'

Shelley paced as much as the confines allowed. 'You should understand, Mary, there are varying kinds of love, mine is the love of one friend for another, and only that.'

He hadn't come near her, the table a barrier between them. 'Mary, whenever you are offered the opportunity to say something you appear tongue-tied and unable to express a single thought.'

Mary jumped to her feet and leaned towards him across the table, her stance importing anger and possibly frustration that Shelley could be so... so pigheaded in not seeing her point. 'Shelley, I am in love with you yet you neglect me. What else can I say? You're forever walking with Byron in the hills, talking with him on Diodati's veranda, or sailing with him on the lake. And sometimes... sometimes I am more at a loss when you seem to take greater interest in Claire's predicament than mine.'

Shelley looked genuinely pained. As a wounded animal will seek to hide, he searched for a place to go, but there was nowhere. Mary believed that had Byron been present, they would probably have gone for another walk, or a sail, irrespective of the choppy, dangerous waters out there.

They parallel the turbulence in here, she thought. And all around us.

Retiring gracefully, he looked out of the window onto a high wall smothered with wind-blown trailing vines.

Sighing, Mary said, 'Dear Shelley, I have spoken out of jealousy. I shouldn't resent Claire but she is the bane of my life without exaggeration. Think how we two used to enjoy ourselves.' Anger intruded. 'Will we ever be rid of her? Get our lives back?'

Mary sat again, her animated fingers stroking the table top, drumming impatiently.

'And now,' she said, anxious to lay bare all her misgivings, 'Lord Byron rejects her and she expects *us* to contend with it.'

'What do you mean?' Shelley turned from the window, his innocent eyes prompting an answer.

'You know what I mean, Percy! That not so pure maid is now transferring *all* her affections to you. Yes you, Shelley, her chief confidant and... friend.' The emphasis chewed at Shelley. 'And here am I expected to sit quietly and bear it. Well no more. *No. More.* I feel there is a depth and durability between you and Claire that I, nor even Byron, can surmount.'

Unknown to her at this time, her accusations would prove well-founded when Byron would confess to another that when speaking of Allegra, his so-called natural daughter by Claire, he would state, "She is no child of mine. She is Mr Shelley's child."

For now Mary must content herself with provoking Shelley into emphatic denial, or a confession.

Is it the price of love? Could anyone tell her? It is part of life – live life and discover, for who is versatile enough to explore the fickle tributaries of the human heart?

'I think I have much in common with Lord Byron,' she said.

'How so?' Shelley hedged, trying to avoiding answering her earlier, veiled accusation.

'Oh Shelley.' Mary's eyes grew softer. 'Is it so hard to see? What I've said, declared my love to you and yet it seems Byron and I still need to find love.

'Do you think for one minute he enjoys these endless, ill-matched affairs? Yes, I believe you do, for man thinks with his loins, not his mind. You have a quick, agile mind, and should therefore consider – free love aside – just what one person can mean to another.'

Again avoiding a direct answer, Shelley argued, 'Mary, whilst Byron and I are so ensconced in our various tête-à-têtes, you accompany Polidori. I have seen you walking with him down isolated paths, or rowing by moonlight on the lake. And, plague upon you, the man plays the role of doctor and sometime baby-sitter to William.'

'What else am I to do?' Mary retaliated. 'You are so... so obstinate. Sit and read all the time? Walk by myself? That is what you would have me do while you do as you please. You should know I am my own woman, with a mind of my own.'

'Oh yes,' Shelley said, boyish face suddenly more adult. 'I'm forgetting you are the daughter of the famous Mary Wollstonecraft and the *immortal* Godwin.'

Impasse.

No matter how much they talked – argued – Mary was sure she would never make him realise. Do I blame my own youth? At eighteen, I am not yet skilled in the ways of the world, or relationships. Perhaps I am infatuated with the idea of love.

She conjured the idea of creation – more precisely: who creates love? And then who creates man to love? And from that, an idea of creating the perfect man, a mechanical man who would do her bidding whenever she wished.

Mary glanced at the small clock standing on the armoire, her mind divorced from the vagaries of her argument and transported to Neuchâtel and its surrounding villages, during their last tour. An area renowned for its clockmakers, she, with Shelley, went to see the mechanical man – built by some unnamed person who had presumably been struck by a series of analogies between the mechanisms of the human body and the intricacies of the clock.

Extraordinary skill and inventiveness were displayed in these 'human' machines – they could write, draw, play music and perform various other chores, some of them appearing very human.

The small, human android gave way to the stoop of Shelley sitting at the table and looking at his boots rather than anywhere else.

Mary's notion of changing life to suit was instantly terminated by a thunderous knock on the door.

Elise's head bobbed around the door jamb. 'I will answer,' she offered in passable English.

A flurry of rain and wet leaves spoiled the polished floor when Elise opened the door to admit Fletcher. He looked bedraggled, and was conscious of his muddy boots further marring the floor.

'Madam, sir,' he said, 'Lord Byron wishes to know if you will be attending tonight?'

Mary and Shelley looked at each other. 'I am coming.' Shelley didn't take his eyes off Mary, daring her to deny him that right.

In view of everything, Mary preferred not to be left here alone.

'Elise,' she said, 'I presume you will attend to William?'

'Mais oui, madame.' Elise smiled. 'I like nothing better than to look after him. It is a pleasure.'

'Fletcher, please inform Lord Byron that we will be there directly,' Mary said.

'If it please you, ma'am, I am to escort you and Mr Shelley to the villa. The path is dark and slippy with the storm an' all.'

'Very civil of you. And Lord Byron.' Mary stood. 'Elise, my cloak with the hood please.' To Fletcher, and ignoring Shelley, she said, 'I shall walk with you.'

GIVE LIFE

'How they undermine themselves,' he said to the one who could not yet speak. 'Listen to them with their petty jealousies, each determined to outwit the other.

'Ah, if only they realised that beyond the human frailties of the mind there lurks something far more profound.

'Let the storms rage... let the lightning's power bring down a more restorative vengeance upon the heads of an unsuspecting world.

'Others will come, take up the threads of our existence and promote them. For now we must remain patient for they will give us LIFE in order to promote their own weak existence.'

CHAPTER 20

'...so besmear'd with blood and dust.'

I

'The alchemist Dippel puts forward some interesting insight into the discovery of the "principle of life".'

On her way to the villa, reliant on the saving arm of George Fletcher to prevent her falling, Mary made up her mind that she would voice a few opinions. Dependent upon how the conversation went, she wanted to show that her formative years had not been wasted through lack of education.

The remains of a roast chicken supper were cleared away by Rushton, who avoided Byron in the event he may be drawn into the conversation.

Byron did no such thing, allowing the young man to go about his business. With only the three of them to clear away for, Polidori and Miss Clairmont still in their rooms, Rushton paused only to say: 'Cold cuts will be put by for your other guests, m'lord.'

'Thank you, Robbie.' Byron and Shelley – distanced by an expanse of table – were pleasantly surprised by the contribution from Mary. Byron more than Shelley, the latter irked because Mary had dared treat him as she had, Shelley blaming both climate and absence from her father as being contributions to her boldness.

Small talk had preceded Mary's comment about Dippel, along with vague references to Polidori's tumble, anecdotes about the lake trip, future ones curtailed by the weather. The chatter did little to ease the obvious discomfort Byron detected between his two guests.

Byron coughed to break the strained atmosphere. 'Did either of you give any consideration to my, er, offer t'other night regarding individual lives, how our way of living affects us?'

Sipping port wine after enjoying a rare cheese made in the area, Mary mellowed. The room's ambience, its richness, contributing to her growing feeling of well-being, further promoted because she did not have to tolerate Claire's morose *visage*.

Following his remark, she confessed to Byron that this was perhaps her intention. 'During our tour in 1814,' she said, 'Shelley

190

and I forged a fascination for the history and folk-lore of the places we visited.'

Byron toyed with the stem of a wine glass, his demeanour uplifted by Mary's willingness to talk. 'Konrad Dippel, a German. I've heard of, and read about him. Go on, Mary, it's good to hear your opinion. Pleased you wish to join in our discourse on the birth of man.'

'Yes, Mary,' Shelley interrupted, a touch condescendingly, 'do enlighten Lord Byron as to how your own imagination functions ' He poured himself wine, the white rather than depressive red. Like Polidori when they last congregated, Shelley felt distanced by something he perhaps feared.

Night: the time of night – a time when he would contemplate his own jottings, and the workings of his mind. How the dark hours would either promote ideas, or scare him because of their complexities.

The fire crackled: lightning... *crackled.*

'We were aboard ship – do you remember Shelley?' She tried to include him, his blasé attitude close to making her want to scream. 'Of course you do. We met three German travellers, Hoff was one, I forget the others, all students of the University of Strasbourg–'

'I remember, Mary.' Claire's voice floated across the room. She stood at the door, her black dress lending an impression of mourning, her sallow complexion hardly enhanced by use of rouge.

Mary looked up, and supposed her sister may be grieving for a love now lost, her own white gown, hem mud spattered from the walk, in sharp contrast to Claire's.

Claire came over, Shelley, ever attentive, such attention not gone unnoticed by Mary, leapt to his feet and pulled out a chair.

Claire acknowledged it. 'I shall take some wine–' She looked at Byron. 'With your permission, my lord.' She sat.

'Drink as you will, Miss Clairmont, it is of no consequence.'

And here they were: two couples, each at loggerheads with their respective partners, neither one admitting to having committed a sin in the eyes of God. Yet not to Shelley's thinking for he sought no god but the one hidden deep within himself.

'We smoked, drank ourselves silly, and laughed a lot,' said Claire. 'No difference really, except hilarity appears absent tonight.' She savoured her drink. 'One of 'em mentioned the name Dippel... alchemist, necromancer, some such thing. Oh and a theologian who thought he'd discovered the principle of life.'

'Mary was just saying–'

'My lord, I heard,' said Claire. 'I wasn't eavesdropping you understand. I have exceptionally acute hearing and when not rendered deaf by the appalling thunder, I find it helps to pick up on conversations and not feel out of it!'

Byron smarted a little, his smile, countering his discomfort.

'Shelley, you read out some of my notes to them as I remember,' Mary offered, slightly uncomfortable herself that Claire had chosen this moment to interrupt.

'I did, for what they were worth.'

Byron, sick of this, said quite rudely, 'Is it necessary to have to bear these petty squabbles? Differences can be aired in private, not at the dinner table.'

'You're a fine one to suggest that, George,' Claire said caustically, the second glass of wine distilling her pallor, evidenced by the colour of her prominent nose. 'You are the one who started it.'

'My apologies, m'lord.' Mary left the chair upon which she'd been seated, situated midway between Byron and Shelley to sit closer to Byron. 'It is true, Shelley and I did have words and it's remiss of us in bringing them to your table. We should keep the conversation lighter, not allow personal differences to mar the evening.'

'You sound like a schoolteacher, Mary.' Claire gave a lopsided smirk, the movement comical. With hair in disarray, her own fastidiousness concerning dress and deportment was lacking tonight.

'You should learn from it, Claire.' Mary sounded determined. 'My writings told of my fascination for the Promethean fire stolen from heaven "to give life, not animation to the inert clay".'

'Not surprisingly,' Shelley said, 'this Dippel had a series of, er, misadventures, while attempting to sell his outlandish alchemical craft. Not unlike you, Mary, though hardly in the alchemical sense. I suggest that you did rather flaunt yourself in a peculiar way.'

'Blame it on exuberance, Percy,' she said. 'Our desire to make an impression. Two years ago, we were younger, influenced by what we saw and experienced. Being more adult affords us additional common sense. Some of us that is.' She glanced at Claire, who ran her finger round the rim of her glass.

Sensing another argument, Byron said: 'I'm captivated by Prometheus.' He offered his profile, though not deliberately. 'Another Greek god,' Inspired himself, he went on, 'Interestingly, his fame was due to his affection for mankind... A touch me I think, for I, too, have given the earth some fire now and again.' His laugh bordered on bawdy. 'Another tale, eh?' He chuckled again.

Unfortunately, no-one joined in and the laugh wavered when Claire enquired, 'Where is Doctor Polidori?'

'Seeking an ally, m'dear?' Byron said. 'Who cares where he is? Probably bringing down his own fire – from a bottle.' More seriously, he added, 'And out of the flaming forge came weapons of war, added to which all the miseries that follow the disruption of a simple way of life.'

He made no further reference and drank his wine, determined not to get drunk. 'Mary, tell me more about alchemy, it intrigues me.'

'Ideas, my lord, simply ideas, and an inquiring mind.'

'Seeking what?'

'The secret of life.' Mary looked intense, this look influencing Byron's answer.

'For to know that would perhaps reveal the secrets of the heart.'

'And for whom does yours beat, my lord?' Claire waited, refused to be melted by his scathing glance.

Surprisingly, rather than being angry, he said, 'I know not, for I haven't found her yet.'

'Or him,' Claire said brazenly, unable to prevent bitter thoughts surfacing, or uncover perhaps the underlying reason behind Byron's rejection of her.

'Claire,' Mary interrupted, 'it is not for any of us to be so outrageously outspoken.'

'Then forgive my offending your susceptibilities, sister.' Claire slurped more wine. 'I suggest truth is better out than in.' Her guffaw gave substance to innocently spoken innuendo.

Byron had been right: they did want a piece of him. 'Madam–' His stare forced Claire to flinch. 'Madam, since your *joke* is obviously shared by us all, I would emphasise that *the reality was endured by you last night!'* He stood and limped to the fireplace, hypnotised by the glowing embers. He collected a log and threw it on, its dampness hissing as flames licked around it, the sound a marvellous precursor to what he would say next. Scowling, he ventured, 'And you enjoyed it! Your ecstatic screams were enough to awaken the dead.'

He looked around the room. 'Pray, don't be embarrassed, for you know my reputation. Aye, and who knows what we may awaken from our nefarious lives tonight, or tomorrow night... Or however long we keep up this charade of *marvellous* living.

'All are gathered here, enclosed by the dark, the storm and the enmity we nurture inside ourselves. I ask again, who will reveal their innermost soul?'

None spoke, thoughts intruded upon by the hissing fire.

'Come, all of you, up from the table and be comfortable, these easy chairs are not here just t'look pretty.'

Byron stiffened, he looked towards the door, left ajar. Polidori, not altogether sure of a welcome, stood there.

'Well doctor, you have chosen to rise from your pit and join us,' called Byron. 'I note you have a sheaf of papers tucked under your arm. We were discussing the alchemist, Dippel before you arrived.' Byron beckoned. 'Come, bring your surly self in here. Sit and entertain us.'

II

From what had already been experienced in these multifarious relationships, emotions ran high, the climate inside a match for the inclement weather outside.

To divide the two households, and so divide the two classes of citizens, it is a fact that the demigods, Byron and Shelley, occupied centre stage, Byron more so than the younger man, for he held three aces to Shelley's one. With their heads in the clouds like one of Shelley's balloons, the duo held court whilst the lesser mortals, Mary, Claire and Polidori, spent their time weighing each word in an almost begrudging, silent adulation. Irrespective of their own opinions, they could not argue that the poets had reason to feel elevated.

They listened. Mary – having had her say over certain matters – chose the right of every woman to alter her opinion. In London, at her first meeting with Byron, she'd taken him at face value – a handsome dandy who had a way with words. Over the past weeks, however, she found herself in awe of his more wayward, sometimes insulting behaviour. Yet, in a way, it prompted her own need to be more outspoken than perhaps she would have been. After all, they were all friends – but then there are so many definitions of the word. For now, she would keep silent and listen.

Byron looked intrigued by the folder Polidori carried.

'It's about Dippel. A coincidence I daresay,' said Polidori, pleased interest had been shown. 'And one I–' He offered a rueful smirk. 'Actually a play I wrung out of myself in the small hours when I couldn't sleep.'

'A play, eh? You must read it to us.'

'Happy to.' Polidori seated himself by the fire. 'It is entitled "Cajetan". The name derives from one of Dippel's contemporary alchemists in Berlin, as well as a version of my own father's Italian name, Gaetano.' He looked at the others. 'You wish me to begin?'

'We do,' said Byron, head resting on the chair back, eyes closed.

Claire sat with Shelley on a silk covered settee, Mary occupying a third, comfortable easy chair. Firelight flared up the walls, the Promethean analogy gaining ground as it spoke to them in different tongues, Polidori's recital – for he was no great reader – falling into a sleep-rendering monotone.

It wasn't the fact that most of this captive audience were drowsy through wine, or their inability to listen that upset Polidori, rather it was Byron's low titter – at least it started off as such, gradually climbing, its infectiousness causing Shelley to join in.

'God in His Heaven, Polly,' laughed Byron, wiping away amused tears, 'whatever induced such drivel? Did you indulge in a sip of Black Drop before you took up the pen?'

'He might have dipped the pen in it,' said Shelley, rocking forward, his own amusement transmitted to the otherwise seriously irritated Polidori.

'I think it's rather good,' Claire said, offering her condolences, ashamed the others should treat it thus.

The comment brought fresh hilarity from Byron and Shelley, Mary agreeing with Claire that they should not be so cruel.

'Words like that... dialogue like that,' Byron said, sarcasm dripping, 'should be condemned. Tell me, Polly, *dost thou* ever read Shakespeare, or Milton? Keats perhaps? ME? Take lessons, doctor, ere your words overlap your mouth and grow so big you can't control 'em.'

Humiliated, Polidori quickly gathered the papers and made to leave.

'Polly, don't be too offended, I've heard worse lines when I was on the committee of the Drury Lane Theatre.'

It poured more oil on already troubled waters.

Polidori felt like a single palm tree on an island buffeted by a hurricane, his defiance bending beneath the onslaught, given over to embarrassment shared by Mary and Claire, but not Shelley. 'I... I...' Polidori stammered, finally blurting: 'Having delivered my play into your hands, I am forced to hear it laughed at!' He turned abruptly and stormed out of the room, his hurried steps resounding with his anger.

Byron stared after him. He sat forward. 'Shelley, why does he behave like a child? Can't he take a joke?'

Shelley could not answer for laughing, corridors and rooms resounding with vitriolic humour, assaulting Polidori as he half walked, half ran to his room.

The door slam effectively cut off the laughter as multitudes of ugly shapes assembled over the Villa Diodati and its occupants.

'Where I alone stand, so shall ye all stand.' Byron had made it up, the words no doubt being personal to him, the others unable to define what he meant.

Something seeded within Byron; tendrils snaked through him whispering, "Beware". For Lord Byron grew afraid that what would be sowed here would herald a time of wilderness wandering, his writings rejected, aims unfulfilled. For is it not true, he reflected, that each man will reap what he sows?

His grin turned sour as he mused on what Shelley might say to the often quoted biblical passage. He being an atheist!

And no prayer could ever put this night's party together again.

Bad weather made it impossible for any walk back to Chapuis, Mary, Shelley and Claire retiring to their allotted rooms upstairs.

III

Something is here, wanting, always wanting.

Byron thrashed on his bed. Fully dressed, apart from his jacket, his clothes creased, he sweated, each breath a burst of heat in the humid, storm-wracked confines of the bedchamber.

Terrified of the future, of facing his peers and admitting to failure, his mind screamed: NOTHING HERE! Equally it contradicted, intent on proving him wrong. *There is! THERE. IS!*

What are you frightened of, my lord? Did Gussie ask that? Or Lucy? Maybe Patrick. *What are you scared of, Father?* Mad Jack? The idea of being penniless with nowhere to wander?

Question. Answer. One answer prompting another question. Never ending.

Life's oppressiveness follows me everywhere, without respite, each day a living year of echoes and recrimination.

A low chuckle in the early hours, the whole of the villa in repose, Mary and Shelley away in their room, no Claire attached like an embryo who refused to cut the cord that united them body and soul.

Body. And. Soul.

There must be a way out. Dream-thoughts assailed him, their own embryonic grip far greater than ever Claire's could be, on him, or her half-sister. These thoughts Byron had carried all the days of his life. Humiliation; elation; repatriation; expulsion and, in the future, retribution. And again, repatriation.

Heart, beat... Keep me alive. Do not be torn for want of love. Be not destroyed.

An image of a grey horse, a dark rider; a blot of shadow – perhaps the image of... a dog? – in a wasteland of mud, a calm sea

breaking on a flat, wind-swept shoreline, dirty, grey-white buildings.
A church.

Projected thoughts? Or real?

He reared up, one hand clutched to his chest seeking the beat of life, proof he was alive.

The room became a living thing, early dawn's wavering changes of light creating patterns. Beyond the window, grey-white mist curled about the trees like a host of ghost dancers who cavorted across the slopes and the barely discernible lake, this stretch of water so like another lake in another time, similar spectres having him to dance to their tune.

'There is a power here,' he breathed. 'A power greater than all of us. None may control it, we haven't the strength.'

Byron pressed himself to the wall, and pulled away, afraid the fabric of the house might draw him in, just as he had thought it would in the lonely, vaulted rooms of Newstead. Unseen forces ingratiated themselves, rendering him powerless; different voices called, reminding him of what had been said, written – words of life and death, remembered, forgotten. Good. Evil. Spirits tapping without, waiting to be let in.

He should be afraid, for the evil outweighed the good, and dictated he see this journey through to the bitter end – whatever it may be.

Byron had little option but to do as dictated, and attempt to rise above petty jealousies conspicuous amongst them all. In this he included himself.

"I suoi pensieri in lui dormir non ponno."

A line he used in his introduction to *The Corsair*, courtesy of his favourite poet, Tasso.

He speaks aloud, 'Within him his thoughts cannot sleep.' He knows it is true.

CHAPTER 21

'Behold – but who hath seen, or e'er shall see,
Man as himself – the secret spirit free?'

I

The second night, following a day of rising late and returning to Elise and their child, the pathetic humour of yesterday best forgotten, the Shelley party – drawn by Diodati's magnetism, as well as their own compulsions and sensitivities – were invited to stay, the ever present torrential rain making any return to Chapuis out of the question.

Talk tonight centred on Percy Shelley's own scientific dabbling. Firelight tinted the immediate seating area, orange-red hues, as Mary suggested, associated with Christmas cheer. Numerous candles and oil lamps contributed their own allure, the ever-present shadows casually scaling walls to spill across the ceiling.

Polidori, though present, his injured foot resting on a stool, smouldered from yesterday's harsh criticism and languished in a corner to the right of the fireplace. By observing, listening, he hoped to draw conclusions from the madness aggravated by weeks of stimulating, sometimes unruly behaviour and comment from the others.

A soberness, extraordinary given previous excesses, permeated the company, each of the five waiting on Shelley.

Fletcher set a tray of fine china cups, saucers, matching teapot and other necessities, on a highly polished occasional table whose Queen Anne legs complemented the dining furniture.

'Thank you, Fletcher.' Mary smiled as he withdrew.

Fletcher turned. 'Will that be all, m'lord?'

'Yes, George, off with you, put your feet up.'

Dressed in a pair of loose fitting black trousers and a charcoal coloured velvet jacket over an open collared white shirt, Byron was the eponymous true lord as he posed by the fire, any trace of his tortuous night evident only in the darker lines beneath his ever-alert eyes.

Shelley's casual appearance overdid the *casual*, his own grey trousers creased. His neckerchief, far from precise, dangled about his neck like an afterthought. He looked preoccupied.

Mary poured the tea and handed Byron a cup. 'Black for you I think.'

'How astute, Mary.' Byron took the cup and placed it on the mantle. Steam curled from it before being sucked up the chimney. More ghosts.

Refreshments served, Claire sipped her own drink. She sat on the edge of her chair by Polidori, while Mary sat with Shelley. 'You were about to tell us of your interests in alchemy, though I'm surprised you embarked on such a course.'

Byron sat opposite Polidori, the substantial distance between them across the hearth underlining their feelings towards each other.

Shelley, in placing his cup on the floor, winced, hoping Mary would not detect anything wrong. His hand trembled, a nervous spasm, blamed on his worrying over what Mary had said last night. He'd secretly resorted to laudanum again, not wishing Mary to know.

A look passed between him and Byron, the latter's hardly perceptible nod giving nothing away. Shelley, to ease his own conscience, had told Byron of his infrequent need for its medicinal qualities.

II

Days ago, purely reciprocal, Shelley offered Byron a potted history of his life, not least that part of it immediately after his expulsion from Oxford when he married Harriet Westbrook.

'She was the youngest daughter of a coffee-house owner. Bless her, she brought money for me from my sisters. Penniless in London is not exactly the thing to be.'

'It is a predicament with which I am well acquainted,' Byron tells him.

'My father disowned me,' Shelley says.

'You're lucky you had a father to disown you. I never knew mine.'

'Is that so bad? Better not to know one, than realise the one you have is a miserly, miserable excuse.'

'Tell me about Harriet, the way you expound her virtues she sounds like a goddess.'

'Hogg, a friend of mine, said words to that effect. "Lovely, bright, blooming and radiant with youth, health and beauty."'

'Virtues indeed,' Byron agrees. 'Can such a woman truly exist?'

'I believed so then. Only a mere schoolgirl when we married, I think out of obligation because she didn't wish to return to school. They taunted her for being the friend of an atheist.'

Byron sees the humour in this. 'We all suffer for our beliefs, m'dear.' Humour aside, his face reflects his own suffering.

'Harriet was naive,' Shelley goes on, 'yet our marriage was, to the greater degree, blissful. She was gentle and faithful.'

'So are dogs, my friend.' Byron's remark draws a look from Shelley.

'I think I said the other day, that your involvement with the ladies can hardly have rendered you so devoid of feeling that you entertain such an observation. You pre-judge.'

'Then prove otherwise.' Byron casts the gauntlet. 'Make me believe your love for Harriet overcame all else. If that be so, then why are you here with Mary?'

Shelley stares off into the distance. 'Harriet. An arduous task, I fear.'

From where they sit in the garden overlooking the lake, this vast expanse of world that confronts Shelley conspires to make him realise that an empty, unfulfilled life may be all he has facing him.

To be like Byron, write like Byron, might be a wish-fulfilment he has promptly set aside. Yet he knows Byron is correct, that relationships can, and do, dip from love, to doubt, to separation.

'After Ianthe's birth, our marriage began to disintegrate. I blame the overbearing and constant attendance of Harriet's older sister, Eliza.'

'A strange situation, with a curious parallel, Shelley. I'm sure it's occurred to you that Claire reflects this. Like a poem written twice. If you cannot achieve a certain rhythm with the first, try it with another version.'

'You make the most pertinent analogies, Byron.'

'No, my friend, life does.'

Shelley can't disagree. 'I despised Eliza, and came to despise Harriet's increasingly extravagant material demands. I wonder, how can materialistic value ever overcome a true and lasting relationship?'

'Because love dies, Shelley. We fall in and out of love in order to feed our own selfish desires. Reasons, man, we always seek a reason, no matter how infinitesimal, we build upon it and thus manufacture a basis for ending an affair, a marriage, call it as you will.'

'By the time I met Mary, my marriage to Harriet was beyond salvation. Oh I made repeated bids for a reconciliation but Harriet removed herself to Bath. With her completely alienated, I began to doubt she'd ever loved me.'

'As you intimated, Snake, you were a convenience. She sought to bask in your growing fame, and because fame does not come overnight, she tired of your frustrating efforts to make it so.'

'I won't argue. Following the separation I began to suffer from spasms of nervous pain, relieved by doses of laudanum.'

'Not all answers repose in a bottle, friend, be it laudanum, opium or brandy. They simply divert what we must inevitably face.'

'And that is?'

'Destiny. Fate. The search for the meaning of existence... in a laboratory, or in that damn lake out there.'

III

'So elaborate, Shelley. What did you find hidden in laboratory chemicals? The truth?'

'Go on, Percy, tell us what you raised.' For the first time, Polidori became sufficiently interested to get involved.

Shelley did manage to take a drink without trembling. 'Science,' he said, 'transformed the world into a place of enchantment.' Such statement made the whole subject of science a challenge for argument. Yet no-one did, all wishing to know more about the scholar who dabbled.

'No takers, eh? Very well, and excuse me if my attitude becomes overbearing.' He scanned the attendant faces, obvious interest prompting a smile.

'As you know, I read voraciously, and converse on quite an extraordinary range of topics, for instance, the aesthetic values of ancient Greece, the virtues of the Roman Republic, the humanism of the Renaissance, and more, including the libertarianism of Rousseau's Social Contract. I did take a few liberties and recast certain aspects into what I term "the Godwinian mould".' He glanced at Mary. 'Blame your father, for I accept many of his views as pertinent to life today.

'I'm told I read some sixteen hours a day on occasion. I have no concept of time when in my books.'

'How on earth do you find time to write?' asked Claire.

'In his sleep,' said Byron, an aware smile begging nothing.

'Believe me,' Mary said, 'he writes as eloquently as he reads. We both read and share our views and critiques on certain authors.'

Polidori squirmed, the room sighing when none chose to elaborate.

'Speaking of books, John,' said Byron, 'did you fetch some?'

'I did. Some interesting tomes amongst them.' But Polidori didn't wish to read, or talk books *per se*, intent on wanting to know more about Shelley. 'What of your family, Percy?' he asked. 'Are they not proud of your accomplishments?' His own prowess when at college added weight to the question.

A cynical laugh burst from Shelley. 'In spite of 'em, I was ostracised by everyone, and disinherited by my conventional, narrow-minded family.' He turned to Mary. 'I'm sorry, my love–'

Mary felt heartened by the phrase and squeezed his hand, happy he seemed to be climbing from the trough into which she had inexcusably pushed him.

'– this is hardly likely to endear me to your father, I gather he was banking on my inheritance!'

'Your letters to him about his views on William didn't actually endear him to you.' Mary hoped it sounded glib enough to prevent him finding fresh fault. Her smile ensured it did.

'That apart,' said Shelley, more relaxed now Mary had not taken offence, 'besides poetry and dialectic, my other fascination was science.'

Byron clapped. 'Hoorah, we're getting to it.'

'Like Godwin,' Shelley said, 'I studied the works of the famous *Paracelsus* who later taught medicine at Ingolstadt. I borrowed forbidden books on chemistry. At Sion House, one of my schools, I came across what are termed androids. Remember, Mary, we saw their like two years ago near Neuchâtel.'

'We did. Fascinating.'

'And these, er, androids actually moved? You saw it happen?' Claire queried. 'Just as we move, hands, arms?'

'Quite so. And they wrote on paper, played instruments–'

'But couldn't think for themselves,' Byron said. 'A rare, and intriguing premise.' He looked at Claire, who avoided him.

'Tell us about your laboratory,' Polidori directed.

'My lab! At Eton my room resembled an alchemist's pit.'

'Dippel again,' Byron suggested. 'You have much to answer for, Mary. From what I've read, his schoolmates nicknamed *him* "the owl".'

'M'lord,' Mary said, 'you're as bad as Shelley for using the night hours. The two of you are without doubt encouraged by Dippel.'

'Dear Mary, Dippel, too, considered himself a superior.' Byron taunted her, wearing his intelligent smirk. 'An individual animated by a higher spirit: it endowed him with exceptional powers and astuteness. By such means he could penetrate the mysteries of the universe. The peasants thought he'd sold his soul to the Devil in return for material advantages.'

Byron caught Shelley's look, shades of Harriet evident before Shelley veiled his thoughts by finishing his tea.

'Engrossing vision,' Polidori said. 'Being a doctor, I share such, for to prolong life we must first understand its vitalities.'

'Dippel did,' said Shelley. 'At least he tried. He was considered a visionary with the powers of divination. Chronicles relating to the period spoke of "scandalous behaviour". After two years at Strasbourg, and owing to a "serious incident", he was compelled to flee under cover of night. Local gossip implicated him in body snatching at the nearby cemetery.'

Claire jumped at this. 'You mean...'

'He dug up graves, Claire,' Byron answered. 'And removed their contents.'

'Oh my – I can't believe anyone would do–'

'The naïveté of youth accompanies your disbelief, my dear,' Byron said. 'While lust and power, the two perhaps sanctimonious longings of women, remain to the fore, then the need to learn fresh, more invigorating concepts can be classed obsolete.' He leaned back, holding court. 'Claire, dig deep into the substances that make up your own being, learn from it. Think, woman; it is how all life is succoured, maintained. A little learning, or refusal to learn, often conspires to become a dangerous thing.'

Byron threw more logs on the fire. 'It's grown decidedly chilly in here.'

'And who is to blame, m'lord?' Polidori aimed it where intended, accusing eyes sparking at Byron.

'It is the air breeds and breathes situations, Polly. And what is said. Ladies–' Byron offered a curt bow, 'forgive my outburst. Claire, I apologise. One shouldn't judge some through their belief in the teachings of others. My analogy was obviously ill-timed. Shelley, you were saying? Dippel?'

'Mm, yes, he... Dippel returned to live with his parents, ingratiated himself in the more serious study of alchemy. He resided near Castle Frankenstein.'

The dull-grey stone of a castle reared. Gripping the northern edge of a vast chunk of rock known as Magnet Mountain, this particular edifice proved awesome to behold in the twilight.

Mary looked away, the words as stark as the fresh, yet old, old image centred in her mind's eye. She looked about her, into shadows gathered in the corners where the light didn't reach, and instantly turned from them, believing what visions she experienced represented a cold, heartless soul whose hour to be born was imminent. And the recurring image appeared as clear now as it had in 1814.

Disintegrating, eroded walls. Twin towers, donjons – an architecture that formed part of this medieval castle named Frankenstein, *whose walls grew, living, from the rock, a dark entrance tunnel enticing the unsuspecting into the very heart of it...*

None noticed her agitation, covered admirably when she poured more tea.

'It will be cold,' said Claire.

'I'll call for Fletcher,' said Byron, 'have him bring more.'

Mary sipped from the cup. 'It is barely warm, I agree, but it quenches a sudden dryness. Shelley, please continue.' Mary sat once more.

Shelley sighed. 'Very well, but I think we should dispense with Dippel. One thing, by heating bones...' Shelley wracked his mind trying to remember. 'Oh, and dried blood–' His hands danced as he fought to recall ingredients from somewhere in his active mind, dulled by laudanum. 'Hair was another ingredient, plus others I don't recall. From this concoction, and mixing them with the product of scrap iron and crude potash, Dippel obtained a chemical called potassium ferrocyanide. Mixed with air it assumed a striking blue colouration. Artists use it in their paintings. Damn fine skies they accomplish, too.'

'Excuse me, Shelley,' Polidori interrupted, 'but didn't the German scientist, Scheele, by taking Dippel's formula and diluting it in some way – I think Sulphuric acid was added – didn't it result in the discovery of Prussic acid? Apparently a very potent poison.'

'Polly, you excel. Meant as a compliment,' Byron acknowledged.

'My own efforts pale by comparison to Dippel, and Scheele,' said Shelley. 'I would return home, hands and face smudged by explosive powders and virulent acids. Still have a few scars to prove the claim.' He giggled. 'Once I half poisoned m'self with some arsenic mixture.'

'It obviously didn't work.' Byron's wry amusement bubbled. 'Don't whatever you do, try Prussic acid.'

'If life treats me well I won't.'

'Shelley!' Mary took umbrage. 'Don't say that, not even as a joke.'

The poet offered a mock bow from his seated position. He then stood and paced, massaging his legs. 'Sitting too long.' His look grew serious again. 'Had a tutor,' he said, 'man named Bethell who suspected I was engaged in nefarious scientific pursuits. Fact is, I was overawed by the new found powers of electricity so I obtained a small galvanic battery while at Eton. Bethell appeared in my room without a by your leave and found me partially enveloped in a blue flame–'

'Not Prussian blue by any chance?' Claire controlled her giggle, the others smiled.

Shelley said, in mock seriousness, 'I didn't plan to paint the ceiling if that's what you infer. We digress. Bethell asked me what I was doing, and I answered–'

Shelley's amusement spiralled at this juncture, his answer tumbling out on a laugh. '"Please, sir..." I said, "I'm... I'm raising the... the devil." You know what he did? Not the devil, Bethell. He seized some of my apparatus from the table and bellowed' – Shelley assumed a lower, more adamant tone as might befit the curious – '"What in the world is this?" Before I could tell him, he was thrown back against the wall. The damn fool had exhibited a very pretty electrical experiment, and received an unstinted discharge.'

'Presumably grabbed Old Nick's tail,' Byron said.

Mary, enthused by the banter, and allowing for the fact that her Shelley held the floor at the expense of Lord Byron, prompted. 'Shelley, you must tell them about your experiment at Oxford. Your friend Jefferson Hogg, what he saw...'

'Come, Mary, let them suggest something, not I.'

'Please, Shelley.' Claire insisted.

'I promise it is the last. How persuasive you are, ladies.'

'What did I tell you, Shelley,' Byron said. 'Men are all slaves to their will.'

'I think, you're right. Truth is, my friend Hogg insisted I show him what my experiments entailed so I turned on this, that and t'other. Crackling sparks flew forth, Hogg begging me to work the machine until it was filled with electricity. His long, wild locks bristled and stood on end... Picture him... he looked like some demented street clown, discoursing afterwards on the remarkable power unleashed–'

A clap of thunder from beyond the mountains made them all jump. Mary's hand flew to her breast, Claire shrieked. Polidori uttered something about 'being cursed for listening to this' and promptly allowed himself to be swallowed into the chair.

Shelley went quiet, he hugged Mary. 'We tempt the Devil, m'lord.'

Lord Byron hurried to the window and flung back the drapes, immediately lit by a charge so brilliant that all there must have thought him a munificent god absorbing the light of heaven.

'A sign,' he said. 'All will be revealed tonight. We shall yet open ourselves to the sins we commit, and as such absolve them.'

In a trice, his countenance changed. Unseen by the others, it grew blacker, thoughts of his own life resurrected from last night, and over many such nights of soul-searching. He cursed the essence of a degenerate family which it had been his unfortunate destiny to be born into.

His heart thumped. As he turned, the forces of nature conspired to fashion a drumbeat, each loud crash, each low rumble a symphony that might have been specially composed for His Satanic Majesty.

Elements combined, nor would they cease until the early hours, when stories had been recited, told, written, and once written, shied away from, with possible exceptions.

Mary dare not look at him, or beyond him to the windows. She avoided the mirror, having seen contained there, in that same vivid luminescence that had lit Byron, a monstrous shape – a man, yet not a man.

The cups rattled on the tray, Polidori's own cup kicked as his startled good leg flew out. He shook, and Claire ran to him, her own fear matching his.

'You did indeed conjure the Devil, Shelley, for he is without, and come a-knocking.'

Shelley's head shot round. He looked at Byron, and stayed quietly pale, his nervous spasms inexcusable, blamed now on Mother Nature.

A lull – calm, sighs of relief, something you could touch, and from them gain solace. Byron, affable gentleman once again, claimed his chair. 'My thanks for the enlightening insight, Percy. Very droll, though the humour contained has been scattered by forces beyond our control. Small wonder all our hair did not bristle and stand on end.'

He sought Polidori. 'And now, a diversion. John, ease your cringing self from the chair, after first allowing Miss Clairmont to unlatch herself from you, and fetch the books you purchased from the Genevan book dealer. Where are they?'

'On the table in the hall, m'lord.' Polidori limped unwillingly towards the door. 'I... I'll get them.'

AND IN CREATING – LIVE!

'The hour is come,' said the dark one.

The other said nothing, for he had not yet been given the power to speak.

'It is sad you cannot voice your apparent yearning,' said the dark one. In truth, my mentor, my guide, my deliverer, has already met me, so I live on the edge of his mind, am already in his writings, have walked beside him in many guises...

'We would welcome you to our dark world: urge you to enter the light, for the clouds are stacked, the sky bleeds, the earth drinks...

'Create. CREATE.'

CHAPTER 22

'Of thee and thine, by forcing some lone ghost...'

I

'Erasmus Darwin's recent experiments place science against religious doctrine.'

Calmer now, and with several books stacked on the table that had held the tray, the storm still voicing contempt outside, Shelley raised the observation relevant to his earlier invective.

'What are you inferring?' asked Polidori. 'That God is angry tonight and is using his own science to punish us?'

'Your cynicism betokens your adolescent thinking.' Shelley was in no mood for petty remarks. His talk, apart from the invited humour, had verged largely on the serious, Shelley adamant he wouldn't have it reduced to the level of the school yard foolishness Polidori excelled at.

Byron's distorted grimace matched Shelley's.

'Darwin presupposes that human life can be created in a laboratory. He is alleged to have made an experiment with a piece of vermicelli. He sealed it in a glass case and it began to move with voluntary motion.'

Mary, ever the devout listener, added: 'Perhaps a corpse could be reanimated.'

Claire visibly shuddered. 'Mary, we've already heard of Dippel digging up the dead, and now you suggest we give them life!'

'Think about it,' Mary went on, shutting out Claire, and agreeing with Byron over Claire's blinkered prejudgement. 'Yes, galvanism had given token of such things; perhaps the component parts of a creature might be manufactured, brought together, and endued with vital warmth.'

Claire excused herself. Without another word she left the room, walked to the main door, opened it, thinking fresh air would do her good. She prepared to look out. A burst of lightning, of instantaneous thunder startled her, within seconds her dress and skin soaked as rain lashed the porch. She slammed the door.

Yet in that heartbeat, she convinced herself that something struggled towards the house. She hadn't sense to realise that she could have seen a tree, a bush, something easily explained.

'Shelley and his stories! And now Mary adds to them!' She stroked her stomach. 'There is but one way to promote life,' she whispered.

Nourished by the thought, she rejoined them, pausing at the wine decanters left on the table by Rushton an hour ago. 'Anyone want wine?' she asked brusquely. She didn't receive a reply, an amused look lighting her face as she studied Byron engrossed in the pile of books.

II

Fantasmagoriana, or Collection of the Histories of Apparitions, Spectres, Ghosts, etc.

After reading the title, Byron slapped the book. 'I do believe I have found the very volume that will enhance these dark hours. The storm lends its own valuable contribution.' He studied the book. 'It is a French translation. I shall read from it.

'Claire when you have availed yourself of more wine, do you wish to join us? I warn you, should you go to your room, you may be dwelling overmuch the reanimated corpses our good friends, Mary and Percy spoke of.'

Claire joined them, sitting as close to Shelley as she dare, a demeaning look from Mary obvious.

An audience of people, held in check by nature, and by nature a group who had conspired in various ways to undermine the very core of it by their outrageous beliefs and practices.

Mary Shelley, courtesan by choice to the indiscriminate selfish doctrine of an atheist.

Claire Clairmont, a young woman partially linked by blood to an outspoken seeker of truth.

Percy Shelley, the poet whose self-esteem had been lessened by his own concepts of a literary genius expecially when he compared himself to Lord Byron.

Doctor John William Polidori, a determined, self-centred student of other people's art – a man who fought to rise above the demeaning platitudes he induced.

And...

George Gordon Noel, the Sixth Lord Byron, a legend: practitioner of self-love, yet a seeker of true love, a poet of renown who unwittingly, and unwillingly, decried his own talent and incurred the wrath of many.

Five people, four of whom formed their own, self-orchestrated sinister quartet. The fifth? Well, she had clung to her own ideals and unwittingly become a party to theirs. Poor Claire, for who amongst them would acknowledge her as less than a troublemaker?

The question begged an answer, but would any offer an honest enough one to give her back the confidence so denied her by Lord Byron?

Many diseases, both mental and physical, are hereditary. Byron inherited his arrogance, his temper, and ultimately his penurious habits, in the main, from his mother. Reared in poverty and obscurity, he unexpectedly became a Lord: enough to upset the tolerance of such a temperament as his. Fortune and eventually misfortune turned out to be unwilling suitors. When he awoke that morning and "found himself famous", it made him dizzy. Reckless, he faced the danger of being swallowed by his own swell. In short, he joined the ranks of those who worship images they create for themselves.

By his own admission, this frightened him. In order to avoid this fear he had a notion to place others before it, use them as buffers to his anger, his notoriety and obvious arrogance.

His mental state, cruel sometimes, set him on a par with the unleashed power of nature, and he supposed that in his attempts to tap, and try to understand the vast sources of the unknown, harness their essence, reasons behind what drove him to live as he did would gain clarity.

From science, and not forgetting the Darwinian theory upon which Shelley had expounded – a combination of science and religious doctrine – essentially flouting the things many believed in, he, Byron, and the others would endeavour to explore the darkest regions of their inner minds in which they might discover all manner of things beautiful and grotesque.

Imagination could be proved to truly exist – it would become – *real*.

Flipping pages, Byron found an appropriate place at which to commence. The others couldn't know what tale he'd chosen and sat nervously expectant, the storm making pulses pound, perspiration a sheen on every shadowed brow and breast.

More logs thrown onto an already roaring fire, Byron stood to the right of it, a statue of light and dark. '"History of the Inconstant Lover",' he announced. Using appropriate intonation as befitted such words, he began to relate the story of a husband who kisses his new bride on their wedding night... '"His lips brushed hers, her hair flowed through his trembling fingers—"'

Byron paused to assess their interest.

Polidori sat forward, eager, anticipating; Claire, oblivious to what Mary would think, clung to Shelley's arm, doubtless thinking of her own and Byron's intimate moments; Mary, alone in the other chair, partially draped in the shadow caused by its high wings, sat prettily, eager to learn. And last, Shelley, the poor man beside himself with unease, and comforted, Byron guessed, by Claire's company, her closeness.

The world turns, he thought before instantly resuming, those few seconds hardly allowing them any complacency. '"The woman, his bride, turned her head, the long tresses falling away from her face... Love turned to horror as the man drew back to admire her porcelain countenance only to find... *transformation!*"'

Another pause, movements, more agitation, never prompted by the storm.

'Go on,' said Polidori, 'don't stop there.'

Claire's eyes told him to cease, Shelley's too. Mary waited.

'"He screamed, fell back, tumbling over the already disarrayed bed linen, for there, *there* before him lay the form and features, the obnoxious putrescence of his first, very dead, wife!"'

How the silence raced in to wrap around the last lines uttered, the shock on their faces like a farewell kiss, their hardly relieved sighs expelled into air the colour of blood and grave worms.

Collecting another book, previously selected, and hardly giving them time to relax from the story just read, Byron, noting their numbed silence, launched with even greater dramatic emphasis into lines from Samuel Taylor Coleridge's *Christabel:*

'Then drawing to her breath aloud
Like one that shuddered she unbound
The cincture from beneath her breast:
Her silken robe and inner vest
Dropt to her feet, and full in view
Behold! Her bosom and half her side,
Hideous, deformed and pale of hue,
A sight to dream of, not to tell!
And she is to sleep by Christabel.'

The only sound to impinge on the awful, subdued quiet was Claire guzzling more wine, presumably to render herself immune from the chilling concepts of stories and poems, the sounds not as funny as might have been, under less disturbing circumstances.

Byron guessed each of them would carry a picture in their mind, not only of the decomposed corpse, but a more clarified image suggested by the poem.

'It's evil,' Claire said, her denouncement clearly a spoken thought.

Lightning and thunder – a battlefield noise of frightening extremes – prompted Byron to say, 'I once saw a tree spun into life by lightning, and a pretty scary sight it was.'

'We... we won't be struck by... by it, will we?' Claire visibly shook. 'Shelley, you tell me that it cannot reach us in here.'

Shelley, instead of realising how utterly frightened Claire had become, said, 'Electricity in whatever form, if not contained, can travel anywhere, even down a chimney.'

Precisely on cue, a log tumbled; a multitude of sparks crackled onto the hearth, flared up the chimney. Claire screamed, her glass tumbled from nervy fingers to shatter on the floor, contents staining the carpet.

A mesmerised Byron watched as it took on an embryonic shape so like the one on the floor of his dressing room at Newstead. New life seeded... being born.

Leaping to her feet, still gripping Shelley's coat sleeve, Claire almost pulled him from the settee. Shelley jerked back, Claire left alone some feet away, shadows curling like fingers as the candle flames, urged by the draught of her passing, crawled more swiftly across walls and floor.

In the mirror, a larger shadow seemed to peer out, find Mary.

Mary, whose thoughts tumbled, enmeshed, and formed the makings of an idea – one so terrible, she might never write it down. A creature born of lightning, of thunder – the son of a far greater mother than the one from whose loins she burst forth.

A mother who died.

But the castle isn't dead. *Castle Frankenstein* wants to live.

III

A little later, nearer midnight, Byron regaled them with a sinful tale of the founder of a race whose miserable doom it was to bestow the kiss of death on all the younger sons of his ill-fated house, just when they reached the age of promise...

'Do you not hear?' said the dark one. 'This tale could be one of my own making, for that phrase "Kiss of Death", lingers, it appeals.

Byron continued: "'The shape was lost beneath the shadow of the castle walls; but soon a gate swung back, a step was heard, the door of the chamber... opened, and he advanced to the couch of the blooming youths, cradled in healthy sleep... kissed the forehead of the boys, who from that hour withered like flowers snapt upon the stalk.'"

Byron finished. Unseeing, he conjured likenesses of beautiful boys... *Edleston, Rushton...* Others he had touched, kissed, loved, not least in Turkey, where the law was less stringent than in his homeland.

Suddenly he snapped back, a lingering, almost sadistic smile playing on his lips. 'I have an idea,' he said. 'We will each write a ghost story.'

Shelley squirmed in his seat bringing a concerned look from Mary. Byron said, 'I take it that doesn't appeal, Snake.'

'H... hardly that.' Shelley looked flustered. 'I don't wish to rebuke the intention. I... I was thinking about my freshman year at Oxford when I wrote a couple of horror tales.' His thoughts took flight. 'One of them, explored a desire for the elixir of life. It led to a compact with the Devil... All sorts happened, seduction, murder–'

'Sounds a bit like us,' Polidori mused aloud. No-one paid attention.

'What of those two poems you spoke of, Shelley?' Byron inquired. 'They held a similar theme as I recall.'

'Yes, "Zeinab and Kathema" was one.' Shelley paused, gathering his thoughts. 'In that my hero encountered the "damp, deathly smell" of his hanged lover, goes mad and hangs himself with a chain.'

'What I've read of yours, m'dear,' said Polidori, 'you tend to pause in dank wastes and putrid marshes, or on harsh crags. Unburied bones is another image – *the field of Waterloo perhaps?* – and... and we have the desolate shore in a howling wind.'

'Indeed so, doctor, but were you to read on, you will find that I do subordinate such elements to ennobling themes.'

'Smacks of a death wish t'me,' said Polidori.

Without recourse to any introduction, Shelley began to recite:

'While yet a boy I sought for ghosts, and sped
Through many a listening chamber, cave, and ruin,
And starlight wood, with fearful steps pursuing
Hopes of high talk with the departed dead.
I called on poisonous names with which our youth is fed.
I was not heard; I saw them not;
When, musing deeply on the lot
Of life, at that sweet time when winds are wooing
All vital things that wake to bring
News of birds and blossoming,
Sudden thy shadow fell on me:-
I shrieked and clasped my hands in ecstasy!
I vowed that I would dedicate my powers
To thee and thine: have I not kept the vow?'

He remained seated, staring at the fire, saying nothing more, his countenance revealing the evidence of effort expended.

'As I said,' Polidori repeated, 'a death wish!'

'It is perhaps what we all court,' said Byron, more subdued, lacking gusto. 'What is that, Shelley? One of yours?'

'He's already confessed his fondness for dabbling in the occult,' Mary answered for him. 'The lines are from his poem "Hymn to Intellectual Beauty".'

'Some beauty,' Polidori said, sarcasm apparent.

'Would that your words smacked of such soul-searching, Polly.' Byron's remark didn't invite comment.

Savouring his wine – his third glass full – and not about to argue, Polidori said, 'I warmed to your suggestion of each writing a ghost story, Noel. 'I'm enjoying this, pity to let it go. Good innovation allows us to freely think.'

Strange thing the grape, more so its debilitating effect on man: it relaxes, makes people less tense, more likely to reveal their secretive self, information that otherwise will remain buried.

Glass returned to the hearth, Polidori rubbed his hands together. 'I shall relate an idea I've been entertaining, invite your opinion before I set it on paper.' His smile announced intent, and overlaid objection. 'My turn, I believe.'

None disagreed, Byron happy to let the doctor continue, wondering if he would make an even bigger fool of himself.

In Shelley's mind, tortuous images reared, horrid visions of women, malformed and threatening, plagued. Mary steadied his hands, her agitation hidden in shadow as she turned to him. Her questioning look gained nothing, her beloved's eyes wide, seeing into a blackness only he conjured.

'I beg you, doctor,' Claire appealed, 'don't frighten us so.' She glared at Byron. 'You,' she said, 'have little or no concern for me.'

'Then go to bed. Dream sweeter dreams.' Byron's smile appeared chilly.

The dare was lost on the others: Polidori considered his tale, Shelley and Mary wrapt in each other. Claire stayed: with no poet to guard her, she gripped her chair arm with one hand, and clutched a fresh glass of wine in the other.

Taking a lesson from previous judgements, Polidori did at least improve his diction, affording his tale a hint of dread. Certainly his idea had some merit, but the tale of a skull-headed lady who was so punished for peeping through a keyhole to look upon some unnameable horror, and reduced to a worse condition than the renowned Tom of Coventry, lacked the necessary rousing ending simply because the poor doctor had no idea what to do with her. The ending put forward trailed into an insignificant blather of possibilities that wouldn't work. In short, it turned out as dire as his play.

Before anyone could appraise it, Shelley, possessed of some insane idea, shrieked loudly, the outburst startling everyone. Claire and Mary tried to reach him, he waved them away. Clutching his head as though drunk, he stood shakily, stumbled into the table, the light from a solitary candle flame defining the horror on his stark face. Like one demented, Shelley grabbed the ornate candlestick, the flame flaring out behind, smoke trailing a pungent aroma of melted fat as he ran, still shrieking, from the room.

'Doctor! Go after him,' ordered Byron loudly. 'His need for a physician is greater than his need of a friend.'

Polidori hurried as best he could, unable to place too much weight on his injured ankle. They heard him calling Shelley's name.

Mary made to follow. 'No, Mary.' Byron steered her to her seat. 'Please, allow the doctor to take care of him. I fear it has been too much for our good Shelley.'

IV

'Your... your tales...' Shelley stammered.

Returned to the group an hour later, he huddled in the corner of the settee, eyes darting everywhere, his breathing slightly worrying.

Polidori had found him curled in a corner of the landing, and eventually succeeded in coaxing him to his room.

'Not that I much liked the idea myself. Being up there, you understand.' Polidori jittered a little. 'Isn't a deal of light 'cept for the lightning. Bit scary.' His slack smile underlined his agitation. 'Once I'd got him to my room, I poured water into a bowl and doused him with it.' He looked at Shelley, quaking in Mary's arms. 'At least it brought him out of it. Gave him a dose of ether, too, that helped famously.'

'Listen, my friend–' Byron went to Shelley. 'If you don't wish to say anything, we understand.'

Claire hovered, heart palpitating. She wanted to hug Shelley, not wise with Mary in attendance.

Shelley looked at Byron, then at Mary. 'Oh my God, I saw... I mean when I heard all this about corpses coming to life, and... and my own recital and thoughts plaguing to such an extent... Oh Mary, I thought of a woman I'd heard of who had... had eyes instead of nipples.' He clutched hold of Mary. 'It... it horrified me!'

The concept sounded startling, the idea that imagination can conjure such a strange, terrible notion centred in all their minds. Even Claire, awash with wine, didn't laugh.

'Taken together with those lines you recited from *Chrlstabel*, and that ravaged female body of the... the female serpent... God, the revelation of that monstrous form! It... It reminded me...'

Shelley couldn't know that his thoughts would be prophetic – six months later his wife, Harrict, mother of his children, would be found floating in the Serpentine, the narrow, artificial lake in London's Hyde Park. A suicide, she wouldn't be found for five weeks, and be judged to have "lain in the water for some days".

More visions to taunt: Shelley's mental state would be further harassed by one he would recall vividly when told of Harriet's death.

Lord Byron paced, his awkward gait beating a new rhythm on the floor. Beyond the window, the fiendish storm had not yet reached the height of its omnipotent power.

Lightning skipped along the Jura; somewhere in the villa, shutters burst open on lancing, distorted lines of light, clattering against the stonework like some hellish applause for the light show; clouds swirled and scurried, blanching as the electrical tumult carved fresh holes in their underbellies.

'Such terrible force,' he whispered.

V

Distanced from the others – apprehensive over Shelley – he sees Claire with her cajolery; Polidori taking Shelley's pulse, and Mary, only Mary, behaving as a lady should, a haughtiness about her that forbade any pathetic exhibitionism. A friend: a lover. Shelley, he thought, consider yourself a lucky man.

He shivers, a cold rants up his back, down his legs.

He recollects stalking through the Abbey's corridors, loaded pistols at the ready. 'Who can ever kill a memory?' he asks. 'Who may defeat the long-dead, yet victorious ancestors? Victorious because we can never chase them from our minds.'

A good evening to start with, everyone mellow from drink. Then we commenced to tell ghost stories. Fun at first, appealed to my humorous trait, but good Christ, it got too sinister. Snake couldn't take it. Too many spirits gathered under one roof–

Like the Abbey, m'lord?

Yes, like the Abbey.

We attracted them, all of us afraid to continue. They warned me. Claire, Shelley, even Polly-Dolly hid himself in his chair at first. Why won't they admit there *is* a presence here. Should have told them I wanted to leave, but their insistence... Polly and Mary made me stay, continue.

Coleridge, you were the one... Christabel, the epitome of womanhood, fair of face, graceful – *Like Shelley's wife?* – Possibly. And the thing that crawled and squirmed... as worms crawl and squirm. Yes, something is here, it's with us now because... because *we have made it!* It's part of all our lives, those parts we have thus far lived.

Easy to laugh it off, pretend it isn't real. Yet I... the others... if only we dare admit to being terrified, and still are. We should end this evening now, pretend it didn't happen. How I wish to leave this place. I dare not because they will wish to know why. What man admits to being scared? Except Snake.

But who wants to know, Lord Byron? The people gathered behind, or the demons of your mind that cavort and laugh, and demand you stay? Who, my lord? WHO?

'*We shall each write a ghost story.* I should not have said that.'

With a lingering look at the others, Byron departs the room without a word.

VI

The hallway explodes with garish light, his features marked, even down to the dimple on his chin.

Lightning. From Heaven? Or from Hell? 'It points fingers at me. Why do I love myself? Hate myself? Selfish, vain, perfidious. Love is never true, selfless love... living for me, never for others. I demand, they supply, I am appeased... Yet only for a short time.'

The other voice intrudes. In his mind, or does some shape hover on the edge of his eye?

You see ghosts, George Gordon; they make you see them; they frighten you. It's why you departed Newstead because they were always there taunting–

'They hurt me.'

NO. You hurt yourself. Inside your mind, a-l-l inside you. And what of the portraits, the sketches done of you? Why so pensive? So sad?

'A happy lifestyle doesn't mean I was happy. Had others not judged me too harshly, then I–'

Only you think yourself a misfit. There is more to life, even beyond the pale.

'I am what I am, and how others see me on canvas, in their sketch books. When I depart this life, I will be what I will be.'

Legacy. How others see you. Only you can know what you will leave behind for them to see.

At his desk, reams of his life are spread before him, Byron totally unaware of how he has come here. Thunder slackens, the wind drops, he hears footsteps in the corridor, light, dainty steps.

CHAPTER 23

'...to receive without discrimination,
any visitor who may come.'

'They are all abed.' Mary stood on the threshold, hazel eyes begging his company.

He bids her enter, what else can he do? Besides, he desires company just as she does. Fletcher and Rushton have retired in this hour after midnight, and as for the others, especially Shelley, he couldn't face them.

'Forgive the intrusion, my lord.' She walked in. 'I saw how troubled you looked when you left. I thought–'

'That I was ailing? No, not in the literal sense.' He stood. 'Forgive my manners. Please, be seated.'

She sat opposite, in the same chair Shelley had used days ago. 'I confess to being fatigued, but my mind is tossing around ideas for a story.' She couldn't guess his thoughts, only surmise, and so could not be aware of his regret at having suggested it.

He said, 'Our talk and readings have undoubtedly reduced our ardour, but like you, my mind refuses to rest. How is Shelley? Recovered?'

'I'm afraid not. We thought it best to call in a local doctor.'

'Our own good doctor isn't good enough to see what ails Snake.' He tittered to himself. 'Forgive me, Polidori and I have what you may call a love-hate relationship. He loves me, I hate him. To think *I* chose *him* to accompany me as physician. Another monkey would have been a better companion.'

'Are you so bitter towards John, m'lord?'

'Too long a tale to tell.' Byron sighed. 'He thinks to match me, better me, and who am I to say he cannot? I have already offered him help.'

'And is the laughter following his reading likely to enamour him to either of you?'

'You speak your mind, madam, I'll say that.'

'Would you have me any other way?'

'The truth, Mary, it is good to tell the truth. Polidori waffles. Why when I peeked at his diary a few days ago... Do I shock your susceptibilities? Ah, I do. Then know me for what I am,

Mary, and for who I am. Polidori states it well when he wrote "I am on the footing of an equal with Byron".'

'He wrote *that*?'

'You are shocked, but for a different reason. There's more. Evidently, he realised he isn't and wrote, "I am nothing more than a tassel to the purse of merit" and "like a star in the halo of the moon".'

'Pretty words, sir, and obviously meant. One's diary is like the heart and should hold and retain its secrets.'

Byron appeared uninterested in the particular subject, but added, 'I judge him too harshly. Perhaps it is myself I should judge. Am I so selfish that I treat others badly?' He met her eyes. 'Of course you know to whom I refer. How is Claire?'

'Claire has retired. I left her, much like my Shelley, frightened out of her wits.'

'Shelley isn't alone, I trust?'

'Doctor Polidori undertook to sit up with him.'

'Mary, I'm not too relieved at that news. Polidori couldn't cure a wart on a donkey's arse.'

Mary tittered, composing herself when Byron glanced at her. 'My apologies. It's not what you said, but the stern way in which it was said. Your brows knit, and your eyes have fire.'

'See me when I'm really roused.'

A second or so slid by. Mary doubted his meaning, considering it as perhaps innuendo.

Thankfully, he indicated the stack of manuscript paper. 'Much to do, so many thoughts, revelations, truths. I tell you, Mary, you look upon a monster.'

Mary balked. 'My lord? Monster? You?'

'Many think so and perhaps I am. But no, I refer to papers you see here. A life, Mary, many lives, all wrapped up in words sewn together with imagination's threads. I *am* Childe Harold; perhaps I am Don Juan. I know I am Darkness. Indeed I am, so do not attempt to contradict me. I am responsible for so much gloom in people's lives, in my own life, that when all are stacked, they make up one impenetrable darkness.'

'You speak of your life, Albé, yet you must attest that all here court their own secrets. My father–'

'I know, Mary. Shelley has expanded on his dislike of Godwin. It is not to any detriment that I say this, only to justify your own needs for a man you love at risk of losing another whom you respect. It may echo my lost relationships.'

'With respect, are there so many, sir? Is there one who is closer to your heart than any other?'

Byron's eyes softened, tempered by a fatigue he couldn't balance. He appraised Mary, the soft, blue gown, the low bodice, slight swell of breasts, her elfin-like features which, in this sulky light, were made softer, her eyes entreating an answer.

'I have high regard for you, Miss Godwin. Do forgive the formality; in a sense it establishes our relationship, ensures a friendly, yet less intimate probability. I see you as a friend and would keep it so.' In this, he would honour Shelley's claim to her.

Mary, unable to outstare him, played with a brooch shaped as a cluster of flowers which pinned her bodice slightly higher than intended.

The silence gave Byron time to note the stark differences between her and Claire, the former not so pushy, the latter a bloody nuisance. Lady and hardly such, Claire over-confident in her claims to ownership. This fact would be substantiated by Mary as conversation developed.

'I have enjoyed a full life, Mary, but I attempt to charge myself to love but one, when another is hardly available to me.'

'Which one? *If* I dare ask.'

He whispered, 'Lucy,' not expecting her to frown as she did. 'You don't approve?'

'Who am I to judge? I'm eighteen and of your acquaintance. I often sit quietly while you commandeer my Shelley for your long talks. You have much in common, yet I feel you use him to satisfy your own conscience. He is your confessor, my lord.'

'Am I not his?'

'In a way, I suppose you are.'

'But I'm taking him away from you?'

What had been a comfortable silence became something less so, Byron galled by this outspoken female who, he estimated, had sought this audience to chide him.

'What of Lucy, then? Let me hear your views. Given that I'd looked upon this as an airing of ideas, I am astounded you make such bold *accusations*. Agree or disagree away, madam, you have my ear.'

I am too young, she thought, and daring to be outspoken to a lord. I've said more than I intended. Yes, she had but couldn't stop the words tumbling out.

'You asked the question, my lord; I answer honestly.' Her conscience bids her leave. She stays, as inscrutable as ever. 'Your liaison with Lucinda is entirely your affair, sir, but to profess a love for her when, if you will excuse me, she is beneath you in stature and class, then I suggest you're wrong. A brief affair, a flirtation, yes, but to confess *love* is a lie, Lord Byron.'

She noted how tense he'd grown, yet this need to declare herself was a temptation she couldn't disregard. 'We have shared secrets, Albé. I speak of London when you were inclined to talk of Claire, how she dogged you. I have respect for you, and hope you feel the same. Of Lucinda, I have heard talk, admittedly through gossip–'

Someone at the Abbey, he guessed. Did not Lucy mention something of what Mary said? He thought she had during a walk in the garden with Patrick.

'–gossip. She is but a worthless servant and a lord should not have feelings for the likes of her. She is the sort to be used for pleasure, nothing more.'

'You speak of respect, yet have the gall to tell me how to conduct my business, my life and my loves. Must I then seek your permission to avail myself of anyone, man or woman, whom I see as someone to care for, to give the benefit of *my* experience. Yes, mine, Mary. Being born into my family ensured I would become a lord.' He stood, anxious to distance himself, angry at her presumptions. 'I didn't ask to be born a lord. I am, first and foremost, a man, with desires, and you must take that as you will.

'You search for love, and so must I. It appears you have found it, I have not. I was a small boy when I inherited the title of Sixth Lord. I'd done nothing to deserve it but believe me, I love to have such a title. I use it to full advantage. Why shouldn't I? It stands me in good stead, opens doors to many who have shown me respect, and some who don't. I confess, I never have gotten used to it, perhaps I won't, purely, and you are right in this, because I never behave like one!

'As to Lucinda, she bore my child, a boy. And no, I cannot marry her. I've told her this but not because of your views, or anyone's, plainly because I do not wish to be tied. Annabella–'

His temper outran him again, and he arrested it. 'It is enough, we are both tired. Excuse me, I would like some privacy.'

Mary took him at his word and went to the door. 'I ask that you forgive the intrusion. I came to speak of ideas, the conversation rambled of its own accord.' She opened the door. 'It is too late for proper conversation.' Quite how she meant this made him wonder.

'Our lives are testy things at best Albé, yet I wonder as to the reason why you cannot marry Lucinda – the *real* reason. Is it because you are a lord, and thus elevated by inheritance?'

Mary tendered a slight curtsey. 'Good night, Lord Byron. I wish you pleasant dreams.'

CHAPTER 24

'And when the grave restores her dead.'

I

'I felt that blank incapacity of invention which is the greatest misery of authorship, when dull Nothing replies to our anxious invocations. "Have you thought of a story?"'

Days spun by, the telling, inquisitive phrase, 'Have you thought of a story?' frustrating Mary until another June night immediately following.

She retired to her room at Diodati, her own and Byron's relationship hardly strained but certainly less intense than of late. They were affable enough in company, Byron tending to shy away from being alone with, or close to her. He preferred leaving that dubious pleasure to Polidori: it kept them both busy and allowed Byron to write more of *Don Juan* and scribble a few lines for another idea before he forgot them.

II

'When I placed my head on my pillow, I did not sleep, nor could I be said to think. My imagination unbidden, possessed and guided me. I saw with shut eyes, but acute mental vision – the pale student of unhallowed arts standing before the thing he had put together, I saw the hideous phantasm of a man stretched out, and then, on the working of some powerful engine, show signs of life and stir with an uneasy, half vital motion...

'Frightful must it be; for supremely frightful would be the effect of any human endeavour to mock the stupendous mechanism of the Creator of the world.

'His success would terrify the artist; he would rush away from his odious handiwork, horror stricken. He would hope that, left to itself, the slight spark of life which he had communicated would fade; that this thing, which had received such imperfect animation, would subside into dead matter; and he might sleep in the belief that the silence of the grave would quench forever the transient existence of the hideous corpse which he had looked upon as the cradle of life. He sleeps; but he is awakened; he opens his eyes; behold, the horrid thing stands at his bedside, opening his curtains and looking on him with yellow, watery, but speculative eyes.'

Everything – all that had been said, done and thought about – tumbles into harsh perspective, even as the inclement weather rages.

Mary sees in the mirror the monstrous, frightful image; in the curtains at the window, its clawing hand reaching above the level of her mind's tide, one huge, stentorious breath sounded in the beat of the wind rattling the window.

No silence of the grave would ever quench this beast's hunger, for it was made up of her foulest nightmares. No ghost story had prompted this, merely brought it living from the deepest recesses of her mind. Childbirth; the deadly dark uterine-like cavern into that cursed castle; the curse of a witch-woman telling her to beware of demons. Of suckling puppies licking at breasts with eyes instead of nipples, those eyes weeping yellow pus, the curtains suddenly torn down – Mary rising in her bed, whimpering like one of those puppies, as the shock of her creation watched from the shadows, one awful, ghastly face riven with grave dirt, hanging there, lit by the force that gave it life – the *true spark of genius.*

Mary Shelley *née* Godwin, would court the spectre for years, and would liken it to all the abhorrent things in her own life, for this creature had only a cold heart.

III

'*You are born, my friend,*' the dark one said. '*You walk the night of centuries – ten million nights down the annals of true literature.*'

The creature, for it was no man in the accepted sense of the word, muttered what could only be interpreted as 'Y-E-S-S-S.'

It sounded like a snake hissing, or the noise a damp log makes when cast onto a hot fire.

IV

Composing forgotten, Lord Byron writes like fury, ideas from his first tour cascading down his mind as a fountain would spew the blood of life.

VAMPIRE.

The word sits as though branded across his forehead – a lightning strike, like the one t'other night, when he was bathed in unholy fire – the spark of his own genius.

They were there, creatures of the nether world, yet only *one* begged to be let in.

We knew they were in residence, spewed from our own drug and alcohol ridden minds, our deepest, innermost thoughts, the ones we prefer to forget. Drugs cannot offer love, only oblivion; they can heighten sexual prowess, they can dull the mind until that poor pathetic scion of thought can hardly bear to think.

There are no monsters other than those we create, or are created for us.

A fifteen year old boy stands alone in a room, the man with him an evil entity, the like of which he never wished to come across.

He wants me to be his slave, thinks the boy. I must refuse. He will hate me for it, I know, but he seeks only to better himself. He has standing, but wants more. He tells me he is only interested in men, never women.

Wealthy, with money and lands, yet he demands extra. Always the one with the power. He hurts many, doesn't care what he does as long as he has fun. They say money talks, I know his did. He always had everything he wanted...

He comes towards me, hands reaching, fondling... he undoes my clothes and throws me across the table... God... NO! NO-O-O-O!

Me, his slave? NEVER. I was a favour, and I rejected him, and what he stood for.

Never love, only lust.

I never speak to him again. No more to do with you, I tell him. Power meant that he always tried to win me as a friend.

He was no friend. Only a seeker of blood, in its varying ways. A vampire.

A lord. A creature of night-time whose lean, hungry preferences dulled many an existence.

In some ways, he made me crave as I do.

He never found love: neither can I.

Is this then the embodiment of man? The curse of his forbears, and the kind word hissed with venom from a dark reptilian, yet smiling countenance?

What am I to write of my life?

Lord Byron sits in the room at Villa Diodati: he languishes in the present, yet contemplates what could well be a stark, unsure future.

Dark, mysterious strangers enter my poetry. Of this *he* is positive, his reasons drawn from the equally sunless corners of his mind and memory.

A father I never knew... Thoughts annoy: friends dead; others no longer friends. Catherine, who both hated and loved me dependent on her choice of drink. Shades of Claire.

Mary Chaworth – *"I could never love that lame boy."* You, too, Mary!

Bell. Didn't want to marry me at first, convinced insanity ran in the family. Damn me, she was right!

And all are gathered here in this villa, a rare spot of beauty invaded by darkness.

People? Demons? Is there much to choose between some of them? I see them now, and you will never imagine how they really are. They take on the shapes of dead people – faces I know – but they have wings like bats and they flit around my mind – inside and out – horrible, grotesque things, so evil they should never be allowed to invade such beauty.

Our space is a private thing, yet what foul beings encroach. I, and the others, feel it, feel *them*.

Shelley: his father; his wife; the ones who expelled him.

Mary: her father's preachings and writings; the death of her mother; the rumours dripping from the tongues of those least understanding.

Claire: her own demands haunt her; her discontent at being used by me... by Shelley.

Polidori: one who sees his jealousy floating in the air, given wings. Glory is his demon. Perhaps my traits have embedded themselves in him.

And out of the dross there is one other: Grey De Ruthyn. Always haunting my mind – the executor of *my* life; who plagues me to beg the knowledge of what I am, what I have become.

Forms of love, but never... never TRUTH.

In *The Giaour*, I wrote of an outlaw who murders a Turk who has thrown his illicit lover into the sea in a sack. 'In none of my Turkish tales do the lovers end well.'

We release all manner of beasts in our imagination. And the drugs deepen such thoughts, bidding us venture where few have been. They are aphrodisiacs offering total elation. Never abuse, more a natural enhancement of sensation.

In *Darkness* I offer my graphic dream of apocalypse, with shrieking birds and vipers.

I think of Shelley, running from the room; my nickname for him, "Snake", and I believe that destiny is shaped by action, what we say, do, accomplish.

We are all *PREDATORS*. We leech off others to further our aims. And what better way than to amaze, frighten and gain followers than to write?

He picks up his pen. And thinks before he writes.

One other watches.

He knows I am evil. I have appeared regularly throughout his life.

I am truly evil, and very real: I look more like death and destruction than any imagination can believe.

I take on many forms – to him I am like the bat – and appear from nowhere. I disappear just as quickly.

He has seen me, and will go on seeing me. It is what makes it easy for him to write about me.

Byron commences to write his essay, his contribution to his own challenge.

> Where there is mystery, it is generally supposed that
> there must also be evil: I know not how this may be,
> but in him there certainly was the one, though I could

not ascertain the extent of the other - and felt loth, as far as regarded himself, to believe in its existence. My advances were received with sufficient coldness: but I was young, and not easily discouraged, and at length succeeded in obtaining, to a certain degree, that commonplace intercourse and moderate confidence of common and everyday concerns, created and cemented by similarity of pursuit and frequency of meeting, which is called intimacy, or friendship, according to the ideas of him who uses those words to express them.

Darvell had already travelled extensively; and to him I had applied for information with regard to the conduct of my intended journey. It was my secret wish that he might be prevailed on to accompany me; it was also a probable hope, founded upon the shadowy restlessness which I observed in him, and to which the animation which he appeared to feel on such subjects, and his apparent indifference to all by which he was more immediately surrounded, gave fresh strength. This wish I first hinted, and then expressed: his answer, though I had partly expected it, gave me all the pleasure of surprise – he consented; and, after the requisite arrangement, we commenced our voyages. After journeying through various countries of the south of Europe, our attention was turned towards the East, according to our original destination; and it was in my progress through these regions that the incident occurred upon which will turn what I may have to relate.

He is alerted to the storm, the sickly yellow light flickering at the curtain...

At once he begins to realise that he is inside the mind of Mary Godwin, actually *seeing* images of some monstrous form that in turn echoes the utter blackness of man's soul.

As one demented, he writes more...

In this situation, I looked round for a place where he might most conveniently repose: contrary to the usual aspect of Mahometan burial grounds, the cypresses were in this few in number, and these thinly scattered over its extent; the tombstones were mostly fallen, and worn with age: upon one of the most considerable of these, and beneath one of the most spreading trees, Darvell supported himself, in a half reclining posture, with great difficulty. He asked for water. I had some doubts of our being able to find any, and prepared to go in search of it with hesitating despondency. but he desired me to remain; and turning to Suleiman, our janizary, who stood by us smoking with great tranquillity, he said, 'Suleiman, verbana su,' and went on describing the spot where it was to be found with great minuteness, at a small well for camels, a few hundred yards to the right: the janizary obeyed. I said to Darvell, 'How did you know this?' He replied, 'From our situation; you must perceive that this place was once inhabited, and could not have been so without springs: I have also been here before.'

'You have been here before! How came you never to mention this to me? and what could you be doing in a place where no one would remain a moment longer than they could help it?'

Hesitant for a minute or so, Byron realises he can only be writing of his own adventures – the rest beneath the trees with Polidori; the ride across the field of Waterloo; a more immediate sensation of *déjà vu*. He sees his own heart pulsing against his shirt. Excitement? Or a need to clear his conscience?

'In the midst of life, we are in death,' he whispers caustically. 'I will see this to an end.' He writes again:

He was silent and appeared to be collecting his spirits for an effort to speak. He began - 'This is the end of my journey, and of my life; I came here to die; but I have a request to make, a command – for such my last words must be – You will observe it?'

'Most certainly; but I have better hopes.'

'I have no hopes, nor wishes, but this – conceal my death from every human being.'

'I hope there will be no occasion; that you will recover, and-'

'Peace! It must be so: promise this.'

'I do.'

'Swear it, by all that.' He here dictated an oath of great solemnity.

'There is no occasion for this. I will observe your request; and to doubt me is–'

'It cannot be helped, you must swear.'

I took the oath, it appeared to relieve him. He removed a seal ring from his finger, on which were some Arabic characters, and presented it to me. He proceeded–

'On the ninth day of the month, at noon precisely (what month you please, but this must be the day), you must fling this ring into the salt springs which run into the Bay of Eleusis; the day after, at the same hour, you must repair to the ruins of the temple of Ceres, and wait one hour.'

'Why?'

'You will see.'

'The ninth day of the month, you say?'

'The ninth.'

As I observed that the present was the ninth day of the month, his countenance changed, and he paused. As he sat, evidently becoming more feeble, a stork, with a snake in her beak, perched upon a tombstone near us; and, without devouring her prey, appeared to be steadfastly regarding us. I know not what impelled me to drive it away, but the attempt was useless; she made a few circles in the air, and returned exactly to the same spot. Darvell pointed to it, and smiled – he spoke – I know not whether to himself or to me – but the words were only, ''Tis well!'

'What is well? What do you mean?'

'No matter; you must bury me here this evening, and exactly where that bird is now perched. You know the rest of my injunctions.'

He then proceeded to give me several directions as to the manner in which his death might be best concealed. After these were finished, he exclaimed, 'You perceive that bird?'

'Certainly.'

'And the serpent writhing in her beak?'

'Doubtless: there is nothing uncommon in it; it is her natural prey. But it is odd that she does not devour it.'

He smiled in a ghastly manner, and said faintly, 'It is not yet time!'

As he spoke, the stork flew away. My eyes followed it for a moment – it could hardly be longer than ten might be counted. I felt Darvell's weight, as it were, increase upon my shoulder, and, turning to look upon his face, perceived that he was dead!

I was shocked with the sudden certainty which could not be mistaken – his countenance in a few minutes became nearly black. I should have attributed so rapid a change to poison, had I not been aware that he had no opportunity of receiving it unperceived. The day was declining, the body was rapidly altering, and nothing remained but to fulfil his request. With the aid of Suleiman's ataghan and my own sabre, we scooped a shallow grave upon the spot which Darvell had indicated: the earth easily gave way, having already received some Mahometan tenant. We dug as deeply as the time permitted us, and throwing the dry earth upon all that remained of the singular being so lately departed, we cut a few sods of greener turf from the less withered soil around us, and laid them upon his sepulchre.

Between astonishment and grief, I was tearless.

Byron relaxed a little. 'There, it is finished, or represents as much as I am prepared to do.' He scrawled at the top of the first page:

Fragment of a Novel (1816) BY GEORGE GORDON, LORD BYRON, June 17, 1816.

In her own room, Mary Godwin read her own notes.

'I have found it! What terrified me will terrify others; and I need only describe the spectre which had haunted my midnight pillow.'

On the morrow she would announce that she had *thought of a story*.

She began that day with the words: *"It was on a dreary night of November..."* and would make only a transcript of the grim terrors of her waking dream.

What would precede this, and follow it, still fermented in her mind.

Sinister twins had been created this night –

A twisted embodiment made up from pieces of humanity, its creator *Frankenstein* writing under the auspicious pseudonym, Mary Wollstonecraft Shelley.

And:

A creature of night, a leech, a predator, given 'life' by an English lord.

This creature would gain prowess, and the shocked audience would be convinced it was one of the best works this English poet had written, until he revealed all in a letter to Monsieur Galignani in Venice on the 27th April, three years hence.

Hate and love? Who knows, for Byron would acknowledge the work as coming from the pen of his Jonah, John William Polidori, even though the idea originated from himself, his travels, his – fears.

Byron couldn't know that his character Darvell would become Ruthven, the name 'borrowed' from Caroline Lamb's own treatment of Byron in her novel *Glenarvon*, in which she would refer to him as *'mad, bad and dangerous to know'*.

In a sense, Caro would have the last laugh.

Was she right, or wrong?

CHAPTER 25

'But die, as many an exiled heart hath died.'

I

The storms were over. In part. The people who visited Lake Léman enjoyed its scenery, drank of its atmosphere; they talked, made love and eventually departed to meet fame, fortune and death.

Romance, love, lust, cruelty played their parts in the hearts and minds of those whiling away their time in a pretty villa, in an equally attractive setting. Motivation? A zest for life, and a fear of death. Of what lay beyond death.

The stormy summer of 1816 prompted autumn's raging winds and with them a more intense impression of foreboding.

Shelley's dreams, his hallucinations, were haunting, terrifying premonitions.

Strange then that Lord Byron should think on those same lines when he prophesied: 'Tragedy will befall all those with whom I've been intimately involved.'

Succeeding years would bring untimely and violent deaths or suicides to all the male members of the Diodati group.

Differences tormented them, not least Shelley's arguments with Byron which caused him to write to his friend, Thomas Love Peacock: "Lord Byron is an exceedingly interesting person and as such is it not to be regretted that he is a slave to the vilest and most vulgar prejudices, and as mad as the winds."

Friendship is fickle, and destructive.

II

On the morning of December 10th, 1816, barely three months after Percy and Mary's return to England, the bloated body of a woman is pulled from the Serpentine.

It is Harriet, child bride of Shelley, mother of his two children, whose mournful note intimated she still loved Shelley.

A death prompts a wedding: out of tragedy comes good. Percy Shelley and Mary Godwin marry at St. Mildred's Church in London on the 30th December, only yards from Harriet's resting place.

Birth. And death. Mary's lot in life. Since the beginning of her liaison with Shelley, the gravedigger relentlessly pursues his work for there seems to be no respite to the tragedy of her young ones as the years pass.

'No, Shelley, please tell me it isn't true. *It can't be.* Not my little "Willmouse".'

Shelley reaches out on that 8th day of June, 1819. He touches the child's peaceful face. 'It is the Roman fever caused it, Mary,' he tells her, trying to remain calm. 'Five days he has taken to die.'

Mary clutches William to her, tears tumbling, bathing her own face and that of William. She gazes at Shelley, the loss of worlds emphasised in her features. 'Three years, Shelley, and now "Willmouse" is the first of our circle to perish. To think I extolled his beauty, even wrote of it in *Frankenstein.* I made him into Victor's brother. Dear God, Shelley, was it a premonition of my own child's fate vividly brought to life when William is killed by the creature on the field of Plainpalais?'

She silently beseeches him to say no, that it cannot be, tell her she is being foolish. No such answer is forthcoming, Shelley too upset and frightened by heathen premonitions.

'It is the end of everything!' wails Mary. 'Must I be so accursed, that all my children die? Is it then true that fiction is merely insight into fact? Shelley, it is so close to truth, it does not beg argument.'

III

Two months and two years later.

Another bottle, twin to one he had at Diodati, sits on another table in a small apartment in a house in Great Pulteney Street. Outside, carriages clatter by in the London streets, newsvendors cry out the news of the day, sights, sounds and smells of the city lost to the man spreadeagled in the chair. A window blind partially shields him from hazy, August sun, his colour unhealthy.

'People,' he mutters. 'Took dinner with that resident... no wonder I'm depressed in spirits.' Bloodshot eyes flitter over his writings, a wealth of papers littering desk and floor.

'Three months in Geneva, an apotheosis of achievement in my short, illustrious career.' He sounds derisory, the past so much less than he'd hoped.

'And that holier-than-thou poet dared dismiss me... Me, John Polidori. Small wonder he redeemed himself and recommended me as private physician to those three prominent English expatriates.' He sneers. 'Horner, North and Guilford... Wasn't my poxy fault they all died in rapid succession.'

The contents of the brandy bottle by his chair leg are low, further depleted as he takes another swig. Lifting the bottle high, he toasts: 'To Lord Byron; if you hadn't recommended me to them they'd still be alive!' He drains the bottle.

Light creeps under the blind as the day sinks into evening, a bloody orb of sun entrapping him in its hellish glow as it peeps between a multitude of chimney pots.

'Thirty pounds. THIRTY. My payment for that wretched book. *And* the buggers labelled me a cheat and plagiarist. Was not Judas awarded thirty pieces of silver for his act of betrayal?'

He rolls the bottle across the floor, too tired to lift up his arm and throw it at something. 'I am related to genius so why am I not a genius?' He remembers names, Walpole, Rosseti. My father translated Walpole's *The Castle of Otranto* into Italian, my sister became the mother of Dante Gabriel and Christina Rosetti, and I... I... Who am I? I couldn't even record my trip with Byron to any great degree.'

The air is stale with his own sweat, the room unaired for days. He massages his head, the pain there irrefutable since the day he was accidentally thrown out of his gig.

Barely able to focus through the effects of brandy and pain, he flips through a copy of *The Vampyre*. 'My dream of fame and fortune. Who can blame me for wanting to claim my due for being dismissed? What did *he* say? Ah yes, "dismissed for his eternal nonsense and *tracasseries* and emptiness". Oh and let us not forget "ill humour and vanity" for they go hand in hand with his own deplorable character.

'What if I did plunder Byron's plot, borrowed from his verse tales, drew on his personality? He deserves to be called vampire. Y'might say he inspired me!'

He lapses into drunken thought, the room's shadows edged darker, reminding him of Diodati, the firelight, the storm, the never-ending belittlement. He begins to laugh. 'They all thought Byron had written it. "A bookselling imposture," he wrote, said he was disappointed in me for writing out his story. Well you didn't want it, m'lord, so I merely took up where you left off. Even Goethe declared it "the best thing Byron had ever written". Damn 'em all, let them think as they like.'

He searches for his bottle again, forgetting what he's done with it. Without a bottle with which to toast him, he says what he intended anyway: 'To you, Albé, for it is *your* story.'

Night eases in, the room dulled, the man barely visible, slumped as he is in the threadbare chair, eyes drawn indubitably to the small, grooved bottle on the table by his right hand. It is the only liquid he has left.

Taking the bottle to the bed, he slumps down, all fight gone. Uncorking it, he pours the contents into a glass, discards the bottle, and raises the glass. 'To Byron, and to Dippel for inventing this concoction. I go like you, a recluse in a solitary, miserable room. To "Prussian Blue". And may your skies, Mr Shelley, remain that blue.'

He drinks it down.

Harsh knocking, a concerned voice. Someone enters the room, but he is too ill to care. Vague fluttering of movement, a startled cry. 'Send for the doctor quickly! The nearest is Golden Square.'

Something pushed down his throat... a bowl held beneath his mouth... bile, water trickling into it, a smell of alcohol impregnating the room. The attempt to discharge the contents of his stomach has little effect. He feels a draught of warm air on his face from the open window. Sounds waver, grow indistinct... shadows gather... shadows with wings beating forever in his brain, before his tortured, closing eyes.

On August 27th, within ten minutes of any attempt to save him, his heart paralysed, John William Polidori, aged twenty-six, and one-time physician to Lord Byron, is dead.

The jury at the Coroner's inquest, unable to decide on "suicide" recorded a verdict of "Died by a visitation of God".

In his disappointing life he perhaps met one along the way.

IV

Sorrow and death undermined what had once been a happy relationship between Shelley and Mary. The dreams were portentous.

Mary, in dire pain through a dangerous miscarriage, viewed Edward Williams, his wife, Jane, and Claire, as they fussed about her. Nearly lifeless, they administered brandy and vinegar. 'It's to keep you from fainting,' said Claire. 'The doctor will be here soon.'

Nerves were frayed, not helped by another prophetic dream of Shelley's.

"I think it was on the Saturday after my illness, June 22nd," wrote Mary, "while yet unable to walk, I was confined to my bed, in the middle of the night I was awoke by hearing Shelley scream and come rushing into my room... He said that he had not been asleep, and said that it was a vision that he saw that had frightened him.

"He dreamt Edward and Jane came into him; that they were in a most horrible condition – their bodies lacerated, their bones staring through their skin, the faces pale yet stained with blood...

"Edward said, 'Get up, Shelley; the sea is flooding the house, and it is all coming down.'

"Shelley got up, he thought, and went to his window that looked on the terrace and the sea, and thought he saw the sea rushing in..."

'Shelley, my love, I know you love the sea and boats,' Mary told him days afterwards, 'but please be aware of your handicap, I beg.'

He looked at her, begging an answer. 'Pray, what is that?'

'Shelley, don't be obtuse. You can't swim! Lord Byron chided you over it. He even saved you near St. Gingoux.'

'I know, my love, you are right, but Williams and I have this notion to purchase a boat...'

Percy Shelley, with Williams, and a boat boy, eighteen year old Charles Vivian, should have sailed early on the morning of the eighth as advised, and not at 3 p.m. They were journeying to Leghorn to meet Leigh Hunt and his family. The boat, renamed *Ariel* by Shelley, in contradiction of Byron's desire to have it christened *Don Juan,* stood too much inshore, the current setting them there.

'They will have a land breeze,' someone commented.

A mate said, 'Maybe. But she'll soon have too much breeze; that gaff top-sail is foolish in a boat with no deck and no sailor on board.'

The same man nodded towards the south west, acknowledging the clouds. 'Black lines and dirty rags hanging on them out of the sky – they are a warning; look at the smoke on the water; the devil is doing mischief.'

A sea fog swirled, it taunted, threw landmarks into disarray, and easily enveloped Shelley's little boat, until distance and grey ghosts swallowed her.

With the sun obscured, the air remained sultry, not one hint of breath in the harbour.

And not one hint of breathable air in Mary Shelley's anxiety.

From meeting the Hunts, Shelley anchored in the lee of Byron's yacht, *Bolivar,* Shelley insisting, 'I wish to catch the breeze tomorrow morning. I'm anxious to return to Lerici at the earliest.'

He studied the sky, ignoring the brief thunderstorm, and Byron's Captain Roberts' warning, 'A tempest is brewing. You'd do well to stay.'

Roberts, a tall, commanding man who felt his words had done more to precipitate Shelley's decision to sail than it had to deflect it, kept the *Ariel* in view to a distance of about ten miles out, off Via Reggio. Then the storm hit and he lost them, the night reminiscent of the evenings at Diodati; driving rain and lightning flashed along the Italian coast.

Shelley was scared, in fact terrified, the earlier squall suddenly a full-throated gale, the white caps tortuous. 'Did we ought to slacken sail?' he yelled to Williams, the sound snatched away.

Young Vivian did his best to steer, the eighteen year old more proficient than Shelley or Williams, irrespective of his young years.

He jabbed a finger through the spray. 'See, there. OVER TO STARBOARD. Another boat!'

Sarsanna, the Genoese sailor, on the poop of his far larger boat, saw the *Ariel*, though the name was obscured by flying waves.

He ordered a course steered towards it, his devious mind considering possibilities. He said to his mate, 'The *Anglaise* poet they call Byron is in these waters. Maybe that is his boat. If he is on board then we are sure to find gold.'

Nearer and nearer, the sea tossing it like so much driftwood, the *Ariel* flew towards the mirage of the other boat...

Two bodies were discovered on the beach off Via Reggio on the sixteenth day of July, 1822. They were buried in sand by the peasants as is the custom with drowned victims.

Edward John Trelawny was born in the same year as Shelley on 13th November, 1792 in London. Like Shelley and Byron, he was a romantic who sought to expunge his early life by immersing himself in his own imagination with rumbustious tales of pirates and adventure.

It was Trelawny, dressed in dark clothes, his cloak flapping in a restless in-shore breeze, who gazed upon the remains.

The furnace Trelawny had made at Leghorn of iron bars and strong sheet-iron, supported on a stand, appealed to him as it would have done to Shelley for it was of the type used by Shelley's much loved Hellenes on their funeral pyres.

He had immediately written to Byron bidding him be with those already assembled by noon the next day.

They burned Williams first, his remains identifiable only by the initials E.E.W. on a black silk handkerchief.

Byron, looking on, muttered, 'The entrails of a worm hold together longer than the potter's clay, of which man is made. Hold! Let me see the jaw,' he added, as they removed the skull. 'I can recognise anyone by the teeth, with whom I have talked. I always watch the lips and mouth: they tell what the tongue and eyes try to conceal.'

A wayward expression lit his face as he thought of Polidori's lies and underhandedness. And also considered those temperamental critics of his work: their eyes spoke many lies.

Byron studied the skull and shot a glance at Trelawny, whose dark countenance, long tails of hair blown by the wind, looked equally morose.

'Can you preserve Shelley's skull for me?' asked Byron.

Trelawny offered a reluctant smile. 'I think not, m'lord, for I have heard you speak often of a certain other skull used as a drinking vessel. It would hardly be fitting that you drink from the head of a friend.'

''Tis a pity then that we may have to pour more wine over his body to make him burn.' Byron's face barely flickered, any humour he might have intended difficult to discern as he watched Williams's remains hoisted onto the furnace situated practically at the water's edge. Once lit, a smell of pine-wood permeated the air; tinder dry, it burned furiously.

Enough for one day, the party agreed to wait until tomorrow before cremating Shelley.

'How did you recognise him?' asked Byron of Trelawny.

Trelawny couldn't look at Byron: instead he gazed onto a quietly rolling sea, about which Mary Shelley had said to Jane Williams, 'That is his grave'.

'Even though bloated and badly mutilated by the water,' said Trelawny, running a hand through his dark beard, biting back his grief, 'there was little doubt in my mind about his identity. Tall, green jacket, a volume of Sophocles in one pocket and Keats's poems in the other, doubled back as if the reader, in the act of reading, had hastily thrust it away.'

'That's Snake,' said Byron. 'Would read sixteen hours a day, so he told us.'

'All too familiar for the body not to be Shelley's then.' Trelawny walked some little distance away. So did Byron, in the opposite direction.

They ordered more timber loaded onto the pyre, Trelawny seeking to avoid any prolonged burning as with Williams yesterday.

The sea – the islands of Gorgona, Capraja, and Elba visible in the near distance – chattered on the shingle; old battlemented watchtowers stretched along the coast, backed by the marble-crested Apennines glistening in the sun, not one human dwelling in sight.

After the fire was kindled they repeated the ceremony, Byron's supposition correct when he saw more wine being poured over Shelley. 'More than he consumed in his entire life,' he said quietly to himself.

Wine, oil and salt made the yellow flames glisten and quiver, the sun's heat coupled with fire heat making the atmosphere tremulous and wavy.

The corpse, after what seemed an interminable three hours, its clothes burned away, fell open, the heart laid bare. The frontal bone of the skull, struck by a mattock while the body was being disinterred from the sand, fell off. With the back of the head lying on the red-hot bottom bars of the furnace, the brains seethed, they bubbled and boiled as in a cauldron for a very long time.

Trelawny, trying to avoid the trenchant fumes lancing at him, could not take his eyes from the unusually large heart that seemed impregnable to the fire. Stepping forward, he plunged his hand into the flames and snatched it from the burning.

Had anyone seen him he would have been placed in quarantine. For this transgression, Trelawny was rewarded with severe burns.

Lord Byron, unable to face it, took to the *Bolivar*, his remorse dispelled by his strength of mind and body, and perhaps his determination not to stare at death face on.

Leigh Hunt, one other in the assembled crowd, remained in his carriage.

Trelawny, after cooling the iron machine in the sea, collected Shelley's ashes and placed them in a box. Pacing solemnly to Leigh Hunt's carriage Trelawny, with due reverence, handed the man Shelley's heart wrapped in a cloth.

'I think you know where this belongs,' he said.

Leigh Hunt nodded, his features drawn like Trelawny's.

V

On the twenty-first of January, 1823, Shelley's ashes were interred in the Protestant cemetery in Rome near the grave of little William.

Mary Shelley gently touched the heart enveloped in fine linen, Leigh Hunt having kept his promise to Trelawny and delivered it to her.

'It is the least I could do,' Leigh Hunt said, further words irrelevant.

'He will remain by my side, his spirit is too restless. My own Shelley.'

Leigh Hunt quietly departed and closed the door.

A heart, and a few other tokens, she knew would aid her in her desire to keep him alive. She kept it in a leather bound copy of Shelley's poem *Adonais* to the end of her life.

VI

'You have placed our daughter Allegra in a convent.'

Byron sits by a table in a room sticky with heat. Claire's words echo, and he recalls his denying the fact that the child was their daughter.

Thoughts insinuate, the events of the recent past upsetting him. Yet Byron believes that in facing up to them he may dispel them altogether.

Allegra was mine insofar as I loved her like my own, but was not in reality mine.

Such a grand way of disassociating himself: he'd said as much to Claire that day in the garden at Diodati – a day when any delusions on her part concerning romance, like the grape without water, curled up and died on the vine.

A year ago, Shelley and I went to see Allegra at Bagnacavallo. You saw her as pale and delicate, Snake, but indulged nevertheless. Such a charmer she was that none punished her for breaking the rules.

By then, Miss Clairmont, you hadn't seen her for two years. Her *mammina* was Teresa, who played with her in the country and took her for rides in her beautiful coach.

I trust you remember when we did meet, you in the public coach coming from Pisa, I in my own carriage. I'm amused to think you were journeying to Florence to look after other people's children!

He re-reads a part of her last letter in which she deplores convent life, and the fact that Allegra is part of it.

> The state of ignorance and profligacy of Italian women, all pupils of convents. They are bad wives and most unnatural mothers, licentious and ignorant they are the dishonour and unhappiness of society... This step will procure to you an innumerable addition of enemies and of blame.

'You blame me, madam.' He speaks aloud, pleased he has privacy at last. 'It is a concept over which I could expend equal blame. I took Allegra for my own because of my love for her. She was adorable and the loss of my true son caused me so much grief.'

His grey eyes, older now, more tired though he is barely thirty-six, harden. 'So much loss in so short a lifespan.' The words strike home, they pain him greatly. 'I wished to pretend she was mine because she was born at a time I needed to love a child. And she was handicapped like me. Suffered and never complained.

'Allegra —' He looks through the window towards the lagoon and the flat, empty stretch of beach. 'Allegra gave more love than ever she took.'

Byron thinks of Shelley. And Shelley's heart plucked out, its beat of life extinct.

Fletcher is by the door: he looks uncomfortable.

Byron turns. 'What is it, man, does the air vex you? I must say it's uncommon hot today and the odour from those swamps tell on a man.' He scans the room. 'And this spartan accommodation hardly befits my standing.'

'It isn't me I'm worried about, m'lord,' Fletcher answers, 'but you. You're the colour of the flaking plaster walls, even they need a paint.'

'You'll be saying I should don my helmet and enjoy a canter across yon marsh.' Byron tries to stand, the heat of Missolonghi, its turgid air, defeating him. 'I fear I have caught a fever, my friend.' A hand scored across his brow is sodden with sweat. 'No helmet then. Anyway, I hate it, an unlooked for penance. Wearing it to suit others, not meself. It is a horror to don it and strut about like I own the place. That head piece is a symbol of war,

Fletcher; it portrays only evil, not good, although I vow it placates those who want to see the soldier.'

He remains seated and asks for some water which Fletcher conveys from another table in the small, confined room of the three-storey building built on ground that slopes towards the muddy shallows of the shoreline.

'Look at this place. Devil take it, it hasn't stopped raining since we arrived. Streets and alleys are mud baths and if I want to take a swim I needs only go to my ground floor. Told Hancock, m'banker, that if we're not taken off with the sword we're like to march off with an ague in this mud basket. Better martially, than *marsh*-ally!'

After sipping the water, he pulls a face. 'Warm, stagnant water. What other things lodge here to plague us, George? Look at it, a camp bed and divans, not much like a campaign headquarters apart from my muskets, pistols and sabres hung on the walls.' He sniffs the water. 'Am I poisoning myself?' Setting it on his table-desk, he ruminates for a few seconds, smiling at simple, pleasurable memories.

'It's good Rushton went home.' He laughs. 'Never forget him at the villa, will you? Poor lad was appalled at what went on there, but I half think he was enamoured with the house like the rest of us. Too idealistic by far. Being shy made him less of a communicator.'

'He talked to me, m'lord.' Fletcher eased himself into a seat. Pushing it back on two legs, he leaned into the wall.

'Look at me, Fletcher. What do you see?'

Never outspoken, Fletcher disliked being placed in this situation.

'Well? Don't be afraid, man. We've been long together, and too long in the tooth to rest on ceremony. Be honest.'

'Well... sir...' Fletcher coughed in embarrassment. 'I, er, see a nobleman brought down to the level of a party o' people who don't know what they're fighting for. Beg pardon, sir, for sayin' it, but they 'ave a cause of sorts, and rightly they should fight for it, but to 'ave you involved when you should be writin' and relaxin'... We 'ad good times at the Abbey didn't we, sir?'

'And you see me as a man who doesn't know his own mind, is that it?'

'I see you as a sick man, sir–' Fletcher looked out of the second floor window, then at the wall, his gaze resting finally on Byron's dress sword standing in the corner. Only then did he look at his master. 'Honour, glory, what is it? Dyin' a martyr's death can only make the world remember you as such, not the man you are... sir.'

He slapped his thighs. 'There, I said t'much already. If you'll excuse me, m'lord, I 'ave other matters t'tend.'

'All right, George. I reckon it's fair comment that after being associated with so much evil in my life, I perhaps wish the world to see me die for a genuine good cause.' He raised a salutary hand. 'The glory that is Greece.'

Left alone, head tilted, Dyron decided that somewhere out there, amidst the mist and marshes, he could hear the solemn beat of a drum.

The bark of a dog – a big animal by the sound – rose above it, the land and buildings absorbing it. 'Bos'n?' he said quietly. 'Inseparable weren't we, until death took you. Friends falling fast about me.'

Fletcher, hearing a sound from Byron's room, rushed back to see his master prostrate on the floor in a dead faint.

Fletcher had guessed right, Lord Byron was ill, very ill.

George Fletcher courted a sense of impending doom.

Impossible to get real expert advice with a gale raging outside, he waited while the none-too-efficient, travelling companion and physician, Doctor Bruno, was summoned.

A small, very precise, yet seemingly agitated man, he was elated at Byron's fever – 'It will cure his tendency to epilepsy,' he told Fletcher. 'I think we should bleed him.'

Fletcher, listless, kept an eye on the weather, high winds speeding into port and so preventing any vessel from attempting to reach this safer haven. Nature ensured that Missolonghi remained completely isolated from the outside world.

Byron, temperature running dangerously high, refused bleeding and yelled out: 'The lancet has killed more people than the lance!'

Bruno did everything to persuade him. That night, after spasms of coughing and vomiting, and barely recognising Bruno, he said, 'There – you are a damned set of butchers. Take away as much blood as you like, but have done with it.'

Had he been *compos mentis* he would have considered the irony following his lecture to Polidori about the leech.

Seeing his master in this state distressed Fletcher, the man worried when he overheard comments from Bruno and other doctors. 'I dislike the apparent inflammation of the brain... you can see it in his features... I think we should bleed him again, ease the pressure.'

'No,' Fletcher said, 'you can't. 'Is lordship isn't eating, and drinks little. 'E can't even keep 'is tea down. 'E 'asn't the strength to suffer it again.'

Byron's hand reached out. He couldn't speak.

Fletcher, sensing the end was near, said, 'Is it pen and paper you're wantin', m'lord?'

A barely perceptive Byron found voice. 'Oh no, there is no time – it is nearly over.' He gripped Fletcher's arm. 'Go to my sister – tell her – go to Lady Byron – you will see her, and say –'

His voice grew indistinct, and Fletcher could only hear his master's rambling. For over twenty minutes, Byron muttered to himself, his words barely distinguishable: 'Augusta, Ada, Hobhouse, Kinnaird.'

'My lord,' whispered Fletcher, 'I have not understood a word your Lordship has been saying.'

'Not understood me?' said Byron. 'What a pity – then it is too late, all is over.'

Fletcher, emotion choking his voice, managed, 'I 'ope not,' before turning briefly away. 'But the Lord's will be done.'

Byron heard this. 'Yes, not mine,' he said. He tried to say more, that well-modulated voice he'd carried for three and a half decades refusing to obey him.

Fletcher leaned closer, hearing: '... my sister, my child.'

Bruno interrupted with a strong, anti-spasmodic medicine, which he urged Byron to drink. Seconds saw him get it down, and further seconds incited him to rant wildly –

'Poor Greece! – poor town! – my poor servants!... Why was I not aware of this sooner? My hour is come! – I do not care for death – but why did I not go home before I came here?'

Somewhere in those dark recesses he hears Lucy's laughter, and the strident voice of a child calling him.

'There are things which make the world dear to me: for the rest, I am content to die.'

It was April 19th; two years ago to the day Allegra had died in the convent at Bagnacavallo.

Days later, a distraught Fletcher told a visiting Trelawny, 'These savages are worse than any highwaymen; they have robbed my Lord of all his money and his life, too.'

'So what did he really die of, Fletcher?' Trelawny asked.

'If you want my opinion, and I'm no doctor, sir, I believe my Lord died from a form of pneumonia. I seen it in the poor, back in Nottinghamshire – the damp and cold, with little or no fuel to burn. A rare form, sir, an' no cure. Them doctors didn't know what they were at.

''E knew 'e couldn't be saved, sir, despite all their efforts. Lord Byron accepted 'is fate, but they couldn't. They wanted t'be the folk who saved 'im.'

Trelawny acknowledged this, aware none speak the truth like a good friend.

'His unhealthy lifestyle caused him problems, Fletcher, as well you know. And yet they seemed not to have contributed to his death. This place, fever rife... That and fatigue left him with little strength to fight for his life.'

'Aye, mebbe, sir.' Fletcher looked down at the shrouded body. 'Savin' 'im would have been to no avail, sir. It was Lord Byron's time to leave this earth and nothin' nobody could do would've prevented it.'

VII

Mary Shelley learned of Byron's death while still in Italy: she collapsed from shock.

In her journal she later noted:

Byron had become one of the people of the grave – that miserable conclave to which the beings I best loved belong. I knew him in the bright days of youth, when neither care nor fear had visited me – before death had made me feel my mortality, and the earth

251

was the scene of my hopes. Can I forget our evening visits to Diodati? Our excursions on the lake, when he sang the Tyrolese hymn, and his voice was harmonised with wind and waves. Can I forget his attentions and consolations to me during my deepest misery? Never.

Beauty sat on his countenance and power beamed from his eye. His faults being, for the most part, weaknesses, induced one readily to pardon them.

She added:

Albé – the dear, capricious, fascinating Albé – has left this desert world! God grant I may die young! A new race is springing about me. At the age of twenty-six, I am in the condition of an aged person. All my old friends are gone. I have no wish to form new... Life is the desert and the solitude – how populous the grave.

CHAPTER 26

'And take thy rest'

I

It is the 21st January 1851. The house is situated at 24 Chester Square, London.

Mary Shelley looks wistfully at Claire Clairmont.

'But it is hardly fair to think of rest,' said Mary. 'None of our dearest ones can ever rest while ever we hold them to our hearts. They are always there, their laughter, their smiles, their wayward antics, aye even their ghostly tales.'

'And that is their legacy.' Claire rose from her chair and went to sit beside Mary on the chaise longue. 'Despite what you think, you and I have much in common, Mary. We are both older and have loved the same men in our different ways. Haven't we both lost their children?'

'Lost hearts.' Mary whispered, the sound like a breath of breeze over myriad graves.

'Were–?' Claire faltered. 'Mary, you and I are half sisters, we haven't seen eye to eye and I admit my own desires persuaded you to take me wherever I needed to go in my search for... for... Mary, I must know, were you and Byron ever lovers?'

Instead of being annoyed, Mary offered a brief smile. 'No,' she said, 'Lord Byron and I were never lovers. We were very close friends. Many, including Percy, remained unconvinced there was no sexual liaison.' She gazed for a while at Claire. 'I wonder, can you say the same? Dare you admit to loving Shelley?'

'I... I loved him. We must leave it at that.'

'Loved him... as a brother you mean?'

'If you wish.' Claire busied herself brushing unseen loose threads from her dress. Somehow, at this age, the red didn't suit her. Why argue? 'I realise I made myself a nuisance both to you and Lord Byron. I grew ridiculous in my devotion to him. He was cruel and selfish, yet I wish to believe he came to realise it. He was fun to be with, but I trust fun and cruelty didn't drive him to behave as he did.'

'To know Lord Byron, is to accept him for what he was. And my Shelley, too.' Mary looked distant. 'Perhaps we were all born before our time.'

'Did you know about the servant girl, Lucinda?'

Mary nodded slowly. 'You obviously do. Lord Byron and I had a talk on that subject. He told me to mind my own business. I do know he visited her as often as he could, and only a chosen few knew of his visits. They were so different. Poor Byron, in such a position he could never provide for her as she wished. They understood each other, and yes, he was in love with her.'

'More than me?'

'I can't answer, Claire. Only your heart can do that.' Mary took Claire's hand. 'You are right, we do have many differences, and it takes a man to see through us, define our feminine wiles.' She laughed. 'Despite what others say, we were acquainted with *men.* Byron and Shelley were friends, make no mistake. Shelley told me they would talk on all matters spiritual, about love and women. Trivial pursuits such as walking, fishing... The main subject was women. You have your answer.'

'You're right, it isn't worth pursuing. Who can know the truth, when the truth has gone with them?'

Claire shivered. 'Those nights at Diodati? Did you... *feel* anything? I mean become aware of a presence, perhaps more than one?'

Mary pondered this, eventually stating: 'The situation bred all manner of disturbing things, yet I believe it was our own problems gave birth to the imps of imagination. Once unleashed, they create, *spawn,* many ideas and thoughts. What is worse, Claire, than our own imagination?'

'Your book appears to be selling.'

'I have Shelley to thank for it, he made me go on and finish it. And Lord Byron. I showed him my notes and he wholeheartedly supported the story. He told me, and I quote: "You are putting into words what the rest of us believe but find difficult to say."'

'This concept of birth and death, and resurrection is intriguing.'

'Indeed it is,' said Mary. Turning to face Claire, she said, 'I don't remember, tell me did you attend the funeral?'

'Lord Byron's?'

'Who else?'

'No... I didn't. I was told that empty carriages formed part of the cortège – an empty gesture without total commitment, a part denial of association. That is what I believe.' Claire wrung her hands. 'What did they know, for they only criticised him, never loved him.'

'Not many years ago certain rumours abounded that two vile persons stole the jewellery that adorned his coronet from the vault in which he was interred. And debased him.'

Claire's jaw dropped. 'How? I mean, who told you? They must have taken it soon after he was buried, and before the vault was properly sealed.'

'How does gossip of such nature start? I will attest that the person who told me can be trusted, and in a position to know. It was stolen by evil people seeking only material gain. They took only what they thought would help them and had no idea what they were doing. You see, it was there for the taking.'

'Those who stole it? Did this person know them?'

'Yes, very well. He thought they were friends but proved their worthlessness when they performed what can only be termed "an act of treachery".'

Claire, on tenterhooks, ached to know. Noting Mary's stoic look, she decided not to press the matter. Mary sensed this and in her own way pre-empted the unvoiced question. 'It would do no good to name them. It is hoped that when they pass from this life, God will find it prudent to forgive them.'

'I wonder, were they really friends of Lord Byron?'

'I'm told they were.'

Claire shook her head, unable to fully accept this. 'You said "debased": in what way?'

'My dear, I hardly like to say.'

'You must... Please.'

'That same person told me that Lord Byron's deformed foot was cut off. By the same people who stole from the vault, I cannot say. I can only surmise that evil people, whoever they were, wanted to portray his deformity as something bad, thinking that to get rid of it would do good. How foolish thought can misinterpret such disabilities.'

Claire, feeling a little shaky, asked, 'Is there more?'

255

'Only from me, sister. I'm of the opinion that when we die, such deformities that blight us when alive, disappear in Heaven and that it is of no consequence at all that his or any body is deformed. These people are totally unaware of any spiritual world and perhaps wished, in their blindness, to make his body more perfect.'

'How? More perfect?' Claire didn't understand the logic. 'To cut off his leg would hardly do that!'

'Even though a person's body ceases to be of earthly use, such persons, in their blind need to correct an imbalance, do it for whatever warped reasons they think fit.' Mary held Claire with a startling stare. 'And that, in my opinion, is evil.'

'Thus the demons of Diodati still linger. Living, they walk amongst us.'

By the fireplace, she contemplated a picture of Byron. One in his youth, with the urgency of life flowing through his veins. She smiled, because she, on those few capricious occasions, had shared that life. 'Why do you keep this, Mary?'

Mary, as guileless as ever, said, 'To remember. As I said earlier, in case you didn't hear me, lost hearts should never be truly lost.'

She looked towards the leather bound copy of *Adonais*, and what it contained.

II

Towards the end of January, Mary suffered a series of fits and lapsed into a coma. It lasted for eight days.

On the first day of February, with dusk darkening the streets, the air outside bitter cold, heralding snow, Mary Wollstonecraft Shelley died.

Percy, her son, and his wife, Jane, were at her bedside.

"...her sweet, gentle spirit passed away without even a sigh..."

Following exhumation of her parents' bodies from the old borough of St Pancras and their transportation to St. Peter's Church, Bournemouth, the two Marys and Godwin rest together.

A piece of Shelley's heart was later interred in the grave.

III

Of those who gathered at Villa Diodati, Claire Clairmont outlived them all.

She died with her memories, at the age of 81 in Florence. She is buried at Campo Santa della Misericordia de St. Maria d'Antella. The inscription on her tomb reads:

> *She passed her life in sufferings, expiating not only her faults but also her virtues.*

All are soon borne away... lost in darkness and distance.

But hearts can never be lost. Once created, they remain *alive.*

> *'My heart is in the vault...*
> *My true heart* is *my spirit ... the physical heart matters not'.*

AUTHOR'S NOTE

In bringing together the lives of well-known, and well-loved literary figures – Lord Byron, Mary and Percy Shelley, John William Polidori, and Claire Clairmont – it has been necessary to use 'poetic licence' in order to unite fact and fiction into an imaginative and subtly disturbing read.

By promoting the realities and complexities of such lives the story becomes a timeless anecdote to charm and terrify the hearts and minds of readers today – especially those who profess an interest in the romance and fascination for the literati of the nineteenth century.

The affair at the Villa Diodati lasted less than three months: the Summer of 1816 promotes an understanding as to why the events play a definitive and intriguing role in the lives of the protagonists. And the effect it has even now.

By reference to innumerable records available, and use of their fertile imaginations, the icons will undeniably live on.

On a personal note, my thanks to Bettina Croft, John Arundel and all at Blackie & Co, for agreeing my suggestion to write the truth. Thanks also to my agent Elizabeth Baker for being there!

Writing the truth? Possibly someone sat at my shoulder, urging me to relate events as honestly as I could.

I like to think that whoever it was, did, and that I have.

Derek M. Fox,
Pilsley, Derbyshire
Spring 2002

DEREK M. FOX is a Derbyshire based novelist and creative writing tutor whose short stories have earned honourable mentions in the USA, not least 4 from his recently published collection *Through Dark Eyes*. 'A name to watch' says Ellen Datlow, publisher of the World's Best Horror and Fantasy.

Following the success of *Heart of Shadows, Lord Byron & The Supernatural*, in 2001, and having completed the Talking Book for this, Derek is now writing a supernatural thriller. Along with several published novels and anthologies, a horror thriller *Jackdaw,* is due from *prime* U.S.A. in 2002. Commissioned stories will appear in anthologies, notably *Cold Touch* from Cosmos Books, and the British anthology, *Beneath the Ground.* A stage play, *Boiler Suits, Bofors and Bullets*, based on workers in a wartime munitions factory, will be staged later this year.

Also check out his column on writing at *thealienonline.com*

Derek M. Fox,
Spring 2002

On 'HEART OF SHADOWS - Lord Byron and the Supernatural' (Published April, 2001)

What they're saying about it

Georgina Papadachi, Reviewer: *'A book that evokes all that is mysterious about Byron and the ghosts at Newstead Abbey. A fascinating read.'*

Denis Robinson-Reviewer for Hucknall Dispatch: *'It tells the fascinating story of the Abbey through Byron's eyes... a gripping new book'.*

Jon Smart - Nottingham Evening Post: *'It is very intriguing and at times quite chilling.'*

Jonathan Oliver - Author: *'The book gave me nightmares - big black dogs and mad monks! An excellent book.'*

Mark West - Author: *'I don't think I've ever read anything like it. Part biography, part fictionalised- biography, part oral history - there's more but I can't put it into words. Very spooky in parts (got me looking up from the book whenever the house chose to make a sound) and well done on getting your research into the book without once becoming stuffy. A terrific job, Derek.'*

David Price, Author/
Publisher: *' The Byron book was pretty chilling stuff, especially when you mentioned the experiences those workers had in their own homes. The ghostly encounters really held it together. Who knows, I might even pluck up the nerve to visit Newstead Abbey one day.'*

Susan Phillips - Author/Publisher: *'As an introduction to the works of Byron, or to the mysteries of Newstead, this book could not be bettered. As a fascinating read in its own right, it will intrigue.'*

Nottingham Today: Article by Ashley Franklyn, Freelance Journalist; formerly critic and reviewer for BBC Radio Derby:
'... has the ingredients of a Gothic horror novel. After reading the history of Newstead's ghostly past , I defy anyone to find a house more haunted in the entire kingdom.'